PRAISE FOR *THE SECRETS OF SAFFRON HALL*

'Emotional and intense, this is a page-turning story of secrets that
echo through time'
Rachel Hore, author of *The Love Child*

'A rich and vivid historical story, *The Secrets of Saffron Hall* is one
of those rare books that is totally engrossing. I loved it'
Nicola Cornick, author of *The Forgotten Sister*

'The past and present are skilfully entwined in this
captivating and emotional debut'
Heidi Swain, author of *The Secret Seaside Escape*

'An intensely gripping, emotional read that kept me turning the
pages until the early hours of the morning. An atmospheric story
sure to please all fans of timeslip novels'
Christina Courtenay, author of *Echoes of the Runes*

'Emotive, immersive and compelling, a beautiful story that
captures the heart'
Liz Fenwick, author of *The Path to the Sea*

'This pulled me in and didn't let me go: a page-turner with such
historical depth and tender touch that it enchanted my heart.
I adored it'
Laura Jane Williams, author of *The Love Square*

'Intriguing and fascinating, a real insight into a turbulent time in
England's history'
Kathleen McGurl, author of *The Secret of the Château*

'A beautifully written story that pulls you in and whisks you away
to another time. Clare Marchant is a fabulous new talent'
Rosie Hendry, author of the East End Angels series

'A charming and engaging mystery, beautifully told'
Jenni Keer, author of *The Hopes and D...*

Growing up in Surrey, Clare always dreamed of being a writer. Instead, after gaining a degree in history and an MA in women's studies she accidentally fell into a career in IT. After spending many years as a project manager in London, she moved to Norfolk for a quieter life and trained as a professional jeweller.

Now, finally writing full-time, she lives with her husband and the youngest two of her six children. Weekends are often spent satisfying her love of history, exploring local castles and monastic ruins with her miniature schnauzer Fred. The family also make frequent visits to the beautiful Norfolk coast where they all, including Fred, eat (a lot) of ice cream.

You can follow her on Twitter here: @ClareMarchant1

THE
Secrets *of* Saffron Hall

CLARE MARCHANT

avon.

Published by AVON
A division of HarperCollins*Publishers* Ltd
1 London Bridge Street
London SE1 9GF

www.harpercollins.co.uk

A Paperback Original 2020

First published in Great Britain by HarperCollins*Publishers* 2020

A catalogue copy of this book is available from the British Library.

ISBN: 978-0-00-840627-1

This novel is entirely a work of fiction. The names, characters and incidents portrayed in it are the work of the author's imagination. Any resemblance to actual persons, living or dead, events or localities is entirely coincidental.

Typeset in Bembo by Palimpsest Book Production Limited, Falkirk, Stirlingshire
Printed and bound in UK by CPI Group (UK) Ltd, Croydon CR0 4YY

MIX
Paper from
responsible sources
FSC
www.fsc.org FSC® C007454

This book is produced from independently certified FSC™ paper
to ensure responsible forest management.

For more information visit: www.harpercollins.co.uk/green

For you, Mum, who always believed in me.

Prologue

1541

Her hand trembled as she dipped the quill into the ink and wrote the words, the script barely legible as hot tears scattered across the parchment and soaked in, swelling the fibres.

Mary, in the arms of our Lord 17th November 1541

Mea culpa, mea culpa, mea maxima culpa

Outside, the dark expanse of heavy grey cloud lay so low it was almost touching the tops of the bare trees. The bitter, icy wind threw sharp flecks of snow at the windows, whistling through the numerous gaps to find its way inside and curl raw fingers around her weary bones. It scarcely mattered. Her heart was already frozen, a hard painful lump, weighted in her chest. No amount of wool garments and fur-lined cloaks could warm her now.

Eleanor knew the chances of such a small baby who'd been born too soon surviving were slim. An impossible wish. But watching her daughter's perfect features turn to alabaster just minutes after she'd arrived in the world was more than she could bear.

And now she sat in the tower, her body poised and still as she listened for the drum of approaching hooves, announcing the arrival of the king's men. Never had she needed her beloved Greville more, but he wasn't coming. The damp rushes at her feet were stuck together in clumps with the blood she'd lost. Her whole body ached. She wanted to lie down on the cold stone floor and let her life slip away with the blood still trickling from her. It stained her hands, darkening them where it had dried, stretching the skin tight over her knuckles.

They needed to leave and soon, very soon. Already they had tarried longer than she'd intended, and there was no time to do what was needed. All she could do was hope that by leaving this message someone would be able to decipher what she was asking, and answer her plea. Her eyes strayed across the floor against her will, drawn to where Mary now lay. Could she hear something? A whimper? The thin cry of distress? No, it was just her fevered imagination and the wheeling gulls buffeted by the winter winds outside the window, crying with her.

With shaking hands she began to write. *infans filia sub pedibus nostris requiescit . . .*

Finally, taking a pressed saffron flower, together with a sprig of rosemary, she laid them gently between the pages, and closed the book.

Chapter One

2019

'Would you like me to help carry anything?' Grandad leant in the study doorway, a mug of tea in one hand and a stack of custard creams in the other.

Amber looked up from the dusty box she was emptying, piling the contents onto the front of the desk where she was fast running out of space. Her pallid face was thin and pinched. Deep shadows smudged like bruises under her eyes reflected the hours she lay awake at night, whilst all around her slept.

'Grandad, you can't lift them. Don't even think about it!' she admonished. Biscuits were probably the heaviest thing he could carry these days.

'You look too pale,' he observed. 'You should eat more.'

Amber ducked her head back into the box she was emptying and rolled her eyes. 'I'm always this colour. It goes with the red hair.' Her parents had used little imagination when they'd named her Amber. Standing up, she placed a

3

handful of old London A–Zs on top of a precarious pile of almost identical copies, dating from the 1950s. 'Really?' She indicated them and raised her eyebrows. 'Were you thinking of doing The Knowledge?' She gave him a wry smile.

It was Grandad's turn to roll his eyes. 'Don't change the subject,' he told her, frowning from beneath his overgrown eyebrows, now almost white, but still holding faint traces of his own auburn colouring.

'So, I've set up a spreadsheet to catalogue everything,' she carried on as if he hadn't spoken, 'and I'm noting the location of the books in the house so you can find them later when you decide what to do with them.'

'That all sounds very efficient.'

'It's what we agreed,' she reminded him. 'My skills as an archivist in exchange for bed and board.' And a place to hide – she left the words unsaid. 'It's just as well I'm here for a year because I expect it'll take that long to log all your books. There are thousands. I knew about the library of course, but I had no idea you'd filled the attics with who-knows-what.'

'Well, that's the problem when you're a book dealer,' he defended himself. 'At auctions sometimes you have to buy a job lot when there's only one book you actually want. I imagine everything in the loft is rubbish, but it needs going through first.'

'Hmm, rubbish is probably the right word,' Amber commented, adding a further two A–Zs to the pile and balancing a tattered copy of *Malory Towers* on top of some *Jackie* Annuals. She had to stop herself from flipping through some of the books she'd found, or the mammoth task would never be finished. At least there was plenty of reading

4

material for the long, lonely nights. The dark hours when it was preferable not to fall asleep, because then she had to wake up, and remember all over again.

Grandad dunked one of his biscuits in his tea and tried to flip the soggy half into his mouth. These days his reactions weren't as fast as they once were, and she heard him curse under his breath as it plopped back into his drink, sinking out of sight. The stroke that had left him with an imperceptible limp and a slight slurring of words when he was tired, had taken its toll on his left arm leaving it weakened and for the most part, useless. And being left-handed made the disability all the more cutting. After a lifetime of quick wit and lightning reactions, she could feel his frustration every day as the new body he inhabited failed him.

'And how are *you*?' He was always tentative about asking, but she was fading more and more every day. Shadows darkened her face, and he could no doubt see pale blue veins tracking across her forehead where she'd pushed back the strands of her short wispy hair.

'Oh, you know, I'm okay.' She knew exactly what he was referring to, but she wasn't ready to talk about it. Not yet. She smiled at him although the wobble at the corner of her mouth belied her reply.

'I may be old,' he said a little too sharply, 'but I'm not stupid. As well as being as thin as a rake, you're looking washed out. You should eat proper food, not just soup and toast or cornflakes. It would help, you know.' His mouth quirked and he raised his eyebrows. His eyes crinkled slightly, a small acknowledgement of his harsh words. 'And every time I go into the kitchen, I find cups of tea you've made but not drunk. What's that all about?'

5

'I don't sleep well.' She shrugged. 'Making tea is a comfort. A little routine I can do without thinking about it, to help clear my mind.' Sometimes, it kept the demons at bay, just for a few minutes, she reflected silently. 'And actually, I don't remember my eating habits being part of our agreement – I'm here for some peace and solitude, and no nagging, thank you.' She moved to another box and began to slam its contents onto the last unoccupied corner of the desk. A thick layer of grey dust rose into the air, a cloud of tiny motes effervescing in excitement at being set free, dancing in the weak sunlight that struggled to filter through the grimy windows. Amber suspected they hadn't been cleaned in the decades since her grandmother had died.

After squashing the now empty box flat with undue aggression, she threw it into the corner of the room on top of a small mountain of similarly battered cardboard. Grandad watched in silence as she pulled another one towards her and ripped the top open, lifting out a handful of books and piling them up.

'I thought your being here and having something to take your mind off . . . things, would perk you up. But that doesn't seem to be happening yet. Maybe . . .' he held his hand up slightly as she opened her mouth to interrupt '. . . being out here in such a remote location wasn't such a good idea. Perhaps if you were with your parents, if you don't want to be with Jonathan, it would be better for you? Kinder for your soul? Sometimes, isolation in troubled times isn't the answer.'

Amber's eyebrows shot up to her hairline. 'Er pot, kettle? Why did you hide yourself away in this big old rambling house after Grandma died, to run your business from behind closed doors? If you recall, you dumped Mum on Gran's family and then ran away to bury yourself in the back of beyond. So excuse me, while I follow in your footsteps. Call it genetics if you like.'

She threw herself down onto the office chair behind the desk making it roll back slightly, and tried not to grind her teeth together. The hall had been in their family for generations and it was part of her essence, her core. It echoed with the souls of their red-headed ancestors and it had seemed only natural to return here when her life had been wrenched apart, to hide from the world. Although she loved her parents, their relationship was often strained and she felt closer to Grandad. She needed to be with him at that moment, and at the hall. So the last person she'd expected to question her decision had been Grandad himself.

As Amber sat down, her grandfather realised that she'd built a wall of books on the desk around her, and was now completely concealed from view. A barricade behind which she was hiding, yet again.

'Just because I did it, doesn't mean it was the right thing to do,' he said into the void where she'd been standing. Turning carefully, letting his legs catch up momentarily with his brain, he returned to the living room and the two-thirty race at Kempton Park.

Once she was sure he'd left the room, Amber got to her feet again. She rubbed at the familiar tears that had started falling with the hem of her T-shirt, tilting her face upwards to try to stop them, but it was a futile gesture. The tracks were almost permanently engraved on her face, so many times had they snaked their way down, to drip off her small, pointed chin. She expected to wake up one morning with the lines indelibly marked on her cheeks forever more, like tattoos. A visible stain of her sorrow, to show the world what a terrible person she was, a failure. Life was hard enough, without a lecture from Grandad, the king of running away, sixty years hiding in this mausoleum of a house.

She'd only got a year's sabbatical from the university, during which she needed to sort her life out, somehow. Decide if she and Jonathan had anything worth saving. The crushing grief, now a familiar friend, lay heavy on her shoulders as she walked through to the kitchen to make a cup of tea she wouldn't drink.

Chapter Two

1538

From her room, Eleanor could hear the frantic commotion in the courtyard below, men shouting to the stable lads and servants, together with the impatient stamping of horses' hooves against the cobbles. The bustling entourage that had arrived seemed huge. Nobody in the house was used to this number of guests and the noise they brought; Eleanor included.

Despite her reservations, she knew what protocol dictated. Her dear father had instilled good manners in her from an early age, and so she prepared to descend the stairs and greet Cousin William, now the owner of her home. It appeared he'd arrived not only with his family, but also a great many others.

By the time she reached the top of the stone staircase, accompanied by Joan, her companion and best friend, the great hall was swarming with people, the stench of damp wool clothing rising up and making her wrinkle her nose. Her eyes flitted amongst them to ascertain which of the many gentlemen, most of whom were still wearing their thick riding cloaks, was her cousin. Watching as the kitchen boy darted about offering jugs of ale, her glance caught on a pair of pale, flinty eyes, which narrowed on hers as they met, and locked. The woman was clothed in a heavily embroidered deep green velvet travelling cloak and stood beside a small, stocky man. Eleanor looked at Joan and together they both raised their eyebrows. Joan smiled and gave her a little nod of encouragement, before leaving her and returning to their room. She needed to do this on her own.

Eleanor pushed her way through the jostling people who hardly noticed her slight form, until eventually she found herself in front of the couple she'd spotted from the gallery above. Close up, William was barely taller than her own five foot three inches, his rotund body topped by a florid face, sweating profusely. Curtseying to them both, she greeted them.

'My lord, lady, welcome to Ixworth. I hope you will be very happy in your new home.'

'Cousin Eleanor, how lovely to meet you.' What he lacked in height, he made up for with the volume in his voice. Eleanor winced slightly as a gust of stale, beery breath assailed her nostrils. 'This is my wife, Lady Margaret.'

Eleanor repeated her curtsey with lowered eyes, but once upright again she stared into the piercing shards burning into her. Why did this woman hate her so much? Her animosity was leaking out of every pore on her pockmarked face. Her fine clothes and furs, the row of pearls sewn onto her fashionable French hood, failed to detract from the ravages her skin had taken. These people were moving into her wonderful home, taking everything her father owned

10

because William was his heir and Eleanor merely a girl who could very soon be homeless, or despatched to a convent. Margaret should be dancing around the room in delight, not looking as if she may shatter into a million pieces at any moment.

'Our fine son, Robert, will arrive in a few days,' William continued. 'He is but a year old and has a slight fever so will follow from Richmond when he is well, and a nursery has been established for him here. We've come straight from court and are of course sorry we were unable to arrive in time for your father's funeral.'

He didn't sound very remorseful, and a series of images flickered momentarily across her vision of the sparse funeral procession behind her father's coffin as it made its way from the home he'd loved to the chapel where he was interred beside her mother.

'Sir William will be sorely missed by the king,' Margaret informed her, 'and I cannot imagine what we will do in this godforsaken wilderness.' Her long nose was screwed up and Eleanor began to realise why she was looking so out of sorts. She bit back the retort that they were more than welcome to return to court because she didn't want them in her home. Except, it was no longer hers. She suddenly couldn't stand the crowd, the oppressive heat and reek of unwashed bodies a moment longer.

'Please excuse me,' she muttered, before darting through the mass of people towards the door.

Once outside, she paused for a moment in the cooler damp air, taking big gulps. She'd been used to seventeen years of isolation and peace; how would she live with a house full of noise and clamour all day long? It was unbearable.

Looking across the pasture, her eyes lifted towards the pale cream sandstone of the priory walls, rising from the marshy ground that surrounded her home. Under the wing of the much larger Thetford Priory, this was a smaller and self-sufficient institution, the monks mostly a law unto themselves. As always it offered her the sanctuary she craved and without a second thought she gathered up her skirts, her feet flying across the ground towards it, running through the waist-high grasses along the well-trodden path.

Slipping through the battered oak door in the priory gardens, Eleanor let her breath out slowly, watching it form into vapour in front of her. Here, she was safe. The empty garden that lay before her filled her heart with calm. The fruit trees and rows of herbs and vegetables, immaculately tended by the monks, were a comfort. Despite the late hour, the swifts were still flitting above her head catching insects, and a pair of finches argued loudly together in a nearby fruit bush. Whatever happened at home, this small corner of her world was a constant. The soothing regularity of the brothers at their daily work, the chanting from the chapel as the flow of the Latin prayer washed over her and cleansed her soul of the uncharitable thoughts she'd had about her cousin.

Bending down, she tugged off a sprig of thyme, rolling the tiny green leaves between her fingers and thumb and sniffing at the pungent aroma they released. A slight rustle disturbed her thoughts, and looking up she saw Brother Dominic making his way towards her. He was her favourite of all the brothers, a dear friend, and Eleanor couldn't help a wide smile spreading across her face, her childlike innocence simmering inside her. A feeling that had been all but extinguished in the past few months.

'Are you visiting, or hiding?' the young monk asked as he grew level with her. He'd only been ordained into the priory the previous year and was not much older than Eleanor herself. She saw in him a kindred spirit, someone who had to conform to the rules laid down, against their better judgement. His eyes, the clearest green she'd ever seen, sparkled mischievously at her under his raised eyebrows, already sure of the answer to his question.

'Of course I'm here to visit,' she replied. 'If nobody knows this is where I am, that is merely a useful coincidence.'

'Has your kinsman arrived yet?'

'He has, along with his wife and a large retinue of other people. The hall was full. I greeted them, before leaving them to settle into their apartments. I doubt anyone will miss me for a while. Or at all.'

'Then come inside and take a cup of mead. The prior will be pleased of some company – he is feeling pained again. This cool air and the damp doesn't suit him. I have made a poultice with cloves and pennyroyal, but it does not seem to ease his aching.'

'You could add some feverfew?' she suggested. 'Or oil of bay berries if you have any?'

'I think we do. That's a good idea, thank you. I'll go and look right away.'

Eleanor found the prior, Father Gregory, in his private solar. From here the sound of the plain song, the deep melodic singing of psalms that undulated and swayed like trees in the wind was louder, making the stone beneath her thin slippers vibrate. He passed her an earthenware cup, and she sipped at the honey wine, feeling its warmth steal down inside.

13

Perching herself on the edge of a bench, she closed her eyes as the peace and serenity of the building rolled over her. She'd visited the priory with her father on almost a daily basis, for as long as she could remember. And now it was her sanctuary, a place where the soft call of routine never varied. All around her change was coming, plucking at her clothes, pulling her in through the sounds of horses' hooves and the shouts of strange men. The news from London grew more concerning, that the king was closing many convents and monasteries and threatening to sweep away the once ordered life she'd known. What would the future hold for her friends? A prickle of fear and premonition crawled down her spine.

'Word comes your cousin has arrived?' the prior eventually said.

'He has,' she replied, distracted from her thoughts, and she explained about the train of people who had accompanied him.

'It's perhaps better not to antagonise him,' Father Gregory reminded her, leaving the rest of the sentence unsaid. She needed to keep on the right side of her cousin: her situation was precarious and he owned the roof over her head. Eleanor frowned and nodded – she understood what was expected of her.

As she gazed out of the window, she realised the shadows were beginning to lengthen. A gentle snore from Prior Gregory alerted her to the fact that she had stayed too long and she slipped through the door into the Lady chapel, dipping her fingertips into the holy water and crossing herself before sinking to her knees in the gloom at the back. Closing her eyes, she murmured the vespers, the familiar evening prayers, whilst the deep plain song continued as a background to her murmuring. The flickering candlelight threw wavering shadows of the hooded brothers across the rough walls and vaulted ceiling. Eleanor lifted her head for a moment, letting the sounds of her childhood seep into her body. She was balancing on the cusp of a new life, all that was familiar about to disappear from beneath her.

Getting up from her knees, she crept through the door and back into the meadow where dusk was creeping in. It wasn't wise to be out after dark, especially when the house was full of strangers. She had no desire to meet any of them outside the protective walls of home.

Chapter Three

2019

The unusually warm late September weather clung on to the last traces of summer, as if loath to let it segue gracefully into autumn. Day after day of dense oppressive heat left the air thick and humid, congesting their lungs. Before she went to bed, Amber opened her windows as wide as she dared, concerned about how old they were. She didn't want them to drop out of the stone mullions. It didn't help though; the heavy, petrified air hung still and silent both outside in the hall grounds and in her room.

She listened to the familiar sounds of the house as it creaked and settled for the night. At her feet, Grandad's huge ginger cat, Gerald, was already curled up fast asleep, oblivious to the sticky conditions. Thinking she'd never be able to sleep, Amber lay down on top of the duvet with her T-shirt sticking uncomfortably to her skin.

She must, however, have dozed off, because she was suddenly woken by a crash so loud it scared Gerald into a shrieking orange ball of fluff. When she opened her bedroom door, he shot out. Her room was lit up by a brilliant harsh blue-white light, which stung her eyes and made her wince. It was swiftly followed by another crack similar to the one that had woken her, a noise that sounded as if the earth were being split in two, followed by a booming and grumbling rolling away into the distance. Then came the welcome sound of rain, big droplets splattering onto the ivy outside. Quickly she shut her windows but left the curtains open, watching the streams of water coursing down the little panes of glass as the storm raged on. She'd bet money Gerald had changed his mind about going outside, and had found a dry spot to curl up somewhere downstairs.

As the wind howled around the building, an almighty bolt of lightning hit the house. Amber heard a loud bang and a sizzling noise as if something somewhere was frying. Gingerly she opened her bedroom door and poked her head out, sniffing the air for the smell of burning. The house was in darkness, but she couldn't smell anything untoward. When she flicked the switch for her bedroom light, nothing happened. The electricity was off. She heard shuffling and grumbling from Grandad's room and she cautiously inched towards it. The last thing she wanted was for him to fall in the dark.

'Grandad, are you all right?' she called into the silence following another crash of thunder, which vibrated beneath her feet. 'The electricity's gone off.'

'Yes, I'm awake – hang on.' She heard his door open a little way along the corridor and as the sky was lit up again, she could see him momentarily silhouetted in the doorway.

'Don't come out of your room,' she called to him. 'I just wanted to make sure you're okay.'

18

'I'm fine,' he tutted. 'We've a lightning conductor on the top of the tower. I expect it's been hit and frazzled; it won't be the first time. There's nothing we can do until daylight though. Can you smell burning?'

Worried, Amber sniffed the air again. 'No I definitely can't,' she confirmed.

'That's fine then, we're not on fire.' He sounded quite cheerful as his words were drowned out by yet another ear-splitting crash outside and the corridor was lit up once more.

Amber gave out an involuntary squeal. She'd never been afraid of storms, but this was something else. 'Are you sure we're safe here?' she asked as her heart rate began to return to normal.

'Of course.' Grandad chuckled. 'This house has survived five hundred years of weather; we'll be fine. It may end up losing a few slates from the roof. We can check them in the morning. Try and get some sleep now.'

She paused for a moment listening to him bumping into furniture, followed by the creaking of springs as he climbed back into bed.

The idea of sleeping through the noise outside, the rain still battering against the window, was laughable. After making her way back to her room she was about to shut the door when she heard the scampering sound of claws on parquet flooring. Gerald raced back in and disappeared under her bed.

Eventually as dawn began to break, the storm moved away to be swallowed up by the North Sea and Amber managed a couple of hours of fitful sleep before being woken by Gerald, with a full bladder, scratching at the door wanting to go out again. Slipping on her dressing gown she followed him downstairs, where his fluffy posterior disappeared out of the cat flap. There was no sign of Grandad even though he was usually an early riser and it was already light outside.

Pushing her feet into a pair of Grandad's far too large wellington boots she'd found beside the back door, Amber stepped outside. The air felt crisper, clearer, and she drew in her breath, enjoying the cool freshness in her lungs, smelling the damp earth and scent of wet vegetation where it had been battered the night before. Mint, chives and wet roses assailed her senses as she splashed through puddles on the old broken brick path leading to the vegetable patch. She was pleased to see the glass in the greenhouse was still intact. Grandad would be relieved.

The lawns were littered with branches and twigs, the remains of the last of the summer flowers scattered across the grass, but Amber barely had time to register them as she plodded on in the cumbersome boots until she came to the reason for the crash they'd heard the previous night. Strewn on the ground at the base of the tower, supposedly the oldest section of the building, were various pieces of rough masonry and stone. She looked up at the tower and could see nothing structurally amiss, although she suspected the local conservationist and listed building planners would disagree with her. Her archiving work would have to pause while she sorted this out.

She retraced her muddy footsteps inside and started to make phone calls to find out when their electricity would be restored and enquiries over the correct protocol regarding the damage to the tower.

By the time Grandad arrived in the kitchen it was past nine o'clock and Amber had organised everything she could, although by that point she was becoming desperate for a hot drink and some toast.

'It's not just us without power,' she reported. 'There are cables down between here and Downham Market. It may be off all day, but they're working on it.'

'No television for me today then.' He pulled a despondent face as he flopped down into a chair at the table. 'But if that's all we've suffered, we can't complain.'

'Actually, it's not all,' she warned him, explaining about the stonework she'd found at the base of the tower. 'I can't see where it's come from, but I called the listed building people at the council about getting a builder and they're coming out to look themselves. If the roads are clear they should be here this afternoon, but when I spoke to them they didn't know if there are any trees down around here.'

Amber was delighted when just before lunch the lights flickered and then came back on. She and Grandad were tucking into bacon sandwiches and their second cup of tea when a banging on the front door announced the council officers had arrived to inspect the tower.

'I must admit I wasn't expecting you to come out so soon,' Amber told them as she took them around the outside of the house. 'If you can maybe suggest a builder, I'll call them to come and have a look.' It was obviously the wrong thing to say. The older of the two men stopped in his tracks making his younger assistant almost cannon into him.

'Mrs Morton,' he began, his voice deliberately slow as if he were talking to a five-year-old, 'this building is grade two listed, little short of a national monument. It may be your

21

grandfather's home, but it's also part of this nation's history and as such you must use a specialist historical building restorer, not any old cowboy you find on Google.'

Amber ground her teeth together as she tried to think of a response that wasn't as condescending as the way he was speaking to her. The younger officer looked suitably embarrassed and gazed around the garden not meeting her eye.

'I'm well aware of the history and provenance of my family home, thank you,' she replied, her voice cool and modulated, 'which is why I asked you here to view the damage, and to suggest who I could call. I have no intention of just searching for someone on the internet.' She strode away across the grass to the tower, stepping over the pieces of debris still lying on the lawn and leaving the two men to follow in her wake.

'So, here's the stonework, but I can't work out where it's from.' She spoke directly to the younger man as he and his colleague removed monoculars from their pockets and used them to silently examine the top of the tower. Eventually he cleared his throat and replied.

'I suspect the crenellations took a direct hit from the lightning last night,' he told her. 'I can see one of them is broken, but it looks to be the least of your problems. There's a crack from the roof about a third of the way along the façade on this side. It travels down to the window frame. You need to get that looked at urgently.'

'So, can you suggest someone who can have a look?'

'We'll leave you a list of approved contractors. They'll have to put up scaffolding first to be able to look properly. It won't be cheap.' The older man had spoken and he almost sounded pleased. Amber's urge to slap him increased. She screwed her hands into fists.

'No problem,' she said airily, 'there'll be insurance to cover it,' whilst fervently hoping her assumption was correct.

Within two days, Kenny Clarke, a specialist restoration builder together with his son Pete arrived with a lorry load of scaffolding. It was stacked up outside the house for three days whilst they, and what felt like a dozen scaffolders, banged and crashed, whistled, laughed and shouted as they slowly erected a huge metal cage around the tower. Amber tried to hide in the office, having realised on day one that if she was spotted in the kitchen, someone would appear at the back door with their tray of mugs and a hopeful smile. It was usually Pete, who had intensely blue eyes that sparkled every time he grinned. There were no prizes for guessing why the other workers always sent him to ask for cups of tea, although when she'd tried to engage him in conversation, she'd discovered that behind his rugged good looks he was very shy.

Now, sat in front of her laptop, a pile of dusty, worn 1950s detective novels on the desk beside her, she couldn't concentrate. The room felt wrong; however, she couldn't put her finger on what was different. As far as she could see none of the furniture had been moved and given the depth of the dust that covered everything, it would be easy to spot if any of the ornaments had been altered. In fact, there was something odd right through the house and whatever it was, she could feel it most strongly in the library, at the base of the tower. With the poor light from the small windows now obscured even further by the myriad of scaffold poles, the room felt strange, edgy. As if it wasn't happy with the work going on outside, which was a ridiculous notion she told

23

herself. Nevertheless the atmosphere had been disturbed and sometimes she was certain someone was watching her, although a quick check of the room proved what she already knew – she was on her own.

Within hours of the two men starting their investigations, Kenny was at the back door, carrying a small package, and asking if he could speak with her and Grandad. His usual joviality had abandoned him, and after inviting him into the kitchen and offering him a chair at the table, she went through to find her grandfather.

'It's a lot worse than I could see from the ground,' he began as soon as they were all sat down with yet another cup of tea. 'There's some major structural work that needs to be undertaken. The crack we spotted is bigger than I first thought and will carry on crawling down the tower wall until the whole corner shears away and it'll all come tumbling down. The window frame is so loose we had to remove it before it fell out and all that ancient glass got broken. Pete found this on the window ledge.' He put the package he was carrying on the table in front of Amber.

Even before she picked it up she knew it was something special and a sharp tingle crawled along her arms, making the hairs stand up. A small rectangular block, roughly wrapped in a clump of embroidered brown linen, frayed at the edges. It was enveloped in a musty smell, with a whisper of spice and incense, reminding Amber moment-arily of her and Jonathan's home and his ancient church next door. As she held it in her hands, she could feel the air around her shiver and distort for a moment. Sliding it onto her lap she tried to listen to the conversation between the other two. Whatever was contained in the old piece of cloth had piqued her interest, but she wanted to look at it when she was on her own.

Following further discussions about the work needed, and despatching Kenny back outside with more tea and some chocolate cake for both him and Pete, Amber went to her office, holding the package tightly against her chest. Laying it on the desk, she gently lifted away the linen wrapping, now yellowed and brown with age and darker still in patches. As she began to unwrap it, her senses were alerted to the pungent, evocative scent of decrepit books and bitter herbs that washed over her and she closed her eyes for a moment. It infiltrated the room like a spirit, there, but not there.

The perfumed air reminded her momentarily of Jonathan and his church. Of his ordination and the soaring voices of the choirboys as they sung the '*Ubi Caritas*', the words spinning across the vaulted ceiling in veneration, while her husband in his black robes lay spread-eagled on the floor that vibrated with the deep powerful notes from the organ. The coloured light streaming in from the stained glass windows shone through the smoke from the incense, creating a misty rainbow. She'd never understood his intense passion for theology and his absolute rock-solid belief in his faith, but now, she wished more than anything she also had that rock to cling to, and save her. She closed her eyes for a moment, letting the faint fragrance settle on her. It was underpinned by a sharp, almost metallic tang of a pungent spice she couldn't place.

Amber turned the fabric over in her hands, examining the heavy embroidery. It looked ancient. Unwrapping it carefully, she lifted it away from the object it covered. She drew her breath in sharply, realising with a shock what she was holding. A tiny leather-bound prayer book, its thick cover enclosing gossamer-thin pages.

Inside the front cover, surrounded by coloured illuminations, exquisite religious illustrations still as bright as the day they were completed, and written in an old English styling that made Amber screw her eyes up, it read:

Sir Greville Richard Lutton, born June 1508
Eleanor Lutton, born 29 November in the year of our Lord
1520

Beneath, in a similar vein and with decoration, was written:

Jane Elizabeth Lutton born 7 August 1534
Henry Greville Lutton born 15 May 1539

A further entry, less illustrious simply said:

Thomas Lutton July 1539

Below the entry for Thomas, it read:

Mary, safe in the arms of our Lord, 17 November 1541
Mea culpa, mea culpa, mea maxima culpa

She swallowed hard. It appeared Mary, just like her own daughter, her tiny Saffron, had not survived her birth. The absolute worst experience that any parent could go through. A pain etched on her heart forever. And why had the author of those words added *Mea culpa*? How could she possibly think it was her own fault? Although Amber knew exactly how that felt, the all-consuming guilt. Opposite the front-ispiece, that first page with the list of births, something else was written in Latin, but scrawled untidily as if written quickly, with none of the artwork that decorated the other page. Amber's eyes caught on the first line, which, she was pleased that due to her profession, she was able to translate.

infans filia sub pedibus nostris requiescit

'A baby daughter lies beneath our feet'

What did the inscription mean? Was it an epitaph to Mary? She could feel her heart beating harder. It was as if the book had found her, had been waiting in the tower for her to be united with it. She and Eleanor, the original owner hundreds of years ago, had a connection through the most painful of reasons, two mothers grieving. Her suspicions were confirmed: this book was definitely very old. Had it been here in Saffron Hall all the time?

Although the house was a fraction of the size it once was, she knew from the records and research already done that in medieval times it had once been a sizeable castle. A book of hours, a small personal prayer book such as this scribed by hand and not printed, probably dated from the fifteenth century, maybe even earlier. It must have been very special to Eleanor. What a find. The air around her crackled and for a moment she thought she'd heard a whisper as the fabric of the building sighed and shifted slightly, almost in antici-pation. She was desperate to decipher the rest of the Latin passage, to discover if it referred to Mary.

Chapter Four

1538

'Sir William has asked to see you,' Joan announced breathlessly as she hurried into Eleanor's bedroom, where she'd been hiding for most of the day, playing cards and watching the relentless rain outside as it threw itself against the window, as if demanding entry. She slapped another card down on the table.

'Why?' She didn't raise her head. Since her cousin arrived a week ago there had been much coming and going of people she hadn't seen before, but nobody had bothered her. She'd hoped they'd forgotten she was there, but evidently not.

Joan shrugged. 'I don't know,' she replied, flapping her arms as if to make her companion move with more haste, 'but it was more of a demand than a request, so best not to keep him waiting. You know how important it is to us both to keep on the right side of him. We are now here as his guests; we no longer have any rights.'

Eleanor tucked the wayward strands of her thick unruly auburn hair under her linen coif and pushed her feet into soft leather slippers, before walking down to the great hall, her steps measured and steady. There was no need to fear a meeting with her cousin, she told herself, although every hair on her skin prickled in trepidation and her shaky breathing belied her external confidence. Joan had spoken wise words: they were now at the mercy of her cousin and although she hated the situation, she needed to remember that. She sensed a tension in the air as if everybody was poised and listening, waiting for something dreadful to happen, and she didn't like it.

She found her cousin sitting before the fire with Lady Margaret. At the other end of the room, platters were being laid out on the table for dinner, and her stomach rumbled loudly. Since everyone had arrived she'd chosen to eat in the kitchen after mealtimes rather than in the great hall, and usually there was little remaining decent food by the time she got to eat. The sharp scent of burnt fat and roasting meat wafted across the vast room towards them, making her salivate.

Eleanor dropped a brief curtsey and stood waiting for William to speak, her eyes staring at the floor.

He twitched his head slightly in acknowledgement. 'Eleanor, finally you honour us with your presence.'

She couldn't think of a response, doubting he'd actually noticed that other than mass she was absent as often as she could be, so she kept her lips pressed shut and said nothing. He sat in her father's favourite chair, and Eleanor bit down on the inside of her mouth to stop fierce tears from welling up as he indicated the stool beside him and she sank down

30

onto it. The rushes, the dried grasses strewn on the flagstones for cleanliness close to where he sat were damp from spilled ale and beginning to smell. Eleanor couldn't help screwing up her nose in disgust. Her father had always been meticulous about keeping the grasses and lavender dry and fresh, smelling sweet, and it relieved her he was no longer there to see what was happening to their home. William cleared his throat loudly, and she was pleased to see even Margaret winced at the disgusting sound.

'Eleanor, my son Robert will arrive within the week. It's just what this house needs, a family to fill it. You understand that it's no longer your home.'

She opened her mouth to point out he was now the closest family that she had, then shut it again, without saying a word. She could tell by the tone of his voice she was an inconvenience to be disposed of as soon as it was possible. Just as she'd suspected. The convent loomed large on the horizon.

'Luckily for you, I have made an agreement for you to marry Sir Greville Lutton. He is a rich merchant and courtier with extensive lands in Norfolk and is prepared to take you, despite the lack of dowry left by your father.'

Aghast, Eleanor didn't open her mouth to argue, shocked into silence. She sat unmoving and not breathing for a few seconds. Marry? Her? And who was this Sir Greville Lutton he spoke of?

She knew plenty of girls were wed by the age of seventeen, but she expected to be consulted, given a choice as her station dictated, as her father would have wanted. As a baron who distinguished himself at the Battle of Flodden and had later been appointed the high sheriff, he would have expected to do this for her. If he hadn't died so suddenly. To her astonishment Sir William waved to a man on the periphery of a group at the other end of the hall who got to his feet and strode over until he stood in front of Eleanor, and then bowed deeply. He was here, now?

'Cousin Eleanor, Sir Greville Lutton.' William made the introductions as if he were supremely proud of himself. He probably was, having successfully rid himself of a relative cluttering up his new home. She looked up at the stranger. He was considerably taller than William and slimmer, with strong, broad shoulders. His dark hair was clipped short as was his beard, and he looked at her with concern. Lines fanned away from his dark brown eyes, and she could just about make out heavy eyebrows. He looked considerably older than she was.

William and Margaret made a big show of disappearing to join their friends for dinner, but suddenly Eleanor's appetite had deserted her. Instead she thought she may well vomit at any moment. Greville sat in the seat William had just vacated and leant forwards, his forearms resting on his knees. His jerkin, doublet and hose were entirely in black, giving him a menacing look.

'I know this is a shock for you.' His voice was deep but surprisingly gentle and cultured. More like her father's than her cousin's. 'But you have nothing to fear. I can give you a safe home, and a good life. I'm a widower and I have a young daughter, Jane. She's almost three years old and lives at my home in Norfolk. After we are wed I will take you there, and I hope you'll grow to love it as much as I do. Unfortunately I'm unable to spend as much time there as I would like. I have trade to attend to in London. I have a

32

successful business importing fabrics and spices from the Far East, and I must spend time at court.'

His words washed over her and she took in nothing. This stranger was to be her husband and she had no say in the matter. Nobody cared if she wanted to marry him or not. Eventually she blurted out the question most prevalent in her mind. 'How old are you, sir?'

He chuckled deep in his throat. 'I'm twenty-nine years old,' he replied. 'I was married to my late wife at the age of twenty-four. She died giving birth to Jane. Now, I need a new wife to run my house and give me sons. You are . . .' He paused and ran his eyes over her slight figure in her dress cut from drab brown fustian, deliberately worn to render her almost invisible amongst the finely dressed visitors, huddled desolately before him. 'You are younger than I would have preferred, given that I have a house and estate to be managed in my absence, but I suspect you are stronger than you look. And you have organised this house for your father, so you will do very well. Tomorrow I'll visit the prior and request the banns are read, and we will be married in three weeks. I'll have just enough time to accompany you to Milfleet before I must return to court. And now, dinner.' He got to his feet and offered his arm to her.

Eleanor shook her head. 'I do not wish to eat, thank you, sir.' She kept her voice cool, but even she could hear the wobble of distress in it. Standing up slowly and keeping her back straight, she walked carefully, sedately, to the stairs and the sanctuary of her bedroom.

Chapter Five

1538

In the early morning darkness, the glowing embers from the fireplace cast a burnished copper glow around the room. Eleanor knew if she called across to Joan, asleep on her truckle bed in the corner of the room, she'd immediately build the fire back up again, but Eleanor wasn't cold. Indeed, her anger burned inside as hot as any furnace. Moving to the window, she sat on the seat, pulling the heavy drapes out of the way. She leant her forehead on the cool glass and watched an owl flying silent and low across the meadow before swooping momentarily out of sight then reappearing to perch in one of the many oak trees scattered across the park. This was her world, the only place she'd ever known. And today was her wedding day.

She knew where Norfolk, her new home, was – not far from her native Suffolk. With frightening tales her father told of its windswept boggy pastures and wild fenlands though, it may as well be the other side of the country, because tomorrow when she left Ixworth there would be no coming back. Sir William wasn't preventing her from taking Joan with her, but everyone else in her life would be left behind: the servants and the quiet monks with their gentle lives, many of whom she considered her dear friends. Her father was gone and now her life here was over.

When dawn began to bleach the sky, the sun a red ball hanging low and steady, shimmering on the horizon, she was still sitting on the window seat. Through the house came the sounds of fires being lit and the preparation for the wedding feast later. She'd barely seen her betrothed since their initial introduction; he'd spent most of his time out hunting with the other guests. No doubt they were all keen to escape the house and the furious yelling of young Robert, who'd arrived ten days previously and had made his presence known, day and night. There was nowhere in the hall to escape the baby's constant angry shouting. Sir William merely laughed, then absconded for the day on his horse. No wonder his wife had a permanent scowl; she probably had a headache as well. At least when he and Margaret were at court she could get away from the din. Here at Ixworth it was far more difficult.

Joan appeared silently at her door carrying a bowl containing steaming water with floating rose petals and, after Eleanor had finished washing, she helped her to dress before they both slipped away to the priory for matins. In her heart, Eleanor knew she'd miss this the most.

Kneeling on the cold stone floor, her eyes closed, she was conscious of Joan's steady breathing beside her as the familiar Latin prayers washed over her, their responses murmured automatically, her fingers clicking through her beads as she

36

allowed her mind to drift. Was Joan as worried as she, at the upheaval in their lives? Her cousin had readily agreed when Eleanor had insisted her companion came with her. But for Joan this was nothing new – she'd come from her own family, distant relatives of Eleanor's mother – to be her confidante as it was deemed Eleanor was in need of gentle female company. Although Joan was the quieter of the two, Eleanor knew her friend had an inner strength she rarely revealed, which would help them both in the new life they were about to begin.

But Ixworth wasn't Joan's home, and she wasn't about to become someone's wife, with all that would entail. Eleanor swallowed hard. She knew what was expected in the marriage bed, and Greville was not a boy of her own age. He'd have expectations – she had no doubt about that. So no, answering her own question, Joan had very little to worry about.

The voices of the monks lifted in the final bars of the 'Te Deum' hymn soaring to the vaulted ceiling as the heavy, cloying scent of frankincense drifted through the nave and the service was over. She'd be back here in six hours, and she'd already been informed they would leave for Norfolk early the next morning. This was it, the final time she'd be alone to say her farewells.

'You go,' she said, 'I'll be back shortly.'

Joan looked unsure. Did she think Eleanor was going to run away? If there was somewhere else to go, she'd have already gone.

'I want to say my goodbyes now,' she added.

Joan's face cleared and she smiled gently, nodding. She gave Eleanor's arm a slight squeeze. 'We need to finish packing the last of your belongings,' she reminded her.

'I've not forgotten – I'll be back in plenty of time. It's going to be a long day.'

Joan disappeared through the chapel door, leaving Eleanor sitting silently in the shadowy morning half-light at the back. By this point the brothers had all dispersed to their chores with just two remaining, snuffing out candles and cleaning the sacraments. Their movements were fluid as if they were contained in an ancient religious dance, their rough wool habits sighing against the floor the only sound they made. Finally they too left and she was alone, with the solitude and silence that enveloped her a comforting, familiar blanket. But she had little time to pause and appreciate. Her time had run out.

Outside, after a brief visit to her parents' grave – there were no goodbyes here; she missed them, but had accepted they were gone forever – she carried on until she reached the priory's physic garden. Carefully laid out in sections splayed out like the rays of the sun from a central bed, each patch contained herbs to cure ailments for a different part of the body. Behind her a separate bed held the plants needed to create dyes for the colourful inks the monks used. As if he were expecting her, the prior was already there, gently pulling the tops from new shoots on a feverfew bush. He straightened and smiled as he saw her, and they walked together to a wooden bench set against the stone wall of the garden. It was a seat her father used to rest on when watching her helping the monks in the garden. Or on the many days she was inside with the scribes watching and copying their painstakingly intricate illuminated texts.

The pair sat in companionable silence for a few minutes until finally he asked, 'Are you ready for your wedding and the next part of your journey?'

Eleanor shrugged. 'I suppose so. I shall miss being here so much. But nothing stays the same forever, does it?' She managed a small smile as if she was trying to reassure him and not herself, and his old hand, the veins bulging and the skin paper-thin, patted hers.

'You speak wise words. Even here in our pious solitude where nothing has altered for centuries, the bells of change may soon be chiming at our gates,' he replied. She knew he was talking about the king's commissioners who were closing down monasteries. Nobody knew where they may turn up next. An air of constant apprehension and dread hung over them, clinging silently to the fabric of their lives. 'Now,' he said, changing the subject, 'I have a gift for you. Not a wedding present, but something especially for you. Come with me.' Getting shakily to his feet, he led the way to a wooden shelter propped against the opposite wall, which contained the monks' gardening tools. Reaching inside, he withdrew a sturdy carved wooden coffer and placed it into her hands. It was heavy and Eleanor put it onto the ground so she could open it and peer inside. It appeared to be full of tiny gnarled onions. She looked questioningly at him.

'Crocus bulbs,' he told her, 'so you may grow your own saffron at your new home. You've seen how we cultivate it here in our stand, you've helped many times with the harvest and the drying, and you appreciate the value the saffron has, both in monetary terms and in its uses. These are your dowry from the priory.' He looked down at her and smiled gently. The smile of a father to a daughter he'd never had.

'Thank you, this is so kind of you. These are very precious to me.' Shutting the lid, she left the box at her feet, dropping to one knee and kissing the ring on his hand. 'You'll be

39

forever in my thoughts,' she promised him, before gathering up her gift and leaving the garden. Determined not to look back, her vision was hampered by the tears in her eyes.

The rest of the morning passed quickly. The smells and noises from the kitchens confirmed how excited the servants were to finally have a happy occasion to prepare for, after the sadness of the previous months. The wedding was a cause of celebration for them, if not for Eleanor, and they were determined to give her an impressive nuptial feast. They had spent days cooking swan, gosling and boar, the cool larder shelves filled with fruit preserves, sweet pastries, tarts and custards together with a magnificent cake.

In her room, with their last chest laid open for the final pieces to be packed, Eleanor sat mutely while Joan decorated her hair. For once it was uncovered, with flowers and pearls wound into the tight, uncomfortable braids against her head. Finally the fine lawn veil, which had been worn by her mother, was pinned on her head. Already she was hurting, in her thoughts and her heart. She wore her best dress, a muted pale blue wool, the perfect foil for the blaze of her hair glowing as if it were alight. Her eyes kept straying towards the bed behind her, the curtains drawn back displaying the embroidered coverlet her mother had sewn during the early years of her marriage before Eleanor's arrival. Her father had often assured her how delighted her mother had been to be having a baby.

Only a few days previously, Lady Margaret had swept into her bedroom uninvited, and inspected the furniture and layout, explaining she would be using the room after Eleanor had left. She'd sneered slightly as she fingered the covers and Eleanor had decided immediately that whatever else was packed into her luggage, the bedcover was coming with her. Already, the room no longer felt like her own, and tonight her husband would be joining her in that bed. She shuddered and Joan tutted as a hairpin fell to the floor.

'Keep still,' she scolded.

Eventually, she couldn't delay the inevitable any longer. Downstairs the previous noise and raucous commotion had abated, the household having already left to line her route to the chapel. The house was silent and Eleanor could hear every shaky breath she took as her heart pounded hard in her chest, a fine sheen of sweat beading on her forehead and sticking the veil to her face.

If she'd been praying for divine intervention, now was the moment she acknowledged that God had let her down. Badly. Prior Gregory had often told her that some things, such as her father's death, were a part of the Lord's great plan, but it was difficult to understand how the Lord thought this was going to improve her life.

'Do not look so despondent,' Joan reassured her, as she handed over a small posy of lavender, which Eleanor tucked into her kirtle beneath her gown. 'Many girls would be delighted to have a handsome husband and a new home awaiting them.'

Eleanor looked at her friend sharply, suddenly appreciating that in Joan's eyes she had more than she deserved, although even this realisation couldn't lift her black mood.

Joan walked in front of her, holding aloft a branch of rosemary, and Eleanor followed slowly, her legs unsteady but with her shoulders back and her head held high as they approached the church. Everyone from the hall was crowded outside waiting, including the servants she'd known all her life, her cousin's guests and of course, William and Margaret. As if their presence would ensure she went through with the marriage. Which she would. She was too much of a coward to run away, or take herself off to a convent. Stood at the heavy wooden door was the prior, together with Greville, dressed in his customary black but this time with flashes of deep, rich scarlet from the inserts in his doublet sleeves. His dark eyes met hers and he smiled encouragingly. Eleanor, still quaking, lowered her eyes and stared at his shining leather boots, so big compared to her small slippered feet.

The ceremony words washed over her bowed head and within minutes it was all over. A heavy gold ring studded with emeralds and rubies was slipped onto her finger and together they stepped inside the church for the wedding mass. Greville offered her his arm and although she wanted to shun him, Eleanor leant on it until she could sink onto her shaking knees. No longer could she occupy the front pew, the family space now taken by her cousin as she and Greville knelt before the altar.

For once, the familiarity of the mass was of no comfort to her and she went through the motions in a daze. That was it. She was married to a man who was a stranger, and tomorrow she'd be leaving the only home she'd ever known. And tonight was her wedding night. Her insides constricted painfully.

Suddenly the service was all over and they were back outside, followed by the rest of the party who were in a buoyant mood as they returned to the hall in the cool afternoon as twilight crept in. Inside, platter after platter of roasted meats, vegetables and sweets were brought out to the guests. The air filled with raised voices as the ale and wine flowed freely. Eleanor would have been surprised at the generosity of her cousin in providing such a feast, but Cook had already told her Greville had paid for everything. She toyed with a piece of manchet, the best white bread that Cook could make, pulling it into crumbs. Her hand felt strange and uncomfortable with the weight of the band of gold now sitting on her third finger. Greville kept putting fine slivers of meat on her plate, but she slid them off and onto the floor where the dogs sat under the table, making short work of them.

Finally a large cake made of marchpane studded with coloured comfits Eleanor had helped make was brought in, and the celebrations dissolved into drunk, unruly partying. Someone was playing a lute, the noise increasing the more wine was consumed. Eventually the moment she'd been dreading arrived as the revellers began to insist the bride and groom were taken to their wedding bed. Good-naturedly, Greville got to his feet and held out his hand to Eleanor, almost lifting her from her seat. As if he could sense the reluctance that was emanating from her in waves, he gave her fingers a gentle squeeze in reassurance.

He led her upstairs and the rest of the guests followed, jostling them forwards and shouting ribald suggestions which, she noticed, her husband frowned at rather than joining in. The party tumbled into the bedroom still singing loudly, but to their surprise Greville held his hands up to quieten them – Eleanor could see that his height and wide shoulders had definite advantages – and announced they could all continue celebrating downstairs because he didn't require any further assistance in the bedchamber.

The response was not polite as he ushered, and in some cases manhandled the disappointed guests from the room

43

until finally, just the two of them were left. He threw another log onto the already blazing fire, causing sparks to splutter up the chimney and the flames to rear up, lighting one side of his face. In that brief moment, he looked like Beelzebub himself and Eleanor resisted the temptation to cross herself. Walking around the room he lit the candles in their sconces while Eleanor stood motionless watching his every move, like a rabbit suddenly spotted by a fox. Joan had left with everyone else and she wondered how she was going to undress on her own.

Silently she began to unlace her sleeves. She felt, rather than saw, Greville move behind her and she paused, holding her breath before recoiling as his fingers wound in her hair, gently removing the pins that had kept it firmly braided to her scalp all day. The flowers, now wilted and limp, scattered across the floor. With two deft pulls of the laces at her back, her gown was loose enough to step out of and Greville laid it over the open chest, still awaiting the last pieces to be packed. Eleanor took off her kirtle and stood in her linen shift, shivering despite the blazing fire and watching his every move.

Her new husband removed his boots and hose, his slim legs looking long and pale in the firelight. He threw his doublet carelessly on top of her dress and within seconds he too stood in his smock, which mercifully came down to his knees. Eleanor averted her gaze, just in case. Lifting the bedcovers back he gave her an encouraging smile before indicating that she should get into bed. She darted across and slipped between the cool linen sheets, pulling them up to her neck, and lay down with her eyes closed, awaiting the dip of the mattress as he climbed in beside her. It didn't happen. Instead, she felt the weight of the blankets on her legs shift, and peeping out from beneath her eyelids, she saw Greville struggling with her coverlet as he pulled it from the bed. What was he doing?

She watched through half-closed eyes as he continued to wrestle with it until it was pooled on the floor.

'I know you're watching me,' he remarked, and reluctantly she opened her eyes properly.

'What are you doing?' she asked finally as he wrapped the blanket around himself. Not before she'd seen his muscular thighs as they disappeared underneath the coverlet. She looked away quickly. He settled himself in the chair beside the fire, his face shining in the firelight. His dark eyes met hers.

'Go to sleep,' he told her. 'We've got a very long journey over the next few days. I want as few stops as possible on the way home.' And with that, he blew out the last candle, leaving just the dull glow from the few embers in the fireplace.

Eleanor rolled onto her back and gazed up at the canopy above her. She knew what was expected of her on her wedding night, and it definitely wasn't lying here in her bed on her own. She cleared her throat.

'Why are you sleeping in the chair?'

'I just told you. We have a long day tomorrow and we'll be gone at first light. Are all your belongings packed?'

'Yes,' she confirmed, 'apart from the blanket you're wrapped in. My mother embroidered it for me before I was born, and I'm not leaving it for Lady Margaret. Apparently she's using this room when I've gone.' He still hadn't answered her question though. 'But, aren't you supposed to sleep in the bed with me now we're married?'

45

She heard him chuckle. 'It's late and we've both had a long day. We have the rest of our lives ahead of us. One night . . .' he paused for a moment '. . . however many nights, won't make a deal of difference. Now, do as you are told. Sleep.'

Astonished, Eleanor rolled onto her side, bringing her knees up to her chest and hugging them against her as she lay in the dark, her eyes wide open. She hadn't been expecting this on her wedding night. All day she'd worried about what would happen in the bedroom and now, nothing. She couldn't help feeling a sense of relief as well as surprise that she was lying in the bed on her own. But it was, she reminded herself, merely a stay of execution. From across the room came slow, measured breathing. It hadn't taken him long to drop off and she needed to sleep as well, but the day's celebrations – if they could be called that – were playing out in her head, turning over and over. She didn't feel remotely tired, and tomorrow she would begin the journey to her new life, in Norfolk.

Chapter Six

1538

Eleanor must have finally fallen asleep, and before she knew it Greville was shaking her shoulder urging her to wake up. A fresh log on the fire was spitting and cracking, although the room was still in darkness. He was already dressed and had placed her folded coverlet on top of the remaining chest.

'We need to be leaving,' he told her. 'I'll call Joan. Do you want something to eat before we go?' Eleanor shook her head and watched as he left the room, leaving the door ajar. She heard whispered voices outside and then Joan slipped in, lighting the candles around the room until it was flooded in soft light. She was wearing her travelling clothes and Eleanor wondered if she'd slept in them, given that she didn't appear concerned by the early start.

Before long, Eleanor was also dressed in her warmest and most robust clothing for the journey ahead. They packed away the last few pieces of their belongings, with the rest of their clothes having already been sent ahead the previous week. Downstairs, the servants paused in their chores to say goodbye to the two women. Some of them had known Eleanor all her life and there were plenty of tears. Both for her and the quiet, devoted Joan. There was no sign of William or Margaret, and Eleanor's own eyes filled as she took a last look around the great hall, still clothed in its night-time shadows. She imagined she saw the ghost of her father sat in his chair, smiling and nodding encouragingly at her, as if giving her permission to start this new chapter in her life. She was turning a page, a fresh start.

'Goodbye, Papa,' she whispered, as behind her she heard the clump of heavy boots approaching. Her husband took hold of her shoulders and turned her around, enveloped her in his strong arms and held her close for a moment. Her face was pressed against the rough wool of his cloak. He'd been striding in and out as the horses were being prepared and there was a layer of fine, early morning dew on him, making his short hair curl into tendrils against his neck and his clothes and skin damp. Eleanor pulled away.

'Here, put your cloak on,' he told her, swinging it round her back and fastening it at the front, 'and we'll be off. We've got a hard day ahead. Today is not a day for endings and farewells, but rather a time for new beginnings. Come.' Taking her small hand in his much larger one, he led her outside where two horses waited, stamping their feet impatiently. She'd been expecting her own mount and she looked around for him.

'Where's my pony?' she asked. 'I'm not leaving him here.'

'Don't worry, he's already gone on ahead. He left yesterday,' he reassured her, 'but you need something bigger and hardier for the long journey, so I had one of my horses brought from

48

Milfleet.' The beast he indicated was fine-looking, with strong lines and a wide sturdy body. It had a gentle face and was snorting quietly, small white clouds puffing out of its nostrils as she patted its soft nose. It was also huge, at least twice the size of her pony. At Greville's behest she placed her shin in his cupped hands and he lifted her up and onto the horse's broad back as if she weighed nothing at all. From her vantage point the ground seemed a long way down, and she wished she was perched on the end of the cart, with Joan.

Dawn was creeping slowly over the horizon, soft shards of light beginning to beckon them forwards. Behind her, the hall and the abbey beyond rose up in a dark silhouette against the skyline and, with a heavy heart, Eleanor kicked her horse forward. Greville followed behind as they rode out of the courtyard, and she willed herself not to look back.

The four-day journey to Milfleet was every bit as arduous and dreadful as Eleanor had suspected it would be. She could hardly blame Greville for misleading her as he had given her fair warning, but nevertheless her mood soured with every mile that passed. The landscape barely altered, a flat expanse of damp, boggy wilderness, rushes as far as the eye could see, broken up occasionally on higher ground by a few rough longhouses or shacks. At first Greville had kept up a running commentary, but as Eleanor's face grew dark eventually he gave up, riding beside her in silence.

When they finally arrived, it was gone midnight. Twice Eleanor's mount had stumbled in the dark, and once she had almost slid off the horse as she fought sleep. Her mood had not improved. The full moon had helped them keep to the narrow dusty track and now it shone down on the castle-like hall, behind which lay ponds, the water still and shining in the moonlight, like glass. Up ahead there was the sound of chains and men shouting as the huge wooden gates below a gatehouse opened to allow the party access to the courtyard beyond. It appeared to be full of people waiting for them.

Gratefully, Eleanor slid down from her horse, pausing momentarily as she felt Greville's big hands around her waist steadying her. After so many hours in the saddle her legs were numb and frozen and without him there, she was sure she'd have stumbled. She kept her gaze steady, looking into his deep brown eyes surrounded by thick lashes she hadn't noticed before, and tried not to show the fear that coursed through her veins. When he offered his arm she took it without a word, and he led her into the great hall.

Inside was bright with burning candles, every corner and alcove lit, and what looked like a dozen or so dogs, milling around everyone's legs. They seemed delighted to see their master, pushing each other away as they shoved their heads against Greville, making him laugh loudly as he shepherded them out of the way.

The great hall was unlike anything Eleanor had ever seen or imagined, the huge space far eclipsing that of Ixworth. The ceiling soared up to elaborate decorations and carved beams, not the rough-cut ones she was familiar with, and even the candle sconces on the walls were ornamental. The walls were covered in thick, deep-piled tapestries depicting hunting scenes and Roman gods in battle. At one end of the room stood a long trestle table, bare of cloth, along which were glowing pewter candlesticks. It all seemed so huge in comparison to everything she was used to, and Eleanor felt small and insignificant. She wondered how she would ever live in this cathedral of a room; it was completely over-whelming. She began to realise her preconceived ideas of Greville's home and his wealth and stature together with that of Norfolk in general, may have been incorrect. Despite Greville's fine clothes and horses she had convinced herself that his home would be grim and austere with few trappings of luxury, echoing the landscape in which he lived.

Someone offered her a cup of ale, which she drank down quickly, not realising how thirsty she'd become. Joan appeared at her elbow and helped remove her travelling cloak. Without it she felt exposed and felt herself shiver, despite the huge fire that roared in the wide fireplace, taking up almost half a wall. She wrapped her arms around herself.

'Are you cold?' Greville asked, steering her towards the fire. 'Stand here, where it's warmer. Are you hungry?'

She shook her head.

'Let me show you to your bedroom then. You can meet everyone tomorrow when you're not so tired.' Putting his arm around her body to guide her through the throngs of people – everyone who lived on the estate seemed to have turned up to meet his new bride despite the late hour – Eleanor found herself climbing a set of dark polished wood stairs, the finials and bannisters intricately carved into oak leaves and autumnal fruit, all shining like freshly exposed conkers. She spotted Joan following them, together with a large hairy hound that seemed rather attached to her, despite her frantic attempts to shoo it away. Greville just chuckled, seemingly unperturbed at the beast being upstairs.

Opening a door, he ushered them both into a bedroom, much larger than the one Eleanor had occupied at Ixworth.

51

Here, another fire was blazing and Greville quickly lit the candles. One wall was hung with thick tapestries, the other three panelled with linen-fold wainscoting, which glowed in the firelight. He pulled aside a heavy curtain in one corner and indicated a large walk-in anteroom, which contained a bed, built into the wall.

'There's a bed here for Joan—' he pointed, before indicating the opposite corner '—and through that door is my bedroom.'

Eleanor couldn't even see where the panels ended and the door began, but her surprise at him having a separate bedroom was written all over her face. She'd anticipated that despite the long journey, he'd be expecting to share her bed tonight. It appeared she was wrong.

'Before I leave you, I have a wedding gift for you.'

He went through the dividing door into his own room and reappeared seconds later carrying something small, which he placed in Eleanor's hands. It was smooth, and had the faint tangy scent of treated skins. The sharp smell reminded her of sitting with the scribes in the abbey as they spent laborious hours writing texts and illuminating them with brilliantly coloured inks, and gold leaf. She'd often sat and practised alongside them with discarded quills and scraps of parchment or vellum that were no longer needed. She'd never have the steady hand or eye for detail they did, but she was able to complete passable, if rather naïve illustrations. It was an enjoyable way of spending the long winter days when bad weather could keep them confined for weeks at a time. And she'd acquired a lot of knowledge whilst chatting with them, learning from their experiences in the stillroom and infirmary. Her handwriting – with all the

52

practice she'd had – was small and neat. A skill that would no doubt be useful when she was helping Greville.

She turned the object over, examining it carefully. A small, heavy book, it was barely larger than the size of her hand. The leather front had been tooled into elaborate patterns and swirls that looked like new ferns, curled around a crest, decorated with brilliant colours. She opened it slowly and looked inside at the Latin words inscribed within.

'Is it a prayer book?' she asked, delighted. 'It's beautiful, thank you.'

'It is.' He nodded. 'A book of hours. See here, it has the stations of the cross.' He showed her the richly illustrated images of the Good Friday journey and accompanying prayers. 'And here—' he turned to some other pages '—are saints days and feast days. It was my mother's, given to her by my father on their wedding day. There are blank pages throughout the book. He had them added for her to write in anything she chose – her thoughts, or prayers. But she didn't use them, so the book is still waiting for someone to make proper use of it. I hope that you'll fulfil my father's wishes.'

Eleanor smiled. She was certain she'd have no problem doing that.

'This is your crest?' she asked, touching the raised design on the front.

'Yes,' he confirmed, 'and now it is yours, too. Given to my grandfather together with this hall, as thanks for his loyalty by Edward the Fourth. See here, there are bulrushes to denote the fenlands we live in, and also here, a heron. This is our family motto.' Taking Eleanor's hand, he ran her fingers over the Latin inscription at the bottom.

'*Dum Spiro Spero*,' she read. 'While I breathe, I hope.'

'That's right,' he agreed. 'There are times in all our lives when everything appears bleak, or broken,' he told her, 'but we must never lose hope that things will get better again.' He looked deep into her eyes as if he was searching her soul and reading what was written there. Maybe he understood more of her distress, how lost and alone she felt, than she gave him credit for. Eleanor gave herself a little shake, and tore her eyes away.

'Thank you, I shall treasure it always,' she told him.

'In case you're wondering, Jane's mother had her own prayer book, which is why fortuitously I still have this one. I think you'll find more use for it.' His beard, always neat despite the long days of travelling, tickled as he bent to kiss her on the cheek, warm against her cold skin, and then he was gone.

Around the edges of the room were stacked the various chests that the two women had spent the past ten days packing, but Eleanor was too tired to find a night rail to sleep in. As soon as Joan had helped her undress, she crawled beneath the covers of her new bed in her shift and lay down wearily as Joan pulled the drapes around her. She didn't hear the sounds of her companion sinking gratefully onto her own mattress, as she dropped into an exhausted, dreamless sleep.

Chapter Seven

2019

Amber's phone pinged with the arrival of a text and glancing down at the screen she sighed, stabbing repeatedly at the power button in frustration until the screen finally went dark. What had begun as an occasional enquiry about her wellbeing was now beginning to feel slightly overbearing and uncomfortable. She knew Jonathan was worried, and she really needed to speak to him to allay his concerns. Not least because if she didn't, he'd start calling the house phone to speak to Grandad, and it took the poor old man ten minutes just to get out of his armchair and stagger to the phone.

He wouldn't leave her alone. She'd already explained on numerous occasions she hadn't left him or bailed on their marriage, but she couldn't be home with him at the vicarage at the moment. All that was there merely reminded her of what wasn't there. He'd cleared out the nursery and put everything up in the loft thinking it would help, but in fact he'd made things worse. As if Saffron had never been. But she was a real person, their daughter. A surprise pregnancy after a course of antibiotics that resulted in her pill failing to work. Amber had been horrified when she'd first seen the two blue lines appear on the test. Jonathan as ever had been far more pragmatic and then within days he'd morphed from sensible, to wildly excited. It had taken Amber several months before she accepted what was happening and had begun to look forward to the new addition to their family and share in Jonathan's mounting excitement. Now, she was crucified with guilt at her initial lack of happiness.

Amber knew if she stood at the window in the now empty nursery, she could see across to the graveyard to where her baby lay. Jonathan found it a comfort being so near; he visited the grave every morning before he unlocked the church. She'd seen him from the window, his lips moving as he talked to their daughter. Or maybe he was praying. She couldn't ask because she didn't want to admit she'd been watching him. At first she'd drifted around the vicarage in a fog, unable to concentrate on anything. Picking up books and putting them back down, unread. Making cups of tea she wouldn't drink. Until after a couple of months, she knew she had to find somewhere she could breathe again. A familiar place that was calling her home.

It was only a ninety-minute drive home from Grandad's and initially she'd agreed to return home at weekends, but that had soon petered out. Jonathan was always working on Sundays and usually prepping for services the day before, and it was a long way to drive just to cook a roast dinner and spend little time together.

And now that he wasn't able to monitor her physical and mental decline in person, he'd taken to texting several times a week. She'd persuaded him it was better if she rang him at a convenient time so she didn't disturb Grandad, but the text messages were now increasing. All she wanted was some peace to breathe, and to grieve for her daughter in the way she felt able to.

Grandad was taking his morning stroll, although Amber had discovered this actually meant walking from the back door to his greenhouse. He sat in there on his gardening stool every day, whatever the weather, looking out over his extensive vegetable plot, which was now completely overrun with weeds. The troublesome unruly plants had grown, for as long as she could remember, throughout the carefully regimented beds from which over the years he'd nurtured enough vegetables to feed the entire British Army. Against the pale brick of the walled garden, espaliered fig trees still produced buckets of fruit every year, most of which lay on the floor, a feast for insects before the autumn rains rendered them down into a sticky molasses of compost.

But he wasn't able to do the physical labour any longer. She knew he hated the weakness he'd been left with following his stroke, and she doubted he'd ever really accept the way things were now. He still made plans of things to do when he was well again, and she hadn't the heart to tell him that day may never come.

Taking advantage of having the house to herself and knowing she ought to return Jonathan's messages, Amber switched her phone back on and walked through the house to find somewhere she could get a decent signal. It was definitely better at the front of the house, but even then it wasn't brilliant. She'd once suggested to Grandad that she climb the tower to find a decent signal, but he'd been vehement in his

57

response, shocking her. And now with the scaffolding up it was structurally unsafe and the door to the stairs remained, as it had always been, locked. Nothing would dissuade him from his decision. He admitted it had been inaccessible for as long as he could remember and nobody knew where the key was, but she was certain there was more he wasn't telling her.

The library, however, was the best room for a phone signal. It wasn't a place she normally frequented, with the ancient leaded windowpanes letting in dozens of minuscule draughts. Little freezing stabbing knives. That was the problem with a listed building such as Saffron Hall: nothing could be replaced, so no chance of sensible and efficient double glazing, and the family had to live with the consequential cold. No wonder that in the winter Grandad sat in the gloom most of the day with the thick old curtains drawn to keep the heat in.

Her phone finally locked on to the weak signal and buzzed at her. Looking at the screen, she discovered not one but four texts and a missed call from Jonathan.

'For heaven's sake,' she muttered scrolling down the texts. They started politely enquiring about her health and asking if they could chat, but by the fourth it said starkly, *CALL ME, AMBER, JUST BLOODY CALL ME*. He might be iffy about taking the Lord's name in vain, but Jonathan was not particular about swearing if he thought the occasion deserved it. Pressing his name in her recent call log – in fact the only name in her call log – she held the phone against her ear, listening to the noise as it connected and imagining him sitting in his study and snatching his phone up, almost dropping it in his hurry to answer it. Jonathan had an A level in clumsiness.

'Hi, Amber?' He sounded breathless.

'Yes, just me. Is this a good time?' She picked up a discarded pen from the sideboard beside her and started clicking the lid on and off, on and off.

'Of course, yes. I was just cutting some of the last dahlias to give to the women on the flower rota this week. They're a bit windblown but they'll do. The flowers I mean, not the volunteers. Sorry, I'm rambling. How are you?' His voice tailed away and she felt compelled to fill the silence she knew would stretch between them until she spoke. She could visualise him, his eyes darting around as if that would help him find the words to say.

They had been such a great partnership from the first time they met when she'd been unlocking her bicycle outside her digs in Cambridge and he was stood there unlocking his own. He had immediately made a favourable comment about her brilliant yellow Doc Martens boots, although she didn't explain until much later the connection between the vibrant hue of her footwear and the name of her ancestral home. Grandad had bought them for her eighteenth birthday and she adored them. It hadn't taken long for her to feel warm listening to his deep melodic voice, and she'd invited him to a gig that some friends were playing at in the college bar that evening. Since that day they'd never had a moment when they couldn't think of something to say to each other. Until now.

'Oh well, you know, much the same as usual. Still working hard on Grandad's books.' She went on to explain about the recent damage to the tower. 'There hasn't been much time to do anything else. I've been out for a walk when it's sunny, but that doesn't happen very often.'

'Yes the weather's been much the same here.' They could both get a qualification in small talk.

'How about you? Anything exciting in Little Walpole?'

59

'Well, there is something I want to tell you, which is why I wanted to speak with you, instead of the infernal texting. This is something that needs to be said out loud.'

For a second Amber's heart beat wildly in her chest and sharp prickles of heat crawled across her face despite the cold draught from the window. Jonathan rarely had anything important to tell her. Had he got fed up waiting for her to go back to her old self, the Amber she used to be? Was he calling time on her retreat, or on her and their marriage? It had originally been her suggestion she took some time out and went to stay with her grandfather, to clear her head. He hadn't been keen on the idea, but when Grandad suggested she could catalogue his book collection, Jonathan had wavered and eventually agreed that maybe it would help.

She realised she'd missed his first few words as she tried to tune in again to what he was saying.

'. . . So I didn't think you'd mind if we went ahead and had it erected. Tony came yesterday afternoon and I helped him do it. It felt important to me I was involved, for Saffron. And it looks just right. I think you'll be happy with it. The Yeats you chose is absolutely perfect.'

Amber realised with a jolt he was talking about the head-stone for Saffron's grave. It felt so long ago they'd chosen it, she'd forgotten it still needed to be put in place. Her eyes smarted as the familiar tears welled up and rolled down her face. The view from the window, the expanse of flat fields beneath the sorrowful wet sky blurred into a wobbly tableau of grey and sepia like an Impressionist painting.

'I hadn't realised it would be finished yet,' she admitted, sniffing loudly, 'or the ground already settled.'

'Will you come home and see it? I think it'll help. I know

it has for me. It's more permanent and a proper symbol she was here. It's telling the world we had – have – a daughter.'

'Yes of course, I'd like that,' Amber replied. She could almost hear the smile on Jonathan's face as if he'd been expecting a different answer. He suggested a day the following week when he had no work and they could have lunch as well. Amber winced. She didn't think she could face the hours of idle chitchat he'd expect. She wasn't the same person anymore; she'd changed forever. If only Jonathan could realise that. Grandad was used to a quiet life and rarely indulged in aimless chatting, so since arriving her ability to conduct lengthy mindless conversations had dwindled to almost nothing. She agreed reluctantly she'd meet him at the vicarage late morning on the day he'd suggested, before ringing off.

Saffron's headstone. It all felt so final as if everyone else, Jonathan included, was moving on. Except she couldn't. She was flailing in her own personal purgatory. A pause between her life and no life, just the darkness she inhabited every day. They still didn't have any official explanation as to why their precious daughter's heart had stopped beating. One day everything had been fine, she was a week overdue, the baby was kicking well and the next, nothing. It had been several hours before she'd realised she had felt no movements. If only she'd noticed earlier and gone to the hospital then, they might have been able to do something. Her fault, it was all her fault.

The stillness surrounding them when the doctor looked up from the scan machine and told them there was no heartbeat. That their baby was dead. A gaping silence sucking the air out of the room and leaving them in a vacuum as they processed the information. Then there was a rushing in her ears, a roaring noise that she realised was coming out of her mouth, but she didn't know how to silence it. And that sound might now be internal, but she still couldn't make it stop.

Amber slumped against the window frame and shut her eyes. It was her fault that instead of being on maternity leave with her beautiful daughter, she was on a year's sabbatical, compassionate leave while she tried to learn how to live this new life. The one with a huge cavernous hole in it, because she hadn't insisted the doctors induce the birth as soon as her due date came and went. While Saffron was still alive. For accepting the medical assurances that anything up to ten days late was perfectly safe. But seven days later they'd discovered it wasn't.

Running her fingers through her short hair she gripped them into fists, pulling the hair taut but not feeling the pain. She was numb, icy; she couldn't see a way to ever feel normal again. As she rubbed the heels of her hands hard into her eyes she smeared the wet and salt down her face, and shivered. The room felt even colder than before. As she turned towards the door, she stilled. There was a shift in the air. A momentary feeling she wasn't alone in the room, and yet she could clearly see she was. It was similar to the way her arms ached sometimes because she was sure she could feel the weight of Saffron lying in them, but she knew it was impossible. They were empty.

It felt so real that someone had been in the room with her for a brief moment. And there was just a hint of a strange smell. Honey, and something metallic. Was she starting to lose her mind? She'd had some counselling after Saffron and was told that with grief, anything was possible. It was simply her addled brain playing tricks on her, wasn't it?

Chapter Eight

2019

'What time are you leaving?' Grandad asked.

'About ten o'clock I think. Traffic will be slow if this weather doesn't ease off.'

'Don't worry about dinner this evening if you want to stay at home with Jonathan. There's plenty in the freezer for me.' Carefully he scooped a blob of marmalade out of the jar with his knife, and they both watched its unsteady journey to his toast.

'No, I'll definitely be back. I only agreed to lunch because by mid-afternoon I can be on my return journey. Jonathan knows I don't enjoy driving in the dark. I'll do an hour's work now before I go, then I've not wasted the whole day.'

Grandad raised his eyebrows. 'I'm sure "wasted" isn't the correct word.'

'Well, no, not visiting Saffron. I don't know about anything else though.' Amber looked down at the cup of tea in front of her, a filmy skin beginning to form on the top. She'd spent most of the night trying to ward away the bleak thoughts crowding her head. Today was a day she couldn't avoid. At some point she had to see Saffron's headstone. She was already hurting so much, it could hardly make her feel worse. And then a strained lunch with Jonathan. Despite loving and missing him, conversely she didn't want to see him. To talk about everything – no doubt she'd be expected to discuss her mental state. Or answer difficult questions about how much longer she'd be staying with Grandad, or how far she'd got with her book archiving. Even in the depths of her despair, she knew she wasn't being fair to Jonathan, shutting him out when he needed her, but she couldn't find a way to let him in.

Getting to her feet, she automatically hitched her trousers up. Even with a high percentage of elastane, her stretchy black trousers still gaped at the waist, and the charcoal grey sweater she was wearing showed deep hollows beneath her collarbones as it almost slipped from her shoulders. She'd lost more weight than she'd realised.

It was chilly in the office, but she decided against putting on the heating, there was little point when she'd only be working for a short while. Switching on her laptop she surveyed the books still left on her desk awaiting cataloguing. There were several first editions that should really be in the library, although thankfully being stored in tea chests and cardboard boxes hadn't done them much harm.

Ignoring what was laid out in front of her, however, she knew which book she couldn't wait another minute to investigate. What she was drawn to, and had been thinking of during the long insomniac hours of the night when the dark pressed in. Carefully Amber took the precious book from the safe. She'd undertaken some initial research, which had confirmed her supposition that it was a book of hours, a personal medieval prayer book belonging to a high-ranking lady. She laid it on the velvet book cradle she'd brought with her when she first moved in. She hadn't expected anything as exciting as this would need her specialist attention.

After pulling on her gloves, gleaming white in their bleached freshness, once again she unwrapped the coarse coverings, this time looking more carefully at what she thought originally had just been a rag. Although textiles were not her speciality, she strongly suspected the fabric was linen and it looked fairly fine, high class, not rough workers' material. This was compounded by the delicate embroidery that appeared to have once been blackwork, the simple geometric embroidery in black silk that was used to decorate the edges of shirts and smocks in medieval times, along one edge. In an age when all fabrics were expensive, they would have still used an item ruined with what appeared to be a dark stain, as a wrapping. She wondered why a damaged cover had ended up around a book as precious as this one.

She ran her fingertips over the thick deep brown leather cover, delicately tooled and engraved into a coat of arms, although it was now shiny and worn in places. It appeared to have originally been coloured, but that had almost worn away as well, just small traces of yellow and red visible. Running her hands over it, feeling gently with her fingertips like reading elaborate Braille, it was almost impossible to ascertain what had originally been there. She carefully turned to the first page and her eyes fell onto the writing she'd observed the previous day. Once again a shiver of distress ran down her spine and made her shudder. She tried not to look at the inscription for Mary, but opening a new document on her laptop she began to make notes. When she finally handed the book over to her colleagues at the Fitzwilliam Museum, she'd like to give them a full research paper as well.

List of births and deaths, she quickly annotated, *but one – Thomas Lutton – does not have proper date of birth, just a month and year beside his entry.*

Opposite the list of names, were the scrawling lines of Latin. It was almost impossible to decipher. She'd picked up a small amount from projects she'd been assigned to at work, but she could only recognise the more popular and frequently used words and phrases. Taking her magnifying glass from the desk drawer, she tried to see if making the words larger would help. She frowned as she squinted at it. What did it mean?

A quick glance at the corner of her laptop screen confirmed what she'd suspected, she needed to be leaving or she'd be late. Her investigations would have to wait, and after carefully rewrapping the book in its bindings she laid it in the safe in the corner of the room. There was a tiny stirring in the pit of her stomach, the smallest butterfly wing of piqued interest. After weeks and weeks of wading through Grandad's collection, maybe she'd come across something exceptionally special.

Amber stopped her car in Swaffham. Driving in the rain had made her eyes feel gritty and her mood, which had improved just a little after her work on the book of hours, was now as damp as the weather outside.

She thought she could do this. See Jonathan, make small talk, avoid talking about the subjects he clearly wanted to discuss but never did because he was too frightened of putting his foot in it. To visit Saffron's grave and see the new headstone, a visible reminder in perpetuity she wasn't able to do that most basic of things and keep her baby safe inside. Now, she wanted to turn around and return to Grandad's and hide. But she couldn't run away forever. And hopefully it would feel cathartic to lay some flowers for Saffron.

After getting out of the car, she splashed her way down the High Street trying to dodge the puddles, and darted into the florist. There was only one flower shop in the town, otherwise she'd have gone elsewhere. This was where Jonathan had brought her to choose flowers for the funeral. Even walking into the shop again, the overwhelming smell of flowers and greenery, of new life, threatened to push her over the edge.

Thankfully the young woman behind the counter was a different florist, so no problem with being remembered and having to have an uncomfortable conversation. Instead, after exchanging pleasantries about the poor weather, Amber was able to ask for a bouquet of gypsophila and leave with her purchase, laying the flowers with their small, fragile white petals gently on the car seat beside her. It was the flower they had chosen to be laid on the tiny white wicker coffin at her funeral, and Amber couldn't think of anything else to buy.

Eventually she pulled up in the lay-by beside the church. Her hands trembled as she wiped her damp palms down her trousers. She knew she should have parked on the drive at home – the vicarage was right beside the church. Through the trees, she could see its dull yellow bricks threaded with ivy. But for the moment, she didn't want to alert Jonathan to her arrival.

Before, in that other life, the one before Saffron, she'd loved being in that house. It was their hideaway from the world. There had been many lively meals with friends, which carried on long into the night. Her academic colleagues from Cambridge were a good match with Jonathan's ecclesiastical ones, together with old school friends and couples from the village, some with small children or expecting their own babies.

The rain had finally stopped, the sky slowly clearing as the constant drips from the trees bounced off her head and shoulders as she walked slowly towards the church. Maybe she should be doing this with Jonathan, but she wanted silence and peace to be alone with her thoughts.

She followed the path around to the back and then across the grass, freshly mown but sodden with the rain, the grass cuttings sticking to her shoes. The area for the children's graves was in the far corner, set slightly apart from the rest. A small cluster of sorrow. Some of the graves were decorated with plastic windmills, soggy teddies and pottery rabbits. Everyone dealing with loss in their own way.

Saffron's pale cream headstone, its gold lettering glistening under the beads of raindrops decorating it, sparkled in the weak sunlight pushing through the clouds. Kneeling beside it, Amber ran her fingers over the engraved words.

Saffron Morton, born asleep 18 February 2019
And stars climbing the dew-dropping sky,
Live but to light your passing feet

It was every bit as permanent as she had imagined. And it hurt, seeing it, just as much as she knew it would. Gently she laid the flowers she had brought on the small bump of grass in front of the headstone.

68

'I'm sorry,' she whispered. 'I'm sorry you aren't here with us, like we planned. I miss you every day and I know your daddy does as well.' Talking to her daughter was easier than she had imagined it would be and she had a small insight into how Jonathan could find it a comfort to visit the grave and talk to Saffron every morning. She got to her feet and retraced her steps towards the car. She knew what she needed to do now, what she'd agreed to, but she couldn't manage it. It was too hard. Another time, she'd go and see Jonathan another time. She was sure he'd understand why she couldn't do this now.

Standing at the window of the empty nursery, Jonathan watched her kneeling at the graveside before getting slowly to her feet and walking away, her head bowed. Minutes later he heard her car start up and drive away. He rubbed the heels of his hands hard against his eyes, stopping the hot tears from running down his face.

Chapter Nine

2019

The following day, Amber was surprised she had no messages. No missed calls or voicemails, no texts. Nothing. Had she got the day wrong? Hadn't Jonathan been expecting her the previous day when she'd raced back to the sanctuary of Grandad and Saffron Hall as if the devil were at her back? She'd be lucky if she didn't get a speeding ticket.

She double-checked her calendar. She'd definitely got the correct day, so why hadn't he called to find out the reason she hadn't arrived for lunch? After his numerous messages previously, it seemed odd. And maybe, she admitted to herself, she was a tiny bit disappointed there hadn't been a single enquiring message. Even she could tell she was being contrary.

Thankfully Grandad hadn't questioned her when she returned, his tentative 'you're earlier than I was expecting,' was met with her terse 'yes, I am,' and that was the end of the conversation.

Amber decided to put all thoughts of Jonathan to one side, at least for a few hours. If she hadn't heard from him by lunchtime, she'd send an apology and explanation. First of all, she was desperate to start some in-depth investigations on the tiny ancient prayer book, without interruptions. Her heart beat faster every time she thought of it, but she hadn't wanted to start an examination of it the previous day after the upset and the drive home. This precious object required a level head. She pulled on her white gloves.

Before she had a chance to start tackling the Latin, however, she was disturbed by a loud thumping on the front door, followed by the doorbell ringing.

Cursing under her breath – she knew for a fact Grandad was outside in his greenhouse – she pulled her gloves off and marched through to the entrance hall, opening the door.

'Oh. I'd been expecting you to call, not for you to drive all the way here.' Her shock at finding Jonathan on the doorstep made her blurt out a less than polite welcome.

'If Mohammed won't come to the mountain.' He tilted his head to one side and gave her a brief apologetic smile, his eyes creasing in the way that had always made her tummy flip. She felt a flush of embarrassment at her behaviour the previous day as she opened the door wider so he could step inside.

'Come in. Coffee?' she asked. 'There's only instant I'm afraid.'

'I'll cope, thanks.' His need to drink thick, freshly brewed black coffee both day and night was a constant source of jokes between them. 'I hadn't realised the damage to the tower that you mentioned was so bad. I saw the scaffolding around it as I drove up from the village.'

Walking through to the kitchen, she explained about the problems Kenny and Pete had discovered. She filled the kettle and took cups, coffee and a teabag for herself from the cupboard.

'I owe you an apology,' she finally admitted, making herself face him. 'I was going to call when I thought you'd be at home and not busy. I'm sorry about yesterday. It all over-whelmed me, and I didn't know what to say to you. I still don't. I did visit Saffron's grave. The headstone looks . . . good. Well, not good. How can anything about her being there and not with us, be good? But you know, it looks like I expected it to. And I still like the Yeats quote. I'm glad we went with it.' She smiled at him gently, softening her features.

'I saw you,' he admitted.

'Sorry? You did? Where?' She was confused.

'With Saffron. I was watching you from the back bedroom window.' She noticed he no longer called it the nursery. 'I wasn't spying, I happened to glance out, and you were there. Then you left and didn't appear at our front door, so I guessed you'd changed your mind.'

She passed him his drink and squeezed the teabag in her cup, throwing it into the food compost bin. No wonder the weeds grew so profusely in the garden, given the size of compost heap Grandad was building.

'I didn't change my mind,' she protested, immediately on the defensive. He must be so tired of her prickly attitude, because it was certainly exhausting her. It pulled her down to a place she didn't want to be. 'You make it sound so fickle. I just couldn't cope with it. I was upset and I didn't want to talk.'

'About Saffron, or about us?' His shoulders were rigid as he exhaled sharply.

'I don't know.' She shrugged. 'Both maybe.'

'We have to talk at some point, Amber.' His voice rose, his knuckles white as they clasped his cup. 'We can't just drift along like this forever.'

'I know, I know, but not at the moment please – it's not the right time. Not yet. Have we had a letter with an appointment to see the consultant? Remember they said we'd get one?' Abruptly changing the subject, she poured milk into her tea and sat down opposite him.

'No, I'll give them a call and chase it.' He took a sip of his coffee and stared out of the window. 'Have you seen Becky since you arrived?' Becky, her best friend and closest work colleague. They'd both started work at the university within a couple of months of each other, Becky as a lecturer in medieval art history and Amber as an archivist in the same department, often working alongside each other on projects. Within hours of being together they had discovered that Becky lived in the same village as her grandfather, and that coincidence had been one of many.

'No, not yet,' she confessed. 'She called me when I first got here and I said I'd get back to her but I haven't yet. I keep chickening out. The less I talk to people, the less I feel able to.'

'Look, I know it's hard to reach out and speak to people, but it may help. She's your friend and she'll want to help you, and if you can't talk to me then maybe to her? Don't be short-sighted, go and have a chat, even if it's just to have a shoulder to cry on.'

'Crying isn't the answer though, is it?' Her hand came down sharply on the table. 'I spend half my life crying but that won't bring our baby back and neither will talking to someone. How can I pretend to be the old happy smiling Amber when that person has gone and I'll never be her again?'

'I don't know, Amber, I don't have all the answers. But I do know that I miss having you at home. It feels so empty, like you've been gone forever. I want our lives to move on somehow. How much longer will the book archiving here take?' He raised his eyebrows at her. This time it was Amber's turn to admit she didn't have any answers.

'There's still over half to catalogue,' she explained. She almost told him about the precious book of hours, but then stopped herself. Just for a little while longer she wanted to keep it to herself, at least until she'd unearthed the secrets it held. 'I can't come home yet. I feel so upset there, reminders everywhere. I feel calmer here, safer. Saffron Hall has always felt special to me; you know that. We both decided to call our daughter after this place because of the bond I have with it, and right now I feel as if it's protecting me from the world.'

'I know how it makes you feel, but is it protecting you from me as well? You don't have a monopoly on being sad.'

'Of course not from you.' As she said it she wasn't sure the words were true, but she hated seeing him this way, his shoulders hunched as he leant on the table, a broken man. 'But you've got your church, and your calling, a reason to carry on. At the moment I don't have that. I don't have anything.'

'You do have something – you have me. Staying here forever and wallowing in grief isn't the answer, Amber. You've pressed "pause" on both of our lives, but somehow we have to try and find a solution.' Jonathan laid his hands on the kitchen table, palms up.

'I'm not "wallowing"—' she made little inverted commas

in the air with her fingers '—I just need a break from life for a little while. Sometimes I really wonder if you know me at all. If you ever did.' She regretted the words the moment they were out of her mouth and she was devastated when Jonathan, her rock, always her tower of strength, agreed with her.

'So do I, Amber, so do I.' Getting to his feet he shrugged his jacket back on, leaving his coffee on the table. 'We aren't getting anywhere. Perhaps you were right not to stay for lunch yesterday. I'm sorry, I shouldn't have come.' Rummaging through his pockets, always full of the detritus of life, he located his car keys. He came around the table and gave her a peck on the cheek; his dry, cool lips there and then gone, so brief she hardly felt it. She moved to hug him, but he wasn't there. The front door opened and there was a moment's silence as if he'd stopped for a moment, then it slammed shut and she heard his car engine start up. The house was quiet again, every fragment of it holding its breath, as shocked as she was.

Amber poured her cup of tea down the sink and immediately began to make herself another. Now she wished she'd gone to lunch with him the previous day. If they'd been in public neither of them would have felt able to throw accusations at each other as they just had. She felt further away from him than ever. She still loved him, she truly did, but from behind the barriers she'd erected around herself she didn't know how to show him anymore. She had no strength left to try.

Leaving her tea beside the kettle, she wandered back to the office, making a mental note to call Becky and see if they could meet up for a coffee. At least then she'd have done one little thing Jonathan had asked of her.

* * *

The book of hours was still resting in the cradle where she'd left it when Jonathan had knocked on the door. She sat back down in front of it, picking up her gloves but not pulling them on. Leaning back in her chair she gazed out of the window, but the vast expanse of pale cloud, the brilliant light of Norfolk so loved by artists, wasn't offering her any answers.

Finally, giving herself a little shake, she turned to the book. It didn't have any solutions, but it might hopefully provide some distraction. She opened it at the front to reread the Latin inscription, which she had now fully transcribed and couldn't stop thinking about.

> *infans filia sub pedibus nostris requiescit*
> *nunc mihi tempus fugit*
> *oro vos et spero in vobis*
> *pro illa*
> *ut ea in pace requiescat*

What did it mean? She opened the translation app she normally used. There were a few words she recognised but not enough to make sense. The translation wasn't completely straightforward, and eventually Amber had before her a passage that she was still unsure of. The hairs stood up along her arms as she read it and she gave an involuntary shudder.

> *A baby daughter lies beneath our feet*
> *time escapes me now*
> *I beseech you and place my trust*
> *for her*
> *so she may be at peace*

77

What was Eleanor asking? This book was hundreds of years old, and yet Amber had an eerie feeling this was a personal message for her, reaching down through the centuries. If only she knew what Eleanor wanted. It was baffling, and yet there was a connection. A plucking at the filaments of time trying to catch her attention.

Leaving the passage for a moment, she carefully turned the page. She gasped with delight at the miniatures that shone out, their brilliance and colours, rich reds and vibrant hues of blue, with flecks of brilliant gold. It seemed as though the book hadn't been opened since it was originally scribed. These illustrations were saints, she was certain, although she had no idea which ones they were. Becky certainly would. Turning the page again, she was keen to discover what other secrets the book was holding between its covers. Despite the Latin, she recognised the first few words of the Invitatory from other prayer books she had studied, followed by Psalm ninety-four, decorated with yet more delicate illumination that surrounded not just the initial letter, but almost half the page. Either the scribe who worked on it had been paid by the hour and had wanted to drag out the time it took him, or he was really devoted to his work. Either way, it was exquisite and incredibly well preserved.

The following two pages were less decorative and contained a calendar of church feasts as she would have expected, but her eyes widened and she held her hand to her mouth as she turned to the next page and discovered not more prayers, but what appeared to be a journal entry written in a different hand. It was decorated around the edge of the page with a careful attempt at some illuminated art in blues and yellows, although not as fine as the previous pages.

Written in the same distinctive handwriting as the entries in the frontispiece of the book, Amber found it almost as difficult to decipher as the Latin she'd struggled with on the front page, but as time went on, she found it easier to recognise individual letters. Whoever had written it had to be well educated – the writing had been precisely executed. Finally, with the assistance of her app, she was able to read the whole thing, tapping into her laptop as she repeated it out loud.

'Eleanor Lutton, born 29 November in the year of our Lord 1520. Married this March 21 1538 to Sir Greville Lutton. I hope my husband will love me and be kind to me.'

This prayer book must also be Eleanor's journal. The names at the beginning and the dates corresponded. Gently she turned to the front again to check, whilst doing some mental arithmetic. In 1538, Eleanor would have been seventeen, so more than marriageable age. Greville had been almost thirty, so quite a bit older. And Jane's date of birth was 1534, so did Eleanor already have a child? A widow at seventeen, she'd have had Jane aged fourteen – not unheard of in the sixteenth century. But the entry said Jane Lutton, so it seemed more likely Greville was the one who'd been widowed, and the little girl was his.

Why did she hope he'd be kind to her? There was something in the way she wrote it. She sounded scared and worried, a little unsure. Amber gave a shudder. Back in Tudor times, she reminded herself, someone as educated as Eleanor must have been, to be able to write in both English and Latin, would have been married for family or political reasons, or money. Not for love.

She must have been muttering to herself out loud as she worked, because Grandad appeared in the doorway, bringing her back to the present day and making her jump.

'I thought I heard you talking,' he said. 'I wondered if you had a visitor.'

'I was working. Wait until I show you – you're going to love this. But yes I did have a visitor earlier. Jonathan was here.'

Grandad raised his eyebrows. 'And?'

'And nothing. We argued, he stormed out. I feel so guilty. We don't seem to be able to agree on anything at the moment. He suggested I go and visit Becky, see if that helps.'

'You should call in on her. She's your best friend and only a mile away. Locking yourself away here with me and my books all the time isn't going to do you any good. You need to go out and see other people occasionally. Have a chat, get things off your chest. Or invite her up here for dinner again?' He reminded her about the time Becky had come for dinner and a tour of the hall when they'd first realised she lived in the same village as Grandad.

'We'll see. I only agreed to please Jonathan. Anyway, come and sit in my chair and let me show you what was in that package that Pete found up in the tower. This is really exciting.'

Jumping to her feet, she held the chair still with both hands, bracing her hip against it while he carefully sat down. He rested his hands on the desk and peered at the book on the cradle.

'A genuine, perfectly preserved book of hours. Not a Voynich – I think it's later than that although it's hand-scribed not printed. But the best part is that it's also been used as a journal. There are some dates of birth in the frontispiece but here, four pages in, is the recording of the owner Eleanor's marriage to a certain Greville Lutton. Isn't it amazing? How come it was up in the tower? Do you suppose it's been here all the time? Do you know who the

Luttons were? Surely someone has been up there and would have found it before now.'

Grandad shook his head slowly. 'I'd forgotten about Pete finding that package. How amazing. I've told you before that there's always been a family suspicion about the tower. I always thought that was tosh. My father told me nobody should ever try to go up the tower, that it may be haunted, or cursed. Not of course that his warning stopped me.' He chuckled. 'When I was a teenager I made a concerted effort to find the key. Some friends came back from school to stay over and we ransacked the house trying to work out a way of getting up there. A dare, I suppose it was, but when my father discovered what we were up to, he went absolutely crazy. I'd never seen him so angry. I've never felt the desire to go up there again; he put the fear of God into me. It seems that the tales were correct, although I doubt the book is cursed.'

'Of course it isn't. And really it should be in a museum. We can donate it to the Fitzwilliam when we're ready, but do you mind if I carry out some research first? I'm wondering what sort of connection, if any, it has with our family. I know Saffron Hall has been in the family for a long time, but I didn't think we'd been living here as far back as this book dates to.'

'I don't have an issue with you investigating it. I haven't seen you so animated since . . .' he paused '. . . since you came to stay. But make sure it's kept in the safe.'

Amber agreed, helping him to his feet and offering to heat some soup for lunch. After carefully wrapping the book in its frayed shroud, she locked it away.

Chapter Ten

1538

Leaving Joan on her own to unpack upstairs, Eleanor sank into a large carved chair pulled up beside the fire in the great hall. In the cold light of day, she could see it was definitely far grander than the hall at Ixworth. But although Greville had spoken of his home so warmly, it still felt more a fortified house than a refined home. And it was grubby too. She flicked the bottom of her skirt, trying to remove the dust on her hem that had been swept up from the floor. No doubt with Greville away at Ixworth and just Hugh his steward in charge, standards had fallen. There were going to be some changes made at Milfleet, although she wasn't sure yet how successful she'd be in achieving them.

Growing up the apple of her father's eye, she'd had such visions for her future. Her father was nobility and a good match for her was expected. Especially as he'd refused to remarry and produce sons to inherit Ixworth, she was all he had. He'd declined to send her away to a fine house to finish her education and to potentially expose her to the right kind of gentleman, because he'd miss her too much. But she'd always expected to be the mistress of a large estate eventually, maybe even go to court with her husband. She wanted to be someone important, treated with respect. And instead, she'd been married off, with no discussion or agreement, to a man who appeared to be nothing more than a merchant and, it seemed, a minor courtier.

Greville had told her he had a fine establishment in London and a warehouse at the Queenhithe docks there, as well as another warehouse in Lynn only three miles from Milfleet. He'd explained how he traded in silks and spices with the merchants who came over from North Germany as if she would be enthralled, but she wasn't impressed with any of it. She'd been sold to him like a chattel or a servant.

There had been a dowry put aside for her by her father. She knew this for a fact because he'd shown her the chest it was kept in, but that gold was no doubt now added to William's wealth – her suspicions were aroused when he had blatantly stated that her father had left her no dowry. The duplicitous toad. At least she'd never need to see him or his mealy-mouthed wife again, but that also meant she'd never return to Ixworth either. And when she considered that, her eyes prickled with unshed tears.

This was her life now. There was no escape. She felt sick. The learning, education she'd acquired with the monks . . . why had her father bothered? All he'd done was ill-equip her for the life she would now lead, in which she'd be forever dissatisfied with what she had, with little chance to use all that she'd learned.

Discontentedly she kicked out at the tired dry strewings on the floor. Out here in this barren landscape the one thing they must surely be able to achieve was to grow plenty of rushes and hay, so there was no excuse for the paltry evidence she could see about her.

Thinking of what may be growing outside, and how she could manage the physic garden, she remembered the coffer of crocus bulbs the prior had given her. That was the only dowry she came with, and when she'd shown Greville he'd raised his eyebrows in amusement and told her she could have as much acreage to grow them as she wished. She'd spent enough hours helping the monks at Ixworth when it was time to pick the small saffron flowers and harvest the precious fronds, before drying them and pressing them into cakes to be easily transported. It would give her great pleasure to have her own small saffron production at her new home.

Now that she was beginning to form a plan, it made her feel a little happier. Her first task was to request – no, demand – fresh floor coverings throughout the house although she supposed she'd be expected to assist in sweeping the old ones up. That was all right, she told herself, she was not a feeble weakling, and she could help with hard work. Then she needed to get outside in that vast, bleak wilderness surrounding the castle and start deciding what she was going to grow.

Before leaving Ixworth, the prior had helped her copy out the layout of his own gardens, and whatever was missing here she would go out foraging for locally. Greville had told her there was a priory at the other end of the village, so she would be paying them and their gardens a visit very soon. She was certain that for a donation to their coffers, she could purchase some new plants to supplement those which were growing wild and hopefully the local brethren were as friendly and kind as the ones she'd left behind. Thinking of Brother Dominic's smiling eyes helped her heart lift slightly. She didn't know how, but somehow she had to try and make this new life a success. Or at least, bearable.

First of all, what was needed was a tour of her new home. Unfortunately though, it seemed her new husband would not be her guide. Greville had apparently disappeared at dawn to ride to Lynn to visit his warehouseman and inspect a recent shipment from Antwerp. Nobody knew when he was likely to return. She'd ventured into the kitchen looking for Hugh, her husband's steward who she was yet to meet, and the cook had all but ignored her, just informing her that he was outside somewhere. He barely paused in his continuous pounding of the dough on the table in front of him. The other kitchen staff all lowered their eyes and looked away. It wasn't exactly the welcome she'd been hoping for.

Just at the point when she decided she'd go exploring on her own, she heard a door bang somewhere and into the hall strode a tall, thin middle-aged man, his hair sparse and grey, his skin tanned dark. He had a lopsided gait as if his legs were uneven.

'Mistress, Sir Greville asked me to show you around your new home as he has been called away on business. I'm Hugh, your husband's steward.'

'I'm pleased to meet you, Hugh,' Eleanor replied coolly. 'I've been waiting for over an hour for someone to come and show me around.' She watched his shoulders lift and then lower as he let his breath out slowly.

'The bull had escaped. It trampled a fence down. Everyone

was needed to help round it up.' He spoke to her through gritted teeth, then turned ready to leave with no apologies for his tardiness. Obviously the bull was more important than she was. Eleanor seethed, lifting her foot to stamp it on the floor, but then lowered it again.

'The strewings,' she said, 'I assume we have fresh in the barn?'

'Yes, mistress.'

'And lavender? Meadowsweet?'

'I expect so, my lady.' Hugh sounded confused.

'Good. Instruct someone to have them all replaced downstairs, please. And to make sure the floor is swept well before the new goes down. I want it done before dinner.' She had to tilt her head back he was so much taller than her, and she looked him steadily in the eye until eventually his lowered. But not before she'd seen the dark flint of rebellion in them.

'Yes, mistress,' he said, 'now if you'd like to come upstairs, I'll show you the rooms up there.' Feeling a little less shaky than she had before, Eleanor swept past him and ascended the stairs.

Upstairs the chambers were pleasant and definitely better furnished than at Ixworth, although Eleanor didn't want to admit it to herself. There had been little point filling the bedrooms with fine furnishings and tapestries when there had only been herself and her father, and half a dozen servants. Joan had slept on a truckle in her bedroom since she'd arrived when they were both young girls, and it had never occurred to either of them to change the arrangement until Eleanor married. She was pleased to see that the room next to hers had been prepared for Joan. Her companion would be delighted to finally have a room of her own.

When she saw the enormous, decorative bed that was her

husband's, she drew her breath in sharply. It was the biggest she'd ever seen. The drapes around it were heavy and luxurious and beautifully embroidered, shining with glossy threads, the mattress so deep she wondered how he climbed up onto it. She stepped into the room to run her fingers down the panels, and to examine the bed she would probably have to occupy before long. She had to admit the room showed her a different side to the man who was now her husband. She hadn't imagined he would enjoy such comfort and realised he was a man she knew little about.

A huge fireplace dominated the wall opposite the bed, and the walls were mostly covered with dark tapestries similar to the ones in her own room. As she went to walk out of the room, Hugh hovering in the doorway as if disapproving of her being in there, she ran her finger around one of the turned posts of the bed. It came away thick with dust. Without a word she held it out towards Hugh as she left the room, not missing the black scowl he gave her. She knew she was fast making an enemy of him, but she'd been able to tell from the moment he'd introduced himself that he had no kind thoughts about her, so she had nothing to lose.

At the opposite end of the dark passage from which the bedrooms lay, was a room that made Eleanor gasp with delight. A solar, with wide windows made of tiny leaded panes, jutted out from the corner of the house overlooking the kitchen garden. Along the top of the window the light shone through small panes of stained glass and a myriad of jewel colours spread across the floor. Three chairs were arranged beside a small fireplace, and at the other end of the room stood a low table. A seat each for her and Greville and Jane, she thought. How long would it be before further chairs would be added as their family continued to expand?

'Lady Elizabeth, Master Greville's first wife, particularly liked this room,' Hugh said, defying Eleanor to say anything bad about it. But there was nothing she could decry about the room. She'd never seen anything so lovely.

'I'm not surprised; it's beautiful. So light – the sunshine through the window makes it sparkle. I shall enjoy spending time here,' she said. Even being polite and saying something complimentary didn't alter the look of disdain etched on his face.

The floor above was dark, but at one end was the nursery wing, which looked warm and cleaner than the rest of the house. There was a fire crackling in the grate and two narrow beds lay at one end of the big room. It was, however, empty of its occupants.

'Where's my stepdaughter, do you know?' Eleanor asked.

'Probably in the orchard – it's where she and her maid Nell are usually to be found when the weather is fine. Or out riding. The master recently purchased a pony for Jane and sometimes she practises in one of the meadows.'

Eleanor nodded. She was keen to meet the little girl who had surely been told that she was to get a new mamma, yet nobody had seen fit to bring her to be introduced. The air of hostility emanating from Hugh appeared to be shared by the rest of the household. It was of no concern, she would show them by her actions who she was, and that she wouldn't be intimidated by anyone.

'I'd like a tour of downstairs now, please.' Without waiting for a response, she swept out of the room and descended the stairs, back into the great hall, still feeling less assured than she appeared. Hugh briefly showed her down the corridor behind the stairs, which contained several store-rooms, a door to the outside and a couple of bedrooms.

'My room, mistress,' he said, standing in the doorway as if defying her to enter. She put her head around the door and noticed how bare and utilitarian it was, lacking in the drapes and tapestries of upstairs. It was not remotely welcoming. How apt.

She'd previously found the kitchen, and once again Cook ignored her as she walked through. Behind the hot kitchen were pantries, a cold store and a stillroom. Eleanor stepped inside the stillroom. The space where the many medications she could produce would be prepared, and the herbs and spices so vital to her work would be stored. This was her territory and she turned round in a full circle, taking in the whole room. It had an air of abandonment and sorrow. Some dusty flagons stood on the shelf, a pestle and mortar discarded on the table with dried seeds still lying in the bottom. As if the previous incumbent had stepped outside for a moment, but never returned. She knew her predecessor Lady Elizabeth had died within hours of giving birth. Had she been working in here and gone into labour, going to her room never to return? It looked as if someone might walk back in at any moment. Eleanor shuddered.

Beyond the stillroom was the dairy, the creamery, bake-house and the alehouse, then a gateway to the yard. In stark comparison to the inside of the house, out here was pristine. Swept clean with several chickens pecking about hopefully, looking for grain. It was lined on one side with the house and two others by barns. The fourth side was open and fell away down a grassy bank.

'Orchard, kitchen garden, home farm.' Hugh swept his arm towards the grass. 'Stables are around to the right, round the corner from the house.'

'Formal gardens?' Eleanor asked.

He gave a huff of sardonic laughter. 'Long since overgrown. They've barely been touched since the late mistress passed away.'

'Physic garden?' she tried again.

'It used to be part of the kitchen garden, but it's not there anymore, just the herbs that Cook uses,' came the reply. She followed him back through the kitchens and into the great hall before going through a low, wide doorway and into another part of the house. It was cooler here, and Eleanor shivered involuntarily.

'Sir Greville's office,' Hugh said, opening a door immediately to the left. A big solid desk took up most of the room, and behind it against the wall was a long trestle table, neat piles of paperwork tidily stacked along it. Similar heaps of paper sat on Greville's desk, together with his inkpot, some quills and a stick of dark red sealing wax. There were also some thin wooden spills for lighting fires and candles, and his heavy gold seal.

'We're in the base of the tower here,' Hugh explained as he led her out of the office and into a small reception hall. 'That path—' he pointed towards a narrow path leading outside from a small door, overgrown with grasses and shrubs and shrouded by dark yew trees '—leads to the chapel.'

'It doesn't look used.' Eleanor frowned. 'Surely the household prays daily?'

'There is another door, mistress, from the garden. A priest comes from the village daily for matins, but only holds mass

91

on Sundays. The household all attend mass, of course.' Eleanor winced at their heathen ways. She already had her suspicions that her new husband wasn't as religious as he should be.

'I want this path cleared,' she snapped, 'and I expect mass to be celebrated every day. Please show me the other entrance.'

Eleanor followed him along the path and inside the chapel, where she was stunned into silence. As she drew in a deep breath, she could feel the icy cold crawl down inside her, a sharp comparison to the warm atmosphere outside. The air was filled with the muted scent of dust and incense, the sunlight filtering through the stained glass and throwing an arc of dappled colours on the tiled floor. But this paled into invisibility compared to the altar upon which sat a glorious triptych, its images of the Virgin Mary and her baby son surrounded by the Magi, their gilded gifts shining out, the jewelled shades from the windows dancing across it bringing the painted figures to life.

'How beautiful,' Eleanor whispered as she walked up the short aisle to genuflect, dropping one knee to the floor and bowing her head in reverence, in front of the altar. 'Has this been in the family long?' She turned to ask Hugh who was still stood in the doorway.

'I don't know, mistress. I suggest you ask Sir Greville.' He shrugged, his disinterest palpable. After taking one last look at the triptych, Eleanor strode out again and walked back towards the hall leaving Hugh to shut the chapel door. She paused at the back door of the hall as she waited for him to catch up with her.

'And the tower?' She indicated the rough, undersized wooden door that opened onto the small vestibule. 'Does this lead up to the top?'

'I believe so, mistress, but only Sir Greville has the key for up there, so you'll need to ask him if you wish to view it.'

'Thank you, Hugh. I'll take a walk around the gardens by myself now.'

He dipped his head and twitched his shoulders as if he was going to bow, but changed his mind at the last moment. Eleanor inclined her head before walking away in the direction he had indicated would lead her to the gardens. She kept her back ramrod straight, her hands clasped at her waist so he couldn't see they were balled into fists. She hoped her face was not as red as she imagined it was, as it burned with suppressed fury.

The man was insufferable. His high regard for Greville's first wife was obvious, and his contempt for her, equally so. She may be considerably younger than her husband, but her position was a fait accompli not just for her, but for the household as well. He might not like it, but they were both going to have to live with it.

She found the orchard and kitchen gardens, shaking her head in frustration at the state of the beds. Some had been dug over and she could see the tops of a variety of vegetables, but there was no sign of a proper physic garden. It was a disappointment; however, she would simply have to start from scratch and lay out her own. She also needed to find a field where she could grow her precious saffron and could already imagine the battle if she approached Hugh. She'd ask Greville directly. As she walked through the overgrown plants, her skirts brushed against leaves that released familiar pungent scents. Her eyes welled up as they reminded her of home. It shouldn't be too difficult, she thought, to equip herself with the means to start producing the medicines and potions she had at her disposal at Ixworth.

Shouting and laughter drifted across on the breeze from the orchard, and going through the gate at the end of the kitchen garden, she followed the noise. At the far end a young woman was chuckling as she chased a small child around an apple tree until they collapsed on the grass, exhausted and giggling. A small flock of half a dozen sheep huddled against the far wall staring at her with glassy eyes as she walked past.

'Hello.' She smiled at them both. 'I heard you playing. I'm Eleanor.'

Immediately the woman, her hood skewed on the back of her head with a lot of her hair escaping, jumped to her feet and curtseyed.

'Sorry, mistress,' she blustered, 'I didn't realise. I thought you were . . . sorry.' She curtseyed again. Eleanor suspected the girl had thought she was one of the new mistress's maids because she was younger than anyone was expecting.

'And you are?' she enquired.

'I am Nell, mistress. Nursery maid. This is Jane, the master's daughter.' She indicated to the little girl who was now silent but remained seated on the grass.

Eleanor knelt down beside her and took her small hand. 'Hello, Jane.' She smiled encouragingly. 'I'm your new step-mamma. I'm so happy to be here at your home.' It wasn't true, but Jane didn't need to know that. She looked up at Nell and indicated to her to sit back down with them.

The child was a perfect miniature replicate of her father. The same dark watchful eyes and almost black hair, but whereas Greville's face was creased with lines, open and laughing, Jane was solemn and unsure. Eleanor could hardly blame her, she supposed, to be presented with a young woman and told she was suddenly her new mamma. For that matter, it was a shock for her as well. Five weeks ago she had never heard of Greville, and now she was a married woman with a daughter and home where she felt that she held no jurisdiction whatsoever. However could she start to change things? Because change things she would.

Chapter Eleven

2019

The following day, Amber mustered up the courage to send Becky a text apologising for her radio silence and suggesting they met for a coffee. She'd spent all night thinking about the tiny prayer book and who exactly Eleanor Lutton was, and she'd already made up her mind to go and investigate the village church that day, hoping to find graves or a memorial there. It was fortuitous that there was a newly opened tea shop in the village, and when Becky replied almost immediately to her message, Amber explained that she wanted to do some historical research at the church and they arranged to meet there that afternoon, from where they could wander to the café for coffee.

As soon as she and Grandad had eaten lunch, Amber set off. She'd expected a text from Jonathan, apologising for his outburst or at least letting her know he was home safely, but she'd received nothing and she couldn't deny the twinge of disappointment she felt. Yet at the same time, there was

97

an excitement buzzing in her chest that she hadn't felt for such a long time she hardly recognised the feeling. Walking briskly down the stony track that led from the hall to the village, she pushed her hands into her jacket pockets and kicked at the rubble at her feet.

There was a sharp, cutting wind blowing off the coast only a couple of miles away, and Amber pulled her collar around her face, the cold making her eyes water. Even when she wasn't crying, her body produced tears as if it was a system default.

The village appeared to be deserted. With no local school anymore, parents were already in their cars on their way to King's Lynn to collect their children, and it was far too bleak for any old age pensioners to be out for a stroll. There was a car in the car park beside the derelict priory, and she could see the flash of a turquoise coat as someone walked around the few pieces of wall that remained.

The main body of the priory, the nave, and also the chancel where the altar stood, had escaped the desecration of the other buildings and was now the village church, and it was into that building that Amber let herself, pleased to be out of the wind.

Grandad had told her about the church and its history previously, but that was when she was a teenager and totally uninterested. Now, Amber could see why he'd been so enthusiastic about the ancient and magnificent architecture surrounding her. This was the nave of the original priory and tilting her head back she could see soaring above her, tier upon tier of Norman arches, appearing to reach up to heaven, the ceiling was so high. In front of her stood a once ornate rood screen, a wooden barrier separating the congregation from the priest, sadly displaying where painted protestant texts desecrated the original decorative saints. Henry VIII had a lot to answer for.

As she wandered around her eyes scanned the plaques on the wall and the worn slabs at her feet, searching for any reference to the Luttons. But there was nothing. Plenty of 'Greens', her grandfather's surname, her mother's maiden name. She knew their family had lived at Saffron Hall for a long time so it wasn't any surprise to find her ancestors honoured by mourning relatives. But she wasn't interested in them; she wanted to find some tangible evidence to link the church to whoever Eleanor Lutton had been. The woman who'd once owned the precious medieval book.

Sitting on a pew towards the back, she leant forward and closed her eyes, waiting, hoping for something. Comfort, a sign, anything, she didn't know what. But nothing happened. If God wanted her to understand why her daughter had died, as Jonathan seemed to think, he wasn't telling her anything today. All she heard was the wind whistling under the door behind her, and the angry squawking of a magpie somewhere in the churchyard.

She sat up again, wondering where Becky was and if she was stood outside waiting when suddenly the door behind her swung open, letting in an icy gust of wind and Becky fell in, slamming the door behind her.

'Blimey it's windy out there!' She pushed her windswept hair out of her eyes and enveloped Amber in a bear hug that threatened to squash all the air out of her. It was, Amber realised as she stood with her face pressed into the rough wool of her friend's coat, exactly what she needed. Hugs weren't very prevalent at Grandad's. He wasn't the touchy feely sort of person, and Amber's own mother had never encouraged hugs or cuddles when Amber was a child. She'd grown up used to a lack of human warmth until she'd met Jonathan and now she realised, she was missing it. 'You're looking far too slim,' her friend admonished as she finally let go of Amber and held her at arm's length giving her an appraising look.

'I've been so busy I keep forgetting to eat.' Even to Amber's ears her defence sounded exactly what it was: a thin excuse.

'Then we must rectify that immediately, let's go to Dolly's Tea Shop and eat cake.' Becky tucked her arm through Amber's as if she may need to drag her friend there.

'Good idea,' Amber agreed, 'but before we do that, I'm just doing some investigations and I need to have a quick look around the churchyard. I'll explain later over our tea and cake but can you help me first please?'

'This sounds mysterious.' Becky laughed. 'And there's nothing we historians like more than a mystery. What exactly are we looking for?'

'Any graves or vaults for the family name Lutton.' Amber held the door open and they both gasped as the cold wind whipped around the edge of the porch and struck them in the face. Becky followed her across the ruins of the priory that surrounded the church until they reached the churchyard. To their left were rows of modern, shiny granite headstones and Amber averted her eyes, fearful that she would see a monument to a baby. Instead she led them over to the older section, now overgrown with coarse grasses in some places as tall as the graves and scattered with cowslips. Pulling the undergrowth to one side, Amber began to scan the graves she could still read for the names she was so desperate to find.

100

'Most of these are too worn away to read.' Becky stated the obvious, and Amber sighed, nodding in agreement.

'You're right, and the ones I wanted to see may well have not been buried here anyway. It would have been a family vault in the church itself, I'm sure, and I looked there before you arrived.'

'Well I'm freezing so can we give this up for now and look again when the weather is warmer? I can hear a pot of tea calling my name from Dolly's.' Becky was already walking back to the gate and speaking over her shoulder so Amber didn't have any choice but to follow.

Once inside the tea shop and quickly warming up over their tea and cake, Becky asked, 'So how are you really? That was a bit unkind what I blurted out in the church, but I was shocked. I haven't seen you for almost two months and you're looking really gaunt. I had a jolt when I saw you.' She put her hand over Amber's and squeezed it, which was nearly her undoing.

'It doesn't get any easier,' Amber admitted, taking a shaky breath. 'Coming out here to catalogue Grandad's books and have some peace was supposed to help but so far I don't seem to feel any different. Every day is still a struggle. I just hurt, all the time. Jonathan came over to see me yesterday but that didn't go very well.'

'How is he?' Becky asked. She'd always been close to both of them and Amber knew that she cared deeply not only about herself, but her husband as well. And she was grateful for that.

'I'm not sure. It feels like he's moved on although you know Jonathan, he never talks about his feelings.' Even as she said it, Amber knew that the words she'd spoken weren't true. He hadn't moved on any more than she had; they were both stranded on an island, but at the moment they were on different ones, slowly drifting away from each other.

'That doesn't mean he isn't heartbroken too; we all grieve in different ways. Give him time, like he's doing for you. And I'm always here if you want to talk.'

Amber nodded. She knew she could depend on her friend. As well as seeing each other at work most days, Becky was also a frequent visitor to the vicarage for dinner and she enjoyed Jonathan's company as much as Amber's.

Abruptly changing the subject to something she felt more comfortable with, and that she knew her friend would be fascinated by, she explained about the ancient prayer book that had been found in the tower.

'How incredible,' Becky breathed, as instantly hooked as Amber had predicted she would be. 'I noticed the scaffolding around the tower – it can be seen all over the village – and I was going to ask what work you were having done. But you say the builders just found it up there?'

'Uh-huh. Grandad reckons that nobody has been up there for hundreds of years. When I used to ask as a kid when we visited if I could go up, he'd just say no, and in that sort of way that told me there was no point arguing. He once said the key was lost and I knew the door at the bottom was locked, because if it wasn't I wouldn't have asked, I'd have just gone up. But when I told him about the book he said his father had told him that the tower is cursed or haunted or something and that nobody must ever go up there so that's why it's remained sealed off.'

'That's amazing. And a bit spooky. So why does it have scaffolding round it?'

'It was hit by lightning in that storm a couple of weeks ago. But actually when they went up to have a look at the damage it appears that it's worse than we thought. It's been crumbling away for years and now has a big crack so they have to almost dismantle the top. One of the builders had to completely remove a window and found the book just lying on the windowsill wrapped up in a piece of old cloth.'

'So, when can I come and see it?' Becky asked.

'I wondered how long it would be until you invited yourself up.' Amber laughed. 'Why don't you come after work tomorrow and I'll cook us dinner? I know Grandad would like to see you too.'

'Brilliant, I'd love that thank you.' They made arrangements for the following evening and hugged goodbye. Amber felt distinctly lighter than she had when she'd walked down to the village. Perhaps Jonathan and Grandad had been right, after all.

After walking back, she stopped on the drive for a moment, admiring the building she'd taken for granted for so many years. As a child, it had always been simply Grandad's home, a chilly and draughty place she'd visited with her parents a couple of times a year. The house had been dark, disturbing and cold in the winter, but it was better in the summer, when she could get out and about exploring. For her mother the trips had always been a chore. Amber suspected she still resented the fact that instead of growing up in the ancestral home with her father, she had spent her childhood in a three-bedroom semi-detached house in Cheam with her maternal grandparents, who were in perpetual mourning for their daughter.

Now, looking at it through adult eyes, she could appreciate

how lovely it was. The tower always drew her eyes towards it, a majestic focal point on the landscape. It felt as if it was part of her heritage, a piece of her soul. Of course, she knew Saffron Hall would be her legacy, the family home and the reason her daughter bore the name of the precious spice, a mark of respect to her dear Grandad and his home. Even though nobody had ever discovered the origin of the name. She was certain it had originally been much bigger, a fortified castle and all that now remained was the great hall and a handful of smaller rooms. It had been divided into a kitchen and reception rooms about two hundred years ago and these days it bore very little resemblance to how it originally looked, with most of the architectural features removed. Luckily the bedrooms above had for the most part managed to avoid the renovations over the centuries, still retaining the huge fireplaces and linen-fold panelling, now dull with age.

The only section that was remotely original and untouched was the tower, which currently looked forlornly out over the surrounding countryside, shrouded in its metallic casing, twice as tall as the house itself. It had always consisted of one room at the base, which was now opened up into the library, behind which was a small vestibule with a locked door concealing the stairs leading to the top. There was the outline of a bricked-up doorway in the little hallway, but having previously looked at the outside Amber couldn't imagine where it led. If only her ancestors had taken more care to log the alterations they were carrying out, it would help her curious nature now.

★ ★ ★

True to her word, Becky arrived the following evening. And after a hastily thrown together pasta bolognese, they decamped to the office. Once they had both equipped themselves with cotton gloves, Amber reverently took the book from the safe and unwrapped it, laying it on the velvet cradle.

'What a find,' Becky breathed, running her fingertips over the tooled exterior. 'Did you say it was wrapped in this cloth when it was found? Where exactly *did* the builder find it?'

'It was just lying on the window ledge in the tower, as if someone had put it down and forgotten to pick it up again. Apparently there's nothing else up there. Given how untidy Grandad can be it doesn't really surprise me that possibly some ancestor just left it there instead of putting it away where it belonged. And how fortuitous for us that they did or it would have been thrown out or sold at some point over the past five hundred years.'

'And what about this wrapping? It seems to be from the same era.' Becky pulled at it gently, examining the fibres.

'I'm not certain, but I believe it may be.' Amber opened it out on her desk. 'See that embroidery? It looks quite simplistic. I don't know a lot about the history of textiles, but I think it's about right for Tudor times.'

'It's quite badly stained as well. I don't wish to sound morbid, but that dark patch there looks like a bloodstain.'

'Oh yuck.' Amber shuddered. 'That hadn't occurred to me, but you may be right. I think I'll be calling in favours with the forensic lab at the university as well then. You've got more influence than me. Could you have a word please?'

Becky nodded, examining the front of the book with Amber's eyepiece wedged in her socket. 'This leatherwork on the front is exquisite, but hasn't fared well over the passage of time. Have you deciphered it yet?'

'No I haven't been able to. It does look quite worn away.'

'What's this writing underneath? A family motto?'

'I'm not sure. I can't make it out. How's your Latin?'

'Not perfect but I suspect better than yours. Let's have a go. Have you got a pen? This first word looks like *Dem*. Or *Dum*?'

Amber screwed her eyes up and tilted her head on one side, running her fingers over the word. 'You're right, I think it's "*Dum*". See if you can work out the second word.' She couldn't help the sharp spike of excitement that leapt inside her.

'I think the first letter is an old S. It's the same as the next word actually; it looks identical. That's odd.' Slowly, they deciphered the next few letters.

'S-P-I or maybe E-R-U. Or O.' Amber read them out. 'It doesn't make any sense.'

'Oh wait of course, yes it does, "*Dum Spiro Spero*".' Becky breathed in sharply. 'I'm so stupid – why didn't I see that? It's an old Latin proverb. "While I Breathe, I Hope." That must've been the family motto of the original owner of this book. How amazing.' Becky sounded as excited as Amber felt.

'Thank you so much.' Amber hugged her friend who was almost jumping up and down in elation. 'I would never have been able to work that out without your help.'

'It was my pleasure. I haven't had so much fun in ages. I know we look at these sorts of things every day at work but that's in the sterile environment of the university, and those are objects with no personal connection. This could be part of your family history. I'm feeling quite envious!'

106

Amber laughed. 'You've been brilliant. And I haven't even shown you inside the book yet. There's a list at the front with the birth dates of the children. Although one of them, Thomas, doesn't have a proper date, just the month and year, I don't think it's his date of birth. I wonder if he was taken in, maybe an orphan from a distant relative, or just sent to live with them by another family member? I'll have to keep reading through it to see if there is an explanation. The other children all have proper dates of birth.'

'Oh I really want to have a good look, but I need to get going now. I've stayed here far too long. My mother has roped me in to join the local yoga class in the village hall so I've got to go. Can I persuade you to come along and join in? It would get you out of the house for a while.'

Amber shook her head. She had far more important things to be doing.

'Quickly show me inside and promise I can come again and look properly another day then,' Becky said. 'I'll bring more cake, and wine.'

'Of course, come any time.' She carefully opened the book at the beginning, on the page with the brightly illuminated miniatures of the saints. 'Aren't they exquisite?' Amber closed it again. She felt a little guilty she deliberately hadn't shown Becky the passage in the front, but for the time being it was her secret. Somehow she was convinced that Eleanor's message was meant for her. And her alone.

As they said goodbye at the door, Becky paused for a moment.

'If you won't come and have a go at yoga, and to be honest I can hardly blame you, I don't suppose I could persuade you to come to the pub quiz with me on Thursday could I? Don't worry if you'd rather not. I can always find a team to join in with. The proceeds raised are for good local causes and I do like to help, but it would be fun to actually have a team of my own for a change. Would your grandfather come as well?'

Amber tried to think of a reason not to go. She didn't feel up to socialising with people she didn't know, but being there with Becky would make it easier.

'Come on, you'll enjoy it.' It was as if her friend was reading her mind, the emotions pirouetting across her face.

'I probably won't enjoy it,' she replied, smiling as she said it, 'but okay, tell me what time and I'll be there. I'll ask Grandad if he wants to come along as well. I might be able to persuade him if I offer to buy us dinner first.'

After Becky's remarks about the potential bloodstain on the wrapping, Amber placed the cloth in a sealed bag back in the safe until she could organise some tests on it. She opened the book again, turning to the page after the one where she'd read about Eleanor's arrival at Milfleet, and discovered a carefully annotated list of herbs. It was like she was glimpsing through a shift in time into the other woman's life. Although it should feel intrusive, instead she felt as if she was being pulled in purposefully, as if Eleanor wanted her to become involved in a story that had played out five hundred years ago. '*Dum Spiro Spero*. While I Breathe, I Hope.' What exactly had those words meant to Eleanor, in 1538? She stared at the book. Was having hope really that simple? And would she ever be able to embrace the sentiment? Leaning back in her chair she stared at the pages open in front of her, but her mind was in another place, slowly mulling over the events and conversations of the previous few days.

Away in the distance, Amber heard the faint peal of the ancient church bells as they rang out across the village, an ageless sound echoing across the flat lands that Eleanor had called home.

Grandad was only too happy to accompany her to the pub quiz when she'd tempted him with real ale and a dinner that would involve proper chips and not the cardboard-flavoured offerings that she put on a tray in the oven. She drove them down and found a disabled parking bay beside the pub door.

Inside it was already fairly full. It was obviously a popular village event. Lots of people hailed Grandad and called hello as Amber steered him towards the last vacant table, before going to the bar to order drinks and fish and chips for them both.

They'd just finished eating and the pub had filled up even further when Becky arrived at their table, together with some sheets of paper.

'I've registered us as a team,' she told them. 'I had to think of a name but my mind went blank. So we're now "Saffron Hall's Heroes". Sorry.'

Grandad gave a big thumbs-up but Amber pulled a face. 'There's nothing much heroic about us,' she replied, 'but I don't suppose it will make any difference to our scores.'

'Did I hear you say you're looking for a hero?' A voice behind her made her twist around in the stool she was sitting on, to see their builders, Pete and his father Kenny, stood behind her.

'If you're here for the quiz then yes, we need all the help we can get.' She laughed, shuffling her seat to one side so the two men could join their table. 'I hope you're both good at sports questions!'

In the end Amber was pleased she'd agreed to go with Becky and although they didn't win or even come in the top three places, they didn't disgrace themselves and she was surprised to find she spent a lot of the evening laughing. Eventually Grandad started to yawn and she realised it was almost ten o'clock.

'I'm going to head home now,' Kenny announced. 'I'll take your grandfather home; it's on my way. You youngsters stay for a last drink. I'll see you later, Pete.'

Amber thanked him and helped Grandad on with his coat before going to the bar for another round of drinks. Driving down to the pub meant that she'd been on orange juice all evening, but Becky and Pete were both walking as Pete was staying with his parents overnight, and they'd ended up sharing a bottle of wine. Leaning on the bar she watched them both chatting and laughing together. Gone was the shy builder who stood quietly in the kitchen while she loaded his tray with hot drinks and packets of biscuits. He was like a different person. And Becky looked about ten years younger as she threw her head back and roared with laughter at something Pete had said. Amber watched his gaze resting on Becky's face and she was certain he was attracted to her vivacious friend.

Eventually it was time to leave and she said goodbye to them both before walking over to retrieve her car, now the only one left in the car park. It was dark and she shivered. Whenever she went out with Jonathan he would bring the car around to the pub or theatre door so she could stay in the warm and not have to negotiate potholed car parks. She missed his quiet, subtly chivalric ways. He would have loved the pub quiz. They often went to the one held at their local and he immediately morphed into a contestant on *Mastermind*, he was so competitive. The thought of him sat alone in the vicarage with a ready meal for one in front of the television instead of being at the pub with her and her friends, brought tears to her eyes. And she knew it wasn't just the cold evening air doing it this time.

Pulling onto the main street through the village, her headlights picked up Pete and Becky ahead of her as they walked along together. They weren't holding hands or even walking especially close to each other, but she could see their arms almost brush together as they moved and she smiled to herself as she turned up the track towards home. When would she be that close to Jonathan again? The casual holding of hands, the presentation to the world that they were whole, a unit.

Chapter Twelve

1538

Eleanor didn't see her husband until supper time on her first day at Milfleet. The household was sat along benches at the long dining table, which stretched across the width of the great hall. She noticed a large carved chair set at one end had been moved to the head of the table and a smaller less elaborate chair had been stationed beside it. She shunned it, however, sitting on the end of the bench beside Nell and Jane, telling Joan to sit opposite her. This resulted in Hugh having to move down from where he usually sat. He opened his mouth as if to argue, but then closed it again, instead glaring at her from his new position. Eleanor studiously ignored him, turning her attention to Jane who was beginning to open up a little, like a tight flower bud slowly unfurling in the warm sunshine.

Eleanor stood to say the '*Benedictio Mensae*' and everyone shuffled to their feet again. Afterwards when they were all seated once more, everybody began to eat. When Greville walked in Eleanor didn't notice him at first, but her eating companions did. All along the table the chatter and noise subsided slightly and people sat up straighter as he strode across the room to the larger chair at the end of the table. He raised his eyebrows quizzically as he spotted Eleanor sat on the end of the bench beside Jane. Pulling at the smaller chair beside his own he held his hand out to her, guiding her out of her seat and onto the chair before sitting down beside her, both at the head of the table. A cheer went up from the garden workers at the far end as she settled in her seat. She smiled her thanks to Greville, but he'd already turned away, speaking with Hugh across Joan who sat studying the food on her plate silently.

Seeing her father, Jane immediately left her seat and ran to him, and he scooped her up off the floor and onto his lap tickling her as she squealed and wriggled ecstatically, wrapping her arms around him. Eleanor smiled as she watched the pair. It was the first time she'd seen this different side of him. Gone was the brisk, serious gentleman, a businessman with no time for his family or his new wife. Here was a man who clearly adored his little daughter, doted on her. Her mind drifted back to her own father and she couldn't help making favourable comparisons.

Finally they settled down, Jane sat on Greville's knee as he sliced meat from the joint in front of him and fed them to her as well as placing delicate morsels on Eleanor's platter. As the chatter around the table resumed, he leant forward to Eleanor and she was conscious of his warm musty smell. It wasn't unpleasant.

'How has your first day at Milfleet been? Have you enjoyed it?'

'Yes, thank you. Hugh showed me around the hall and the gardens. I am most impressed with the chapel, although it does need a proper clean. The altarpiece is wonderful. I've never seen anything like it. Do you know where it came from?'

'It arrived in a consignment from Amsterdam and I gave it to Elizabeth. I'm pleased you like it.' He smiled at her as she nodded.

'I'm concerned the household do not attend prayers often enough.' She glanced at him out of the corner of her eye, wary of his reaction. She had only just arrived and it was a criticism of the way his home was managed and in particular of his steward, but Greville didn't seem concerned.

'Then you must arrange things as you wish,' he told her. 'Tell Hugh which services you wish to be held, and that the servants and family must be present.' She wasn't sure it would be as easy as he predicted, but whilst he was in a generous mood she continued with her requests.

'Would you object if I create a new physic garden in part of the kitchen gardens?'

'Of course not. You're mistress here now and you may do whatever you wish in the hall grounds, inside the house and the chapel. Just ask Hugh for whatever you want. And outside you need Simon, my estate manager. I'll introduce you tomorrow.' She was certain the steward wouldn't be as generous and benevolent as her husband suggested.

'Also, will you take me up the tower please?' she asked, nibbling at the cheese he placed beside her meat. She wasn't sure if he'd agree.

He paused. 'Yes, but I need to take you up there myself. Nobody else has a key other than me, although I'll show you where it's kept.'

115

As the meal broke up she spotted Hugh speaking to Greville in a low voice and gesticulating towards the table, but Greville just shrugged and turned away, earning her another black look from the steward.

Taking her hand and tucking it into the crook of his arm, Greville led her through the door at the far end of the house and into his office at the base of the tower. Immediately she could see the furniture had been moved a little since she'd been shown the room earlier, and a small writing desk was squashed in beside his much larger one.

'I've had this desk put in here for you. My late wife had it in her room but rarely used it. For if you want to write letters, or whilst you are working on the household accounts.'

'Thank you,' she said with delight, 'it's lovely.'

'I'll illuminate on everything here—' he gestured towards the trestle table weighed down with documents '—in due course. You can't learn all you need to know at once. But now, let me show you the tower room.'

Dropping to his haunches, he crawled under his desk and collected a key from a small shelf that was hidden away on the wall beneath it, and he led the way to the back hall, unlocking the door she'd seen earlier.

'The stairs are steep,' he warned and she hitched up the front of her skirts to prevent herself tripping as she followed him. The steps were indeed steep and she was out of breath by the time they got to the top where there was another locked door, leading into the room. Occasional arrow-slit windows let in just enough light as they ascended the steps. The darkness of the stairwell was in direct contrast to the bright room at the top, with two walls set with windows, the tiny panes of leaded glass ensuring the room was flooded with light. Surprised at what she had stepped into, Eleanor screwed her face up against it as she turned slowly in the centre of the room. There was a fireplace directly above the one in the office downstairs.

'What is this room used for?' she asked eventually. 'I don't understand, why keep it locked?'

'These days there are fewer reasons to lock it,' he agreed, 'but there have been times in the past it's been a helpful hideaway. And you can see horses arriving from many miles away, so it's a good lookout. That's always useful. If you look through this window—' with his hands on her shoulders he steered her over '—you can see the sea. Now, as my wife—' his voice grew serious '—I'm going to show you something. A secret. There is nobody in this world still alive, who knows about this apart from me. And now, you. And we must keep it that way.'

Eleanor turned, his hands still firm on her shoulders so she was facing him. He was closer than she thought and her face almost touched the thick dark wool of his doublet. She could feel the warmth emanating from him. When she tilted her head back his eyes, almost black beneath his equally dark straight brows, were staring into hers as if weighing up whether to divulge his secret. Her heart thumped hard in her chest, suddenly so close to him, and she wondered if he could feel it as well, through their clothes.

'My lord?' Her voice cracked slightly and her hands felt clammy. He let go of her shoulders and as his arms fell, he caught her fingertips with his own before leading her over to a corner of the room, close to the fireplace.

'You must promise never to tell anyone what I'm about to show you.' She was afraid of the serious tone in his voice and she nodded mutely. 'Sometimes, it's necessary as the head of the household, to hide things. Money, jewellery, things that may be taken. Things we don't want others to know about. Even from those who profess to be one's friends. Do you understand?' She nodded again although, in truth, she wasn't sure what he was talking about. 'If you ever need to keep something safe when I'm not here, this is where you put it.'

Letting go of her hand, he began to kick away the old, tired rushes on the floor until he had cleared a space, leaving one flagstone uncovered in the middle. Kneeling beside it, he slid his fingers under a hidden lip she hadn't noticed at one end and lifted the slab completely out of the recess in which it was sitting, revealing a dark hole beneath. Eleanor's mouth fell open in astonishment, and then as a rank, mouldy smell crawled out of the space, she closed it again quickly, holding her hands over it and screwing her face up in disgust.

'It does smell bad, I know. The air goes stale under here. This slab I've just moved is much thinner than normal ones, so it's quite light. I think if you needed to, you could move it with no problem. My father and grandfather had occasion to hide wealth from those who would take it, so if you ever need to do the same, you know where the key is kept. No one must know of this. Not even Joan, or Hugh. Understand?'

'Yes, I promise.' She moved a little closer to peer inside. 'How big is it?'

'It's quite deep. If you need to put something in, knot it on a rope. There's a hook here at the top to tie it on to, so you can haul it back up.' He replaced the slab and together they kicked the strewings back over it. Eleanor doubted she would ever need to hide her few pieces of jewellery or

118

money in there, but she felt by Greville showing her she'd somehow passed a test in trust. She wouldn't let him down.

'Have you had reason to hide anything in there?' she asked, wondering whether her husband had secrets to conceal.

'No, not in my lifetime. But we can never foresee what the future may bring. So we must always be prepared.'

After following him back down the precarious steps, she excused herself for a moment in the office. Sitting at her new desk and taking up her quill, she opened her prayer book and turned to a blank page, the vellum thick and smooth.

We arrived at Milfleet last night. We rode for many days – I lost count but maybe four or five and I was tired. I slept many hours. Today my husband's steward Hugh showed me around my new home. It is larger than Ixworth but does not fill me with joy. There is much to explore, a chapel close by the hall and many acres, enough to plant the saffron I was given. This building does not feel like home but I hope I can make it so. It holds secrets that I must not divulge, for I have promised my husband. I was introduced to Jane to whom I am now mother. She is quiet and shy but I hope we will soon be friends.

Closing the book again, she ran her fingers over the smooth lines on the front, the proverb of which her husband was so proud. *Dum Spiro Spero*. She did not know how her new life was going to unfold and if she would face times when she'd cling to those words that were now hers, too.

Chapter Thirteen

1538

Two days later Greville warned her that he must soon leave again for London. 'Before I go though, we will have our neighbours come and join us for dinner, they wish to congratulate us on our nuptials. The Derehams live close to us at Crimplesham and the family have been good friends with mine for many years. Their son Francis is currently staying with their distant kinsmen – the Howards at Lambeth. He and his brother Thomas attended the priory school at Beeston Regis although they are younger than I, closer to your age I imagine. I believe Francis is shortly to travel to Ireland and I am curious to know what news he sends.'

Eleanor was delighted at the thought of entertaining guests in her new home. Her life growing up had been so quiet and now that she was married she had been worried that things would carry on in the same way, stranded in the middle of nowhere and cut off when the weather was bad.

'We must look through our dresses,' she told Joan, 'and

see how we can smarten them up a little. I have some ribbons in my sewing box.' Her friend was as excited as she was and they spent a happy afternoon, the most relaxed both of them had been since arriving at Milfleet, sewing silver threads and pearls to their best hoods and sleeves.

The day of the dinner arrived, and Eleanor was pleased to see that in accordance with her instructions to Hugh, the strewings in the great hall had been refreshed and laid with lavender. Cook had suggested roast swan, gosling and rabbit, and she'd been happy to leave him to the culinary decisions.

A commotion in the courtyard and the dogs barking heralded the arrival of someone and Eleanor hurried into the hall with Joan close behind to greet the guests. She immediately warmed to Isabel Dereham and soon the three ladies were sat beside the fire chatting whilst Greville disappeared into his office with John, eager to discuss Francis's fortunes.

After an expansive meal that finished with stewed plums, cheese and pastries, Eleanor and Joan took Isabel outside to enjoy the warm spring air. The formal garden was still completely overgrown and untidy, and Eleanor reminded herself that she needed to organise the gardeners to clear it up. She was beginning to realise that Joan was right: she couldn't be seen to be weak. The servants would only respect her if she behaved as her new position befitted.

Within twenty-four hours of Eleanor's first experience of hosting at Milfleet, Greville had left for court. A cloud of dust disappearing into the distance. Eleanor didn't know whether she was pleased, or disappointed. Or angry. He still hadn't made an effort to join her in bed, and finally she'd broached the subject with him. If he found her physically repulsive, why did he marry her? After advising her of his desire for sons, he'd need to bed her at some point. Even she knew that. Eventually she couldn't wait any longer and she had questioned him. He'd brushed away her questions.

'You're young, and this is a strange new home. I want us to delay until the time is right, when you've settled in properly. When you're more relaxed and used to the ways and the people at Milfleet, then you'll be ready,' he chided her.

'It will be my first time,' she reminded him, 'and I'm nervous. You delaying the inevitable is not contributing to my feeling relaxed.'

'That is precisely why we are waiting.' He wrapped his arms around her thin shoulders and pulled her close to him so she could feel his heart beating against her own. 'I want your first time to be memorable for all the right reasons. It should be special. Not just for it being your wedding night with dozens of rowdy guests below us shouting coarse encouragement. Not because it is your duty and you simply want it over and done with. When the time is right, we will make love because we both want it. I can be patient until then.' For a moment she leant against him and enjoyed the warmth and security of his nearness.

'And when will you take me to court with you?' she asked, her voice muffled in his jerkin. 'Surely I am not expected to spend the rest of my life abandoned in this wasteland?' Isabel Dereham's description of London life had made her hanker to experience the delights of court even more.

'There is plenty of time for that – do not fret,' he reassured her.

But now he'd returned to London, insisting that as well as business that needed his attention, their future prosperity depended on his position amongst the courtiers. He had already explained his role as a merchant was merely a means to an end, making money and more importantly contacts to raise his profile within the king's inner circle, so he had to be seen to attend court. Promising he'd be back as soon as possible, and having introduced her to Simon, his estate manager, he reminded her that she had carte blanche for any land she required for growing plants.

Eleanor was feeling alone and out of her depth, and she wasted no time in finding Simon as soon as Greville had left, requesting land on which to grow her saffron. She also informed him she'd be taking over a section of the kitchen plot in which to create a proper physic garden.

'We can get any medicines and cures from the monks,' he protested. 'They've an infirmary for the village, not just for themselves. You don't need to worry about growing herbs to make them yourself.'

'Good, then they'll have plenty of herbs from which I may purchase cuttings,' she replied. 'I intend on using the stillroom for making my own potions and medicines as I did for my father. I was taught by the monks at Ixworth Priory and I'm very proficient. Please arrange for one of the gardeners to dig over the places we discussed, and the strip of home meadow is to be ploughed by the end of June. It will need ploughing at least three times, and dressed with a substantial amount of manure. This is extremely important, or the saffron won't grow. I'll need help to plant my crocus heads as well.'

'That'll depend on who's available. It's a busy time in farming.'

Eleanor frowned. 'Not as busy as when we'll need to harvest each flower by hand,' she warned. Turning from him and striding back into the house, the effect was spoiled slightly as the pattens she wore to protect her shoes slipped on the muddy ground and she almost fell over. Once steady again, her diminutive frame remained straight and upright as she marched away, and she held her head high. She intended to start as she meant to go on and wouldn't let the servants think they could bully her, just because she was young and not Lady Elizabeth. She'd noticed the respect they accorded her when Greville was at home had slipped somewhat, and she was determined to correct that.

Two days later, the areas she'd denoted in the garden had been dug over and raked, then laid out in eight dark patches of shiny soil, perfect rectangles edged with small wattle fences and awaiting plants. They smelled of richness and fertility. Eleanor had already found lavender and feverfew, rosemary and mint growing wild around the garden and she took a spade and replanted them, pressing them into the new beds. It was a start, but she needed a lot more. She spent an evening carefully writing a list in her book of hours so she wouldn't forget anything.

The following morning she attached the book to her girdle with her purse of coins and, along with Joan as chaperone, they headed off towards the priory at the other end of the village.

They were warmly welcomed by Prior Matthew, and shown into his private parlour for wine and cakes. Eleanor felt her whole body relax as she immersed herself in the recognisable sounds and smells that surrounded her. She hadn't realised how tightly her insides were coiled, but the ambience and familiarity that curled around her started to relax her taut muscles. Faintly from below, she could hear the soothing, rolling sounds of Gregorian chant, the voices swooping and dipping like the summer swallows and making the floor beneath her feet vibrate. She could feel it through the supple leather of her boots and she found herself considering the very real worry that the rest of England's monasteries may yet be disbanded. The smiling face of her friend Brother Dominic swam into her thoughts and she wondered how he and the brethren were faring.

'I am pleased to see that your establishment has not been closed down by the vicar-general,' Eleanor said quietly. She felt Joan stiffen beside her and was surprised at her own daring. Any mention of the king's actions could be seen as treason if someone wanted to take her words the wrong way, but she was fearful especially for her old friends still at Ixworth.

The prior inclined his head. 'We too are relieved,' he agreed, 'and for that we give thanks to God.' Automatically the three of them crossed themselves.

The air hung heavy in the silence as they considered the terrible measures that may be coming. Changing the subject, she briefly explained to Prior Matthew the reason for her visit.

'Villagers usually come to the infirmary and see Brother Rufus if they're ill,' he told her, 'but I can see why it would be easier for you to make your own medications for your people at Milfleet. Do you have much experience in the stillroom?'

'I do. Before I was married I lived a quiet life with my father, spending many hours at the priory near our home. The brothers taught me how to scribe, to read and write in both Latin and English and some French, and also how to make a great many treatments and cures.' She felt her face light up as she remembered. The prior took the two women down to the garden, and left them with Brother Rufus, who was happy to give them a tour of the grounds and as Eleanor read from her list, he dug up seedlings of a great many plants, laying them in the panniers Joan was carrying.

'Do you grow saffron?' Eleanor asked.

'We do have a stand.' The monk pointed to the far corner of the meadow next to the garden in which they were stood. 'If the weather is kind to us we usually harvest in September. It is a helpful addition to our medical store cupboard, and also for adding to some foods especially in winter when stocks are low and the meals we eat are bland and unappetising.'

Eleanor thought of the wine and cakes she had just eaten. She'd bet her bag of coins the prior never had dull, unappetising food even in the depths of winter.

'I'm afraid we don't have any spare crocus corms,' he added.

'I have some of my own,' she confided. 'I was concerned whether they would grow out here, with the fierce easterly winds. At Ixworth we were further inland and warmer. It's quite close to Walden where they grow a great many plants.'

'I've heard of Walden,' he replied, 'but we've never had problems here with the climate. At Walsingham Abbey they grow a prodigious amount of saffron, almost as much as at Walden I believe. Thankfully though we don't get a lot of rain in the summer, and they seem to thrive in the conditions.'

Eleanor counted out some coins and handed them over to Brother Rufus. They may be neighbours, but he charged a high price for the plants. No doubt all going into the coffers to pay for the prior's sweetmeats, she thought. She was happy though with what she had been able to procure and, more importantly, the confirmation of the favourable growing conditions for her crocuses. She knew she had enough bulbs to grow three times more plants than the size of stand the monks had. And in a couple of years, her corms would be big enough to be split again, instantly doubling the yield. Yes, she'd had an extremely profitable day, and not just in the new plants they carried home.

Eleanor soon set about re-establishing a working stillroom. If the staff were surprised that the new mistress was not afraid to get her hands dirty, they kept their opinions to themselves. She pulled out her durance apron and set about cleaning the room before restocking it with the equipment she needed. At her behest Hugh sent one of the servants to Lynn for the few pieces she couldn't find in the kitchen or storerooms, and she wrote to Greville in London asking him to find the finest French or Venetian glass items for her still. Every day she visited her physic garden to ensure the new plants were flourishing.

Spring turned to summer, and still Greville didn't return. Eleanor found herself missing him less and less as her life fell into a new, well-ordered routine. Every morning she and Joan walked across to the chapel where the parish priest took matins, and often mass as well at Eleanor's request. Various members of staff would also attend, but she made it clear to Hugh she expected everyone to be present on Sundays, and she was pleased to see every pew occupied each week.

Jane had lessons to do in the mornings, but when the weather was fine Eleanor would join the little girl in the garden to play after dinner, allowing Nell a precious hour to herself, which she looked grateful for. If the weather was bad they would play in the solar. Joan made no show of hiding how much she disliked the intrusion, preferring the peace and solitude she had been used to at Ixworth to sew in silence, but Eleanor needed to make an effort to get to know her new daughter. With all the difficulties involved in adjusting to living in her new home, she'd only concentrated on her own feelings of unease, forgetting about how the little girl was coping with having a new mamma. It appeared her father made few appearances in the day-to-day lives of those at the hall, but at least she, Eleanor, could be a proper parent to the child.

Sometimes after dinner, she would follow Nell and Jane upstairs to the nursery, where Jane played with a collection of roughly carved but obviously much loved animals, which Greville had brought back from London for her. They were rubbed smooth from hours of play, the colours now gone. Kneeling on the floor, Eleanor happily joined in a convoluted game involving the animals journeying to London to visit the king. Any mention of the city made Eleanor wonder when the time would come for *her* to visit court, and maybe even see the king himself. She could hardly suppress her eagerness.

Eleanor received two letters from Greville. The first one told her of the damasks and silks he'd bought, promising her he would bring some home for her to make a dress, and of the dinners he'd taken at the Mercers Company and how he had been invited to join the Merchant Adventurers' Company. He was extremely pleased as it was considered a great honour and would help his business transactions. His second letter explained he'd been delayed in London, but hoped to be home by harvest time. He added that there were rumours at court that the king was looking to increase the number of monasteries he was closing to include ones that were currently still active and Eleanor felt her blood run cold. That would mean her new friends at the priory at the other end of the village. New friends as well as old.

She'd replied dutifully, not mentioning what he had told her about the king's plans. She was beginning to realise that her husband was not as devout as she was and didn't fear the religious upheaval as she did. Instead she described to him how she filled her time, although she suspected he wasn't interested in her mundane life buried away in Norfolk. She also wanted to ask if she could use the room at the top of the tower in which to dry her saffron when the time came. She was worried he'd say no, so she deliberately delayed sending her request until it was too late for him to refuse. The fact was, she needed somewhere dry and warm where she could light a fire, a room with no draughts. And somewhere she could prevent anyone wandering in, or stray animals blundering through. The saffron fronds would be thin and weigh almost nothing. They mustn't be disturbed, or the entire crop may be lost.

When July came, the furrowed strips along the meadow were ready, as promised. Eleanor had informed Simon she'd need six men to help plant the bulbs and despite his protestations, her workers were there waiting. Not a man amongst them, however, but six willing children to carefully push the bulbs in as she demonstrated. They were more than happy with the sweet marchpane and groats she handed out as payment. She then took it upon herself to walk up and down the path left between the rows of bulbs, watering them.

★ ★ ★

130

The summer blazed on, day after day of wide, deep blue skies that met the shimmering line of the horizon until they melted together under the relentless burning sun. From the tower, as promised by Greville, Eleanor could see the sea, a thin line of deep slate grey on the horizon between the sky and the dunes.

She'd ordered the watering of the saffron and herbs to be as late in the evening as possible, to stop the water drying before it had a chance to seep into the dusty soil. By midday it was too hot for anyone to work outside, and she began to cut short her games with Jane so she could lie on her bed in just a shift and try to cool off. The linen stuck to her skin in sweaty patches. Outside her window all was still, the buzzing of sleepy flies the only sound as the birds fell quiet in the oppressive, wearisome heat. Although she would have liked to visit the sea, which she was certain would be gloriously cool, she knew that riding in the hot weather would be horrible and exhausting, not worth the prize of enjoying the water lapping at her feet.

Then, in the turgid stillness, terrible news arrived from the village. A sickness had spread through the infirmary at the priory killing three villagers, a peddler and four of the more elderly monks. It was thought the peddler had brought the disease, and within a day they were all dead. Eleanor immediately forbade anyone to leave the house, but her preventative methods were too late. One of the dairymaids, Ruth, had visited her betrothed in the village the night before anyone had fallen sick. She'd been too afraid to admit to the clandestine meeting because she knew she'd be in trouble, so she said nothing until she collapsed in the yard.

Straightaway Eleanor ordered that a pallet be put in an

empty outhouse as a temporary infirmary. She knew it was imperative the girl was kept quarantined, and forbade even her mother from visiting. There were five younger siblings at their home who needed protecting. She prepared a tisane of rue, marigold, feverfew and burnt sorrel, and took it with cups of small ale, making the girl drink everything she gave her. She was thankful that her hours spent in the stillroom at Ixworth, learning beside the monks from a young age, had given her such a wide knowledge of medications. She knew she'd been correct in insisting she had her own herb garden here at Milfleet; Brother Rufus was of no use to her now. Each visit she made to Ruth was in a fresh apron, which was then put in a pot to boil as soon as she removed it. She had no idea if the girl could be saved, but she was more worried about the sickness spreading to others.

Finally after three days of wavering between life and death, Ruth turned a corner and began to improve. Eleanor insisted that she remain in her makeshift room for a while longer and she sent broths, and later pies and jellies to her. After a further two weeks she was happy Ruth was well enough to return home, and Eleanor ordered that the straw pallet be burned. She left the door to the outhouse open and told Hugh to ensure the walls and floor were sluiced with hot water steeped in rosemary and marigold. She expected him to make a churlish comment, but to her surprise he agreed to arrange what she'd requested.

'We all thought she'd die,' he told her. 'What you did, curing her, was most surprising. The sickness always kills. You could teach those monks a thing or two.'

Eleanor laughed, flushing with embarrassment and gratitude. 'Everything I know about medications, I've learned from monks. I was just lucky with Ruth. She was strong and healthy so the sickness couldn't take hold of her like it does weaker people and the elderly. We must be on our guard at all times though. In this heavy heat, with no sign yet of it breaking, the sickness could reappear at any time.'

Returning to the stillroom, Eleanor couldn't resist a small smile of satisfaction to herself. It was only a beginning, but was there a tiny crack in Hugh's wall of ice?

Chapter Fourteen

1538

The harvest began, but still there was no sign of Greville returning and no letter either. The warm days continued and the golden fields were soon dotted with bushels of hay, the barns filling with the satisfying bounty, and finally the pale lilac of the crocus flowers began to unfurl and open their petals, displaying their wealth that swayed within. The monks had taught Eleanor the optimum time to take off the flower heads, and as it was now late September and most of the harvest – apart from the fruit – had been safely collected, she was able to garner the assistance of enough workers to endure the backbreaking picking of the flowers.

At the end of the first day, her back and legs sore from the constant bending down to collect the flowers followed by the arduous task of removing the threads, Eleanor went to find somewhere quiet to sit for ten minutes. She let herself into the office, which she always left unlocked. A sudden scrabbling in the corner of the room indicated to her that she wasn't the only occupant of the room, her arrival obviously disturbing whatever had made the noise. She had her suspicions and made a note to ask for a rat trap.

It was then that she noticed a letter for her, left on the corner of her desk. She'd been out in the field since first light and hadn't seen Hugh, so no doubt he'd left it where he knew she'd find it. Breaking open the seal she immediately recognised the hand of Brother Dominic, her face breaking into a wide smile at the thought of news from her friends. The letter was dated in August and began with an update of his fellow brothers, and how well their saffron was growing, which made her nod to herself in agreement, her own harvest's success due to the prior's confidence in her. Then as she continued reading she slipped into the chair beside her, unable to believe the words. It seemed that the vicar-general's commissioners were to pay them a visit at the priory in Ixworth. She knew that they had been closing down the smaller establishments but discovering that it may be about to happen to her friends, people she had known for most of her life, hurt her deeply. Cromwell's men would take everything that could be sold and throw the brethren out. She could only hope that they would be given pensions and accommodation but there were no guarantees.

Sitting down at her own desk, she opened the book of hours, laid in front of her. The familiarity of the monks' neat lettering, so painstakingly scribed, momentarily brought tears to her eyes, as memories flooded back. The initial page of miniatures of St Andrew and St Philip were exquisite, decorated in a spectrum of reds and blues together with elaborate touches of gold, followed by the calendar of church feasts she knew so well. The blank pages, sewn into every section and numbering twenty in total, were an incentive Eleanor couldn't ignore. Turning back to the flyleaf, she dipped a quill in her bottle of ink and carefully wrote

Our first saffron harvest has begun. I am beginning to feel at peace now in my new home and am so pleased that my crocuses will bring forth the riches they promised. But news from Ixworth and Brother Dominic fills my heart with dread for the fortunes of my friends.

She then sprinkled some of the fine sand from the silver shaker across the wet ink and waited for it to dry, before shaking the sand onto the floor. As she returned to the illuminated page, drawn to its colours, she ran her fingertips over it as an idea for beautifying her prayer book began to form in her mind. The monks at Ixworth had shown her how they made their coloured inks from scratch, although her father, like her husband, purchased them ready-made. If she asked Greville to bring home some gum arabic when he returned from London and she could find oak galls locally, she too could make her own inks for decorating the entries in her prayer book.

Later, she found Joan and showed her the letter she'd received.

'I'm so worried for our friends,' she confessed. 'What can I do to help them?'

'Nothing, I fear.' Joan put her arms around Eleanor and held her close. 'We're too far away now. And even if we weren't, I can't think of any way that we would be able to help them. To go against the vicar-general and his men would be tantamount to treason and could end very badly. It's the king's orders, and we are all powerless.' Her words were meant to comfort, but Eleanor still felt anxious, and helpless.

The harvest was long, slow, arduous work. Far more back-breaking than Eleanor had appreciated when she'd worked with the monks collecting the tiny red stamens in the priory gardens at Ixworth. Every morning at dawn, the pickers needed to be in the field gathering in the flower heads that had opened in the first rays of sunlight that day. By the time the sun was high in the sky and the day was at its hottest, Eleanor and Joan were in the tower room sat at a trestle table, carefully extracting the tiny golden threads.

Later they were able to lay the dried fronds onto the special drying papers to press them into flat, round saffron cakes, as she'd been taught. As well as being the only place in the hall where she could ensure the threads wouldn't be disturbed by draughts, it also meant that people who didn't appreciate its importance – she counted everyone in that category – couldn't accidentally disturb all their hard work. And the large windows allowed the room to warm up during the day from the now softer, autumnal sunshine.

She kept watch over her hoard every day and collected several rats in the traps she'd laid to ensure nothing would spoil her crop at the last moment. Her heart throbbed with a dull melancholy as she remembered the days of autumn past and the sharp peppery scent of the saffron being dried at the priory. She missed home at that point more than any other since she'd arrived at Milfleet.

As promised, she spoke with Cook and told him she wanted to organise a feast to celebrate the inaugural saffron harvest. At first he was dubious, especially with the approach of Advent and the fasting that would be required, but she insisted it was the perfect time and ordered the slaughter of several animals.

Using the tiniest amount of her precious crop, she made small spiced cakes with honey and nuts that came out of the oven a glowing yellow and were immediately hugely popular. Even Eleanor couldn't deny the flavour was like nothing she'd ever tasted before, and secretly she thanked the prior for such a wonderful wedding gift.

The party was in full swing. The whole household and gardening staff, along with their families, were sat on the benches around the edge of the hall, their bellies full and their cups filled with wine or ale. Eleanor was sat in the middle of a bench with Joan one side of her and Jane on the other. They were enjoying the bowls of glazed nuts and sugared fruit, which Cook had placed on the table. Some loud and raucous singing of folk songs had begun. Most of them were local songs unknown to her, but Eleanor clapped her hands in time, smiling at Nell who'd got up to dance with Roger, one of her hardest-working harvesters. Were they courting? Eleanor realised she'd been so tied up in her own life since arriving at Milfleet, she'd neglected her role in watching over her household staff.

Through the noise, with Jane now sat on her lap and joining in the clapping with her sticky, pudgy hands, Eleanor noticed that the dogs who had finished their nightly forage under the tables and were collapsed and dozing in front of the fireplace suddenly jumped up, their noses quivering and their heads cocked to one side. They ran to the door that led out to the courtyard, barking and snuffling their faces against the heavy tapestry, which was pulled across the door. She looked across to Hugh who got to his feet, but not fast enough as the curtain was pushed back and Greville strode in. He was wearing a thick grey travelling cloak with a fur collar drawn up around his face against the cold night air, and his cap was pulled down firmly over his ears. His legs were immediately buffeted by the pack of dogs ecstatic to see their master as he looked around incredulously at the now silent revellers, before turning his questioning gaze on his wife.

'Is this how my house behaves in my absence?' he asked, his voice booming as he walked further into the room, his eyes never leaving Eleanor's face. 'What, pray, are we celebrating?'

'We are rejoicing at the successful harvest of my saffron,' she replied, her words cut off as he kissed her firmly on her lips, his skin cold against her warmth, before he took Jane from her and swung the little girl into the air, making her giggle with delight.

'In that case, if we have something to celebrate, we must all continue with the party.' Pouring himself a beaker of beer, he downed it in one swallow before sitting astride the bench next to Eleanor, and balancing Jane on his knee. Around them the noise started up again, if a little more subdued than it had been before.

'So, wife, what exactly is this saffron harvest you talk about? I've just sold a barrel of saffron from Venice for a very healthy profit.'

'I can show you,' she told him, 'in the morning. But first, try . . .' She reached across the table and grabbed one of the few remaining buns and passed it to him. Raising his eyebrows he pulled a piece off and ate it slowly, his eyes not leaving her face. Then, in two huge mouthfuls the remainder of the cake disappeared. He washed it down with a glug of his drink.

'That's very good,' he told her. 'I've never had cake so fine, not even when I'm at court. I'm looking forward to learning more about your saffron.' His eyes held hers and he nodded once, slowly, as if beginning to realise something. A smile crept across his face.

'Everything I know I learned from the brothers at Ixworth.' She paused for a moment and then decided to broach the subject that was worrying her while her husband seemed to be in an expansive mood. 'And lately I have discovered they may be closed down by the commissioners. How can that be right? They will have nowhere to go. They have devoted their lives to God and to helping others.'

'It is the way the king wants it, and none of us should be questioning his decisions.' Greville dismissed her concerns sharply and left her in no doubt to whom his allegiance lay.

'Helping others,' she repeated sharply. 'People like me,' she muttered under her breath, 'and by giving me the crocus bulbs that now lie under your ground, which have given us the finest saffron, people like you too.' Eleanor was not happy, but knew when to keep her thoughts to herself. She could never accept the tearing apart of her religion, however her husband felt about it.

A flushed, pink and slightly sweaty Nell appeared, ready to take Jane to bed. Greville kissed the top of his daughter's head and went to lift her off his knee and pass her to Nell. Jane, however, had different ideas and instead she scrambled over his lap and onto Eleanor's, wrapping her arms around her neck and planting a noisy kiss on her cheek. Laughing, Eleanor reciprocated, before handing her over to the waiting Nell.

Greville took her hands in his. 'It seems you've settled in to Milfleet very well,' he said smiling. 'I've never seen Jane so attached to anyone. You've brought her out of her shell. She was always such a quiet child.'

Embarrassed, she looked down at her lap. His hands were still cool from being outside and she was conscious that he was rubbing his knuckles back and forth across the inside of her wrist.

'She's a lovely girl,' she replied. 'It's not hard to find a place in my heart for her. I do hope you don't mind us having these festivities. I promised the outdoor workers because they toiled so tirelessly to bring in the saffron. Tell me, though, what you're doing home. We weren't expecting you.'

'The servants are obviously enjoying themselves,' came the reply, but he was laughing as he said it and Eleanor knew immediately he didn't really mind the celebrations. 'I saw an opportunity to leave London, and I took it,' he explained. 'The king has gone to stay at Richmond and I suspect that nobody will notice if I'm away for a little while. I'll need to be back in London in January and the roads may be treacherous by then. It could take several weeks for my return journey. But right now—' he looked around the hall '—I don't think anyone will notice if my wife and I leave the party.' Grasping her small hand in his, he led Eleanor upstairs to his bedroom, her heart thumping hard, in rhythm with her feet on the staircase.

She hadn't been in his chamber since that first day when Hugh had shown her around the house. Now, with a fire blazing and the candles lit, the room felt more alive and welcoming. But it didn't allay any of her fears, which were knotted in a hard lump in her chest. She knew what was about to happen, that the time had come.

Standing behind her, Greville began to slowly unlace her

142

dress. There was none of the unthinking and cursory movements as when he'd done it before, on their wedding night. Then, he'd helped her because there was nobody else in the room to do so, but now as she stood with her back to him he was running the backs of his hands tantalisingly over the ridges of her spine with each pull of a lace. She could feel the heat of his body close to hers when she was finally able to step out of her clothes and she was in nothing more than her shift. With shaking hands she reached up and removed the plain coif from her head, together with the pins in her hair until it fell in a heavy rippling wave almost down to her waist.

She could hear Greville moving about the room taking off his clothes, but she did not dare turn around. Although she knew the basics of a man's anatomy, she wasn't sure she actually wanted to look at it. He blew out the candles one by one until the only light was the flickering flames from the fire in front of her. As the bed was behind her, she knew at some point she was going to have to turn and face him. As she moved though, she felt him stood beside her and then strong, bare arms lifted her as if she weighed nothing and carried her to the bed. His chest was naked and she briefly felt the coarse hairs of his chest rough against her cheek, and smelled the acrid tones of sweat before he laid her down on the mattress and climbed in beside her. Carefully he pulled off her shift and dropped it behind him onto the floor. She shivered, even though she wasn't cold.

Leaving the drapes open, the firelight played on the curves of her body as leaning up on one arm he murmured, 'I've waited a long time for tonight. Do you think that we are now both ready?'

Eleanor nodded mutely, her heart thumping hard in her chest.

Stroking his hand down her hair, he added, 'Don't be afraid, Eleanor, I won't hurt you.'

Chapter Fifteen

2019

Amber slept badly. Her dreams were peppered with snippets from her argument with Jonathan as it churned over repeatedly in her mind until she'd examined it from every angle and still didn't have the answers she was seeking. Finally, with her head thumping and tinnitus hissing in her ears from lack of sleep, she decided to give up on the idea of dozing off again and got up at five o'clock to further explore the precious book of hours.

Down in the office and still in her pyjamas, Amber lifted the book out of the safe and laid it on the cradle. She needed to call the university and see if they could forensically examine the fabric the book had been stored in. She shuddered slightly, remembering Becky pointing out that the stains looked like ancient blood. She feared her friend was right.

Turning the pages, she marvelled once again at the exquisite illuminated decoration. She planned to translate what had been scribed, but she suspected these were probably psalms, and possibly also extracts from the gospels. What she really wanted to examine though were the entries made by Eleanor and discover if there were more explanations about Mary. She couldn't stop thinking about the passage at the front of the book, and what it could mean.

Finally she found a page with the handwriting she could now recognise, this time written in English and decorated with borders of flowers describing Eleanor's arrival at what Amber presumed was her new marital home. Her heart bled for the young woman who seemed from her words, to be lost and alone.

We arrived at Milfleet last night. We rode for many days – I lost count but maybe four or five and I was tired. I slept many hours. Today my husband's steward Hugh showed me around my new home. It is larger than Ixworth but does not fill me with joy. There is much to explore, a chapel close by the hall and many acres, enough to plant the saffron I was given. This building does not feel like home but I hope I can make it so. It holds secrets that I must not divulge, for I have promised my husband. I was introduced to Jane to whom I am now mother. She is quiet and shy but I hope we will soon be friends.

Amber put her hand to her mouth and reread what was written. She leant in closer, sure she'd somehow seen something that she'd misread. But no, it was there. Saffron. Eleanor was writing about saffron. The word leapt out of the page at her. Slowly she read through the passage again, her mouth forming the words silently. She was sitting in Saffron Hall – what was the connection between her family home and Eleanor's Milfleet?

Amber had suspected that Eleanor had lived somewhere locally but had so far deliberately not allowed herself to even

146

consider that she'd lived in the very same house. The family folklore, the stories her grandfather had told her spoke of the pale crocuses that had once been grown here. That gave forth the deep golden spice for which she'd named her daughter. A little girl whose head had been surrounded by wisps of pale red hair so like her own, but not yet the burnished bright copper hers had developed into as she'd grown up.

She carried on turning the pages of the book. Its age meant that she had to use extreme care, but she was desperate to find more entries in Eleanor's hand and it was not long before she was rewarded with another entry.

I have shown Greville where we dried and prepared the saffron. The tower, which holds its own secrets close to its heart, will hold this one too. No harm must come to the precious spice.

It was a sign. More proof, if it were needed. She had been using the tower to dry her precious saffron. Was it the tower, Grandad's tower, currently encased in scaffolding? The connection. Amber's baby – Eleanor's spice – Eleanor's baby. A thin gossamer thread, a bond between the three of them. She drew in a deep lungful of air, hoping to catch a hint of that smell, the suggestion she was now sure indicated that Eleanor was with her, but there was nothing.

She leant back in her chair, feeling her heart beating in her chest. What of this Milfleet? Where had it stood? Was it actually Saffron Hall? It all seemed too much to simply be a coincidence, the description of the tower and the growing of the spice after which the hall, and so much more, was named. She turned back to the passage written at the beginning of the book, the plea for her baby daughter, which she was so desperate to understand. And what of the other three children listed at the very front of the book? Had they lived and played in Eleanor's saffron fields?

Hearing Grandad clumping slowly down the stairs, she waited until she recognised the pause as he got to the bottom where he always stopped to catch his breath, then she called out to him, suggesting he came through to the office to see what she'd discovered.

'Any idea where Milfleet was, or is?' she asked, after explaining what she'd just discovered.

Grandad shook his head slowly. 'I've never heard of it,' he admitted, 'but feel free to research the deeds and family papers if you want, and see if there's any mention of it. They're in that wooden box in the bottom of the safe. See if they give you any clues. Now—' he'd clearly had enough of discussing his home and wanted breakfast '—tea and toast?' He shuffled out, leaving Amber pondering. Everything she found in this little book was creating more questions than answers. Could it possibly be true? Had she unwittingly uncovered the origins of her family home's name, the one she'd chosen for her own daughter? The reference to saffron had piqued her interest further. She'd have to be careful her research didn't turn into an obsession.

A Google search brought up nothing. There was no mention of Greville, or Eleanor, or any of the children. That wasn't surprising though, if they were only minor nobility in rural Norfolk. If they'd lived in Norwich, a thriving port in medieval times, there may have been better records. She tried looking for the history of the Milfleet area of King's Lynn, but all she could uncover was that it had originally been the name of a boundary stream. No sign of any castles or Tudor halls. From Eleanor's brief description, her new home sounded sizeable. Everywhere she turned, the possibility of Saffron Hall having originally been Milfleet felt stronger.

Whilst she was on the internet, Amber quickly opened her email. If she could arrange for a remote login to the academic search engines she used at work, she may be able to uncover more information. She thought nostalgically of how, with a proper mystery such as she was uncovering here, her entire department would have become involved and she realised with a start how much she missed them all. She quickly sent an email to Becky's university account to request the login.

But her inbox displayed something she wasn't expecting. An email from Jonathan. Having failed to produce a response to his texts, he'd obviously decided to fire off an email. The subject line was blank and, surprised, she opened it, her eyes growing wide and her face pallid as she read the contents.

Amber,

I'm sorry we quarrelled when I visited you. It's not what I wanted or why I came. I thought when you decided to take some time off from work it would give us precious space to be together and grieve for Saffron, and try to move forwards. But that isn't happening. It feels as if we're slipping further apart and I don't know you anymore.

I never wanted our lives to come to this, but if neither of us are happy maybe we would be better off apart, permanently.

I love you, but I don't think I can be whatever it is you need anymore.

All my love, forever, Jonathan xxx

Amber leant back in the chair, her movement making it swing from side to side. Her chest was tight with suppressed hurt and despair. She wanted to hit reply immediately and hurl accusations back at him, but just for once she sat on her hands and stopped herself. Did he want a divorce? He seemed to be hinting at it, even if he didn't actually use the D word.

She hadn't 'moved out'; that was a ridiculous thing to say. They had agreed she'd stay with Grandad and help him with his books whilst she recovered from the trauma of what had happened. If he wasn't happy about her temporarily moving out then he should have been more vocal when the arrangement had been suggested. Then he turned up at the hall being defensive, and suddenly it was all her fault? He seemed to have given up on their marriage, which wasn't what she wanted. At least, she thought it wasn't.

She quickly fired off another email to Becky, asking her friend if she was available that evening for a chat. She knew she couldn't put it off any longer; she had to open up about the state of her marriage. Or the non-state of it, which was closer to the truth. She also wanted to share what she'd found in Eleanor's book, and ask Becky's thoughts.

Becky replied, proposing that if Amber didn't mind risking her dodgy cooking she could join her that evening for dinner. Her parents had disappeared to Australia to visit her sister, so they would have the house to themselves. She replied to the email with a thumbs-up emoji and added, 'I'll bring wine!' before turning her attention to the new stack of boxes she'd asked Pete to drag down from the loft the previous day. She needed to make good use of anyone with muscles at the hall.

Conscious she was abandoning Grandad for the evening, Amber took a break from the archiving to have afternoon tea with him. Sitting in the kitchen with a cup of tea and a cheese scone, they were interrupted by Kenny's now familiar knock on the back door.

'That man can hear the kettle boiling from the top of the tower,' Amber grumbled as she called to him to come in and went to get another mug from the cupboard. One look at his face however, told her he wasn't simply in the kitchen to cadge a hot drink. 'You aren't looking your usual cheerful self,' she told him, passing him a cup of dark, stewed tea, just as he liked it. He took a long, loud slurp, running his hand through his springy hair and showering the table with tiny pieces of grit and mortar dust.

'I just wanted to give you an update,' he told them, 'and I'm afraid it's not good news. The crack looks to be a lot more extensive than we'd first thought. We're probably going to have to take the whole corner of the tower down. It'll mean removing the other window, two walls and possibly the chimney as well. The conservation people will need to agree everything up front, and want to supervise it all of course.'

'And how expensive will it be?' Amber asked.

Kenny shrugged. 'The longer the scaffolding is up, the more we get charged for it, and we're being billed by the week for that. And all whilst we're here on site, we have to charge as well I'm afraid.'

'Oh well.' Grandad sounded resigned. 'There's no point worrying about the money; the repairs have to be done. I'm just the custodian of the hall ready to hand it over to Amber eventually. If you need to take the whole tower apart to repair it, then so be it.'

'I don't know yet if it'll be the entire thing, but yes, it may come to that. Thanks for being so understanding.' Kenny drained his cup noisily. 'I'll let you know what the conservation chaps say.' He left them to their tea, now feeling subdued at the thought of their beloved tower – so synonymous not only with the hall but also the surrounding village – permanently disappearing from the skyline.

It was still daylight when Amber set off for Becky's house, but at Grandad's insistence she slipped one of his numerous torches into her jacket pocket. The sparse village street lamps didn't extend to the track that led to the hall, and she agreed with him that if she stumbled in the dark and hurt her ankle he'd be of no use on a rescue mission.

'Don't wait up,' she told him as she said goodbye. He raised his eyebrows at the neck of the bottle of wine poking out of her bag, but said nothing. She was relieved about his lack of comment – she'd swiped it from the pantry and she was hoping it wasn't an expensive vintage. Tonight though, she really needed a glass – several glasses – to help her relax. Jonathan's email kept churning over in her head and she'd read it several times, looking for hidden meaning between the lines.

'Something smells good,' Amber remarked as she followed her friend through the boxy modern house into the large light-filled kitchen at the rear and handed over the wine. Becky dug in a drawer and pulled out the corkscrew, making quick work of opening Amber's wine.

'Pheasant stew, I found a lot of meat in the freezer. I hope Mum wasn't saving it for a special occasion. Dad's friends with a gamekeeper near Holt and he often arrives home from the pub with a brace of birds. I cooked this for Pete last week and he enjoyed it.'

Amber raised her eyebrows at the mention of Pete's name, but said nothing. After placing two steaming bowls of food on the table and passing Amber her cutlery, Becky slid into the chair opposite.

'It's very kind of you to make dinner for me though.'

'Nonsense.' Becky waved her hand. 'It's the least I can do, and you and Jonathan have had me over for dinner countless times. I'm on a mission to feed you up now.'

Remembering her husband reminded Amber why she'd arranged the visit and she explained the gist of the email she'd received.

'He didn't actually say he wants a divorce but that was the impression I got . . .' She tailed off.

'I'm sure he doesn't. It sounds to me like he's frustrated, and don't forget he's grieving too. And the harsh reminder, her grave, is there where he works every day. I wouldn't be surprised if he isn't also questioning his faith after what happened. No wonder he's lashing out. He's trying to open some sort of communication between the two of you so you can move forward. Whether that's together or apart I suppose he isn't sure, but what he's realised is that just standing still isn't working anymore. At least not for him. Did you mention before that you're due to meet with the obstetrics consultant soon?'

'Yes.' Amber nodded. 'I need to chase it. Jonathan said he would but I expect he's forgotten. The hospital should have pathology reports to show us, so they'll know why Saffron died, what could be done differently next time. Ha.' She gave a hollow laugh. 'As if there'll ever be a next time.'

Becky put her hand over Amber's. 'Early days, remember,' she reminded her. 'It's still early days. *Dum Spiro Spero*. While I breathe, I hope.' She smiled supportively. 'So keep breathing right now – that's all you need to do. Why don't you chase

153

the appointment and let Jonathan know? It's keeping the channels open between the two of you. Now, have you made any progress with the book of hours?' Deftly she steered the subject onto something Amber was happier to talk about.

'Yes, I managed to translate a Latin passage on the first page and it's very odd. I could probably do with you checking if I've got it right. I copied it out to show you.' Rummaging in her bag she pulled out the notebook in which she'd originally written out the translation of the cryptic passage and opened it up, pushing it across the table. Becky's lips moved as she read the passage.

'You're right; it is a bit strange. Tell me, Dr Watson, what you have deduced?' she asked.

'It was written by Eleanor, because the writing is the same as the other pages. But in comparison, it's quite scruffily done. It has blots and some words written twice where the first is too scratchy to read, but writing with a quill and ink meant that in order to be neat someone had to write slowly. I don't understand it. It seems to say her daughter died, but honestly I'm so screwed up I can read that into almost anything these days.'

Becky smiled gently. 'No, I think you're right about that. But why isn't she at peace? Do we know anything about the baby from any other entries?'

'I've only read the first couple of pages.' Amber explained about Mary's entry on the first page. 'I don't know if the baby daughter mentioned is Mary. Or why below that entry she says it's her fault. Her grievous fault, in fact.' Amber couldn't help the wave of empathy that burned through her whenever she considered those words.

'You're going to have to read the rest to see if you can

find out. And you need to research the family as well, try and work out if they're your direct ancestors.' Taking their bowls to the slow cooker she refilled them with stew. Amber hadn't even realised she'd eaten all of hers.

'I know, as well as Mary there is also Jane, Henry and Thomas. I need to keep reading to discover if there are any other mentions of them.' Amber explained that was why she'd asked for help to access the more informative academic search engines via the university. 'And the other thing I discovered was that Eleanor was growing saffron at Milfleet. Coincidence, or what?'

'More than a coincidence I would say, given the name of your grandfather's house. There must be a connection between Milfleet and Saffron Hall. Do you think they are actually one and the same place?'

'I don't know, although it does seem likely. We've only ever known it as Saffron Hall, but Grandad told me where all the old deeds are kept, so that is something else I need to look at,' Amber replied.

With dinner finally finished and the wine bottle empty, for the first time in a very long time, Amber felt full. She thanked her friend once again for the advice and dinner. Becky brushed away her thanks, just pleased that she'd been able to help in a small way.

'I've forwarded the login details you asked for as well,' she added.

Dusk was already falling as she left and Amber was relieved that Grandad had the foresight to suggest she took a torch. The potholes in the track would be a hazard in the dark. Small creatures and birds scuttled in the hedges either side of the torch beam as she disturbed them walking past, and she paused for a moment to watch the pale, silent flight of a barn owl as it circled smooth and low over the field, looking for dinner.

Ahead, the hall rose up, dark and foreboding in front of her. Grandad had left the light on beside the front door, but the rest of it lay in semi-darkness, small narrow windows staring blankly down at her, black against the deepening midnight sky. Her eyes were drawn to the tower, now completely encased in the scaffolding and barely visible. It looked so solid, a symbol of her family's heritage, and yet according to Kenny it was anything but.

A cold wind swirled around her, seemingly from nowhere in the still night, rustling the leaves on the trees beside her. Above her head she heard it whistle through the holes in the tower's stonework, creating a moaning sound like someone was crying, howling. A noise she remembered from that hospital room months earlier. A primal moan of horror and distress. She shuddered, trying to stop her overactive imagination. But still the tower gazed down at her, dark and, for the first time in her life, threatening. She put her head down and hurried inside. She definitely needed to look at the old records for the house.

With a freshly made cup of tea and now wide awake with curiosity, Amber decided to look through the box of paperwork Grandad had told her about, and see what was in there. Opening the safe, she took out the documents, some of which looked ancient. It was useful having a family home that had been passed down through so many generations, but not one person knew where the starting point was. And it was annoying nobody in the family had ever felt the urge to write up the genealogies, which would have saved her many hours of research now.

Her mother was an only child and so was she. It had been

instilled in her from an early age her mother had no interest in ever living here and that when Grandad died, the hall would be hers. Jonathan jokingly referred to it as the retirement home, because his job meant they wouldn't be able to take up full-time residence until he was no longer working in the clergy. She'd always thought there would be plenty of time to research the place then, but the hall seemed to have other ideas.

Unfortunately the papers and deeds weren't in chronological order, and Amber spent the next hour going through thick packets of documents that were not relevant to her at all. Why had people kept so much rubbish? Bills of sale and receipts for almost everything imaginable, as well as several land sales, no doubt due to crippling inheritance tax in years gone by. Now the hall had less than thirty acres, all of which was rented out to a local farmer. There was a good-sized lawn as well as the vegetable garden and several overgrown patches that had been left to grow wild, and a small piece of woodland, but she deduced from the deeds spread out in front of her that at some point in the nineteenth century a large swathe of hundreds of acres had been sold. It also appeared a further hundred acres had been sold by her grandfather in the 1950s.

Surely that amount of land was unusual for a house that was not overly large? She began to wonder whether the hall held more secrets close to its chest as she continued to rifle through the papers, desperate for something to spread some light on her suspicions. Eventually in a package tied with frayed red legal ribbon stuck together with shards of red sealing wax, she found it.

A drawing of the hall. She knew it. It was instantly recognisable with the tower to one side looking exactly the same as it had hours earlier when she'd been stood looking up at it. The rest of the building they now inhabited, however, was only about a quarter of the size of this diagram. It looked like a medieval stone castle, with not only the great hall they now lived in, but also a large chamber beside it, two parlours and numerous other rooms. Beside the plan for the main house was a smaller building entitled 'chapel'. Amber drew her breath in sharply. At the bottom of the page in faint but easily readable ornate lettering, it was dated 1541 and beneath the date the name Milfleet had been scored through, and replaced by the words Saffron Hall, lavishly penned.

She exhaled slowly, her heart beating hard in her chest. She was right: Saffron Hall had originally been Milfleet. Eleanor's home. The book of hours had always been here in its home. Harbouring a secret and waiting for the right person to find it and answer Eleanor's plea.

Now wrapped in acid-free tissue paper, the book sat on top of the document chest in the safe where Amber had placed it and she couldn't resist taking it out again – she always felt drawn to it, unable to stop herself. She laid it on the cradle and opened the first page to look again at the passage as if by staring at it for long enough, it would give up its secrets. But it didn't.

'What are you beseeching us to do?' Amber whispered.

A baby daughter lies beneath our feet
time escapes me now
I beseech you and place my trust
for her
so she may be at peace

158

'I can't help you, Eleanor, because I don't understand what you're asking.'

As she sat in the thick velvety darkness, she felt the hairs on the back of her neck stand up. That same strange feeling she'd had in the library previously. The air felt still and soft, as if it was waiting. Listening and watching her. Trying to speak to her, if only she could understand. Again, the faint scent of honey and this time, the sharp tang of pepper drifting on the air, pungent. Amber sat motionless and turned her head to one side.

'Eleanor?' Her voice cracked a little. 'Is that you?' She held her breath for a few moments. 'Please, tell me what you want.' She knew that Eleanor was trying to reach out to her; she could sense it. A lost soul, imploring her to understand. Just like Jonathan was. Her eyes slid to the darkest corner of the room where the shadows collected, brooding and silent. Amber's eyes filled with tears, which began to run down her face, spurting from her in an explosion of grief, sorrow and the sudden understanding of all she had put her husband through. He was the person she loved more than anyone and she'd inadvertently pushed him away because she couldn't deal with her own emotions. Why had she done it? He was already hurting and she hadn't listened.

Instead she had switched her attention to help someone else, a person who wasn't there for her, someone from the past. Not someone who could hug her, comfort her as her husband could. How had she been able to feel Eleanor's sorrow and desperation when she hadn't been able to feel it from her own husband? She'd been blind. Somehow she needed to heal the rift before it was too late. To make them whole again, if she could.

Chapter Sixteen

2019

It didn't take long for the planners to put in an appearance, their car swinging into the drive as Amber boiled the kettle for their builders' first round of tea of the day. She was disappointed to see it was the older of the two men who'd originally visited and, with him, an equally morose-looking colleague.

'Oh great, the Chuckle Brothers,' she muttered as she watched them put on their hard hats from the window and slowly begin to climb the scaffolding in Kenny's wake. She could hear Pete already working away at the top, the continuous chipping at the wall reverberating through the house. By this point, it was a background noise she barely noticed.

They were up there longer than she'd expected, and then they arrived at the back door asking to come in and speak with Grandad.

'He's still in bed,' Amber told them. She'd heard him moving about upstairs and she hoped he stayed out of sight until the visitors had gone. Their self-satisfied, officious attitude was extremely annoying. As soon as they stepped into the kitchen their eyes were darting about, taking everything in. If they hoped to see some of the medieval historical detail they were going to be out of luck. This room had been gutted in the 1970s and the furniture and fittings all dated from that period. It was, she'd told Grandad on several occasions, the ugliest room in the hall.

'We can wait, if you'd like to wake him.' Uninvited, they both settled themselves at the table.

'No, I wouldn't, thank you,' Amber snapped. 'Whatever you need to say, you can say it to me. What's going on up there?'

The planner who had been so dour on the first visit repeated much of the bad news Kenny had explained before, although he managed to sound a lot more pleased about the situation. Amber had no idea why he was relishing delivering the verdict, but she wasn't going to let it affect her.

'Okay, well obviously the work needs to be done.' Amber kept her voice as blasé as she could, looking across to Kenny who'd followed them in and was leaning against the door, his hard hat still crammed on his head. 'I'm sure you can keep me up to date with everything, can't you?' she asked him. Kenny nodded and smiled and it occurred to her he was probably as unimpressed with the council officials as she was. She ushered them all back outside, the banging and scraping continuing relentlessly above their heads. It appeared they were going to be listening to it for a long while yet, and she was going to have to break the news to Grandad.

When he eventually arrived downstairs, Amber quickly brought him up to date about the plans for the tower, brushing over the severity of the situation so as not to worry him and because she wanted to move on to the excitement of her previous night's discovery.

'I've been through all the old house documents – I didn't realise you had so many,' she exclaimed.

'I've collated them over the years, when I found extra pages hidden away in the library and various places around the house. I even found one of the land sale documents in an old biscuit tin in the pantry, can you believe it! So, what have you found?' He raised his eyebrows and waited expectantly.

'This house was definitely once Milfleet, Eleanor's home. I found a document that clearly shows that it was renamed in 1541. I found some drawings, what look like plans for an extra piece of building, and they were dated 1541. In those days it was a much larger fortified hall, more like a castle. We're only inhabiting one corner of the original building. I'm going outside to explore the gardens, see if I can find any old remains. Do you want to join me, help me look? It appears there was once a chapel as well, did you know?'

'No I didn't. Do you know where it was? I've never found any signs, but other than mowing the lawn I didn't really bother exploring the woodland and overgrown parts of the garden.'

'Well I'll go out and have a search around, and report back. Eleanor had a physic garden with some ancient herbs, but that will be long gone.'

'Unless it was where my vegetable patch is now? We know it was the kitchen garden when our Victorian ancestors put up that brick wall. Who's to say it wasn't originally a physic garden?'

Her excitement spiked. Amber pulled some boots on over her pyjamas, grabbed her phone to take pictures, and marched out amongst the vegetables and weeds, the morning frost sticking to her legs where tall grasses brushed against them. She couldn't wait to get started and if she'd turned around, she'd have seen Grandad watching her, a contented smile on his face.

The vegetable patch, however, was an anti-climax. After centuries of being dug over and replanted there was no indication that Eleanor had once used it for her precious herbs. Amber tried not to feel too disappointed. She knew in reality it was a fruitless search, but she was so desperate to find some indication, a sign, Eleanor had once lived there. And what she was particularly anxious to discover was a relic of the saffron crops, although she knew from a quick piece of research the bulbs only lasted about twelve years so there was no chance of finding anything.

She thought of Eleanor walking the same dark corridors and looking out at the same changing landscape as the seasons rolled over her, and it probably looked very similar even in the sixteenth century. The same flat, desolate vista with rich, fertile soil in which to grow her precious saffron.

She did manage to find some pieces of a stone structure or wall under a huge patch of brambles a short distance from the tower. It had been encroached on by the patch of woodland to one side, oak and sycamore saplings, wild garlic and bindweed slowly claiming back the land for themselves. Even with a sweatshirt on she couldn't avoid a myriad of scratches together with several nettle stings as she attempted to scramble closer to have a look. The vegetation had however had the advantage of many years to claim the derelict building for itself, and she knew she'd need shears and some leather gauntlets before she could investigate any further.

Unfortunately, as Grandad now employed a jobbing gardener from the village to mow the lawn and keep on top of the weeds in the flower beds, a quick rifle through his shed produced nothing robust enough as the type of tool she needed. After washing the mud from her arms and applying antiseptic cream to both the scratches and stings, she went into the office to find a signal and send her pictures to Becky, and ask if she had any garden tools. Whilst she was there, she fired up her laptop to check her emails and as she was typing, a text arrived from Jonathan. She hadn't heard from him since his email and after her awful realisation the night before, and she felt guilty she hadn't yet replied to him. Her heart banged uncomfortably when she saw his name appear. She was afraid to know what he wanted to say next, but she couldn't avoid it. She clicked on the message.

Mr MacKenzie the consultant. Appointment next Wednesday at two-thirty. Is that okay with you?

She took a deep breath, shuddering it into her lungs. She knew she needed to go; it was closure. Or not. A final explanation of what had happened, if a reason had been found. Or, a question mark to hang over them both for the rest of their lives. Either way, she had to go, for Saffron's sake. And she needed to have a heart-to-heart with her husband so they could both start moving forward. Now she knew that too.

Yes thanks, that's fine. See you there.

She thought for a moment and added a kiss before she pressed send. How could she start the most important conversation of her life with him? She didn't know, but it had to be done. Picking up her phone she quickly typed: *Meet in the coffee shop first? One o'clock?* and sent it before she could change her mind. She needed him to know she wanted to be with him, to be married to him, even if she didn't feel ready to be back there, so close to Saffron. Not yet. And, she still had unfinished business here. The cataloguing of Grandad's books had taken something of a back seat over the past week, but she was becoming increasingly desperate to discover whatever Eleanor was trying to say to her.

Feeling guilty about how little archiving she'd achieved, Amber spent the rest of the morning working on the books, hauling boxes through the house and enjoying the fact that the physical activity took her mind off the appointment only six days away.

She received a response from Becky at lunchtime, explaining there was a large selection of her father's garden tools, which Amber was welcome to borrow, and they arranged that Amber could call in on her way home from the supermarket later that day, once Becky was home from work.

Grandad agreed, reluctantly, for Amber to take three boxes of books to the recycling centre on her way. He suggested she took them to the charity shop, but Amber refused. 'Nobody, but nobody,' she told him, 'wants old and torn copies of the London A–Z. They're only fit to be recycled into, I don't know, toilet roll probably. I'll take this box of children's books to the charity shop before I go shopping, I've double-checked them and there's nothing of any value.'

Arriving at Becky's later that afternoon, her car now filled with bags of food, Amber was more than happy to drop exhausted into an armchair. In exchange for a coffee and a slice of cake, she explained about her discovery in the grounds, along with her new-found knowledge that the hall had once been Eleanor's home.

'That's amazing.' Gratifyingly Becky was as excited as she was. 'Have you been able to unravel anything else regarding the mysterious Latin passage, the one about the baby?'

'No, not yet. It still makes no sense. I'm hoping the ruins I've found are actually the original chapel and maybe we'll find something there, a clue of some sort. Yikes, I just thought—' she paused for a moment '—might there be old graves in there?'

'Unlikely.' Becky shook her head. 'Usually bodies are exhumed and moved to more modern graveyards if a church or chapel is deconsecrated. Although I seem to recall that little chapels attached to houses were mostly only used for services and prayer, and their dead were buried in family vaults at the parish church.'

'Well we already know there isn't a Lutton family vault.' Amber couldn't hide the disappointment in her voice.

'No, unless it's documented somewhere, I don't know if you'll ever find where they're buried. It doesn't seem to be locally.'

Amber glanced at her watch. 'Bugger, look at the time! I need to get back – I've still got the shopping in the boot. Can you give me a hand with your gardening tools please? And I'll see you tomorrow for more explorations.'

They agreed a time for the following day and Amber drove home, promising herself a long soak in the bath and, afterwards, a few more pages of Eleanor's book. She'd had a busy day, but one filled with activities that had, for the most part, taken her mind off the thoughts that tumbled around her head. The looming appointment the following week, which she didn't want to go to, and a conversation she needed to have with her husband. Which she didn't know how to start.

Chapter Seventeen

2019

As Amber soaked in the bath the high of the day seeped out of her until she felt as cold as the water she lay in. Instead of spending the evening reading through Eleanor's book, she spent it curled up under her duvet, arms around her knees, feeling black and morose, shrouded in the dark night.

She'd finally fallen asleep at past midnight, but as she succumbed to the heavy weight of sleep she felt herself falling into a dark void where she wasn't certain if she was awake or asleep, or simply dreaming. She was walking. No, half walking and half running, stumbling along a dark corridor. Someone was with her, holding her hand and pulling her along, urging her to be quick. The hand in hers was delicate and cold, sharp stones from a ring digging into her palm, and she could feel the brush of heavy skirts against her legs although she could tell from the ease of her own movements that it wasn't her wearing them.

And there was someone else with them. Every few steps she'd falter and trip against a child who seemed to be caught up in the voluminous fabric swirling around them. As she hurried along trying to keep up, she could hear a woman's voice whispering to her, the words catching in the deep blanket of darkness.

'Come, come quickly. You must help, help me now, please. Now is the time, before we are too late.'

'Eleanor, is that you?' Amber spoke the words and yet she couldn't hear them. It was as if her voice couldn't connect through the centuries, a thick padding of time stopping her words from getting across. 'What do you need me to do? Please, tell me,' she pleaded into the silence, the heavy shadows creeping around her. Finally they'd stopped running and she felt a soft breeze on her face, lifting the tendrils of her hair. 'Tell me,' she said again. Looking down she saw the pale face of a small child lit by a single candle flame. Dark haunted eyes in a small waif-like countenance that gazed up at her in silence. Whoever held on to her hand, however, was stood outside of the candle's sphere of light, shadowed from view.

'Help me now, please help.' She heard the words again although she knew the voice she heard was not that of the silent child. And then, they were gone.

Eleanor sat up with a gasp, switching on her light and looking frantically around the room. All was silent. There was enough moonlight filtering around the edges of the drawn curtains for her to see there was no one in the room, but something had woken her. That feeling again of someone else stood beside the bed, holding their breath. She couldn't see or hear anything, but she knew they were there.

'I know you're here,' she whispered. 'Who are you? Is it you, Eleanor?' Still no sound was forthcoming, but the yearning desperation that had pervaded her dream filled the room. Then, just as suddenly as she knew she wasn't alone, the presence was gone. A momentary chill in the air and the now familiar sharp, metallic smell: the honey, steel and freshly mown hay that prickled at her nostrils.

She stretched her fingers. They felt cold and tight, as if they'd been clasped too firmly by another. A gentle breeze rustled against the curtains from the open window and Amber lay back down, her eyes open. She wasn't afraid, more intrigued. Someone, or something, was here in the house but there was no malevolence; it was more that they were trying to attract her attention. Like a toddler who tugged repeatedly and wordlessly at your clothing to get you to notice them, without telling you what they wanted. The thought of it tore at her heart. It was frustrating; she didn't know what it was she needed to do.

Becky was on the doorstep at ten o'clock. Amber's head felt fuzzy. She'd lain awake until long into the night, and she was still feeling out of sorts. She led Becky across the lawn to the undergrowth surrounding the stonework she'd discovered the previous day, and told her of the strange feelings she'd been having that she wasn't alone, and her dream the previous night.

'I've never seen anything, not once,' Amber asserted. 'I just kind of know someone is there who needs my help, and they don't mean me any harm. Do you think I'm losing my marbles?'

'Of course not,' Becky reprimanded her. 'Our minds can

work in strange ways, especially when grieving. People report seeing their deceased loved ones when they're mourning.'

'But I'm almost certain it isn't Saffron. I don't know, it's as if they want me to know they're there, because they are waiting for me to help them, and then this strange smell afterwards. It's not unpleasant either.'

'Smelly ghosts — that's a first for me,' Becky teased. 'So you think that maybe it's Eleanor? You've been pretty caught up in her story and your investigations.'

'That was my first thought as well. Her message at the beginning of the book, asking for her daughter to be at peace. Whatever it means, I'm sure she's depending on me to work it out. No pressure then.' She laughed.

The two women began to hack away at the brambles and elderberry bushes that surrounded the almost hidden derelict walls. They'd taken precautions and worn thick gardening gloves and long-sleeve jackets, but they were both sweating profusely after thirty minutes. Pausing to remove her coat, Amber stepped back to look at what they'd uncovered. She was conscious that they were working in the shadow of the tower as it cast a cold pall over them. It felt ominous and made her shiver despite the sweat that clung to her. Already at her feet she could see the outline of three low walls, with various pieces of stone scattered on the floor and around the outside. One wall was completely missing. She found herself wishing Jonathan was here as well; he loved being out in their garden.

'Well this was definitely a building of some sort, but there's not a lot left. I wonder where the rest of it went,' Amber said as she looked around trying to work out the perimeters of the building.

'Once it was all derelict the locals probably nabbed the stone for repairs elsewhere. That used to happen all the time. The priory next to the church has almost none of the original walls left because it's all been built into the local farms and cottages.' Becky scuffed her feet across the floor of the old building, kicking the debris aside. 'There are some tiles on the floor here but I'd say they're a later addition to the original building.'

Amber joined her. 'I was hoping for a crypt, something like that. I wonder if I can get some archaeology students to come out with the ground-penetrating radar. They'll be able to tell if there was a space under the floor. It would only cost me a couple of crates of beer. I wish we knew if her family were buried in the village. And if they're not there, surely they must be under here?'

'I'm as puzzled as you are,' Becky admitted.

'Are you two auditioning for a garden makeover show?' Pete's deep voice boomed down from the top of the scaffolding and was followed by a bellow of laughter from Kenny, which rang out across the hall grounds.

Pushing her hair stuck against her sweaty face out of the way, Amber laughed and called back. 'Instead of the wisecracks, clever clogs, why don't you come down and help?'

To her astonishment, ten minutes later Pete appeared beside the ever-growing pile of green cuttings they'd pulled out of the ground. She saw Becky give him a swift grin before turning even pinker than the digging had made her, as she quickly bent over to pull at a trailing piece of bramble.

'So, why all the gardening?' he asked.

'There are some ruins of an old building here,' Amber explained, deliberately not mentioning her search for Mary, or the book of hours. 'We're clearing it so we can get a better look. You're welcome to help if you want?'

'We're just about to go to the suppliers for some more lime mortar so I can't hang around for long. But pass me those shears that you're waving around like a deadly weapon, and I'll get some of these nettles cut.'

In the fifteen minutes it took for Kenny to appear at the bottom of the scaffolding, Pete had cleared a large space at one corner of the chapel. Amber had carried on pulling at some bindweed, but out of the corner of one eye she noticed that Becky had stopped working and was watching Pete as he sliced through the vegetation. She also didn't miss him wink at Becky as he straightened up and handed the shears back, her friend flushing and smiling at him.

An hour later the floor was completely revealed, but there was even less to feel optimistic about.

'I'm fairly certain there's no crypt,' Becky admitted. 'There would need to be a door in the floor to it. Or at least cellar steps on the outside of the building, and there's no sign of that either.'

'Cellar,' Amber repeated, 'cellar, why didn't I think of that? There's one here at the hall, although I've never been down. I don't know when Grandad last went into it either.' She paused for a moment and gave a little shudder as she mulled over what had just occurred to her.

'You've lost me now.'

'The beginning of Eleanor's message in her book of hours states, *"My baby daughter lies beneath our feet."* Maybe the baby was in the cellar? I thought it was an epitaph she'd put on the baby's grave – that's why I've been looking for it. But maybe she hid the baby in the cellar.'

'That's a bit gruesome.' Becky's face paled. 'Why would she do that?'

'I don't know, but more and more I feel as if Eleanor is visiting me, because she wants me to help her in some way and I'm trying to work out what it is she wants.' Amber thought of the child in her dream. 'I think it's to do with baby Mary.' The two women looked at each other for a moment, deep in their own thoughts, trying to understand exactly what they may be caught up in.

'Why does she smell funny though?' Becky asked.

'You'd smell funny after five hundred years. Let's go and find Grandad and ask him about the cellar. And get a cold drink.'

Grandad had dozed off and Amber was reluctant to wake him. Instead they took the glasses of squash into the office and she flicked through her notebook until she found the translation of the Latin passage.

'See? Her baby daughter lay beneath her feet, so she must be buried somewhere in the grounds.'

'I doubt it's the cellar. They would have made sure it was consecrated land in those days. Even though we haven't found a grave, she must be in the graveyard or a family vault elsewhere.' Becky took the translation from Amber and studied it as if it may suddenly give her a clue.

'But then, why this bit about "I beseech you"? It's like she's desperately asking for us to do something for her. I need to know what it is.' Amber ran her hands through her hair.

'Have you read the rest of the book to see if there are any more clues?' Becky questioned.

'Not yet,' Amber admitted. 'I've been allowing myself a few pages at a time, but you may be right. Perhaps there are clues elsewhere. I've been transcribing it so I can hand over a research paper to the museum when I donate it, so it's taking a while to read through.'

The sound of a cupboard banging told them that Grandad was now awake and making himself a drink. Amber and Becky went into the kitchen and asked him about the cellar.

'I've not been down there for years. It's empty; there's no boxes of books if that's what you're wondering.'

'Not books, no,' Amber replied, not wanting to tell him what she really thought might be hidden.

He rummaged in a drawer, before eventually – with an exclamation of pleasure – he removed a large rusty key.

'You'll need a torch,' he reminded her, throwing it onto the table. Amber took her phone from the back pocket of her jeans and switched the torch on.

'Coming?' she asked Becky. The truth was, she was a little frightened about what she may find in the cold and damp darkness beneath the hall, and she really wanted someone with her.

'Absolutely.' Becky got to her feet. 'Lead the way.'

The door to the cellar was behind the kitchen in a passage that led to some empty storerooms. Amber turned the key and pulled hard on the door, stuck fast in its frame. Eventually after several hefty tugs it fell open, almost knocking her off her feet. She tilted the torchlight down the stairs, which fell away into the blackness. A copious layer of cobwebs clung to the walls, dancing in the sudden draught.

'Yuck. I'd forgotten about spiders.' Amber shuddered.

'Scaredy-cat, shall I go first?' Becky asked. 'I don't mind a few spiders. Pass me your phone.' Squeezing past, she set off down the stairs with Amber following close behind, trying not to brush against the walls.

'Mind the stairs,' she reminded Becky. 'They may be unsafe.'

'Don't worry, I'm taking it slowly. And they should be okay — they're stone.'

When they got to the bottom, Amber looked around in disappointment. She'd been expecting passageways, cellars and maybe even a tunnel with no idea where it would lead. Something straight out of Enid Blyton, or a gothic horror novel. Instead, all they found were three long, low rooms, with brick vaulted ceilings. They were all empty. Amber walked up and down examining the floors and walls, looking for anywhere that someone may have buried a baby. But there was nothing.

Disappointed, they returned to the kitchen. Amber switched on the kettle before dropping down on a chair.

'That's that then. I don't have any other ideas. I don't know what the passage means. I have no idea what she's saying to us.'

'Don't worry.' Becky patted her hand. 'Sometimes it takes time to see the full picture. We'll solve it in time. Try looking at it from a different angle. Keep reading the book — there may be more clues in it.'

Amber nodded. She didn't know what Eleanor was relying on her to do, but she wouldn't stop until she'd found out.

Chapter Eighteen

1538–39

Eleanor was keen to show Greville how she was using the tower as a drying room for the saffron fronds.

'I keep the door locked at all times. Nobody else comes up here but me,' she promised as he followed her up the stairs. She felt a small twinge of guilt at the lie she'd just told him, as the mental image of Joan working alongside her flitted across her mind. But her friend could be trusted and her assistance was necessary in the drying process. 'I've told Hugh that even the tiniest draught could ruin the whole process so he doesn't question why I'm not allowing anyone else in. And I attend to the fire myself to ensure it's the correct temperature. I believe I've got it right. The saffron looks and tastes as it should. And I've started making it into these squashed cakes, which will be easier to transport. Because this is the first year of growth for these bulbs, this is the finest quality *saffron du hort*. It's usually only used for medicinal purposes.'

She picked one up to show him as she stood in the

middle of the room, surrounded on all sides by trestle tables laid out with the tiny pieces of deep red spice. The room was filled with the heady, almost intoxicating aroma of heavy sweetness, with a sharp metallic tang and, somewhere in the air, the lustre of warm ginger. Greville looked around in amazement.

'I had no idea you had cultivated so much,' he admitted after a moment. 'I thought you were growing a little in your physic garden with your medicines.'

'I asked you if it was possible for me to have a strip of the meadow,' she reminded him sharply. She wanted to stamp her foot and was having trouble hiding the exasperation in her voice. 'I brought a great many crocus bulbs with me. This saffron is worth a lot of money to you. To us.'

'I import saffron sometimes,' Greville replied slowly. 'I don't know how yours will compare; it looks darker in colour. Although the cakes I ate were delicious and had a piquancy I've never tasted before. I'll take a small amount back and see what some of the spice merchants think of it. I can't say fairer than that, can I?' He kissed the top of her head and tapped her on the bottom and then he was gone, taking the stairs back down two at a time. Eleanor expected to hear a crash as he missed his footing and fell to the bottom. She was slightly disappointed when it didn't come.

How dare he think her saffron was a lesser quality than that which he'd bought from the Ottoman Empire? She'd seen the quality of the fronds Cook was using; she'd taken some into her stillroom. Its taste was bland, barely a hint of the hot, sharp, woody flavour hers tasted of. The Ixworth Priory saffron had been a superior quality, and now hers was as well. Then let him see what the London merchants thought of it. She placed another log on the fire, and picked up a thread carefully between her thumb and forefinger, holding it beneath her nose. The familiar and unique scent was almost overpowering. She stroked it gently over the soft, sensitive skin of her upper lip. It was dry; it was ready. Tomorrow she'd finish making up the cakes before packing them away and putting aside a small amount for Greville to take when he returned to London. In her book of hours, she kept a journal of all that happened.

I have shown Greville where we dried and prepared the saffron. The tower, which holds its own secrets close to its heart, will hold this one too. No harm must come to our precious spice.

Her busy daily routine barely altered, even though Greville was in and out of the house all day. She still had requests for her medicines and was often outside at dawn with Joan, the pair of them foraging in the undergrowth, despite the seasonal drop in temperature and the occasional rim of crisp white frost that lay in icy tendrils across the plants they sought. Brilliant spider webs clung to the hedgerows, sparkling with damp droplets and wavering precariously as she swept past, holding her warm fur-lined cloak against herself. She felt the sea salt in the air, rough against her skin, and tasted it in the sharp winds that blew across from the coast, making her eyes water. It was the wind that brought the Hansa, a group of tradesmen and merchants from the Baltic seas and Germany to their shores, people Greville was keen to trade with, but it felt spiteful and harsh on her cheek. Eleanor wondered if the traders were of a similar disposition. Greville was happy to take their money, but he was never complimentary about their temperaments.

At night though, it was now very different. She could hardly understand why she'd been so nervous of lying with Greville, when now she was impatient to leave the rest of the household and hide with him behind the drapes around his bed.

'Do you see now, why I insisted we waited?' he asked one night as they curled up together, their skin cooling in the night air. Eleanor was drowsy after their lovemaking and she smiled.

'I can only think that I was denied this pleasure for longer than was necessary, husband,' she murmured, 'but I am willing to forgive you.'

Greville gave a growl of laughter deep in his chest, and in one movement flipped her body under his, as he rolled on top of her.

Advent soon arrived, with its hours of fasting and masses every day. Eleanor told Hugh the whole household must attend chapel every morning, and although his eyes slid across to Greville hoping for a contradiction to her order, it was withheld and her husband nodded in agreement. She suspected it was the first Christmas at Milfleet during which the religious services would be strictly upheld.

Everyone in the house was excited for the festive season, Eleanor included. Cook was preparing many special dishes for the twelve days of Christmas and had ordered in a great deal of meat, which now hung in the larder, the blood dripping darkly onto the sawdust below. As she walked past every day to the stillroom, the metallic odour of the meat began to turn Eleanor's stomach and she started to hold her breath and scoot past until she could get outside and gulp in some fresh air.

As the days went by, the nausea caused by the meat increased until finally she noticed it was almost constant. A quick calculation on her fingers confirmed what she'd already begun to realise, she'd missed two of her courses. Hurrying to the solar, she found Joan executing some fine stitching on a tear in one of Jane's dresses.

'Have you come to join me?' she asked smiling as Eleanor walked in. 'The light will only be good for another hour or so.'

Sitting down beside Joan, she grasped her small hand with her own.

'I think I am with child,' she whispered as if she could scarcely believe it, let alone say it out loud. Her friend was far more delighted than she was.

'This is wonderful news,' she exclaimed, dropping her sewing in her lap and clapping her hands. 'A new baby in the house, how exciting! Are you sure?'

Eleanor, who was certainly not as enthusiastic as Joan, nodded slowly. 'I believe so. I've counted the months. And I feel queasy every day. It used to begin at morning time, but now it seems to persist all day long.'

'That is to be expected of course,' Joan replied. 'Have you told the master yet? He'll be hoping for a boy, of course.'

'Not yet, I'll tell him later.'

'You don't seem as happy with the news as I'd have thought?' Joan raised her eyebrows and studied her friend's face.

'There's nothing to be happy about,' Eleanor burst out. 'Women die in childbirth all the time. Like my own mother. Like Jane's mamma. But of course Greville will be delighted with the news. Why else did he marry me? Someone to help him run the household during his long absences whilst he enjoys London life and goes to court, and to produce sons as if I am a brood mare or one of the cows out in the pasture. It's all I'm good for.' She didn't care if she sounded harsh, she was frightened and before Joan could remonstrate,

Eleanor jumped to her feet and ran along the corridors to her bedroom where she leant on the door as she shut it, and burst into tears. Until she'd said the words out loud, she hadn't really considered the dangers involved. The fact was, this development just made her even more of a chattel. Carrying his baby branded her as belonging to Greville. Which she did, whether she liked it or not.

She didn't get a chance to tell him the news of her condition for another two days, as word came he was staying in Lynn to help unload a large shipment that had just arrived. He wasn't sure how long it would take, but his note assured her he'd definitely be home for Christmas Day.

Eleanor was no longer as excited about the festivities as she had been, battling every day with the nausea that swamped her. Joan had taken to preparing mint tea for her, adding some grated ginger from the kitchen. It only slightly alleviated the sickness. Eleanor tried adding some of her saffron, which helped a little more.

Greville arrived home late on Christmas Eve. The house was by this point in a heightened mood of anticipation for the festivities and Joan, Nell and Jane had decorated the great hall with holly, ivy and yew, together with huge bunches of mistletoe. The yule log had been dragged inside with much excitement hours earlier, and decorated ready to be burned over the following twelve days of celebrations. Just for once, Eleanor was not disappointed at the sparse Christmas Eve provisions, the lack of meat, fish and dairy eaten during Advent was no hardship while anything rich just made her stomach churn unpleasantly.

Greville found her sitting on her own in the solar, watching a heron standing perfectly still at the edge of the brook that provided their water. The Mill Fleet. The bird could stand for hours on one spindly leg, its life in a vacuum of watching and anticipating. And often not achieving the thing it waited so patiently for. She knew how it felt. She turned to face her husband, a ready smile on her face. He smelled of damp and winter, as he gathered her against him, pressing her into the thick wool of his cloak and speaking into her ear.

'Almost Christmas, my little wife,' he said. 'Are you excited? I've missed you and your warmth beside me at night.' His hot breath tickled her ear and made her giggle. She wanted to be cross with him, but it was hard.

'I have news.' She turned her head sideways so she could speak without being muffled by his clothes. Loosening his arm slightly he cupped her chin and turned her face up to his, concern in his eyes.

'Is everything all right? Hugh mentioned no problems when I saw him downstairs.'

'There's nothing wrong. Well not that concerns Hugh. I believe I am with child. Our baby. I think it will arrive sometime around May Day.'

Greville whooped so loudly, she suspected that not only had the whole household heard, but probably the village as well. The heron below took to the air on graceful wings and disappeared into the approaching murky dusk. Carefully he led her back to the chair she'd been sitting on, and settled at her feet.

'This is the very best of news. Are you feeling well?'

'I've been better,' she admitted, 'but the nausea is not quite as bad now as it was, and I'm just eating small amounts and avoiding greasy meats.'

185

'Whatever you want, just ask Cook. Jellies, custards, anything. Are there any herbs that will help? As soon as Christmas is over I must return to London, so I can send anything you require. Nothing but the best for my child. A son, I hope.' His face appeared a little flushed and he couldn't contain the wide grin that was steadily spreading across his face, his eyes sparkling.

'You're leaving again straight after Christmas?' Eleanor echoed, immediately catching on to the one piece of news she didn't want to hear.

'I must return, I have business to attend to. And I need to be seen at court often, to be noticed. Already I've stayed away too long and I'll miss Christmas there as well.'

'When will you return home again? In time for the birth?' She reached for his hand and clasped it in both of hers.

'I don't know – hopefully, but I cannot promise. I'll take the sample of saffron that you gave me, and see if there is any interest in it.'

Eleanor's heart sank. Childbirth was no place for a man so it didn't matter if he was at home or not, but she would feel safer knowing he was nearby instead of seven days' riding away. She knew he was trying to placate her with his offer of showing the merchants her saffron, but now she had far greater concerns on her mind.

The Christmas festivities flew past. Eleanor enjoyed them as much as she was able, although a heavy weariness saw her in bed every night, long before the carousing downstairs had ended. Despite her assurance to Greville that he didn't need to leave the fun and games just because she was, he nevertheless followed her to bed where she slept soundly enclosed

186

in the warmth of his strong safe arms, her back pressed against the firm heat of his body.

Finally it was Plough Monday and as everything returned to normal after the festivities, Greville could delay his return to London no longer. His journeyman, Ralph, had left with a cartload of luggage and goods from the warehouse in King's Lynn five days previously. If he rode hard, Greville could arrive at his London home only a day or two behind him. Already he was distant, his mind on what he needed to do when he got there. His family seemed all but forgotten; Eleanor felt his spirit slipping away hour by hour, even though physically he was still with them.

On the morning he was leaving, there was a lot of commotion in the great hall as everything was prepared. One of the London apprentices, John, who had travelled up with Ralph, was to ride back with Greville and the two men stood chatting, oblivious to the frenetic activity around them. Nell had developed a soft spot for John, her previous beloved all but forgotten, and her eyes were as red-rimmed as Jane's, who was crying loudly for her papa. Finally, irritated by the pair of them, Eleanor snapped at Nell to take Jane and return to the nursery. She was feeling out of sorts herself, although she wasn't going to let Greville see how disappointed she was that he was leaving her. She didn't need other tearful people making the situation worse.

Retreating to her desk in the office, she pretended to work at her accounts as if it was a normal day. Eventually, just as she thought he may leave without saying goodbye, Greville appeared in the doorway.

'Well, little wife—' his deep voice stayed her hand on the counting board '—I must away. We want to travel a fair distance before it gets dark.' She laid down her quill and went to him, breathing in his warm smell of sweat and peat smoke. He'd been warming himself in front of the fire. Would this be the last time she'd be in his arms, safe and secure? She didn't voice the words as they rose unbidden in her head. She mustn't think the worst. Instinctively her hand moved to the mound of her stomach and she tried to block out her fear for the ordeal ahead she must endure.

'I have the saffron.' He patted the pouch he carried. 'And, I hope, your love.' He placed his hand over his heart, then laid it over hers. 'Rest well and do not do too much,' he continued as he moved his hand gently over the now visible swell of her stomach. She'd already had to ask Joan not to lace her gown so tightly, and they would begin the task of letting out the seams of her dresses that day.

'I promise,' she agreed, 'but please if you can be spared at court will you come home when the baby is due?'

'I'll try,' was all he would agree to. He bent down and his soft warm lips met hers briefly, and he was gone, shouting roughly for John. There were raised voices outside and the clatter of hooves and then they were away, the sound of the horses receding into the distance as people inside went about their business as if it was a normal day, not, as Eleanor felt, with a part of them torn from them.

When had she started to feel like this about her husband? He'd been a stranger who'd taken her away from everything that was familiar to a home she didn't know. But now she could feel that cold winter spite buried deep inside her starting to thaw, and a new warmth and affection growing. Tiny buds of love like the crocus flowers, unfurling and creeping through her.

Chapter Nineteen

1539

Life soon settled back into the normality and routine that existed when Greville was away. Eleanor strongly suspected life had been a lot more lax before she arrived at Milfleet, but now the staff had no choice than to continue working hard at their tasks all year round. She may be growing larger day by day, but she didn't relax in her strict attitude to responsibilities where the house was concerned.

The deep winter snow eventually melted away leaving behind tiny pale shoots pushing their way through the sodden earth. Fresh, brilliant green spring buds and soft pink blossom appeared on the trees, with a promise of warmer weather and longer days. Everyone's mood lifted with the better conditions, even though they were observing Lent and their meals were accordingly dull and severe. Eleanor insisted on reading from her book of hours at supper, before everyone began to eat.

In March two letters arrived. The first was from Isabel Dereham and described her busy and colourful life in London where they were visiting for the spring. There was also a letter from Greville. Eleanor was surprised to read the latest gossip from Whitehall, that Thomas Cromwell was currently trying to arrange yet another marriage for the king. He described how the court portrait painter, Holbein, had been despatched to various parts of Europe to produce some likenesses for the king to see. It seemed that one heir wouldn't be enough for King Henry and he was now thinking of filling the nursery further.

Her face lit up with delight, though, as she read how well received her sample of saffron had been, and that he had sold the whole crop to the king's Clerk of the Green Cloth for an incredible twenty sovereigns. She had to read it twice, mouthing the words out loud to make sure she hadn't misread. That amount of gold was a small fortune. The clerk had said it was the finest quality he'd ever tasted. She was to bag the remainder into sacks and give it to Ralph who was on his way back to Milfleet to take it to the port at Blakeney and, from there, London. Eleanor squealed in delight. When he'd been home, Greville had been dismissive of what she'd grown, and questioned its quality. Now though, it had earned him a huge profit. With a swell of pride, she picked up her book of hours and under her previous entry, began to write.

Today came a missive from my husband. The saffron I grew last year has been sold to the king's kitchens for the princely sum of twenty sovereigns. For the spice that I grew. My dowry from the old prior will produce more riches this coming season, for the crop will be even bigger, and next year even more so. I am filling our coffers with gold, and this pleases me greatly.

Selecting a second quill she carefully decorated around the edge of the page with a deep red-gold ink, which she'd made herself with some of the saffron she'd taken from her stillroom, smiling as she worked.

The cool spring gave way to warmer weather as summer approached. Eleanor was now very large, feeling heavy, swollen and uncomfortable as the baby inside her stretched its limbs out, pushing her stomach into grotesque shapes. She knew it wouldn't be long before she'd be confined to her room and the stifling hot atmosphere, awaiting the time the baby would come. In the meantime, she tried not to think about the inevitable. She helped Joan with stitching tiny garments and repairing the bindings and swaddling stored away since Jane had been born. There was no point in sewing new items if the old ones could be reused.

Her evenings were spent working her way through a selection of crocus bulbs she'd lifted the previous year, carefully separating them as she'd seen the monks do. She warned Simon they would need twice the amount of meadow ploughed for this year's crop. He looked surprised but nodded his agreement, wordlessly. Eleanor was determined to be out in the fields joining in when it was time to plant the extra bulbs. Before that though, she had to get through the ordeal of childbirth, which grew closer every day, like a terrifying storm on the horizon crackling with lightning. She couldn't run from it, or fight it – all she could do was endure what it hurled at her when it finally broke. And pray she'd still be alive when it had passed.

Eventually she couldn't delay her confinement any longer. The midwife from the village, Mrs Copdyke, had been alerted. Eleanor had met her previously when Simon's wife Alys had given birth to her latest child, and she seemed personable enough. She was certainly proficient and well thought of locally, and if rumours were to be believed she'd delivered every person who worked and lived in the castle and the village. Which would make her at least one hundred years old Eleanor thought wryly, if she believed the tales. Alys had six strong children, five boys and her new baby daughter, so the midwife's competency was not in question. No doubt Greville would be ecstatic at a similar tally of children, but Eleanor hoped she wouldn't have to endure childbirth quite as frequently as Alys had.

Once the room had been prepared for her confinement, there was nothing to do but wait in the stifling heat, the thick, static air pungent with sweat and almost unbreathable, as the fire blazed day and night as tradition dictated. Combined with the now burgeoning weight pressing into her lungs, it meant she spent most of her time propped up on her bed, leaning back a little to give herself more space to breathe. Joan had covered the windows with tapestries to ensure the room was in darkness other than candles and the forever burning fire. Any suggestion that Eleanor whiled away the time sewing, or reading from her prayer book was met with short shrift.

She tried to keep her eyes averted from the cradle in the corner of the room, a constant reminder of the ordeal to come. Now, she didn't care if the storm rolled over; every day felt like an eternity of waiting. There had been no further letters from Greville. She made sure Joan asked Hugh every morning and evening. His promise of trying to be home for the birth had been empty.

Finally, as Eleanor awoke one morning, dragging herself awake after yet another night of fitful, patchy sleep, her size now too big to find any position in bed comfortable, she was aware of a painful tightening underneath her belly. By the time she had realised it was there, it was gone again.

But fifteen minutes later, while she washed in the luke-warm water that a kitchen girl had brought in, there was another. It was strong enough to make her catch her breath and stop what she was doing. She hoped Joan wouldn't notice, but her ever-watchful friend missed nothing. She was like the gyrfalcon watching the hedgerows for any sign of movement.

'Are you feeling pains?' Joan asked sharply. 'Is it time? Is the baby coming?'

'I don't know, I think . . .' She paused again as her belly tightened into a hard ball. 'I think it may be. I woke up with this tightening, and now they are more frequent and becoming more painful.'

Joan gave a small satisfied smile and clapped her hands, not seeing the scowl Eleanor gave her in the murky darkness. She was terrified of the ordeal that awaited her, and Joan was almost skipping around the room in excitement. The fact that perhaps her friend was also sick of spending all day and night confined with her grumpy self didn't cross her mind. The message was sent to Mrs Copdyke as Eleanor began to pace up and down the room, making a pathway in the rushes beneath her feet as she swept through them countless times. Joan had pulled the birthing chair into the centre of the room near to the roaring fire, but Eleanor growled 'not yet' and tried to kick it as she walked past, so it was hastily tucked back in the corner.

The midwife was attending another birth and it was two hours before she arrived; by which time Eleanor's waters had broken, a cascade of fluid splashing across the floor and up Joan's dress, and her pains were coming every few minutes. Joan had ordered the cleaning of the floor and fresh rushes, but Mrs Copdyke told the servant girl not to bother. She could tell it was almost time for the birth and the floor was about to be covered in a lot worse. This time when the birthing stool was put before the fire, Eleanor didn't say a word. She'd been humming under her breath as the pain worsened and she sank down on the chair, supported from behind by Joan as she bellowed whilst the waves of pain crested over her, leaving her breathless.

Within minutes and after two further agonising contractions, Mrs Copdyke said, 'Here comes your baby now,' and with one final push, Eleanor's baby arrived. The midwife triumphantly held it up, pink, squalling, slimy with blood and white grease, thick dark hair plastered to its roaring head.

'A boy,' she announced, 'a big, bonny boy.' Quickly she tied off the cord and cut it, passing the baby to Joan so she could concentrate on delivering the afterbirth.

A boy. Eleanor couldn't help a small smile of satisfaction as she looked across to where Joan was wrapping him up. Their eyes met and she smiled at Eleanor and gave a quick nod of approval, a job well done. His crying had subsided and Joan held him up for Eleanor to see, his dark hair sprouting above big dark eyes so like Greville's.

'No denying who his father is,' the midwife remarked. 'Looks just like Miss Jane did when she was born.' Eleanor didn't want to think about Greville's first wife giving birth whilst she was still so afraid. Infections and complications often crept in and killed in the days after birth. But looking at her tiny, perfect new-born son, her heart combusted with heat at the instant love she felt for him. She wasn't going to die, because he needed her. And, she realised with sudden conviction, for the rest of her life she needed him.

Once she was back in her bed, the room cleaned and the baby laid in the heavy dark oak cradle that had been brought upstairs from one of the storerooms a few weeks previously, Mrs Copdyke was ready to leave. Joan counted out the shillings already agreed for payment.

'Would you like me to find a wet nurse?' the midwife asked, gratefully pocketing her fee. She'd doubled what she'd ask a villager but Eleanor had agreed to pay it without question: she needed the best midwife at any cost. Mrs Copdyke knew if Hugh discovered her duplicity he'd be demanding the excess back and it would undoubtedly disappear into his own pocket.

'No, thank you.' Eleanor shook her head. 'That won't be necessary. I shall be feeding him myself.' She wasn't letting him out of her sight. Joan's eyes widened in surprise. She was most likely about to agree to the suggestion of a wet nurse, but then considered her friend's stubbornness and kept quiet.

As soon as it was just Joan and herself in the room, Eleanor felt able to relax. Joan told her a letter had already been despatched to London, and all the members of the household were keen to see the new arrival. Eleanor, still petrified of diseases, only allowed Jane and Nell in to see him.

'What shall you name him?' Jane asked, peering at his tiny sleeping form under the bedding.

'Henry,' Eleanor replied, 'for the king. And my father.' She had no doubt her husband would want to decide what their son was called and probably call him after himself given it was his firstborn son, but he wasn't at home and the baby would be baptised within the next day or two. So she would choose, and Henry Greville Lutton it was.

Greville finally arrived home three weeks after Henry's birth. Eleanor was still lying in, but there had been a steady stream of visitors to her room. She heard a commotion in the great hall and was about to ask Joan to investigate when the door burst open and in walked her husband. He brought with him the welcome smell of fresh air, horses and warm meadows, and never had Eleanor been happier to see him. She'd just finished feeding Henry and his face, now beginning to fatten up and lose its pinched new-born look, was warm and flushed. His long dark eyelashes lay against his cheeks as he slept, the silky black thatch of his hair springing haphazardly about his face. Joan and Nell had both tried keeping it flat but as soon as Eleanor removed his bonnet it bounced free.

Perching on the edge of her bed, Greville ran his finger down her cheek.

'My clever girl,' he said softly, 'you've given me a perfect son.' Eleanor couldn't help a small smile of self-congratulation. He was right. Childbirth had been a painful experience and she was immensely proud to have produced such a flawless, sweet little boy. Greville scooped him up from the crook of her arm so he was resting against his father's chest. Despite the rough wool of Greville's travelling clothes, Henry didn't stir.

'I'm sorry I wasn't here when he was born. I couldn't get away from court. I came as soon as I could.'

'It's a shame, but it's done now. I hope you like the name I chose?' Eleanor was still stung that he hadn't been home when she needed him, but she wasn't going to voice it. Not now, when it was too late anyway.

'I love his name. He looks like a Henry. Are you well?'

'I am, thank you. I'm bored of sitting in this room, but I cannot be churched for another week, so here we stay. Thankfully I'll be up and about in time for the crocus planting in four weeks. Can you look for me please to see that half of home meadow is ploughed and ready? I asked Joan to check but honestly I think she will say anything to placate me. I need to be back in my stillroom soon, before the stocks of some of my basic cures begin to run low.' Already her thoughts had begun to turn towards the many other ways in which she ensured the house kept running smoothly. Producing an heir was only one of her numerous roles, or so it felt.

Greville chuckled, the deep vibrations of his chest disturbing Henry and he stirred momentarily. Lifting his head up a little and opening his unfocused eyes, he looked at Greville before he frowned and closed them again.

'I think he is not much impressed with me.' Greville laughed, laying his son in the cradle. 'I'll go and run your errands, sweet wife. You're not to worry or it will curdle your milk. Joan can make up some of your ointments. She can always bring them to you to check them though I know she is as proficient as you in the stillroom.' His eyes crinkled up as he looked at her, the deep velvety brown making her smile in return. It appeared that finally her husband was beginning to appreciate all that she did. 'And you will sit and watch the gardeners and farmhands plant the bulbs. I forbid you to join in.'

She waited until he'd left the room before looking across at Joan and rolling her eyes, making her friend smile. She'd suspected he would stay her from any heavy work so soon after the birth, even though she was fast regaining her strength. Even if she wasn't able to push the bulbs into the earth herself, she would certainly be out in the field, watching and checking. If the crop was planted incorrectly there would be no saffron in the autumn so she needed to ensure every piece of the planting was carried out correctly, the right distance between the bulbs and all set properly. Nothing must happen to prevent this year's crop succeeding and yielding more, much more, than before.

Chapter Twenty

2019

Amber had read Eleanor's plea so often, she knew it off by heart. But still it didn't make sense.

'I still don't understand what you're asking me to do,' she said into the empty office, her words echoing off the walls. 'Please, show me what it is you want.' There was no stirring of the air, no acrid trace to indicate that Eleanor was there.

'Grandad, can you think of any clues? Anything I've missed?' she asked.

'None at all. There's no helpful family folklore or tales passed down through time I'm afraid. Nothing. I'm sorry I can't help you,' he replied.

'It's okay. I've only got five months left here though, and I feel I can't move on with my life, with this unresolved.'

'Amber.' His voice was unexpectedly sharp. 'You came here because of the huge sorrow in your life. You need to resolve *that* and move on, not merely swap it for a potentially five-hundred-year-old tragedy belonging to somebody else.

You may have to just let it go. When I suggested you came here to help with my books it was to give you space to grieve and then be able to move on with your life with Jonathan. That is the most important thing to concentrate on.' He paused for a moment and took a deep breath before adding in a gentler tone, 'Don't you have an appointment with the consultant today?'

'Yes, I do. But no I can't let it go. Eleanor needs me to resolve something vital for her, for her baby Mary. I just need to find out what it is.' But, she acknowledged silently, her confused state of mind and unanswered questions about Mary was only part of the problem. She had just as many unanswered questions about her own baby, and her relationship with Jonathan. She had to admit Grandad was right: they were the people now, in the present, who really mattered and she needed to remember that, and prioritise them.

'Anyway, I must get ready; Jonathan and I are meeting early to have a chat, so I'd better get dressed or I'll be late.' She poured the tea she'd been making down the sink, and rinsed her cup out.

The hospital car park was as usual completely full, and cursing under her breath, Amber drove round and around watching for someone about to leave. Already wound up like a tight spring, teeth gritted and a fine sheen of sweat steadily washing away her hastily applied make-up, a battle to find a parking space was the last thing she needed.

'Bingo,' she muttered as an old couple she'd been watching totter across the car park finally got into their car almost right beside her. She slid her car into the space. After a quick check that she still had lipstick on her lips and none on her teeth, she grabbed her bag and hurried to the coffee shop. They had just over an hour before their appointment and already her legs felt shaky. She tried to walk as fast as she could, but it felt as if she was clambering through deep snow, her breathing laboured and her heart pounding.

Jonathan was already sitting at a table with two cups of coffee in front of him and she flopped into the chair opposite, her limbs heavy and aching.

'Hi.' His smile was tentative, but the tilt of his head, his creased eyes that lit up as he saw her were so familiar, it made her heart hurt. His shirt collar, badly ironed, was open; she could see him swallowing hard, his Adam's apple bobbing up and down as he said, 'I got you a coffee. I hope that's okay.'

'Oh perfect, thank you.' She took a large gulp. 'I've been driving around the car park for ages.'

'It's a nightmare,' he agreed. 'I've only been here a few minutes myself.' There was a pause as if he was wondering what to say next. Too afraid to say anything. Together they both said 'how are you?' then laughed.

'I'm okay,' she replied. 'Still sorting through mountains of books. I met up with Becky and you were right: I should have contacted her sooner. She's been great. She's been helping me with a kind of project I've been working on.'

'Project?' Jonathan's eyebrows rose. Amber told him about the book of hours she'd found, and explained about Eleanor's disturbing passage at the front of the book.

'And there are moments sometimes when I can feel her with me, as if she's urging me to unravel the message. Becky and I have been exploring, but we've found nothing. Although it's been fun looking. Grandad told me this morning I should give up on it, but I can't.'

'It sounds very interesting.' He hesitated for a moment as if considering his words carefully. 'But please don't take on more than you're able. Remember to look after yourself first, yes? Although you certainly seem perkier than I've seen you in months,' he admitted. 'I suppose it's good for you to do if it's giving you something to concentrate on.'

'There's something else though that it's made me understand.' Shakily she took a deep breath. 'I haven't listened properly to the people closest to me. Those I care about most. I've been so caught up in my own grief when I should have been looking beyond what was going on in my head to what you were feeling as well. I've shut myself away instead of opening up. As I was trying to reach out and communicate with Eleanor, her lost soul and the all-engulfing sadness that surrounds her, it made me realise that I haven't been doing the same to you, the person I love most in the world. What you said in your email, you were right, and I'm sorry. So sorry. I've not forgotten about Saffron,' she was quick to reassure him. 'There isn't a moment that goes by the memory of her isn't in my thoughts. But it used to fill all of my head without space for anything else, and now there's a tiny edge between the membranes round my brain, where sometimes I'm able to think of other things. Of you.'

He smiled gently and reached out with trembling hands to take hers in his. He closed his eyes for a moment, breathing out slowly.

'I understand,' he reassured her. 'I can wait. I'll wait forever.' She looked into his eyes, his kind eyes that were never reproachful, never blaming, and she felt her own fill up. She rummaged in her bag for tissues.

'I brought a new packet.' She laughed, holding them up

and sniffing. 'I didn't think I'd need them before we'd even got into Mr MacKenzie's office.'

They realised it was time to leave, and carrying their drinks they walked together along the corridors to the maternity wing. Amber's heart was thumping hard, remembering the last time they walked the same route. At that point, they already knew their baby daughter was dead. The scan the day before had confirmed the reason why she hadn't felt any kicks during the previous twenty-four hours, but she had to return the following day to be induced. If she'd thought the walk to the delivery unit had been long that morning, it was nothing compared to walking out the following day, her belly and her arms empty.

Jonathan caught hold of her hand and squeezed it as if he knew what she was thinking. The same thoughts that were probably screaming through his head too. After all he'd lost his daughter as well, and she should have been thinking about his grief, as well as her own. She gripped his hand tightly and gave him a watery smile.

Unfortunately the consultant's office was situated in the maternity out-patients and they had to sit in the big waiting room, slowly filling up with women for the afternoon clinic, almost all of them with extended pregnancy bellies, clothes pulled tight across bulges, and many with rampaging toddlers running around fighting in the toy corner over the broken plastic offerings. Amber studied her feet, waiting for their names to be called. She was desperate to be out of there. After what felt like a lifetime but was probably no more than ten minutes, she heard a voice call them through and, turning, she was pleased to recognise Lily, the midwife they'd been assigned to for the birth.

'I didn't expect to see you.' Amber smiled. 'It's nice to see a familiar face.'

'Of course I'm here; it's continuity of care. I was there for Saffron's birth so it's important I'm here now for you.' She put her arm around Amber's shoulders and gave her a comforting squeeze as she steered them into a bright office. Mr MacKenzie was in his sixties, his white hair thinning and a gathering of lines quilting his face. He stood up and shook hands, introducing himself. With her pregnancy being uneventful until the final tragic hours, there had been no reason for Amber to have ever seen the most eminent obstetrician in the department. Even the delivery of the awful news that her baby had died had been delegated to a registrar. The consultant opened the notes before him, and skimmed over them as if he was trying to remember who they were, and why they were in his office.

'First of all, let me offer my condolences.' His voice was sonorous, slow. 'I know this is the meeting no couple, no parents want. And I wish it was one I didn't have to do either. I also wish I could now give you a reason, some evidence as to why your daughter's heart stopped beating, but sadly we don't know, for sure. The pathologist's examination of the placenta shows it had begun to disintegrate and it was without doubt not working efficiently. The reduced blood flow to your baby quite possibly contributed to her heart not being able to cope. Although we can never say with a one hundred per cent conviction, I would say this was the most likely cause.'

'So . . .' Amber's voice shook and she cleared her throat before continuing. 'Why did the placenta stop working properly? Was it something I did?'

'Absolutely not,' he was quick to reassure her. 'I know it's what we medical people say, but it really was just one of those things. There was no way of predicting it. Your baby was a little small for full-term, but not enough that it would have rung alarm bells. As I said, we'll never know. It goes without saying that should you decide to have another baby in future, we'll do more regular ultrasounds on the placenta and umbilical cord during the pregnancy to make sure everything is working as it should. We'd induce the baby at thirty-eight weeks, before the placenta was getting towards the end of its maximum efficiency.'

They were asked if they had any further questions, but there was nothing left to say. It hadn't been anyone's fault, although Amber wanted to blame someone and so she blamed herself, even though she knew it was pointless. Nothing would bring Saffron back.

Before they knew it, they were back in the car park. The meeting had barely taken thirty minutes and Amber remembered hardly any of it. They walked in silence until they reached Jonathan's car, both of them bound up in their own thoughts. Glancing into the passenger window, Amber was saddened to see empty supermarket sandwich boxes and crisp packets abandoned on the seat. She used to insist on making him fresh sandwiches and fruit if he was out and about all day, and now he was having to buy mass-produced offerings and no doubt eating them on the move. Her eyes welled up again, just when she thought she had no more tears left.

'I don't know what I was expecting,' he said as they stopped walking and he unlocked the car, 'but now I feel a bit empty.'

'I agree,' she replied, blowing her nose. 'It feels so final.

That's it. There's nothing left to be said now. It should feel like closure, but it doesn't.'

'I don't think we'll ever get closure. We just have to live with the people we've become, the couple we now are. If we can.'

'I suppose so. I don't know where we go from here. I just wanted answers, a way forward, but we don't have any. Maybe when my mind has got around what the doctor's just told us, when I've made sense of it all?'

'It's fine – there's no hurry. Just try to stay in touch though now, please? Try to keep talking? It's been really lovely to see you today, even in such sad circumstances.'

Amber nodded and smiled. 'You too,' she said, putting her arms around his waist and laying her head against his chest, 'you too.'

By the time she got back to Grandad's, her journey hampered by tractors and school-run traffic as she drove along the country roads, it was already dinner time. She sent a quick text to Jonathan to let him know she was back safely, and went in search of something to eat.

Feeling a little more relaxed after a cup of coffee and a toastie, Amber decided to spend the evening reading some more of the book of hours for any clue or reference that may help solve Eleanor's request. After turning a couple of pages, she found another entry in Eleanor's distinctive writing.

Today came a missive from my husband. The saffron I grew last year has been sold to the king's kitchens for the princely sum of twenty sovereigns. For the spice that I grew. My dowry from the old prior will produce more riches for this coming season, for the crop will be even bigger, and next year even more so. I am filling our coffers with gold, and this pleases me greatly.

From what Eleanor had written, her saffron had produced a very good profit. She certainly seemed pleased and Amber made a quick note to look up a conversion table and see how much twenty sovereigns would have been worth in present day.

The words on the page were so neatly scribed, the pride in their impart evident, Amber could feel the thrill Eleanor exuded. She was rightly proud of what she'd produced. Amber was beginning to see that there was real meaning and truth in the proverb on the front of the book: *While I breathe, I hope*. Eleanor always had hope. She always believed – she had no choice but to believe – that things would get better. Nobody can ever predict the future so it was up to her to try to make sure her future was positive.

Could Amber do that? Finally, it felt as if she was breathing. And now she believed that, in time, she could hope, too.

She awoke the following day in a better mood. Outside, the blue sky was a backdrop to a stunning mackerel cloud, its ragged herringbone flakes of pale white stretching into the distance and she sat on the back door step with her morning tea trying to imagine the house bustling with activity, as it would have been in Eleanor's day. Chickens wandering in and out, and no doubt numerous dogs getting under people's feet. It was disappointing she didn't have a floor plan to work out which part of the original hall she and Grandad were now living in. It had to be the great hall, divided up over the years into smaller more practical rooms. What a shame it now bore little resemblance to a majestic Tudor castle.

Once in her office, she abandoned any pretence of working on cataloguing Grandad's books, and retrieved the book of hours once again from the safe. She opened it gently, rereading the saffron entry again just to feel the same thrill of delight, of connection, before turning the page and ploughing on.

There were more psalms and prayers, then just as she began to wonder if Eleanor had written any more, another entry. This one was short.

Henry Greville Lutton. Born 15 May 1539. Deo gratis.

She quickly checked the beginning of the book with the list of births. Yes, Henry's was there. He was her firstborn, and because there was no mention of a death she assumed all had gone well. Lucky Eleanor. In an era when infant mortality was so high, she'd carried and delivered a healthy baby son. Something she, Amber, hadn't been able to do, not even with all the medical knowledge, equipment and expertise that the twenty-first century had to offer. Because it was her own body that had failed her, and failed Saffron.

Henry's birth announcement was surrounded by flowers, leaves and tiny birds, all finely decorated. Amber smiled. The new mother must have had time on her hands lying in after the birth and had obviously spent hours on the elaborate illuminations. This wasn't a hastily written diary entry, this was an important entry and she couldn't help feeling happy for Eleanor's obvious pride.

On the following page was an itemised list of clothing, dresses, shifts and shoes, followed by: *ordered for Thomas, for he has nothing*. Amber remembered how Thomas didn't have a date of birth entry like Henry and Mary did, and now Eleanor was ordering clothes for him. She knew in Tudor times a boy would have been dressed exactly the same as his sisters until he was about seven years old so at least that gave her a hint that Thomas was a young child. Amber hoped she would find out more about this elusive boy, and what he meant to Eleanor.

She ran her fingers softly over the decoration around the proud notice of Henry's birth. 'Good job, Eleanor,' she said into the silent room.

Chapter Twenty-One

1539

Despite Greville's protestations and concern, eight weeks after Henry's birth Eleanor was out in the meadow supervising the farmhands, as they ploughed and re-ploughed and dressed the land ready for the planting of the new corms. The small baby lay in a basket at the edge of the field while she worked during the morning, and she left him inside with Nell and Jane in the afternoons when the sun was at its hottest. Sleeves rolled up, she helped the workers, pushing the bulbs in before moving on a couple of feet and repeating the action. Her body, which had filled out during pregnancy, was still curvaceous, but swiftly returning to her slender pre-Henry lines. Greville may have chosen a girl for his wife, but she knew she was maturing into a woman and she hoped he still thought he'd made a good choice.

The bulbs had been in for barely a week when Greville came to tell her he was returning to London. She was sat in the solar with Henry on her lap, who was smiling his broad contented smile down at Jane, who played by Eleanor's feet. Jane adored her baby brother and he was equally enraptured with her. His eyes had remained as dark as when he'd been born and although his thick thatch of black hair had worn thin at the back where he slept, the rest framed his head, sprouting out at wild angles. He was a perfect miniature of his father who was as taken with him as the rest of the household, now laughing as Henry gurgled and waved his pink chubby arms at Jane.

'He's a fine lad,' he said, proudly. 'The first of many in the nursery I hope.' Eleanor looked at him from beneath her brows and pursed her lips.

'Not yet, I pray,' she answered. He had returned to her bed after her churching, but she was secretly drinking a tisane of rue with mint and some of her own saffron, which she hoped, together with the fact she still insisted on feeding Henry herself, would prevent another baby. A wise woman at Ixworth had once visited the stillroom to buy some rue when Eleanor was there, and had told her it was needed for a villager who'd recently birthed her tenth child and was desperate that there wouldn't be more. She'd made her smell the herb and told her that she should always remember its pungent acerbic smell and the valuable properties it held. Eleanor was pleased that she had. The household took a lot to manage and there would be another saffron harvest in two months' time, if not sooner. She didn't want to be feeling sick and tired when she needed to be out in the field, as well as constantly up and down to the tower.

'I have had word from London: I must return, and soon,' Greville explained.

'It is so urgent? We will miss you—' she couldn't hide the disappointment in her voice '—especially at harvest.'

'A new act is going to go through parliament soon,' he explained, 'to clarify that we are still to follow our Catholic beliefs even though the king is now the head of the church, and I would do well to be there. Although our neighbour at Framlingham, the Duke of Norfolk, is in favour of this law, others such as my friend Cromwell are vehemently averse to it. I am treading a fine line and trying to remain out of any debates. At present, I am supporting neither of them, but rather trying to keep a foot in both camps. Whilst Norfolk is our neighbour, Cromwell is a powerful friend. There are those who would rather England be completely Protestant.' He rolled his shoulders around as if loosening them, then let out a deep breath.

'Why would they want that?' she asked. 'The changes that have already been made are just appalling – surely we can't endure yet more. This all sounds like something that you should be staying well clear of.' Eleanor chewed her bottom lip. 'Please, Greville, take care.'

'Of course I will, but in order to rise up through the ranks at court, I need to be making connections with those who have the ear of the king – you know this is so.'

Eleanor couldn't hide her concern. It appeared Greville would do almost anything if it would further his position. 'I can see you must indeed go to court to find out the truth of these matters. When will you leave?'

'A week at the most, I expect. We should make good time if the weather holds.'

'And will you be home for harvest?'

'It's possible, but I cannot say for certain. Ralph should

be here from London within days, and I must speak with Hugh to arrange the packing of my clothes.'

'They've barely been removed from your chests since you arrived,' Eleanor replied irritably, but she was talking to herself – he'd already left the room. And although she may have him physically for a few more days, she knew mentally he was already gone. She wrapped her arms tightly around Henry, kissing the fluffy hair on top of his head, her eyes filling with unbidden tears.

It was later the same day whilst Eleanor made a balm to soothe the chest of one of the old farmers who had bronchitis, when she first saw the boy. He was sitting crossed-legged beside the fire in her stillroom, using a pair of bellows to keep the flames burning. His waiflike face was dominated by huge, deep grey eyes and his solemn countenance touched Eleanor. She was certain she hadn't seen him before and she wondered why not, when she thought she knew all of the servants' children.

Over the next few days she looked out for him, watching him. She asked questions, but nobody seemed sure exactly whose child he was, and her curiosity was aroused. Eleanor was concerned whether he was even being fed; she suspected he was scrabbling for scraps alongside the dogs. There was certainly no spare flesh on him. She started to ensure she always had some food – fruit or a piece of warm bread – in her pocket for whenever she saw him.

When she asked Hugh, he replied that Thomas was one of the garden lads, but none of the outdoor workers knew of him. It was as if he just appeared one day, sleeping under a frayed blanket on the kitchen floor. On one occasion she'd asked him if his parents worked in the house or lived in the village, but he simply gazed at her with his big eyes and didn't answer.

'Greville.' She had to raise her voice. Everyone was at supper and the hall was full of noise. He leant in close, putting his hand on her back so he could hear her and she was immediately conscious of the warmth of his body, his musky smell combined with wood smoke from the fire. She felt the first stirrings of desire, buried since Henry's birth, roll through her belly and she gave herself a mental shake. There was another child who needed her attention. 'There's a little boy called Thomas,' she continued. 'He's usually in the kitchen or the stillroom when I'm working in there. He's so small and slight, I'm sure he's underfed and I can't find out who he is. He won't speak and nobody seems to know where he's appeared from; do you know whose child he is?'

Greville sliced another piece of meat from the platter in front of him, folding it in half as the hot fat dripped off his fingers, and took a bite. He looked down the table at the household, searching their faces.

'I don't know who you mean.' He frowned. 'Is he here now?'

'No.' She shook her head impatiently. 'He never sits at meals. That's why I'm not sure if he is getting any food – he's so thin. I've given him bread and cheese and some pottage whenever I see him, but I'm worried he isn't being fed properly as nobody is taking care of him.'

'Where is he usually found?' he asked, and she explained how she saw him usually in the kitchens or beside the still-room fire, anywhere warm.

Wiping his hand before taking hers, Greville told her to

215

come and she followed him to the kitchen, where a handful of staff were still preparing food. Thomas was nowhere to be seen. Eleanor had seen him earlier while she was preparing a tincture for Nell, who was complaining of a headache. Was the stillroom fire alight? She crept inside so as not to frighten the boy if he was there, and sure enough he was curled up on the hearth in the warm, beside one of Greville's favourite deerhounds, Bos. Both dog and boy were fast asleep, but hearing his master approach, the dog climbed sleepily to his feet, his feathery waving tail moving across Thomas's face and waking the boy too.

Seeing Eleanor and Greville there, he jumped to his feet, his lower lip quivering and his brows knotted in fear. His matted hair was stuck up on one side and his cheek was flushed from where he'd been sleeping against the dog. Eleanor crouched down to take his hand, smiling encouragingly as his eyes slid from Greville across to her. Gently pushing Bos away from him, Greville knelt down to Thomas's level.

'So, who exactly are you, Thomas, eh?' he asked. The boy kept his eyes on Eleanor although they kept flicking towards Greville as he cowered away, afraid of what might be coming next.

'We won't hurt you,' Eleanor said gently. 'We just need to know who you are, and where your parents are. How old are you?'

Still no reply was forthcoming.

'Hold on, I have an idea.' Greville got to his feet and left the room, only to reappear a minute later with a small round platter that she recognised as one that Jane used. On it were some scraps of mutton, a chunk of bread and some pieces of cheese.

'Not much left now,' he said ruefully, putting the plate on the floor in front of Thomas. 'Here you go, small boy, are you hungry?' Still the child stood silent although his attention was firmly fixed on the food at his feet. Greville pushed Bos out of the way as the dog nosed interestedly towards the platter. Eleanor picked it up and held it out to Thomas and he grabbed a handful of bread with one hand and the meat with the other, and began frantically cramming the food in his mouth.

'Slow down, slow down – you'll choke.' Greville laughed, scooping the child up. He sat down on the stool that Eleanor used to rest on while she worked, and placed Thomas on his knee. She could see the bones sticking out down the boy's spine and his ribcage visible through the thin shift he was wearing. Did he have nothing warmer to wear? She really needed to find out who was responsible for him. She could see that although he was intent on eating the food that Greville was holding, he was sat as far away from Greville's body as he could, stiff with fear.

Hurrying back into the hall, which was beginning to empty as supper came to a close, she found Nell taking a tired Jane up to bed. She followed them and rummaged through Jane's cast-off clothing, selecting some linen smocks and warm, thickly lined dresses together with a pair of knitted stockings.

Back where she'd left them, Thomas had finished eating but was still sat rigid on Greville's lap.

'I've got him some warmer clothes,' Eleanor said holding them up. 'Jane's clothes that are now too small for her.' She noticed that despite the fact that Thomas was more relaxed with her than her husband, he hadn't even turned to her as she walked back in the room and continued to stare straight

217

ahead. As she moved towards the boy, her movement caught his eye and he gave her a tentative smile. She held the clothes out towards him.

'Shall we get you into something warmer?' she suggested. Still he sat silent. Greville sighed.

'I tried asking him again who he is,' he said, 'but he isn't answering. I'll send someone to the village tomorrow to make some enquiries.'

'Greville, do you think maybe he can't hear us?' Eleanor asked. 'Because he didn't realise I'd come back into the room until I was almost standing in front of him where he could see me.'

Greville nodded slowly. 'It's possible,' he agreed. 'It would explain why he can't talk. If he's become lost somewhere he wouldn't be able to tell anyone.'

Eleanor's eyes filled with tears. 'But surely his parents will have been looking for him?' She gulped. 'Wouldn't they?'

'I don't know. But we'll see what can be found out tomorrow. How long has he been here for? And how do we know his name is Thomas?'

'I don't know when he arrived. I noticed him working the bellows for me in here; I think Cook pushed him in here out of his way. He's been here ever since. I did ask the kitchen staff whose child he is, but they all said they had no idea. I've asked outside but nobody there knows who he is either. He hasn't just materialised from nowhere. It's a mystery. Hugh called him Thomas, but I think he just pulled a name from nowhere.'

Greville got to his feet and passed the child to her. Holding him for the first time she was astonished at how little he weighed compared to Jane, and standing him on the floor beside her she gently removed the grubby torn shift he was wearing revealing his pale skinny body, ribs poking through the skin, which was marked with a myriad of scars.

'Oh, Thomas,' Eleanor whispered, 'how have you arrived here?' He started shivering and she quickly pulled on several layers of the clothes that she'd brought downstairs until he looked warmer, and considerably bulkier.

Greville returned carrying a thick heavy blanket. He folded it into a small envelope beside the fire and she tucked Thomas in, so just the child's sand-coloured tufty hair was poking out of the top as he climbed in. Bos settled back down at his feet.

Adding some more logs to the dying embers, Greville said, 'I'll tell Hugh that someone is to make sure the fire in here is kept burning day and night, and Thomas is allowed to sleep in here. I'll try to find out who he is or where he's from. Looks like we have another addition to our household eh?'

The following afternoon before he left, Greville came and found Eleanor in the garden, as she pulled dead flower heads from the chives with undue force. She knew the time was fast approaching when Greville would have to take his leave and the thought of it, the dangers he may face, were always at the forefront of her mind, twisting her heart into a hard, painful knot. She had taken Jane outside to help, but the little girl soon lost interest and skipped away to chase the sheep trying to graze quietly in the orchard. Her place had been taken instead by Thomas, who crept behind Eleanor, stepping in her footprints as silent as ever.

'I see your shadow is ever-present.' Greville laughed, nodding his head at the mute boy. Jane was making enough noise for everyone as having spotted her father she was shrieking and jumping around him until he swung her in the air. Putting her down again he held his hands out to Thomas, but the boy stepped behind Eleanor's skirts, burying his face in the folds.

'Were you able to find out anything further about him?' Eleanor asked, stroking the boy's fine hair. His head pressed against her thigh. She'd insisted Nell bathed him that morning to make sure he had no lice and apparently he'd been less than enthusiastic, but he looked much better with shining hair and skin glowing pink.

'I found out some information,' Greville replied, 'but it's not very helpful to us. Someone in the village remembered there being a small child at the priory, so I went down and spoke with the prior. He then directed me to Brother Thomas who confirmed he'd found a small boy who matched our Thomas's description asleep amongst some sacks of produce that arrived from Lynn. He wouldn't or couldn't speak. They called him Thomas because he followed Brother Thomas around and slept on the floor outside the dormitory like a small dog, waiting for him. Then one day he just disappeared – he must have wandered up here.'

Eleanor felt tears burn at the backs of her eyes as she cupped the small boy's chin in her hand and tilted his face up so she could look in his eyes. 'I think Tom is a perfect name for you,' she told him, 'and you will stay here as part of our household and maybe one day learn a trade. That's all right, isn't it?' She looked at Greville, worried he might not agree, but he was smiling and nodding.

'Of course it is, we don't want you wandering off again anywhere else, small boy.'

Eleanor felt her heart melt just a little bit more as she regarded her husband. The arrival of Tom had displayed another side of him. She knew him as her husband, a man who supported her in the growing of her saffron, who was kind and gentle towards her at all times, as well as a sensual, generous and considerate lover. At court he embodied another persona, a popular, rich merchant, but someone not to be crossed. And now here she could see how his kind and tender heart was not just for his own children, but any who needed him. He was a man and a master who wore a coat of many colours and she wondered how she could have been so dismayed by him when they'd first been introduced. How blind she'd been then.

Tom regarded him silently and Eleanor wondered if he realised that his fate had been decided right there, amongst the tall dry grasses and first stirrings of autumn.

Once Greville had left for London, the house felt empty. Her bed was deserted and cold, and it was only the exhaustion of the long days that ensured she was asleep as soon as she lay down. Her love for him had grown slowly, stealthily, yet was now entwined around her heart like the tenacious ivy that climbed the trees beyond the castle walls, and she was devastated he'd gone again.

Eleanor spent many days waiting and watching for the crocuses to begin to open until finally, the day came. She walked her regular well-trodden path to the meadow at daybreak, her skirts catching on the crisp foliage at the edges of the fields as she moved past. Although the days were still warm, the nights were cooler now and the scent of autumn hung heavily in the air. The smell of vegetation dying and the damp soil of ploughed fields. She had tied her shawl tightly across her body against the early morning chill, and the sky above her was already a pale, milky blue. The sun sat on the horizon shining weakly through the trees and dappling the light with the leaves yet to fall.

As she stood at the edge of the field, Eleanor's smile creased her face. The small lilac-coloured flowers, which had the day before remained tightly furled, were now beginning to open. They had to harvest every open flower head in the next few hours, because by twilight they would die and be of no use. Tomorrow and potentially for the next two to three weeks they'd be out in the fields doing the same.

Simon and a group of workers were assembled and ready to begin harvesting soon after Eleanor had fed Henry and broken her fast. Most of them had helped to harvest the previous year, and understood the importance of carefully picking the whole flower head, and whilst they started, Eleanor demonstrated to the new workers what needed to be done. With the doubling of the crocus field, she was going to need every pair of hands available.

Once everyone was hard at work, she joined them for a few hours, enjoying the camaraderie, jokes and laughter of the workers, together with the warm sun sinking into her shoulders as she bent over. By midday, she disappeared back into the house, knowing Henry would be hungry and that she needed to have the tower room ready for the first baskets of flower heads to arrive. She'd left Joan in charge of laying and lighting the fire, but she herself had swept the floor and laid fresh hay and herbs. Although the slab on top of the hiding space blended in perfectly with the others, she was always wary of someone else discovering it. For this reason she insisted that only Joan was allowed in the tower with her, and her friend was ready and waiting. The baskets of flowers were left in the hallway at the bottom of the stairs.

The following weeks were exhausting. The work felt never-ending and so much harder than the previous year's harvest. The long hours, and the necessity of going to the nursery every three hours to feed Henry and going to him during the night as well, all took their toll on Eleanor. Nell suggested once again that a wet nurse should be found, but she refused.

'It's only a few days more,' she argued. 'The drying will be over a day or so after the last day of picking the flowers, and then it's all done.' Despite her exhaustion, she cherished the bond, the closeness with her son. She wasn't prepared to give that up yet.

Finally the saffron was ready, tied up in sacks and stacked up in the tower room. Pale hessian bags through which seeped the sharp smell of the spice they held. Eleanor had taken a good-size bag for her stillroom and for Cook, but she was pleased at the quantity remaining, which were waiting for Ralph to take them to Blakeney to meet the boat that would take them to London.

She was disheartened when a letter came from Greville telling her that regretfully he wouldn't be able to return any time soon. The repercussions of the king's new Statute of Six Articles, which had reinforced the Catholic beliefs and intro-duced harsh punishments for those heretics who did not practise them, were still being felt. Allegiance to His Majesty was more important than ever. With many evangelicals being imprisoned, Greville reminded her that duty and loyalty to the crown was everything. She understood the delicacy of everything happening at court, but it was still a disappointment.

Greville also wrote that he had heard from Francis Dereham in Ireland, although it didn't sound as if his visit had been as profitable as he'd hoped. He was already talking of returning to England, and maybe finding a place in the king's retinue. She knew from her letters that Isabel had lately returned to Norfolk and she wondered how Francis was going to secure a place at court.

With little chance of Greville arriving before the Christmas merriments this year, Eleanor knew there was also no likelihood of another saffron baby being conceived in the aftermath of the festivities.

Winter arrived early with a sudden fierce intensity that shocked everyone. Autumn had been pleasantly mild and the late warm weather had resulted in very few illnesses requiring Eleanor's medications, meaning she'd been able to stockpile ointments in readiness for the cold weather.

But now all vestiges of the forgiving rosy autumn had gone. Quietly, flecks of snow began to fall, silent and white; slowly at first, but soon becoming faster as they swirled in the wind and covered every inch of the countryside with a heavy, thick blanket. The air was bitterly cold, bruising the lungs of anyone unfortunate enough to be outside.

Everyone in the hall tried to invent jobs for themselves to avoid going outdoors. The priest failed to turn up for matins and Joan complained as she stumbled back to the house through the crisp white snow shining with a brilliance that hurt the eyes, along an icy path that one of the gardeners had dug to the chapel. Eleanor had wrapped a shawl around her neck and mouth to keep warm so didn't bother replying to Joan's grumbling as she went to record the bad weather in her book of hours.

The cold months stretched ahead, despondent and uninviting, and she yearned for the warmth and cheer only her husband could bring.

Chapter Twenty-Two

2019

Surrounded by antiquated volumes of *Encyclopaedia Britannica*, Amber heard her phone ping with the arrival of a text. It took several minutes of shuffling the heavy, dusty volumes about on her desk until she could retrieve it, and see the message was from Becky. Keen to get a grip on the cataloguing she was supposed to be doing, and spending many hours at her laptop entering the contents of the library into her spreadsheet, she hadn't seen her friend since their fruitless attempt to find Mary's resting place. She hadn't even found time to read any further in Eleanor's book, putting it out of her mind and concentrating on the task in hand.

Faculty annual party, next Friday afternoon. Do you feel up to it?

Amber leant back in her chair. Did she? The annual party for the professors and staff was usually a boisterous affair, starting very sedately with Prosecco and afternoon tea, but often carrying on at a local pub until closing time. She and Jonathan attended every year and always enjoyed it immensely.

Amber frowned. She needed to do it; she couldn't hide away forever and at some point she would have to face everyone. And she'd have Becky there for back-up. Replying to the text she confirmed she'd be delighted to attend with her friend, then quickly sent another message, this one to Jonathan, asking him if he'd be able to go as well. A smile spread wide across her face when a reply came back almost immediately, saying he would love to.

After she'd returned home from their appointment at the hospital, she'd found herself missing him in a way she hadn't since moving into Saffron Hall. Slowly she felt the first fragile shifting of her heart repairing. He was an ally not an enemy, someone in the same boat as she was, adrift. Finally she felt as if she was paddling towards him, instead of away.

A quick rifle through the clothes she'd brought to Grandad's confirmed what Amber already knew. She had nothing suitable to wear to a party. When she'd packed her suitcases all those months ago she'd thrown in her scruffiest clothing. It hadn't mattered what she'd been wearing as she'd had no intention of seeing anyone other than Grandad.

So she found herself wandering around King's Lynn trying to find a suitable outfit that wouldn't cost much money, especially as she needed some shoes as well. After finally tracking down a dress in a small boutique, she felt she'd earned a cup of coffee and a rest before looking for a pair of heels. Sitting down at a table at the window of a coffee shop, she sipped at her drink and enjoyed watching the busy Saturday shoppers, the groups of teenagers wandering aimlessly, the parents trying to hurry along their bored and dawdling children. She realised she could look at mothers with buggies now without a lurch of sickness rising up in her throat, and she was thankful for that small victory.

Suddenly Amber thought she'd seen someone she recognised and she pressed her face closer to the window. Yes, she was right, it was definitely Pete. She recognised his profile as he turned and looked down. But what she hadn't expected to see was that he was holding the hand of a young boy who was half walking, half trotting to keep up. They were walking towards where she was sitting and she almost lifted her hand to wave, then lowered it again. The child, chattering away as they walked along, was the absolute double of Pete.

It was of no concern to her if he had a child, but did he have a wife or girlfriend as well? Someone was that little boy's mother and she was going to have to tell Becky. She had the uncomfortable feeling this information was going to hurt her friend.

Friday arrived all too quickly. Starting to have second thoughts about having to go and meet up with everyone, Amber reluctantly slipped into her new dress and the boots she'd bought to go with it. Her hair, grown out of the harsh, stark pixie cut she'd insisted on having soon after she'd had Saffron now reached below her chin in soft curls and she clipped each side back with slides inlaid with mother of pearl.

She and Grandad had lunch together; Amber had cooked a huge cottage pie. The dean's generosity with the Prosecco was well known, and Amber knew a decent helping of stodge was required to soak up the inevitable alcohol she'd be plied with later.

'There's plenty left over,' she told Grandad as they ate. 'I've put some on a plate in the fridge for your tea, so you can just put it in the microwave.'

'I don't think I'll need another portion today.' He laughed. 'I won't want anything else other than a cup of tea and a couple of custard creams.'

Suddenly, the thought of sitting with a cup of tea in front of the television and relaxing for the afternoon sounded absolutely blissful, and Amber wondered, not for the first time, whether to call Becky and cancel. Invent a sudden illness and cry off. She knew it wouldn't fool her friend though, who'd drive straight up to check on her, as they'd been swapping selfies of their outfits a little over an hour earlier.

This was the first time she'd seen most of her colleagues since Saffron's birth, and she wasn't looking forward to that aspect of the afternoon, seeing the pity stamped on their faces. She felt paranoid they'd all know she wasn't currently living at the vicarage with her husband.

With a heavy heart she picked up her handbag when she heard the toot of Becky's car and stepped outside the front door, a big smile plastered firmly, if not sincerely, on her face.

'Fake it till you make it,' she muttered under her breath as the door slammed behind her.

The journey to the party was the first time the two women were together since Amber's shopping trip, and Amber knew she was going to have to say something about what she'd seen. Better that Becky knew now, before she fell headlong in love with Pete. She'd seen the way they looked at each other, and she knew that they'd been on several dates. She cleared her throat.

'I was in King's Lynn last weekend,' she said, 'shopping. And I um, I saw Pete.'

'Oh yes?' Becky was trying to pull out onto a busy roundabout and wasn't paying much attention, so Amber stopped talking and waited until they were once again moving down the A47.

'So, when I saw Pete,' she started again, 'he was with a little boy. Who looked remarkably like him.' She paused again, her eyes on Becky who was watching the road. To her surprise though her friend's face lit up with a huge smile and her eyes sparkled.

'That must've been Callum. Pete's son with his ex-girlfriend. He has Callum on alternate weekends. Pete doesn't think he should introduce us yet, which I agree with, but fingers crossed, one day soon I'll be able to meet him. It's still early days, Pete and I.'

Amber sighed with relief, her breath leaving her in a long hiss. 'I'm so pleased. I didn't know about his son and the ex-girlfriend and I've been so worried about telling you and making you upset,' she exclaimed.

'He told me about Callum and Katie on the night of the pub quiz. It's never been a secret. It's one of the reasons he lives in King's Lynn – so that he's close by.'

Amber leant over and patted Becky's shoulder. 'That's brilliant and I hope you get to meet him very soon,' she said.

The room at the university was already full of chattering people, jewel-coloured dresses dotted amongst the men's smart trousers and shirts. Just for once people had made a sartorial effort. Having previously arranged with Jonathan that she would meet him there, as she would get a lift with

231

Becky, Amber scanned the crowd looking for him. Here and there waiters flitted through the gathering with trays of champagne flutes and orange juice. Amber smiled politely whilst sipping from her glass as she looked around, conscious of dozens of pairs of eyes trained on her, and a general air of benign sympathy.

Becky had been pounced upon and dragged away by a group of her fellow historians, leaving Amber stood on her own looking for a friendly face, all the while feeling as if she were an island that everyone was skirting around and not approaching. Unsure of what to say to her.

Just at the point when she was going to escape to the toilet where she could lock herself in and nobody would be able to stare at her, there was a shift in a group talking to the dean and as they moved, she spotted Jonathan. He was stood on the edge of a cluster of her department colleagues. Their eyes met and his face lit up as he held his hand out towards her. She hurried over and ducked under his arm, finally feeling safe, anchored beside him.

'All right?' he mouthed as he pulled her tight into his side and kissed her briefly on her cheek and she nodded, before turning to greet the rest of the group as if she'd seen them all just weeks previously, not the eight months whilst she'd been absent from work. She watched them visibly wilt with relief. There wasn't going to be an uncomfortable conversation, at least not today. These people were her friends and she knew they all wished her well.

As usual, the party carried on into the evening as more and more alcohol flowed and a hog roast began dispensing pork rolls. Becky met up with Amber as they piled their plates with food.

'I'm starving,' Becky exclaimed. 'I can never resist pulled pork.'

'Me too,' Amber admitted, 'despite a hefty lunch with Grandad I'm feeling a bit light-headed now.'

'I'm having this and then I must head home. Do you want a lift? Or will you be able to catch a ride with Jonathan?' She'd already spotted the couple appearing relaxed together.

'He'll drop me off, I'm sure. Thanks for the suggestion that I came. I almost cried off, I was so concerned about seeing everyone I know, but I was worrying over nothing. It's been lovely seeing all the familiar faces and everyone's been so kind.' Amber rested her plate on the table to free up both arms, wrapping them around Becky.

'Well of course, you are very much loved – and Jonathan. Everyone just wants you both to be okay. Nobody here will judge you.' She hugged Amber back. 'You've been through the worst thing imaginable and we all want to help.'

'Thanks, what would I do without you?'

'Translate all your own Latin?' Becky replied and they both laughed and said goodbye, agreeing to meet up at the weekend. 'And for goodness' sake find some time to read more of Eleanor's book,' she reminded her as they parted. 'I'm desperate to know what else she has to say.'

'Becky's got to make a move.' Amber offered Jonathan a piece of her roll as she caught up with him. 'Are you okay to give me a lift back please?'

'Of course.' He nodded. 'You can come home for tonight if you want as it's closer, and I'll drop you back in the morning?'

Six months ago his suggestion would have filled her with horror, but to her surprise she didn't recoil at the thought of being back in their home and she heard herself agreeing, quickly calling Grandad to explain about the change of plan.

It was dark when they arrived back at the vicarage, the shadowy shapes of the trees swaying in the breeze against the pale stone of the church walls. Amber followed Jonathan inside, feeling slightly shy, and uncomfortable. She knew that in his head, it was still her home and everything was normal, but it didn't feel like home now. Did she belong here anymore? Everything felt different even though superficially it all looked the same. As if home was a jigsaw puzzle, all the pieces were assembled, but she was a part that no longer fitted.

The furniture was still in the same place, although she noticed instead of the annoying film of dust that had coated everything when she used to half-heartedly undertake any housekeeping duties, it all shone. The mismatched mahogany pieces they'd picked up in second-hand shops over the years were all gleaming, everything looking similar in the uniform sheen and smell of proper wax polish. Whoever had taken it upon themselves to turn the vicarage into a show home, obviously didn't subscribe to the 'Mr Sheen randomly sprayed around the room' method of cleaning Amber used.

She followed him into the kitchen, which thankfully felt more familiar, and flopped down into the small wooden carver armchair that had always been hers. A pile of post lay on one end of the table, Jonathan's favourite method of filing, together with a solitary plate still covered with that morning's flecks of jam and toast crumbs. Amber felt the uncomfortable prick of tears at this visual evidence of her husband's lonely life. She had left him to this.

'Coffee? Tea?' Oblivious to her guilt, he filled the kettle and scooped the plate off the table and into the sink.

'Coffee please, you'd better make it strong. I drank more of that Prosecco than I'd intended.'

She watched him as he filled the cafetiere, put cups onto a tray and decanted milk into a jug. He'd undone the top button of his shirt. He always looked less like a vicar without his dog collar and more like the real Jonathan, the man she had loved and married. The man she still loved. When would she feel ready to move back here, to step back onto the merry-go-round of the real world? Although she missed being with him, small filaments of the dark cloud still lurked at the edge of her conscience, the knowledge that all was not as it should be. Somehow she had to accept the new status quo to be able to move forward. Whilst she breathed, she had hope.

'I'd better google some train times for the morning.' She followed him through to the living room as he carried the tray with their coffee, sniffing at the all-pervasive wax polish smell. 'Did someone get a bit slap-happy with the furniture polish?'

'The flower-arranging ladies. They drew up a rota for cleaning the vicarage. I tried to tell them it wasn't necessary, but you know how forceful they can be. They're only allowed to do downstairs. I told them I've been cleaning upstairs. I didn't want my underwear drawer reorganised into colour coordination. They also keep putting home-made meals in the freezer. If I have to eat another watery shepherd's pie, I might puke.'

Amber laughed although she felt her insides tighten up with misery. She could just imagine the village busybodies gossiping about her abandoning Jonathan when he needed her most. Being a rubbish wife. Not capable of being a mother. Well, how could she blame them, when every word was true?

'You don't need to get a train back,' he told her. 'It's my day off tomorrow. I can drive you back.'

'Are you sure? I don't want to put you out – you get precious little free time as it is.'

'I'd like it. It'll give me a couple of extra hours with my wife.' He smiled as he passed her cup of coffee, with just the right amount of milk added.

They sat in companionable silence and watched an episode of *Silent Witness*, and it felt like a normal evening. How they used to be. Before everything went wrong. Finally at eleven-thirty Jonathan switched the television off, yawning widely.

'Do you want the spare room?' he asked tentatively. Amber suspected he'd been worrying about the sleeping arrangements all evening whilst outwardly concentrating on the television.

'Not unless you want me to sleep in there?' she replied after a moment, unsure of his own feelings. 'We're a married couple – nothing's changed that. I don't think it's inappropriate for both of us to sleep in the same bed if you're okay with it?'

The way his face lit up as he smiled his agreement made her heart beat faster. There was a reason why she'd been attracted to the blond-haired green-eyed young theology student all those years ago and it was his completely open smile, the way it made his face shine and his eyes sparkle. He had the most honest, welcoming face of anyone she knew. There was no side to him. With Jonathan what you saw was what you got; he liked everybody and it was no wonder his friendliness was always reciprocated.

She followed him upstairs and into their bedroom. There, placed on her pillow as they had always been, were her pyjamas. Matching Jonathan's ones left on his. She realised with a wrench of her heart that he had carried on doing everything in exactly the same way, as if waiting for the day when she'd return. They both lay in the dark side by side, wordlessly, until Jonathan reached over, pulling her in to his side, and she curled up under his arm in the same position she'd slept during all the years of their marriage. Gently he kissed the top of her head and within minutes they were both asleep.

The next morning she dressed in an old pair of jeans and T-shirt she'd unearthed from the bedroom cupboard, relieved that before she had left for Grandad's she'd thrown away all her maternity clothes so there were no nasty surprises when she'd gone looking for something clean to wear. It all smelled quite musty and she wished she'd borrowed Eleanor's housekeeping rules and laid lavender between the layers of stored clothing.

Downstairs she found Jonathan finishing his toast. He jumped to his feet as she walked in, cramming the last of his breakfast into his mouth.

'Cup of tea?' he asked. 'I need to go and unlock the church, then we can be on our way. Do you want to walk across with me?' He raised his eyebrows.

'Yes, please, I'd like that. And to say hello to Saffron.'

'Of course.' He grinned and she couldn't help a small smile in return. He picked up his keys from the hall table and she followed him outside.

The church was as familiar to her as home. She suddenly realised where she'd recognised the waxy aroma in the vicarage from; it was the same beeswax that was used to clean the church. But here the polish had to fight with the achingly familiar musty ancient air, which enveloped her in nostalgia and sorrow. She sat in the pew she always sat in on a Sunday, and closed her eyes, listening to Jonathan bustling about in the vestry. She waited, wanting to feel more. That shift in the atmosphere when she knew she was no longer alone, but there was nobody here. Who was she expecting, Eleanor? Saffron? She wasn't sure.

Jonathan finished his tasks and together they walked around the exterior of the building to the back of the churchyard. He caught her fingers in his and squeezed her hand as they walked in companionable silence.

'Hey Saffron, look who's here.' Jonathan spoke easily. He came every day to talk with their daughter and Amber felt a shaft of guilt that she'd abandoned them both. As before, the grave and surrounding area were beautifully tended and a small posy of wild flowers spilled out of a vase in front of the headstone. A tiny pottery puppy had appeared.

'Alfie Byrnes put it there,' Jonathan explained as Amber bent to pick it up. 'He said it wasn't right that Megan has so many toys and Saffron doesn't.' Amber smiled as she put it back, glancing across to Megan Byrnes' grave, covered in toys and bunting. Children seemed to accept the demise of a baby so much easier.

'Saffron would be nearly nine months now,' she said, the words choking her, 'sitting up, crawling maybe, and playing. It's so unfair.'

Jonathan's arm went around her shoulders. 'You're right: it *is* unfair. But she wouldn't want us to be trapped in a bubble of mourning forever, would she? We can move on from this, together. Remember the proverb from the book

238

of hours you told me about? While I breathe, I hope. We've always got hope and we'll never forget her. Saffron will forever be our firstborn, our daughter.'

'Of course she will. Always.'

It was mid-morning when they arrived back at the hall. They found Grandad sitting in his greenhouse, his eyes twinkling with pleasure at seeing the couple walking down the path towards him, holding hands.

'You're a sight for sore eyes,' he greeted them. 'How was the party?'

'It was good, thanks.' Amber grinned. 'As usual there was a lot of booze. For a job with such a staid reputation, professors can certainly shift a ton of alcohol.'

'Are you putting the kettle on now you're back?' Grandad waggled his eyebrows hopefully and, laughing, Amber returned to the kitchen to do as he bid.

'Let me show you the prayer book,' Amber suggested to Jonathan as she threw teabags into the mugs she'd taken from the cupboard, 'maybe you'll have some thoughts on the strange passage at the beginning; Becky and I have run out of ideas. But, I have discovered that Saffron Hall was originally called Milfleet. The owner of the book, Eleanor, lived here in this house. Isn't that cool?'

She led him through to the office and passed him a pair of cotton gloves before donning some herself and retrieving the book from the safe, laying it on the cradle in front of him, open at the front.

Jonathan leant forward and squinted at the entry, his lips moving soundlessly as he read it slowly to himself, pausing as he attempted to translate the ancient Latin. Eventually he flopped back in the chair and looked up at Amber, stood beside him.

'My Latin isn't all that good these days. I can recognise "*in pace*" and the line "*infans filia sub pedibus nostris requiescit*" but I'm lost on the rest. What does it say?'

Amber thumbed through her notebook until she found where she'd written out the translation, and passed it to him, waiting quietly whilst he read it. Finally, when she could bear the silence no longer, she said, 'What do you think she's asking? What's she saying to us?'

'I don't know. Her baby is buried somewhere. And it's not where she wanted it buried? She is asking the reader to do something. Find the baby perhaps? I don't understand why she has no time. Is she running away, or was she dying? Are there any other clues in the book?'

'I'm only about halfway through, but so far there are no other clues, although it's a fascinating insight into Eleanor's life. Becky and I have looked all over for where Mary is buried, but we've found nothing.'

And then, just as it had happened before, she felt something shift in the air around them, and she knew they weren't alone. She gripped Jonathan's arm hard and as his puzzled eyes met hers she pressed her lips together giving a tiny a shake of her head. It wasn't just her imagination: there was somebody, or something, in the room with them. Not moving, not making any noise but definitely there. Amber closed her eyes, wondering if it would help open some sort of communication. The smell was back as well, stronger than ever before. Sharp yet sweet, the mellow dustiness of freshly mown hay, and meadowsweet. Amber decided to try speaking to her.

'Eleanor, is that you?' she whispered, into the silence,

holding her breath as she waited for a reply. None came. No sign she was there, no furniture being thrown across the room or paintings falling from the wall as happened in films. Just a loosening of the threads of time that separated them, a sigh in the air all around and a feeling of sadness draped across her like fine gauze, together with that familiar evocative smell. If only Amber could work out what it was. And then, just like before, suddenly she was gone. The scent still lingered but somehow she knew the other being in the room was no longer with them.

'Did you feel that? She was here in the room, just for a few seconds I was aware of her. A slight shift in the air as if she drifts through from her time to ours. I'm sure it's Eleanor. I've stayed in this house countless times over the years, and never have I felt anything frightening or strange happen. It's only since the book was found and I read her message she's started appearing. After the tower was damaged. Although even the word "appearing" is a bit of an exaggeration because I've never seen anything. I just kind of know when she's with me. And, I get an overwhelming sensation of sadness when she's here. That scent, can you smell it? It's really odd, kind of spicy. Do ghosts smell?'

'I don't think we can call her a ghost.'

'Then what? An apparition? Given that she doesn't appear, that isn't the right word either.'

'I don't know. Lost soul is probably the best description, or spirit. She isn't at rest because someone needs to fulfil her request. But maybe the scent you could smell is from someone harvesting something nearby? You know how sounds and smells can travel in the country if the wind's in the right direction.'

'No.' Amber shook her head. 'I've smelled it before, but it's only in the air when Eleanor is with me. I have to solve this message, before I can move on. I can't bear the thought that she's been waiting hundreds of years for someone to do it. I won't let her down now.'

'Well, you know where I am if you need me, if I can be of any assistance.' Jonathan got his feet and held his arms out to her, and she stepped into them as if it was the most normal thing to do. 'Thanks for a great evening yesterday, just being together at home was lovely.'

Amber nodded, her head against his chest. 'I enjoyed it too,' she answered. 'I hope we can do it again soon?'

He squeezed her tightly and kissed the top of her head, then let her go, clearing his throat and saying huskily, 'I hope so too. I'm sorry, but I must make a move. Today's my only free day this week, so I must go and do some shopping, and I've got to finish a sermon.'

'No rest for the wicked eh?' Amber laughed.

After Jonathan had left, she found the place she'd reached in the precious book and carried on reading, her heart feeling lighter than it had for months.

Chapter Twenty-Three

1539–40

Christmas was merry. The wind had finally turned and brought milder, wetter weather, which meant a constant passage of muddy footprints across the floors, but nobody minded. Everyone was in an expansive mood, looking forward to the feast and festivities, especially when Greville arrived unexpectedly from London, taking advantage of the warmer weather and easier travel on the roads.

Eleanor tried to encourage Thomas to reach the same level of excitement as Jane was exuding, but it wasn't easy when she couldn't explain to him what was happening. He'd seen the kissing bough brought in and looked intrigued but clearly had no idea – or any memory – to connect it with. Taking him by the hand she showed him the ever-increasing specialities accruing in the pantry, making exaggerating signs of rubbing her stomach in antic-ipation and even pinching corners of marchpane to slip into his mouth. Tom smiled and nodded, but she knew that as much as he loved anything sweet to eat, he still had no idea what was in store.

Greville was also in a buoyant mood. The saffron he'd taken to London had been sold once again for the king's tables, and the remainder had carried on the journey to Calais. With the increased quantity together with the acknowledgement of its superb quality, it had brought him a further substantial profit. The coffers had never been so full. He was talking of a new wing being built onto Milfleet, as befitted a gentleman who was now so well respected at court.

'When we were married who would have guessed that the quiet, shy, frightened girl would blossom into a woman with skill and expertise to grow us an empire, out in the meadows of Norfolk. I had not realised that you would bring such shrewdness and expertise with you. I am very lucky to have you as my wife,' he admitted.

His good mood meant everyone was happy. Writing in her prayer book, Eleanor couldn't help a feeling of smugness as she recorded the end of the year, and the twelve days of festivities.

The New Year is upon us and we must bid farewell to 1539. All is well here at Milfleet. Our beautiful Henry continues to thrive. Jane is growing into a young lady. A new addition, Tom, is now part of our family, and secretly I pray that his real family do not come looking for him. He is a help to me in the stillroom with his ability to smell and taste things I do not notice. My husband is most pleased that our second crop of saffron has raised so much revenue and is so well regarded. I am much pleased that the increase in our fortunes and his place at court is entirely due to me.

As soon as the festivities started, Tom began to enjoy them every bit as much as the rest of the household. Eleanor knew he couldn't possibly understand the religious aspect of what they were celebrating. Indeed, although she took him to mass, he was unable to hear what was being said and so he constantly fidgeted and scuffed his feet, clearly bored and having no idea why he must sit on an uncomfortable pew in a cold building. The only part of the chapel that had ever caught his attention was the triptych on the altar she had admired when she'd first arrived. He loved to stand in front of it, closely examining the painted people. If there was no one else present, Eleanor would lift him up so he could reach out with his small fingers and run them over the images, a broad smile on his face.

But all too soon, it was twelfth night, the yule log had burned away, the Lord of Misrule had had his fun, and Greville announced he intended to take advantage of the still-mild weather and return to London.

'I know you would rather I stayed here, my little croker,' he said, using the local name for saffron growers, as he stroked the top of Eleanor's head. She stood, still clothed in her night rail as he had interrupted her getting dressed to inform her he would leave later that day. 'But we both do very well out of not only my being able to trade in London, but more importantly being present at court. The money your precious spice has brought us means I am now most popular with the higher ranked gentlemen and I am confident this may soon put me before the king's gaze. Wouldn't that be a fine thing for us both? And it's your proficiency and knowledge in growing the saffron that will bring this to pass. I admit that I had not believed when you first explained that your saffron would amount to much, but all that I now am can be attributed to your skills.'

Eleanor nodded, her heart sore at the thought that he would probably be gone again for months. 'But when may I come to court?' she questioned. It wasn't the first time she had asked and she knew what his reply would be, before he said it.

'One day, my sweet, one day. At present we need you running Milfleet and bringing up our children and most important of all, growing our saffron. Without all that you do here, I wouldn't be in the position at court that I now am. I'll never forget how much I owe to you.'

She nodded despite the shaft of wretchedness that struck through her. London was a place she could only dream of, but she knew that for the present, her place was at home. They both needed Greville to be at court and relaying the news from London, and she was increasingly concerned about the tales that were being told about Cromwell, now that the vicar-general and his commissioners were ransacking monasteries and making the brethren sign the Oath of Supremacy. All around her, the world she'd known was roiling as if caught in a tempest.

Later that day, she chanced upon Greville and Hugh sat in the office. She was walking through from the main hall and paused in the doorway as she heard their low voices. Hugh had spoken and she'd missed what he said, but then her husband replied, 'I've already said no, it's too dangerous. She is still young and could innocently say something untoward. A word out of place can get to the wrong people's ears and a reputation, a livelihood, is ruined forever. There are too many people at court willing to pull others down to help their own attempts to get within the king's inner circle. I cannot push her into that pool of rats. Especially as her strong faith and friendship with the monks could cause her to speak out of turn.'

So that was that then. She had no doubt who he was speaking of, and she wouldn't be going to court any time soon. Was it really as unsafe as he was inferring?

Chapter Twenty-Four

1540

Four months later, it appeared Eleanor's concerns about what was happening at court were justified. One of the villagers arrived at the back door to the hall to tell them a group of gentlemen on fine horses had arrived at the priory. Eleanor was worried. She'd heard tell of monks who refused to agree to the new ways being tortured and executed, and she didn't want that happening to any of her friends. And all the ancient relics were being destroyed across the country. How could that be right? The priory had a beautiful golden coffer, decorated ornately with exquisite gemstones and containing a relic of St Philip. Surely nobody would damage something as holy as that?

She wondered if the king had lost his senses, first deciding he was head of the church and no longer part of the Holy Roman Empire, and then destroying all the statues and relics, and taking the wealth from the monasteries. And, she had been told, throwing monks out onto the streets sometimes.

Though many did receive a pension, they'd spent so many years in the priory they didn't want to live back in the villages, no longer fitting in. She kept her thoughts to herself though. She knew better than to voice her opinions out loud. Even as far from court as they were. Her husband was in the thick of it, and she didn't want to put him in danger.

The first inkling that anything was amiss at the priory at the other end of the village came three days after she'd heard the commissioners had arrived. A slightly damp, screwed-up piece of paper was pushed into her hand as she was crossing the yard carrying empty buckets to the creamery. She was helping the new dairymaid who was tiny and could barely manage two buckets at a time.

She walked, carefully avoiding the dung that had not yet been shovelled up, when suddenly in front of her stood a small village boy, not much taller than Tom. He thrust the note at her and before she could open her mouth to ask what it was, he was gone.

Putting down the buckets, she opened it up. It was a piece of thick parchment, now grubby and rough around the edges from being passed from hand to hand.

My lady, it read, in well-rounded unfamiliar handwriting, *I am at your mercy. The vicar-general's men are here and demand not only our money but also our precious relic, which is to be burned. They have already desecrated many of our statues and paintings. All of my brothers and I must sign to agree to the new prayer book, but I cannot. I must flee with our most holy relic to a land where my beliefs are not a heresy. Or die in the trying. If I do not sign, I will surely be executed.*

I beg that you may help with my passage to Cley, where I'm told a boat will be waiting to transport myself and Brother Rufus to safety. We cannot pay you money, gold or plate, as it was all taken away these two days hence. But I can give you something of equal value, for we still have our sacks of crocus corms, which the commissioners have left alone. I cannot risk you sending a reply to this, in case it falls into the wrong hands. Myself and Rufus will leave tonight, and hide by the old oak on the common. If you're unable to help, then I understand and God be with you.

Prior Matthew had signed it with his seal. Eleanor wondered how he'd managed to smuggle it safely from the priory.

She had to help him; she had no choice. He was old and she couldn't bear the thought of him being hanged, or burned to death as a heretic. It was only right he be allowed to travel to somewhere safe, and even more so that the relic be hidden before it was destroyed.

It was such a dangerous game to be playing and Eleanor felt a hot wave of fear wash over her when she considered the ramifications of what she was being asked to do. For both her family and Greville, if she were to be discovered everything that her husband had worked for at court would be swept away like sand on the beach. All gone. He would be vehemently opposed, furious, if he knew what she intended. She hated going against what she knew he'd say, and she would make sure he never found out.

Because whatever peril she was about to walk into, she had no choice. She had to do it. For the brothers at the priory, for her faith, for her God. She wondered how, practically, she'd be able to help. Her first problem would be going to the oak where they would hide as it meant getting out of her bedroom at night, unseen. Although Joan now had her own chamber, she'd recently taken to sleeping on the truckle bed in Eleanor's bedroom whilst Greville wasn't at home to join his wife. She either needed to find a reason not to go to bed, or she'd have to sneak out of the room when Joan fell asleep. This seemed the safest option since if she didn't go up to bed Joan might come downstairs looking for her.

And then she had another problem: where could she hide the fugitives? It needed to be somewhere completely concealed. Suddenly, she realised she had the perfect place. Although she was attempting to do something her husband would be so against, he had unwittingly given her a space in which to hide her two friends. Nobody apart from her knew about the hole under the floor in the tower, and now she could use it for what it was intended for. On that first day in her new home, Greville had told her: 'It is to be used to hide things you do not want others to know about,' and that was exactly what she intended.

As the evening dragged on, Eleanor sat beside the fire, her embroidery abandoned on her lap as she gazed into the flames, a plan slowly forming in her head.

'I am going to warm some milk before bed,' she told Joan. 'Would you like some?'

'Thank you, that would be lovely.' Joan smiled up at her, completely innocent of her friend's ulterior motive.

Once in the kitchen, Eleanor put a pan of milk onto the trivet beside the fire, which was always burning, and then nipped into her stillroom. She knew exactly which jar she wanted, moving quietly to the powdered valerian root and taking a large pinch between finger and thumb. Nobody would be surprised to see her coming out of the stillroom or adding herbs to a drink, but she didn't want Joan to know.

As soon as the milk had heated she added the herbs and hoped it wouldn't alter the flavour. She stirred a big spoonful of honey into both beakers. Joan had developed a sweet tooth over the past couple of years and she would appreciate the addition to her drink.

Sure enough, she drank it down as soon as it was sufficiently cool and didn't make a comment about any unusual taste. Eleanor exhaled slowly, peeping through the steam of her own cup and breathing a silent gasp of relief as the milk disappeared.

As soon as Joan started yawning, and with feigned tiredness of her own, Eleanor suggested they went up to bed. It was already dark and she suspected she had about an hour before she needed to be at the common. Plenty of time, assuming Joan would now fall asleep quickly.

The dull rumble of Joan's sonorous snoring could be heard on the other side of the drapes around Eleanor's bed within ten minutes of her snuffing the candles out. Eleanor was thankful she had always been very particular about drawing the drapes, because even if Joan woke during the night – which rarely happened, and with the addition to her drink tonight hopefully even less likely – it wouldn't occur to her to check in on Eleanor.

Eleanor lay in the dark for what she imagined was about half an hour. Her mind was churning over and over as she continuously debated with herself if she should be undertaking something so reckless, and all that she stood to lose. When she imagined the faces of the children and the thought they may grow up without her, she almost talked herself out of it, but then she thought about having to confess to God that when she'd been called upon she had done nothing, and knew it wasn't an option. She slipped out from behind the drapes on the side of the bed furthest from Joan and tiptoed to the door. There was no furniture to trip on but inevitably her feet made the strewings rustle as she moved. She held her linen shift up around her knees so it didn't also contribute to the noises she was making.

Squeezing through the smallest gap possible into the corridor, she paused for a moment, alert to any noise. Was anybody still about the house? She couldn't meet anyone or her secret would surely be discovered. In the darkness it was easy to imagine all kinds of horrors and a scuffle beside her foot set her heart racing until she realised it was just one of the many mice she shared her home with. All around her the dark pressed down on her through the silence.

Slowly she crept towards Greville's bedroom, feeling along the panelled wall with both hands until she felt the door-frame under her fingers, and the cold of the door latch. She carefully put her hand over the top to muffle the click and she slipped through the opening and into the room. She hadn't dared enter through the interconnecting door as it had always creaked loudly and would have immediately given her away to Joan.

It was cold inside; no fire was lit in there when the master was away and the air smelled sour. Eleanor had thought ahead and left a wrapped bundle of clothes on the end of his bed and slowly she inched towards it with her arms outstretched until they made contact with the fabric roll, containing a pair of Greville's hose, and an old jerkin. It would all be too big for her but that couldn't be helped, she was certain it would be far easier to scurry along outside wearing men's clothes, with no layers of skirts to hamper her. Pulling on the hose, she tied the garters tightly and tucked an old linen shirt into the top, covering it with the jerkin. It still carried a faint scent of him and she held it up to her face, breathing deeply, a rush of longing washing over her, coupled with a feeling of guilt at what she was about to undertake.

The clothes felt so strange, so light and comfortable that she wondered if she'd be able to walk properly with her legs free of the cloying heaviness of her skirts. But in fact it was much easier, and she found herself wishing not for the first time in her life that she'd been born a boy. She'd hidden her own boots with the bundle, and before long she was dressed, her plait coiled into an old cap. She couldn't help a small smile imagining what she looked like, dressed as a boy.

Downstairs, thankfully, all was quiet. The fire although damped down still threw out some light and warmth as she took a thin sliver of wood to light a candle. She was extremely relieved that, unlike Ixworth, there were no servants sleeping in the great hall, although she could hear snoring and some movements from behind the kitchen door.

A small scuffling noise made her stop, her heart beating even harder in her chest as she turned to look behind her. From around the kitchen door she could see in the shadows the face of her sweet Tom. Thank goodness she'd seen him or he'd have followed her as stealthily as a cat and that was the last thing she needed. Putting her candle on the floor she ushered him back to his bed in the stillroom and tucked him tightly into his blanket and kissed his head. At least she knew he wouldn't be able to tell anyone what he'd seen and just for once, she was profusely grateful for that.

Taking the candle, she let herself through the door to the bottom of the tower and after a quick visit to the office, she slipped outside from the side door close to the chapel. She took the key with her just in case and locked the door after herself, heaving a shaky sigh of relief and leaning for a moment against the stone wall while she waited for her heart to stop hammering so hard in her chest. Holding her breath, she turned her head to one side listening for the sounds of the dogs that often prowled the exterior of the hall, but there was nothing.

The night was clear and the moon already high in the night sky, hanging against the inky darkness studded with stars. Though Eleanor knew her way to the common easily, it helped having the brilliant moonlight to light her way and, feeling so strange and free in the men's clothing, she was able to run at a speed she'd never achieve in her own garments. Small creatures and birds scurried out of her way, disturbed by her hurrying past, sweeping against the undergrowth as she skirted around the edges of the fields. The cold night air escaped from her lungs in small white clouds, which dissipated against her face, and tiny droplets of dew clung to the hair that had escaped her cap and lay in tendrils on her cheeks. The intoxicating smell of wild garlic, released by her pounding feet wafted up, made her stomach growl. She'd been too nervous to eat much at dinner earlier.

Slowing down as she approached the tree, she was alert for any signs the missing prior and his treasure had already been noticed and the commissioners were giving chase. An owl hooted softly above her head before silently gliding out into the open, making her start. She crept towards the oak, stopping every few yards, her head cocked and vigilant as she listened, but all was still and quiet. This was her last chance to turn around and go and get back into bed. Nobody would be any the wiser, in the morning the two men would be gone and she could do what her husband would want and expect. Even as she thought about it, she knew she couldn't do it. From the moment she'd read the note from the prior, her path had been chosen.

As she reached the tree, the moonlight showed two crouching figures, their dull brown habits camouflaging them against the foliage perfectly. She bent over as she hurried closer until they noticed her and jumped to their feet.

There was no time for effusive greetings. Eleanor wanted to get them both back and hidden as soon as possible. She was relieved they hadn't brought a horse, which would have been impossible to hide.

'My child, I'm so pleased you are able to help us,' the prior began.

'Shush,' Eleanor interrupted him. Didn't he realise the mortal danger he was putting them all in? She didn't want pleasantries.

'We need to get moving, and quickly,' she told them. 'Are you sure you weren't followed?' Her eyes met those of Brother Rufus who was stood behind the prior, and she saw him nod. 'Keep down and close to the hedges then,' she added before turning around and deftly she picked out her route back to the hall.

The journey back took longer as Eleanor repeatedly stopped and waited for her accomplices to catch up with her, their long habits hampering their easy passage. Brother Rufus was weighed down by a large blanket containing their possessions and, she assumed, the priceless relic. She heaved a sigh of relief when they arrived back at the exterior tower door with no mishaps. Eleanor put her finger against her mouth to ensure absolute silence before slipping the key in the door and slowly opening it, poking her head through the gap to make sure all was clear and leading them into the small vestibule behind the office. She then took a second key from her pocket, which she'd collected from the office before she'd left, and unlocked the door to the tower before ushering the two men up the stairs and locking the doors behind her.

Thin strips of moonlight shone through the arrow-slit windows in the tower, giving them just enough light to see by to ascend the steps, although the prior stumbled twice, almost falling backwards the second time. He was prevented from doing so by Rufus who threw his weight and their luggage against the old man, slamming him inelegantly onto the stairs, and making Eleanor want to wince and cheer, all at the same time.

Finally, they were in the tower room, which despite the late hour was lit up by the bright moonlight streaming in through the window. Eleanor passed the men a flask of ale, which she'd taken up there earlier in the evening.

'This is perfect,' the prior whispered as he turned on the spot admiring the room with its saffron-drying trestle tables still lining the walls. 'We will only need to depend on your hospitality for two days, then we'll need to move on in order to be at Cley when our passage arrives. But if we can wait in here until then, all will be well.'

'I'm afraid you won't be in here.' Eleanor was blunt. She needed to get the two men swiftly out of sight, and her voice was hard. Going to the slab on the floor, she bent and lifted it out of the way. The two men's mouths opened in astonishment.

'You'll be down here,' she told them. 'It's not a huge space, but it's big enough for you both to sit. I've got some food—' she indicated a package that was lying on the floor '—so you'll have to make do until I can sneak up tomorrow night with more and let you out for a while. I'm sorry but it's the best I can offer you,' she added before the prior could open his mouth to say he didn't want to be in a hole under the floor. It was there, or nothing. 'And you'll have to keep completely quiet,' she warned. 'If the commissioners come here, they'll search the house and that will include the tower. I'm the only person apart from my husband who knows about this hiding place, so as long as you stay completely silent, you should be safe.'

Quietly and without argument Rufus dropped their luggage into the hole and jumped in after it, then guided the prior in. The moment they were both crouched on the floor she pulled the slab back over and kicked some of the disturbed strewings over the top, before creeping back downstairs. She locked the door and replaced the key, then ran on her toes back upstairs. Joan was still asleep and Eleanor was able to strip herself of Greville's clothing, wrapping it back into a tight wad and hiding it under her mattress. She'd put it back in his room as soon as Joan got up and left the room the following morning; in daylight nobody would question her going into her husband's bedroom.

After all the excitement and tension, sleep evaded her. She lay on her back with her heart still racing as her imagination played out a dozen scenarios where they were caught out by the commissioners lying in wait. But the most dangerous part was yet to come. She had to keep the two men hidden and get food and drink to them for two days, during which time it was quite possible the hall would be ransacked if Cromwell's men came calling.

She could almost feel the heat of the flames of a heretic's death licking at her feet and melting her skin, but she was sure that was nothing compared to the burning wrath of Greville if he were ever to discover what she'd done. Never as devout as she was, he'd been perfectly happy to go along with the king's religious changes and the closure of the religious houses. Which wasn't how Eleanor felt. She was learning to keep her true beliefs to herself, and go along with the changes to ensure the safety of her family.

Finally, the night sky paled as the first fingers of light painted the horizon with soft insipid gold and she fell into a fitful sleep, her dreams every bit as frightening and dramatic as the thoughts that had tumbled through her head while she lay awake.

Chapter Twenty-Five

1540

Eleanor's plan to prevent Joan knowing anything of what she was doing fell to pieces the very next morning. In her haste to get back to bed before she was discovered missing, she hadn't pushed the bundle of clothing far enough under her mattress and to her dismay as Joan moved about the bedroom assisting with ablutions and dressing, she heard her exclaim, 'What's this pouch of rags doing here?' as she pulled them from their hiding place and began to lay the items on the bed. 'Have you seen these?'

'Shush yes, be quiet!' Horrified, Eleanor snatched them up and tried tying them into a small ball again. 'Sit down here, and I'll tell you, but you mustn't breathe a word and for our Lord's sake keep your voice down.' Quickly in a low voice she explained everything that had happened since she'd been passed the note the previous day.

'Wait, what? I don't understand. There's a hole under

the floor of the room where you and I dry the saffron up in the top of the tower? And they're in there now?' Joan's whispering was frantic and heated as she tried to comprehend what Eleanor was telling her. 'Why have you done this? We'll all be killed if Cromwell's men come looking. This is the most stupid, selfish, reckless thing you've ever done!'

Eleanor was so shocked at her friend's outburst for a moment she couldn't speak. In all their years of friendship, never before had Joan been so forthright. She was confronted once again by the enormity of what she was doing.

'The only person who'll be killed is me, because you can feign ignorance and everyone else *will* be innocent. If you don't want to help me that's fine – I understand – but I have to do this for my faith, and my friends. I just ask you not to tell a soul or hand us over.'

Joan's face was black with fury and her mouth a thin line of disapproval, but after glaring at her friend for several long moments as if she were thinking carefully about the demands made on her, she eventually nodded.

'I won't say anything,' she agreed in a low voice, 'not for their sakes, but for yours. Because I care very deeply that nothing dreadful happens to you.'

'Thank you.' Eleanor put her arms around Joan and pulled her stiff, unyielding body to her own for a moment, before slipping into Greville's room through the dividing door and returning his items to where she'd found them.

She let out her breath slowly. Why hadn't she confided in Joan from the moment she'd received the prior's letter? Her friend had always been so loyal, and whatever happened, she knew Joan would always stand beside her. Her heart felt slightly easier with sharing her burden. She knew with absolute conviction she could trust Joan with her life. Over the next day or two, she may need to.

They broke their fast quietly, the children having already eaten and the servants eating wherever they were working, so their meal was consumed quickly whilst Eleanor made small talk about flowers that could potentially be planted alongside the box in the new knot garden. Joan nodded mutely, not really listening to what her friend was saying and constantly alert, waiting for the shouting of the king's commissioners at the gatehouse.

Wrapped up in their warmest cloaks with their faces turned to the weak sun, they walked around the garden far from anyone who may overhear them.

'I cannot abide this,' Joan burst out. 'I'm so afraid. For you, for all of us.'

'If they're discovered I will say I acted alone, of course I will. I'd never tell anyone you were privy to my actions, so you're quite safe. We both are. Nothing bad will happen,' she reminded her, sounding more confident than she felt.

Eleanor spent the rest of the day troubled and unable to relax, despite her assurances to Joan. She sat in the office all day other than at mealtimes and when she attended mass. Nothing would have alerted the other occupants of the house to something being amiss faster than her missing church. The only time she'd been absent from her pew was whilst she was in childbed. Keeping to her routine was key. Her working in the office all day was not unheard of, and it meant she could prevent anyone coming into the tower wing of the hall. There was no reason anybody should, but she felt happier being on guard. She was also able to slip upstairs with some more substantial food she'd collected from the larders, together with another flask of ale.

Later in the afternoon she decided to show her face around the house to allay any suspicions, and she joined Joan in the solar. It was whilst she was bent over her embroidery, unpicking the stitches she'd sewn untidily three times, that she became aware of men shouting in the courtyard and people running about inside the hall. Immediately her head shot up, her eyes wide with horror as they met Joan's.

'God save us, they've been found,' Joan whispered dropping her sewing into her lap and frantically crossing herself.

'Say nothing,' Eleanor muttered, jumping to her feet and hurrying downstairs. To her surprise the door to her office remained closed just as she'd left it. How had the men been found if nobody had been up into the tower?

Hugh ran through the hall and as she spotted him, she called out. 'Hugh, what is all this commotion about? I can hear men shouting from upstairs. Has someone been injured?' The last time there had been such an uproar one of the tenant farmers had been kicked by a horse and had bled to death, despite her best efforts to save him.

'Apparently the prior and the precious relic from the priory have gone missing and the commissioners have been ransacking the villagers' houses looking for them. There is much anger because they've turned the places upside down and broken furniture. Belongings have been thrown out onto the street. There is a real danger the villagers will turn on them and blood will be shed. Word is that they will come here too, to search the hall,' he said breathlessly as he bent over, his hands on his knees and his chest heaving.

'Here? They'll come to search here?' Her voice was

high-pitched and she cleared her throat as she tried to sound more normal.

'Of course, mistress, they'll leave no stone unturned but don't worry, we have nothing to hide. And I'll accompany the men around the house and grounds so they don't damage anything.'

'Very well, but please keep me informed.' She managed to keep her voice modulated.

'Yes, mistress.' He gave her a short bow and hurried out to the courtyard, which was filling up with even more irate villagers. Eleanor's heart felt heavy. She had no doubt that what she was doing was the right thing, but she didn't want the villagers to suffer. And now, it seemed, the men would be coming here in pursuit of the runaways.

Back upstairs, Joan was stood at the window watching the people running about outside.

'Are they found?' she whispered.

Eleanor shook her head. 'It's been noticed they are missing, and now the village has been ransacked in the search for them. The men will be here in due course, without a doubt. We can but hope they do not venture into the tower.'

'Eleanor, you need to wait until nightfall, and get them away from here. I do not care what befalls them and their precious relic, but I do care what happens to this house and the people in it, and so should you.'

'Of course I care about everyone who lives here, but I can't send them away.' Eleanor was resolute. 'Now is the worst time to try moving them, when everyone is out searching. Where would they hide while they wait for their passage to be ready for them?'

'I don't know. In a shepherd's hut or barn? Out in the open? It's only two days at most.'

'Only two days in freezing temperatures, and the prior is old. No, I said I'd help and I intend to carry on. This is the Lord's work and I must do what is right.' She sat back down and picked up her embroidery, but made no attempt to carry on with it.

Outside in the corridor, she heard the sound of footfall and quickly she put her finger to her lips to silence Joan just before Hugh walked in. He bowed briefly.

'Have they been found?' Eleanor mentally congratulated herself at her calm outward composure.

'Not yet, my lady, I've just come to ask that neither of you nor the children venture outside until they are captured. I'm expecting the vicar-general's men to be here within the hour.'

'Really? Is that necessary?'

'I believe so. These men are criminals now and if they are found on our land, I don't want you to be falsely accused of harbouring them. Better that you stay inside.'

'Very well. Bring the commissioners to me when they arrive.'

'Of course, mistress. I'm expecting them before nightfall. They'll probably ask to stay here overnight and search when it is light in the morning. I will instruct that beds are made up.' He left the room, and Eleanor sank onto the nearest chair.

'You have to get them away and now,' Joan hissed, but Eleanor just shook her head. Joan glared at her, making the sign of the cross before hurrying from the room. Eleanor heard her voice in the hall below. Whatever else happened she knew she could rely on her friend not to say a word, however much she disapproved of what she was doing. If there was one quality that was threaded deep within Joan, it was loyalty to herself. She really hadn't appreciated it enough, until that moment. Her friend had followed her to Milfleet without a word of complaint, despite the fact that it was quite possible she wouldn't get the opportunity to meet a husband of her own. She'd been with Eleanor during the long hours of labour and confinement with Henry, and she played with all the children as if they were her own. And during the saffron harvest she worked long, long hours alongside Eleanor. Always without a single word of complaint, or reproach. And in repayment to this steadfast devotion, she'd brought extreme danger to their home and refused to listen to Joan's sensible advice. She didn't deserve the faithfulness her friend showed her, but she was extremely thankful for it, like never before.

She ran from the solar and into her office, shutting the door to the main house behind her. Outside she heard the occasional shout, but most of the servants had now returned to their work, losing interest once they decided nothing was going to happen, and nobody had seen the fugitives. Inside the hall, everything was quiet. She'd have to go up the tower and warn the two men.

Unlocking the tower door, she crept stealthily up the stairs, into the room, and she quickly dashed across to the loose slab and lifted it. Inside the two men screwed their eyes up against the last rays of daylight.

'Eleanor.' Brother Rufus looked extremely relieved to see her. 'What's going on? Even in here we could hear shouting from below. Are we forsaken?'

'Not yet.' She shook her head. 'But it's known throughout the area you are missing, and the relic as well. They are out looking for you at this very moment.'

'Do you think they'll come to Milfleet and search here?'

'I'm certain of it. They have already ransacked the village, which is why there was an uproar earlier.'

'How long have we got? We must run,' Rufus exclaimed, trying to clamber out of the hole.

'I cannot run,' the prior moaned. 'You go, Brother Rufus. Take the relic and leave me here. I'll return to the common and pretend I was ill and confused, and accidentally wandered from the priory.'

'No, you won't,' snapped Eleanor. 'Nobody would believe that. You may be old but you are not infirm in your mind. You must both remain hidden in here. I told you nobody knows about this space. Just keep completely quiet and I will come back when I can, but whatever happens, don't call out if you hear anything in case it isn't me. I'll bring more food and ale when it is safe to do so. If you make a single sound, it will mean the end for all three of us and our heads will be on pikes outside Norwich gaol.'

She pulled the slab back and rearranged the rushes on top. When Greville had shown her the space under the floor, she'd never imagined she would need to use it for such a dangerous reason. Now her life depended on it remaining a secret, here in the room that still clung on to the soft scent of her saffron.

She locked the tower and returned to the great hall, which was filling up for supper. From the kitchen came the aroma of meat roasting for dinner, but with her whole body alert and on edge as she waited for the commissioners to arrive, she knew she wouldn't be able to eat anything. She cursed herself for forgetting to take food up to the tower, because she had no idea when she'd be able to get up there again with something.

Soon the hall was filled with all the members of the household, all with an opinion as to where they thought the fugitives – now numbering five after the gossips had spread the story far and wide – were hiding.

'Have you had confirmation of the commissioners' arrival?' Eleanor asked Hugh, helping herself to food she knew she'd be unable to eat. Her stomach gurgled and she thought her bowels would turn to liquid.

'Not yet,' he answered her, 'but I'm sure they'll time it on purpose so they have no option but to spend the night here. It's bound to be far more comfortable than the priory dormitory and better food as well. But don't worry, mistress, I'll deal with them. These men are good at their jobs. They are very thorough and it won't take long to search the hall and outbuildings and discover the vagabonds are not here. If they have any sense they'll have disappeared to King's Lynn and onto a boat to take them abroad, so I don't know why the commissioners are searching around here instead of riding out that way. You have nothing to fear.'

'Thank you.' She smiled weakly at him, feeling no better but relieved he was attributing her pale and pinched face to the upset to the household potentially being turned upside down during the search. She wanted to pull him up on his terminology calling men of God 'vagabonds' but she knew better. Those two men had done nothing other than devote their lives to God, and now the king, greedy for their wealth, wanted to take everything from them for himself. It was only right they were trying to escape to a land where they would be treated with the respect they deserved.

'Please find our guests a room for the night if required in that case,' she told him.

'I've already seen to it,' Hugh replied. 'I've organised for the room next to mine to be made ready.'

Eleanor nodded. Hugh's room off the great hall was down a long corridor. It was far enough away from the tower that no nosy visitors might accidentally wander that way in the night. But just to make certain, she'd be locking the door from the hall that led to her office and, beyond that, the tower stairs. When the office was searched she'd make sure she was there as well, supposedly supervising to ensure nobody read any private correspondence of her husband's whilst they were rummaging about. More importantly, however, she'd make sure there was plenty of disruption and noise to alert her two fugitives that danger was close by.

As the hall began to clear after dinner, Eleanor told Joan she intended to have an early night. Whilst people were still milling about, it had been easy to hastily lock the door to the tower wing and she then retired with Joan to her room, where they huddled in front of the fire, talking quietly for fear of being overheard by servants who may be in the pay of the vicar-general's men. They could trust no one.

'I did not wish to meet with the commissioners tonight,' Eleanor confessed. 'I'm frightened enough and I don't want nightmares. I know you disapprove—' turning to Joan, she took both her hands in her own '—and I want you to know that I thank you from my heart that you have not said anything about Prior Matthew and Brother Rufus. You've always been so devoted to me and I haven't ever thanked you for everything that you do. But know this, I truly love you for everything that you have ever done for me.'

Before she went to bed, Eleanor knelt on the floor and began to softly recite the vespers, her lips moving although almost no sound came out. Finally she rose and blew out the candle, climbing into bed and lying in the thick black darkness, listening intently.

After what felt like ages but was closer to an hour she heard the clatter of horses' hooves in the courtyard, and men's voices shouting. 'They're here,' whispered Joan, but Eleanor couldn't reply. Her mouth was so dry her tongue was stuck to the roof and she doubted she could utter a word.

Chapter Twenty-Six

1540

With barely two hours of fitful dozing, Eleanor was awake as the first high-pitched strains of the dawn chorus began. The new day was beginning and who knew if she would be laying her head on her own pillow by nightfall. Whether she would see Henry grow up. And who would take the time to converse with Tom, using the sheet of pictures they had created together? Her eyes prickled with tears. How stupid she'd been agreeing to harbour the monks and bring this extreme danger to their door.

Waking Joan, she insisted they both washed and dressed despite the early hour. She needed to be in the great hall and able to supervise anything going on in the house.

Downstairs, the servants were surprised to see the two women up and about, but wisely kept their opinions to themselves. The household was already in turmoil with the arrival of important visitors and Eleanor didn't want any more gossip. Someone must have told Hugh though, because as they sat down to break their fast, he hurried over. His hair was spiky where he'd obviously leapt out of bed and got himself dressed without washing, and his usually clean-shaven face was rough with dark stubble, flecked in places with grey.

'My lady, is everything all right? It's not yet half past five, you do not usually rise this early?'

Eleanor had been expecting his question and was ready with her reply, one that showed no fear of the commissioners. 'Hugh, there are a great many mice in my bedroom. I have lain all night listening to them, as has Joan, and I cannot stand it any longer. It sounds as if there are dozens of them, probably rats as well – the noise they made scuttling about. Kindly ensure they are not there by bedtime tonight for I have had no sleep whatsoever.'

Surprised, Hugh agreed to ensure their immediate exter-mination and he hurried away with a perplexed look on his face. Whilst the house was of course overrun with vermin they did not often venture upstairs when there were rich pickings to be had in the kitchen and the grain store. She hoped she had laid the suspicion that there must be an unholy infestation if she had heard so many upstairs. It would give him something else to worry about when he had the commissioners to deal with as well.

As he disappeared into the kitchen, Joan raised her eyes from her plate to meet Eleanor's. They both knew the only thing that had kept them awake during the long hours of darkness was the panic over the search to be undertaken in a few hours' time.

After eating, they were forced to spend a further hour sat beside the fire in the great hall before the commissioners eventually showed their tardy faces. Eleanor did not care how late they had arrived the previous evening, she wanted them on their way as soon as possible and then she could get the prior and Brother Rufus far away from the house. She didn't dare disappear to the solar, or stillroom, or her office as she usually might, in case they appeared ready to start their search. And she wouldn't countenance them staying under her roof for another night.

The commissioners seemed eager to get finished and move on, not hiding their disagreeable thoughts on the barren Norfolk landscape and how unfavourably it compared with their comfortable, fashionable London homes. Hugh took them outside to start in the barns and outbuildings, and afterwards they slowly made their way through the cattle sheds and dairy, then by late morning they were back in the house once more.

Hugh suggested they ate dinner before they continued the search in the house, and Eleanor almost screamed in frustration. Her captives had now been shut in their hiding place for many hours. Would they even have survived so long in the small space?

She had already told Cook dinner was to be a normal meal; he was not to produce special food for their visitors. They were no guests of hers. So a pottage with mutton and leeks was served with rough brown bread and a platter of fruit, and after thirty minutes Eleanor rose from the table and went to her office. Nell and Joan were to take the children outside to play so they weren't in the nursery while it was being searched. Or ransacked, Eleanor thought viciously as she'd already seen the way the workrooms behind the kitchen had been pulled apart. She'd told Hugh to ensure that nothing in the stillroom was touched, and none of her glass broken.

Finally after listening to the sounds as they moved from room to room, Hugh and the commissioners arrived at her office.

'Gentlemen.' Her voice was cool and she gave them a tight smile. 'I trust you have not found your fugitives?'

'No, my lady, we've found nothing. I suspect they are somewhere hiding out in the countryside, but it won't be long before they are uncovered. Monastic folk are used to the luxurious trappings of life and comfortable living. Not as Saint Benedict prescribed at all. They won't survive long out there, especially at this time of year. We're almost done here, only this room and the tower to search.'

Eleanor looked around the office, her eyes wide. 'I hope you can see there is nobody hiding in here? Just myself, getting on with my work as usual.'

'Indeed we can. And your steward informs us there is only a single tower room above us? And you are the sole bearer of the key to that room?' She knew it irked Hugh that he didn't have a key or even know where it was kept. Her heart by this point was beating so fast she thought it may burst from her body.

'That is correct, I have it here.' She pulled the key from her pocket, relieved she'd had the forethought to take it from its hiding place before she had a room full of people watching. 'Let me show you the way.' As she stood up, her knees were shaking so hard she thought she would fall down at their feet. Her breathing was ragged, wheezing slowly in and out of her lungs as she desperately tried to remain calm. If she could just stay strong for another few minutes, they'd be safe

274

and she could let her friends out of their cold dank prison. If indeed they had survived their incarceration.

Sweeping from the room as best as she could on her trembling legs, she led the way to the door at the base of the tower stairs. The commissioners gave a cursory glance around the small hallway, where only thirty-six hours previously the two men they were seeking had been sat with her.

As she began to climb the stairs, she chatted loudly to the two men, discussing the weather and had they thought the mutton at dinner had been a little tough. Thankfully their corpulent size and shape, no doubt due to the fine living their jobs gave them, meant they soon fell behind her as she hurried up the steps, used to their steep incline and the slippery nature of the damp stone. She called back to them exclaiming what a tiring climb it was as if they hadn't already realised, but that they would be able to see for many miles and out to sea when they reached the top. She smirked to herself. As if they'd care about the view, by now they must be desperate to finish and be on their way. She'd hoped they would change their minds and turn around halfway up the stairs, but resolutely they carried on.

Opening the door at the top she held her breath. The two men were only about a dozen steps behind her. If there was anything amiss she'd have no way of preventing them from seeing. Thankfully though the room looked exactly as it had done when she had shut the door the previous day. She let her breath out slowly and silently, stepping into the room.

'Look, gentlemen, you can see the sea from here, and my husband's fine estate to the south. We're able to see anyone who is approaching along the road towards Milfleet. This house was built in a very good position do you not think?'

275

She chattered on aimlessly as if she thought they might hear the breathing of the two men beneath their feet.

One of the men sniffed the air and frowned. Eleanor felt her entire body stiffen. Could he smell the acrid scent of sweat on the frightened men, the odour of fear hanging in the air? She blinked slowly as the full horror of what may unfold in the next few seconds flashed before her eyes: the children left homeless and penniless, and Tom wandering the countryside again fending for himself. And she and Greville dying heretics' deaths. She shuddered.

'There is a strange smell in here, my lady,' he said, turning his head to one side as if to place it. 'A smell of spices. Sir Greville is a spice merchant is he not?'

Eleanor breathed out a long sigh of relief. 'He is,' she agreed, 'but what you can smell in here is the saffron we grow. It is dried after the harvest and that is done in here, on the trestles you see around the edges of the room. This is why the door is always kept locked, so that during the harvest nobody can wander up here and spoil the precious spice, before it is ready.'

'It is well known in London that your husband has made a good fortune through his saffron crops,' the other commissioner commented.

Eleanor inclined her head, but said nothing. She knew her husband's rise in stature at court was common knowledge and was not surprised that Cromwell's henchmen had heard of him. He was now a well-regarded figure. He'd told her there were always people at court jealous of the sudden increase in others' wealth.

'Have you seen everything you need to now?' she asked with feigned politeness, moving towards the door and waiting for them to follow. She allowed them to walk down first, so she could ensure the door was locked behind them.

'Can we offer you some sustenance before you leave?' she enquired once they were all back in the great hall. In reality she wanted them gone as soon as possible, but knew she needed to keep up her hospitable pretence for as long as it was required.

'Thank you but no,' came the reply. 'We must make good use of the daylight that remains and return to the priory. Tomorrow we will have to try searching elsewhere, or return to London and explain to Cromwell what has happened. He's not going to be pleased.' The two men bowed to her before following Hugh to the stables where their panniers were already on their saddles and the horses ready to leave.

Eleanor waited a further thirty agonising minutes until she was certain they had gone and weren't coming back, and Hugh had disappeared about his daily business. She went and sat in the office, a quill in her hand but writing nothing, listening quietly to the noises around the house. Only when she was as certain as she could be that she wouldn't be disturbed, she crept through to the tower room and up the stairs, carefully locking the door at the bottom behind her to ensure nobody would follow.

She hurried up the stairs and into the room, locking the door behind her and lifting the slab away from the hiding place and peering in. The smell that rose up made her gag and the pile of clothing inside didn't move for several seconds. She closed her eyes. They were dead. All she'd wanted to do was save them and in trying to do that, she'd killed them both. But then a small scuffling noise made her open her eyes and she gasped and put her hand over her mouth as she saw the heap begin to slowly move and the two men unravelled themselves.

She held out her hand to Rufus to steady him as he crawled out, remaining on all fours as he crouched on the floor, barely able to move.

'Help me,' he croaked to Eleanor before leaning back into the hiding place to drag out the prior who was still breathing, but looked extremely pale with a desperate yellow-grey tinge to his jowls. Lying on his side on the floor, he didn't move while Eleanor briskly rubbed his hands between her own. His skin felt icy cold and stiff, and pulling out a flask of beer she'd hidden in her skirts, she dribbled some between his parched cracked lips, making him wince as it ran over the bloodied edges.

She passed the flask to Rufus who drank greedily. There was barely any left by the time he handed it back, but he was able to get to his feet and stagger to a bench and sit down on it, slowly stretching each of his limbs. Eleanor could hear the cracks as his joints protested. Reaching into her pocket she threw across a small pouch of food.

'I need to get medicine for the prior from the stillroom,' she told him. 'He's in a bad way. And I'll collect more ale and food. Can you try and get him to eat something while I'm gone?' Rufus, still stretching and wincing, nodded.

'Wait,' he croaked as she got to her feet. 'Have they gone? We heard them up here earlier. I feared they would hear the frantic thumping of my heart.'

'Not above the sound of my own,' Eleanor answered, 'but yes, they left about half an hour ago. We need to get you both moving about and able to travel so you can be waiting for your boat and away from these shores in the next couple of days.'

She disappeared downstairs and into the great hall, which was empty save for a young house maid sweeping up the old rushes and Joan, sat beside the fire playing cards. By the way her head whipped around as Eleanor entered the room, it was obvious she had stationed herself where she could discover what was happening as soon as possible. She looked enquiringly at Eleanor as she approached.

'Joan, I have some work to do in the stillroom, could you please assist me? It will take the two of us to lift the flagon.' She made sure her voice was loud enough for the servant girl, and anyone else who may have been listening, to hear. Hugh was a good man, but at the end of the day she wasn't sure how well she could trust him.

Together the two women made their way through to the stillroom at the back of the house. The kitchen was unusually empty and as she walked past the table, Eleanor snatched up the remains of a loaf and some figs, and carried them with her.

As soon as they were in the stillroom and the door shut, she hissed at Joan, 'They're alive, but only just. I need some soft food, a bowl of custard or pottage for the prior. He's very weak. Can you go back to the pantries and see if you can find anything please? Without being seen? I'm going to make up a tisane with some mallow and sage, and also find some of the ointment with oak bark I made last summer. I'll put it all on a tray under a cloth in case anyone stops us. We'll say the medicines are for you if anyone asks, so please look as wan and ill as you can. Nobody will look under the cloth if I've said it's for you.'

Joan gave Eleanor's arm a squeeze of solidarity before nodding and without a word she slipped back to the pantry while Eleanor began to assemble the items she needed. She was more thankful than ever for her friend's loyalty. The tray was almost complete when Joan returned with several slices of beef and a dish of custard.

'I told the kitchen lad I missed breakfast,' she said, laying the food on the tray. 'He wasn't much interested. He told me Cook is outside with the farmer choosing a pig to slaughter, so now is a good time for us to help ourselves to whatever is in the kitchen.'

'Good, thank you. Can you collect some beakers of ale as we walk back through? Then follow me to the office. We'll stop there for a few minutes to make sure nobody is paying attention to what we're doing.'

The return journey to the tower went without a problem and while they paused in the office, listening to the movements around the house and the shouting of the children playing in the garden, Eleanor let out a giggle of relief.

'I've never been so scared in my life,' she admitted, 'and I hope that Hugh is now in my chamber looking for all those non-existent mice!' Joan laughed with her, until the two women were leaning against each other helpless with mirth, their nerves making them laugh all the more. With the coast clear, Eleanor sent Joan back to the hall as a lookout while she climbed up to the tower once again.

The prior was now sitting on the bench beside Brother Rufus, propped up but still looking very pale. He'd aged thirty years in two days and his sallow face was a myriad of deep lines etched into the skin. Eleanor put her tray of medicines and victuals down, handing them both beakers of ale. The prior's hands were still shaking so violently he almost spilled his drink, but he managed to swallow the contents down without stopping, and then Rufus poured some of the contents of his cup into the prior's as well.

'I can bring up more ale,' Eleanor promised, 'and I have a tisane that will help with any aching muscles, and ointment for sore skin. There's more food and a soft custard for the prior as it's easier to swallow. After dinner tonight there'll be leftover stew or pottage I'm sure. But as soon as the house is locked up for tonight I'm afraid you need to be gone from here. I hope you understand that? I cannot take this risk any longer.'

'Of course, and we can never thank you enough for all you have done for us,' Rufus replied.

'Your reward will come in heaven,' the prior whispered, smiling at her and squeezing her hand gently.

'Some of your reward will come a lot sooner than that,' Rufus promised her. 'All of our crocus corms will be brought over in the next day or so. It seems the commissioners are only interested in solid gold they can melt down for the king, not the gold that grows in the fields.'

She left them and went back to her office to wait until it was dinner time. Picking up her book of hours from her desk, Eleanor read through the prayers, reciting them quietly to herself, gaining some comfort from the familiar Latin. Thank goodness the king's men did not decide to take it from her, if they had even noticed it on her desk. Although she recorded all the comings and goings and everything of any importance in the house in her book, she knew she could never write down the danger she had brought upon the house and her family. And her husband. If what she'd done had got to London, Greville would have ended his days in the Tower; she had no doubts about that. Instead she carefully wrote the date and underneath she began to scribe:

I received a missive from the prior. He remains at the priory although the brothers have now dispersed. But now he must leave too. He has safe passage to his new home together with his most sacred belongings that he cannot be parted from. He waits here in that place where he shall not be found until his boat leaves from Cley, two days hence.

We were visited by the king's commissioners, which gave me great fright. Joan was almost overcome, but nothing was found. Our saffron has saved them. And his most holy treasure also. Deo gratis.

With dinner eaten, the house began to quieten down for the night. Hugh explained to Eleanor that despite an extensive search, he'd found little evidence of mice in her room or any of the others that adjoined it. She managed to look surprised, but promised she would send Joan to find him if the same thing happened again once they were in bed. She smiled as she turned away, knowing no such intervention would be needed.

The two women went upstairs and sat on Eleanor's bed as they waited until they were absolutely sure nobody was still moving about below them.

'You don't need to come down with me,' Eleanor reassured her. 'I'm just going to let them out of the side door and then they'll have to fend for themselves. I've done all I can. I can't risk accompanying them any further. I've got the food I took after dinner in my office and all the doors through there remain locked.'

'Of course I will go with you,' Joan replied firmly. 'You have taken far too many risks on your own these past two days. Now, I intend to help, albeit at the end. I'll remain in the great hall and if anyone appears I can speak to them loud enough to alert you.'

'Thank you, you've been such a help to me. Such a good friend. I can never repay you.' Eleanor hugged her before they both crept from the room, tiptoeing on the dry rushes, the smell of the fresh lavender and rosemary that had been laid that day after the futile mouse hunt almost making them sneeze.

It took less than ten minutes for the two men to be laden down with food and ale for their journey, Brother Rufus adding it all to the large sack he was once again carrying, their precious relic safe for another day. As soon as they were away from the door, Eleanor quickly locked up, saying a brief prayer under her breath for their safe passage. It was over. She had done all she could.

Two days later, as she was working in her stillroom, there was a knock at the door and one of the gardeners was stood there.

'There's been a delivery from the priory,' he told her, ''tis outside.' He stepped backwards waiting for Eleanor to follow. There in the barn, as promised, lay a dozen large sacks of crocus bulbs. She shuddered as she thought of what this saffron had almost cost her. The terrible risks she'd undertaken pushed its price way beyond the gold that would fill Greville's coffers. She'd never be able to tell him that the riches that pleased him so, had almost become his downfall.

Chapter Twenty-Seven

1540

My dearest wife,

I hope all is well at Milfleet, and you and my children thrive. There is much happening at court and I must remain for the present, although you know I would prefer to be at home in Norfolk with you. The king's new wife, Anne of Cleves, has arrived in England but she does not hold the beauty promised in her portrait. I have spoken with some courtiers close to the king and they say he is most angry with both Holbein and Cromwell. It is rumoured that the marriage has not been fulfilled.

So, you will see I need to be here in these times of turmoil as there may be opportunities to further myself once the king's temper has abated. He is insistent on ridding himself of the new queen. Cromwell's friends are leaving his side in droves. I fear his star may no longer be in the ascendance but like everyone else, I will watch and wait.

Look after our home and children, my little croker, and I will write again soon.

Your devoted husband, Greville

The months passed quickly as the seasons came and went, the weather and religious festivals keeping time. A small package arrived from Isabel Dereham with a gift of ribbons and silk threads inside and Eleanor wished she could see her friend and sit with her as they had before. But Greville remained in London as the king attempted to orchestrate another divorce and Eleanor pined for him. She was frightened that Thomas Cromwell, Greville's former friend, was now being ostracised, shunned by the king, and whether that would affect her husband.

Henry grew sturdier with every passing day as he approached his first birthday and to Eleanor's relief he was rarely ill. Nell took him outside to play in almost all weathers and he could be found all around the grounds or house, always smiling and laughing.

He was a sharp contrast to Tom who, despite having settled in well to his new life, seldom left Eleanor's side and refused to go outside and play with the other two children, however often Nell tried to encourage him. His scrawny body didn't bulk up despite the vast quantities of food he ate and he could have benefited from some warm sunshine, but he'd only venture outside when Eleanor was with him. She tried to find a couple of hours every afternoon to sit in the newly formed knot garden with Nell and Joan if the weather was clement, and then he was happy to run about and play with Jane as Henry tried to follow on unsteady legs.

It was into this happy idyll that Greville arrived home unexpectedly in the late summer of 1540, seeing an opportunity to escape for a while. The king had found himself a new wife and despatched Cromwell to the block in obscene haste and all was calm again – for a while at least.

Greville's popularity at court continued to bloom and Eleanor couldn't help a feeling of pride as she surveyed her tall, muscular husband clothed in his new fashionable London attire, doublets well cut from the very finest damasks and velvets with slashes of deep Tudor green, and scarlet. She knew that whilst his importing of spices and silks had always made him a very good and profitable living, it was nothing in comparison to the fortune her saffron had now created for him. In the fields even now, the tightly filled buds began to push their way through the soil, the whole life cycle beginning again. Although Simon had told her that here in Norfolk it was tradition to split the bulbs every seven years, she had every intention of lifting them to split them next spring, following the three-yearly cycle used at Ixworth.

'So, for what reason have you come home to your wife and family?' Eleanor asked with a little smile as she and Greville sat down together after dinner. It was a full twelve hours since he'd arrived at Milfleet, but the first time she'd had a chance to speak with him alone. No sooner had he arrived but the combined forces of Hugh and Simon had carried him off to discuss matters they'd decided were not of her concern. She could feel her nerves flinch with irritation at their dismissal of her once Greville was home and in command.

'And why do I need a reason? Why wouldn't I want to be here?' he asked, his wide, familiar grin flashing and dark eyes making her melt inside. She'd been childish and immature to think of him as a boorish old man when she had first laid eyes on him. Now she was proud he was her husband, a fine handsome man.

'Court life is not something I choose for pleasure,' he reminded her. 'It's a necessity if I want to increase my standing and position. And that is what every gentleman wants, to be noticed by the king. I know you understand I need to spend the majority of my time there, being seen as much as possible. Mingling with all the right people. But London is never pleasant in the summer and the king is still at Oatlands, completely besotted with his new bride Catherine so it's a good time to slip away, to spend some time with my wife and family.'

He cupped her face in his large hand and smiled into her eyes. 'Henry is growing into a fine boy, but there's always room for more sons in the nursery.' He raised his eyebrows and she smiled tightly, giving an almost imperceptible nod of agreement. It was inevitable that he would want another child soon, although she wouldn't ever be ready for the discomfort that pregnancy brought, the pain and worry of giving birth. Everything had gone well last time, but that gave her no guarantees.

Though his arrival meant she was no longer expected to deal with any business issues, Eleanor's day-to-day life carried on much as before. There were medicines to make and herbs and flowers to collect whilst they were still plentiful. And wherever she went, Tom quietly followed, carrying a basket for her, almost as big as he was.

The balmy summer days flew past until it was harvest once more. This year Greville was available to help the workers out in the fields, his muscles rippling, shiny with sweat as his smart London gentleman clothes lay in a chest in the bedroom and his dull brown, coarse work trousers and white linen shirt made him indistinguishable from his tenant farmers.

Eleanor, suddenly realising one afternoon that Tom was not with her, went outside looking for him. She stopped one of the dairymaids and asked if she'd seen him.

'Yes, mistress, I seen him with the master.' She pointed towards fields of barley still waiting to be cut, and Eleanor went to investigate. What could they be doing together? He'd told her only that morning the barley wouldn't be ready to harvest for another week.

She saw them almost immediately. Greville was walking the length of the field, the ears of the crop brushing his muscular thighs, small insects flying away. Sat on his shoulders, was Tom. Occasionally, Greville would pull a weed from the ground and pass it up to Tom, who was holding a bunch of them tightly in his hand. The afternoon sun, slanting through the trees, lit up the crop like liquid gold as it swayed from the movement of Greville striding through it, a sea of rippling life. Her eyes filled with tears of joy. She had thought that he hadn't much interest in this new member of the household. An interloper in their family wearing his daughter's clothes and forever in his wife's shadow. And the difficulty in communication meant Greville easily became frustrated, his arms waving wildly and pointing, which produced no response from the quiet boy.

She was wrong. He was making time trying to connect with their new son, even though it wasn't easy. As they turned at the end of the field and began to make their way back, Tom spotted her, his face wreathed in smiles, such a rare sight as he waved his hand full of wild flowers and weeds at her, almost falling off his perch in the process. She heard the booming of Greville's laughter and Tom looked down with delight. He couldn't hear anything but she was certain he felt the vibrations of laughter as they moved through Greville's body.

Later that night as they lay in bed, she thanked him for making an effort with Tom.

'He must be so shut off,' she said. 'It's easy to forget he's even there as he makes no sound. He looked so happy out there with you today.'

'I enjoyed being with him. I love playing with Jane and Henry, but they're noisy and demanding. Jane doesn't like it when the attention isn't on her.'

'That's true.' Eleanor laughed. 'She's been the centre of attention her whole life, and unfortunately Henry has rather upset that.'

'Tom asks for nothing. He has no words to do so. Any tiny fragment of interaction he revels in; his face lights up when he knows you're trying to connect with him.'

'And the time I've put in trying to devise ways of being able to communicate with him have repaid me many times over. Now he knows the names of all the herbs I use, the medicines I create. He knows what's dangerous and must only be used in minute quantities. He can recognise the smells and taste of every product I put into a potion. Even if he just sniffs something he can point to each picture of the separate plants I've sketched for him, and his own artistic skills are incredible: he can illustrate perfectly any of the foliage we collect. He's always correct – it's amazing. It's as if because he has no hearing or voice, his other senses have become so much sharper, and if I mouth words slowly he can recognise some of them now. He's a real help to me in the stillroom, but I wish he would play more, behave like a normal little boy. Not simply a shadow in the spaces I've just occupied, because it's where he feels safest.'

As September began, once again Eleanor was watching. And waiting. Every day at dawn she took the well-worn path, now dry and dusty after the long summer days, to the saffron stand. She hurried to check as soon as she was washed and dressed, wearing an old hessian apron, ever hopeful that it would be the day.

Sweeping past the rest of the household breaking their fast, Greville, who by that point knew her routine, would snatch up bread and cheese and fruit from the table and follow her, walking beside her as she strode towards the precious crop, passing her food as they went.

And finally, her observation, her diligence with weeding and tending the plants was repaid. As the couple emerged from between the cool hedgerows, beneath a sky on fire with the morning rays illuminating the clouds into a vibrant orange, a rippling arena of pale lilac flowers lay before them. A carpet that curled and waved in the soft wind, rolling gently to and fro. Above their heads a skylark called, its song soaring across the landscape.

Greville caught hold of her hand and stopped for a moment. 'It's beautiful,' he said quietly. 'I hadn't realised that such riches could begin their life in this glorious display of beauty.'

'It is,' she agreed, crouching down to break off a flower head. She laid it on her palm and with her forefinger and thumb she lifted apart the petals to show him the three dark red fronds like tiny tongues that lay within.

'It's as if they are so delicate and pretty to detract from the secret they're hiding,' she said. 'When I'm sad, when you're in London and I'm lonely, I think of this crocus stand undulating under the autumn sun, and it never fails to make me smile.'

'Now I've seen it, I will always think of you here, when I'm away. Just as beautiful as you look now, the expanse of swaying lilac flowers, your power, laid out before you. I'd like nothing more than to lay you down now amongst the blooms and make love to you. But I suspect you'd have words to say about that.'

Eleanor laughed. 'You're right, I would! There is no time for lying down, here or anywhere else. It's now the hard work begins. Many long days, nay weeks, of toiling here in the field and up in the tower room. I need to go and find Simon to tell him that today we start. He'll be expecting me and he has the workers ready to begin. I know they resent this harvest when they've almost finished bringing in the fruit and grain. That's why I always throw a big party to celebrate and say thank you for the extra work – extremely hard work – the saffron causes.' Clutching the flower in her hand, the strands marking her palms with dark red stains like stigmata, she went in search of Simon.

The harvest was as successful as previous years, but the increased number of plants and flower heads meant the workload was also far heavier and the pale, dark smudges beneath Eleanor's eyes deepened as she spent hour after hour in the tower room. Before long the floors were thick with the discarded flowers, a fragrant carpet that clung to their skirts as the women moved from room to room.

After seventeen long days, finally it was over. The saffron

was finishing drying and the maids had been released to their normal duties. Joan examined her dark orange stained fingers.

'It will be weeks before I can work with any white linen,' she complained. 'I'd forgotten how much the saffron stains everything. There was so much this year as well. Do you really need to grow so much?'

Eleanor nodded, her own hands as stained as Joan's. She was looking at the harvest, so brilliantly golden that it appeared to be lit from within as if it contained the sun, piled up around the walls of the room. Her mind was occupied not by the ache that spread down the backs of her thighs to her feet and knotted at her shoulders so tightly she could barely move her head, nor the fact she was so tired she could lie down on the carpet of dead flowers and fall asleep there and then. Instead she was thinking of the increased wealth her husband had gained, now giving him even more of the recognition he deserved at court. And it was all down to her, she thought, a satisfied smile spreading across her face. She was orchestrating his place at court and that could only result in him being noticed by the king. Now it was only a matter of time.

Their family would be great, rich and powerful. Norfolk had its fair share of powerful families so why shouldn't the Luttons be another Norfolk dynasty recognised by the Tudors? Little Henry may only be in the nursery now, but she was making sure his future shined as brightly as the gold she grew. It was worth every ache in her body.

Greville had previously warned her he would need to return to London as soon as the saffron was ready to be shipped, and he already had a boat waiting at Cley. He'd decided that this year he'd sail with the precious cargo, but Eleanor was not happy about his decision.

'But the seas at this time of year can be rough and wild,' she argued. 'Why don't you ride to London and meet Captain Wyatt when he gets there?'

Greville had brought his ship's captain to Milfleet when the *Elizabeth Jane* had been berthed at King's Lynn the previous year. The fact that his ship was named after his first wife no longer upset Eleanor as it once did – she knew she had completely changed his life for the better and she was utterly confident in his devotion to her. She had liked the shy, quiet captain, but she could tell he'd rather be at sea with the waves and seagulls as company rather than having to mind his manners at his master's home.

'This is valuable cargo, I want to make sure it is safe on every part of its journey to our destination.'

'If the boat is caught in a storm we won't just lose our saffron, we may lose you as well, husband. We can always grow more spice, but we cannot replace you.'

Greville laughed. From her position, with her head lying on his chest in the inky black dark of their bedroom, she felt his mirth rumbling against her face.

'Some would say the cargo in this case is more valuable than its owner, so I'm pleased you don't agree with that sentiment. I have, however, made up my mind. We will unload half the saffron in London, then the remainder will carry on its journey to Calais, where I already have a buyer for it. The French will pay an even higher price for our precious crop than the king. But the riches I can gain from providing the court with such fine spices can be gleaned not only from the coins in my coffers and the plate that now adorns our table, but also with the connections I'm making and the doors that are opening in the great halls and palaces of

London. Talking of which, I shall delay my departure for a day to pay a visit to the Derehams again. Their son Francis has now returned home from Ireland and I'm interested in how his visit went. Do you recall me telling you that he once lived with the Howards, and was a friend of our new queen Catherine before she went to court? He could prove to be a useful association and friend. He wrote to say he will be in Norfolk but a few days, which is why I decided to delay my leaving.'

Eleanor was delighted to have the opportunity to visit their neighbours, and to see Isabel again. It was the first time she'd had the chance to go visiting since moving to Milfleet, and she took a great deal of care with her coiffure and clothes, keeping Greville waiting a full forty-five minutes longer than he'd wanted, after their intended leaving time. His eyes sparkled with admiration, however, and he nodded approvingly as she walked over to where her horse was waiting. Her stocky white palfrey, which rarely got enough exercise, was dancing sideways, as eager as Greville to be on their way. Eleanor barely had a chance to arrange her carefully selected gown and cloak, before her mount darted forward and clattered out of the yard, Greville on his huge black mount close behind, with two of their grooms following.

Thankfully after a brief canter to work off some of its energy, her horse calmed down and they were able to ride together, admiring the fiery oranges and reds of the late autumn trees. Already the track was thick with crisp dead leaves and spiky green chestnut cases, and Eleanor was dismayed to see how heavily laden with berries the holly and rowan trees already were. The bright red against the dark glossy foliage may look attractive, but it foretold of a harsh winter, which she always dreaded.

The Derehams' home was impressive. It was less fortified than Milfleet, more a family home as Ixworth had been, though substantially larger. Built with fashionable narrow dark red bricks in a smart herringbone design inset between pale oak beams, beneath a bowed roof. The numerous windows let in plenty of light and Eleanor was delighted to sit in the small parlour, a warm fire burning in the grate, and talk about children and sewing with Isabel whilst Francis and Greville disappeared elsewhere.

Eleanor was taken with the young man. With his shoulder-length, dark curly hair and merry eyes, he was very good-looking. He'd bowed low and kissed her hand, making her prickle with fascination, and she would have liked to sit and talk with him, but found herself being ushered away as the gentlemen disappeared into the back of the house.

She managed to see him again briefly before they left, and was unable to tear her eyes away. He shone like a god, his handsome face and deep brown eyes that lit up with a boyish smile ever flickering at the edges of his countenance. She couldn't quite place what it was about him, but he behaved as if he didn't have a single care in the world and truly believed everything and everyone was set up on a stage before him for his own pleasure and enjoyment. This poise and confidence streamed from him in waves of contentment and joy. How could anyone not be smiling when in his presence?

As soon as they were riding home again, Eleanor couldn't wait to question Greville about him.

'How was your meeting with Francis?'

'It went well. I wanted to reconnect with him because

I saw him in London briefly a few years ago and he'll be heading back to court very soon. You remember I said he was once good friends with his kinswoman Catherine, and is hoping to become reacquainted? You can see a connection may be fortuitous for me. And in return, I can introduce him to business acquaintances of my own, who will help him to garner some wealth. We agreed to meet up in London and I offered him a room in Cheapside, should he require lodgings.'

'Is he betrothed to anyone?' Her mind had drifted to Joan as she was busily mentally arranging a marriage between them.

'He's just told me that he and Queen Catherine lived as man and wife when they were both living with the Dowager Duchess. Can you believe that? I told him he must keep that information to himself now she's married to the king, or he won't be needing a room with me because he'll be residing in the Tower. I confess I'm not entirely sure he was listening to my wise advice. He admitted his heart has been broken by the news of her marriage.'

'Oh, I had wondered about him being a suitable husband for Joan.'

'Joan? No that's not a match I would agree to. Francis has his sights set on court and a high-ranking role there. Joan isn't a proper fit for court.'

Eleanor's shoulders slumped, any ideas of marrying him to her dear companion dissipating like the morning mist burning away under a rising summer sun. 'I hope he does heed your advice then, so that pretty head of his remains on his shoulders.'

Greville laughed, kicking his horse into a trot. 'I'm certain he's clever enough to steer clear of any sort of trouble,' he reassured her. 'I'll make sure he's well looked after. I know his sort. He intends to present himself to the queen's court, so he may prove to be a useful ally to me. Very useful.'

Smiling, Eleanor rode after her husband, pleased Greville was making friends in all the right places. Their sun was most definitely in the ascendance, and she felt invincible.

Chapter Twenty-Eight

2019

Finally the end of the book archiving was in sight. Amber had worked her way through the mountains of boxes around the hall, and now there was just the dark, musty library left. And the stark realisation that her sabbatical was coming to an end and soon she'd have some decisions to make. But first, the library. Many of these books had been sat on the shelves for possibly hundreds of years, untouched and uncared for by numerous ancestors who'd filled the room with volumes of books they'd never read, and subsequently left this forgotten part of the house to slowly crumble away. Thinking about the precarious state of the tower above her, it made her slightly nervous about working in there, but it was easier to set her laptop up in here than carry everything back and forth to the office.

In this room it was fairly simple to deduce how at some point a previous occupant had altered the original floor plan of this part of the hall. One end of the room still retained a low-beamed ceiling leaving it dark and gloomy, but then it opened up into a much lighter, airier space, part of the original great hall with tall windows set on top of dark wooden panelling that reached halfway up the walls. It was in this brighter end where Amber positioned herself at an old oak pedestal desk with the window behind her to give herself as much natural light as possible. She began to lift the heavy, dusty books from the shelves.

Working in the library prevented her from taking any breaks from her task to read a few extra pages of Eleanor's book. Instead she'd have to wait until mid-afternoon when she'd finished working for the day. After showering off the grime that clung to her skin, clothes and hair, she'd have a cup of tea with Grandad before settling down for an hour or so to continue with her research. The Latin was so difficult to decipher that after sixty minutes she usually got a headache and was forced to give up for another day.

She was beginning to wonder if there were any more clues to be found in its pages, but she had nowhere else to look so she ploughed on even though Eleanor's entries were few and far between amongst the prayers and psalms. Each time she turned the page though and found something written in Eleanor's familiar lettering, she felt her heart thump with excitement and pleasure. The now recognisable style of her illumination jumped off the page, usually decorated with small pale lilac flowers, golden apples and herons, or falcons.

So it was with delight that, late one spring afternoon as the skies were darkening outside her window and night was beginning to crawl in, Amber turned the page and discovered another of Eleanor's entries, with a tiny monk and a rabbit decorating the edge of the page. Amber's face lit up with pleasure and, grabbing her pencil and pad, she attempted to translate it.

As she flipped from her translation app to the book and then to her notes, she began to feel the hairs stand up on the back of her neck. This entry wasn't a list of herbs, or description of an illness and its remedy, or a favoured recipe, nor was it a vivid description of Eleanor's saffron cultivation. This was an account of something that had happened. Amber was convinced this was a report of a real incident.

Despite the dull throbbing ache behind her eyes as she screwed them up, trying to decipher the words, she couldn't stop working at it. It was almost midnight by the time she'd translated the whole passage, having long since said goodnight to Grandad and promised him she'd soon be following him up to bed. By the time she'd finished she was sick with exhaustion and couldn't make head nor tail of what was written in front of her, even though she was certain the significance it held was more important than anything else she'd read so far in the book.

But she was beaten. Her hands were shaking with tiredness as she returned the book to the safe, closed her laptop and went to bed, where she lay in the dark, her heart beating fast with excitement that maybe she'd somehow inadvertently found the clue, the breakthrough she'd been looking for to help Eleanor. If only she could understand what it all meant. First thing in the morning she'd call Becky and see if her friend had any spare time to try and help decipher what she'd translated. With a contented smile on her face she finally drifted off to sleep.

Becky was at work the next day, but she promised Amber

she'd be at the hall by early evening, for which Amber had to be grateful, and wait patiently. She distracted herself with a trip to the supermarket, followed by making lasagne and a lemon meringue pie. There was no point staring at her notes trying to play detective. She needed Becky's expertise to bounce ideas off and it was better to distract herself in the kitchen. Grandad was delighted with the rare culinary feast, especially when she agreed to his request to make some jam tarts. He kept asking when they would be eating like an impatient five-year-old but Amber insisted they waited for Becky.

The tarts were just coming out of the oven, the jam bubbling over and burning the pan on almost every one of them, when Becky arrived. After an agonisingly slow dinner during which Amber had to stop herself whisking plates away before people had barely taken their final mouthful, they settled themselves in the library with Amber's notes laid out across the desk in front of them.

'I'm not sure if I've even got this right,' she began, suddenly doubting herself, 'the tiny letters, the way her words change from Latin to French as she swapped between different languages as if she couldn't remember the word she wanted in the one she was writing in.'

'Is it going to lead us to Mary? Help us understand her passage?'

'No, I don't think so, not that I can work out, anyway. This is something completely different. Exciting, but scary. Shall I read out what I think it says?'

'Yes, go on, I'm intrigued.'

Amber drew in a breath slowly, as if preparing herself, and began to read. *'I received a missive from the prior. He remains at the priory although the brothers have now dispersed.'*

302

'Did this have a date?' Becky interrupted. 'Was she talking about the dissolution of the monasteries?'

'Oh yes sorry, this was November 1540, although I can't work out which day. But yes, right in the midst of the dissolution.' She paused, then continued with her reading. *'But now he must leave too. He has safe passage to his new home together with his most sacred belongings that he cannot be parted from. He waits here in that place where he shall not be found until his boat leaves from Cley, two days hence.'*

'*A place where he shall not be found.* It sounds as if she was hiding him. But where?'

'Hang on, there's a second entry on the next page. This must be afterwards.' She continued reading from the pages in front of her. *'We were visited by the king's commissioners, which gave me great fright. Joan was almost overcome, but nothing was found. Our saffron has saved them. And his most holy treasure also. Thanks be to God.'*

'Bloody hell. Excuse my French.' Becky breathed out slowly. 'What does it all mean?'

'I think she hid the prior – and maybe a second monk as she definitely says "them" not "him" – and helped them escape. The commissioners came looking for them, so did that mean they refused to sign the Oath of Supremacy? They'd have been burnt as heretics. I'm guessing the sacred belongings she refers to were maybe relics? I need to take a walk to the priory ruins and see if there's any information of what holy relics they had kept there. If records were kept. The most important thing here is that her saffron apparently kept them safe. How? Did she hide them in the fields? Maybe the hedgerows around the edge – they'd have been far denser than they are nowadays.'

'But if it was November, surely it would have been really cold. To become a prior he'd have been — for those days — an old man and possibly frail. The saffron grass wouldn't grow tall enough to actually hide in the fields and not be seen. Where else could they have hidden away so well that a bunch of ruthless men couldn't find them? From what I've read about what happened during that time, they would have left no stone left unturned. Eleanor was lucky they didn't burn down the barns just to make sure.'

'Wait.' Amber held her hand up as her brain jumped ahead in a train of thoughts. 'Barns, maybe you have something there.'

'Is that where the crocus bulbs were stored?'

'Not that year — I've already read they weren't lifted after the harvest, even if they were going to be split it was done before the growing season. They reaped the grasses that grew after the flowers as cattle fodder. What I've just remembered is that when they harvested the saffron, the threads were picked from the flowers to be dried into cakes and that was a delicate operation, so it needed to be done well away from the rest of the household, somewhere where they wouldn't be disturbed by draughts, people bustling in and out. A safe haven. And . . .' she paused for a moment as realisation slowly began to dawn '. . . Eleanor also described how the pale flowers left a deep fragrant carpet on the floor.'

'That she could hide someone underneath?' Becky was incredulous. 'That deep?'

'I don't know. But I do know where they did the preparation of the saffron. And it's the one place we can't go. The tower. Her safe haven.'

'Well that's put the kibosh on that plan then. As you say,

there's no way we can go up the tower at the moment – it isn't safe. We'll never know if that's where she hid a fleeing old man and his casket of old bones.'

Amber giggled at her friend's obvious contempt of the relic. 'That's a little irreverent of you.'

'Not at all,' Becky defended herself. 'We know he was the prior and it sounds like they were escaping with some sort of religious relic, which were usually some ancient body part purportedly from a saint, or a piece of the cross. It may be interesting from a historical aspect, but I've never believed in the healing properties or possibilities of divine communication from something ancient and religious.'

'Anyway—' Amber ignored her friend's rant '—who said it's unsafe to go up there?'

'They're taking it apart, as we speak,' Becky reminded her in a patient voice. 'You can hear them. Actually if the wind is in the right direction you can hear the banging all over the village. I hope you aren't intending to climb up the scaffolding? I can't imagine Kenny or Pete agreeing to that.'

'No, I expect you're right, but I'm determined to go up there and have a look. I'll just have to go up the stairs. You know Grandad has always warned me off the tower, that it's foreboding and scary, but nothing will stop me from investigating. I feel compelled to go and look. I have to put aside my fears and do it. You don't have to come with me, if you'd rather not – I completely understand. But I need to see if there are any signs the brothers were ever up there.'

'After all this time? I'm sure Eleanor made certain every trace of them had gone.'

'I know, but she's the one who wants me to go and investigate. I can feel it.'

Her determination, however, hit a brick wall when she asked her grandfather if he knew the whereabouts of the key for the door at the bottom of the tower.

'I have no idea where the key is,' he reminded her. 'Remember how I was told as a child not to go up there under any circumstances and what happened when my father found out I was intending to defy him? And now, the tower is unsafe as you well know. It's in danger of falling apart. There's no way you're going up there.'

'Grandad, we both know it isn't cursed.' Amber sounded more bullish than she felt. Supposing it was? She gave herself a mental shake. What terrible thing could occur now? Her baby had died; she wasn't even living with the person she loved most in the world. There was nothing awful left to happen. And anyway, she didn't believe in luck, or spells or hocus-pocus. Grandad was looking very unhappy. Whatever had been said to him all those years ago, still made him afraid, eighty years later.

'Nobody knows where the key is,' he reiterated, 'or has ever known. It's been locked up for so long. But that doesn't matter as you'd come to serious harm if you go up there now while the work is being done. If you must go, although I'm asking you explicitly not to, please wait until Kenny has finished.'

Amber knew she couldn't wait. Whatever Eleanor wanted from her, it was becoming more urgent and she was going up there to look at any cost. Even if she wasn't going to confess it to Grandad.

Chapter Twenty-Nine

1541

Eleanor received a string of letters from Greville in the early spring of 1541. More than she'd had in the whole four years of their marriage. Every time one arrived her heart leapt in the hope that it may tell her that he was coming home. Or that she was finally invited to court. She would never have believed when she was first told she was to be married to this man that she would love him and miss him so much that her whole body, her very being, ached for him. In the beginning of their marriage he would go away to London and she wouldn't hear from him at all, sometimes not even to inform her he was returning home, and she hadn't particularly cared. But now, every week that he was away felt like a month as she waited for him to return.

And this new gentleman, merchant and courtier couldn't resist keeping his wife up to date with everything currently going on in his life. Eleanor was excited to read what he had to divulge, even though she'd rather that he was there telling her in person. If she closed her eyes she could imagine herself there with him, seeing the opulent fabrics and clothes, the dancing, the tumbling fools and smelling and tasting all the exotic delights the court had to offer.

His first letter arrived only three weeks after he'd returned to London following the New Year. Eleanor found Joan, full of cold and huddled in front of the fire in the great hall.

'A letter, from Greville,' she exclaimed happily, waving the parchment in the air. Joan raised her eyebrows and putting her sewing to one side, waited for the latest news.

'My dearest Eleanor,' she read, *'I have good news to tell. I have been summoned to join the entourage of courtiers when the king and our new queen, Catherine, travel on their great procession to the North of England in the summer. This is a great honour for our family. We will be gone for several months. I shall leave Ralph in charge of the business in London. I have hopes that during our travels I may be able to put myself before the king and be favourably noticed.'*

'So Greville has a proper job at court? With the king?' Joan asked.

'I don't know exactly,' Eleanor admitted, 'but isn't this wonderful? Before we know it I'm certain we too will be at court and seeing all the splendour with our own eyes. I can hardly wait!'

'I won't rush upstairs to start packing my chests.' Joan's response was sharp.

What happened at court rarely affected them, tucked away in the flat barren landscape of Norfolk. She'd realised the harsh truth years ago, and no longer cared who was flirting with whom, nor what the king did. Although she was interested in what the queen was wearing, and the fashions at

308

court. These would eventually filter down, albeit diluted, to her own little world.

And both women were ever conscious about how the newly reformed church now dictated the ways in which they were allowed to pray. Neither of them had been happy with Hugh's insistence on the changes to the chapel that Greville had ordered and the removal of the familiar statues and the glorious triptych. Eleanor had taken the beautiful object and hidden it in her room at the bottom of a chest. Tom adored it and she wouldn't see it go up in smoke with the other icons. Maybe one day she could display it once more. She and Joan agreed together privately they had been incredibly lucky that the commissioners had ransacked the hall but not even noticed the hidden chapel. They couldn't risk such dangers again.

The letters from Greville continued to arrive, full of the delights and excitement of court life and news of the preparations for their journey around the country due to start in June. The king and queen and their retinue would leave as soon as summer arrived in London: it wasn't a place to stay in hot weather with the inevitable appalling stench and, often, sickness. Travelling around the country, they'd eventually arrive in York where the king could make those who'd been involved in the Pilgrimage of Grace pay their penance. Greville's latest shipment of silks had been sold straight to the king and then presented to the queen and her ladies, putting him in an even better mood.

Then in April, a letter arrived saying he would be returning home for a few days, after a visit to Collyweston Palace, where the Great Progress was due to stop on its way north to York.

Every morning Eleanor woke up on her own in her bed and wondered if it would be the day when Greville would arrive. She was bubbling over with anticipation and excitement.

In reality his arrival came quietly, and without the fanfare Eleanor would have provided for him. A week of heavy rain had laid a damp and despondent atmosphere over the hall. The thick, cloying mud from outside was being tracked inside, despite Eleanor's constant insistence that everyone wore pattens over their boots and did not simply tramp the wet and muck throughout the house. Hems became muddy and the rushes underfoot stuck to shoes and skirts as everything became coated in it. Even the food seemed to taste of it.

Inside the hall, both Jane and Henry, deprived of their outside activity day after day, were like caged animals, fractious and very noisy, running around the hall as if looking for a place to escape. Even Tom, usually so mild-mannered and always so silent, was not happy. He would stay close to Eleanor when she was working in the stillroom and there hadn't been any walks to collect supplies for over a week. Most afternoons she'd find him silently lining Jane's wooden animals up along the window seat in the solar and gazing out at the continuous rain running in rivulets down the tiny panes before finding tiny spaces where it could roll in, leaving pools on the sills.

So when Greville finally arrived home through the drenched landscape, there were few people outside to see his horse galloping along the road. And no sounds of hooves, their thundering absorbed by the sodden ground. Even the dogs were lying in front of the fire trying to keep warm, and it wasn't until he strode into the hall followed by his apprentice John, their saturated hats and cloaks moulded to them and water dripping onto the floor, that the household realised the master was home.

Eleanor, sat in the solar, was alerted by the sound of the hounds, finally awake and barking in excitement, their noise reverberating around the house. Tom, who of course hadn't heard any of it, continued with his game until the movement of Eleanor, dropping her sewing and running out of the room drew his attention, and he followed her to see where she was going in such a hurry.

'Wait a moment – I'm really wet.' Greville laughed as she threw herself into his arms.

'I don't care,' she replied with a wide smile, stepping away for a moment as he removed his cloak. 'I'm so happy to have you home. We didn't know when to expect you.' She followed him over to the fire where he stood with his clothes steaming, and ordered beer and food to be brought.

'I saw an opportunity and asked to be spared for a week, whilst we are stopped at Collyweston. I can't stay any longer than seven days and must then ride to rejoin the others at Stamford. I have brought something exciting to show you. Let me eat and drink and change into dry clothes, and I'll show you. Hello, young Tom.' His attention was diverted as he noticed the small boy stood to one side with his back against the panelling, quietly watching. Greville held his hand out and immediately Tom's wary countenance was split by a huge grin as he trotted over, sidestepping the hand stretched out towards him and pressing himself against Greville's leg. Despite his wet clothing, he laughed as he picked Tom up.

A moment later as his arrival became known throughout the house, there was a whirlwind on the stairs and Jane

311

rushed across the floor almost knocking Tom to one side as she greeted her father. Henry was more sedate, toddling steadily towards his mother whilst watching Greville carefully, unsure of who he was.

'Have you forgotten me, my son?' he asked, swinging the small boy into the air, tossing him up and catching him. It only took a few seconds before Henry was smiling and giggling with the rest of them, and Eleanor had to insist that Greville went and changed into dry clothes.

It was much later before he finally had the chance to show Eleanor what he'd brought home, the source of his excitement. He took her into their office and she noticed the usual paperwork piled on the trestle table was pushed to one end, leaving the rest of the space clear. From his travelling coffer on his desk, he collected a thick piece of folded vellum and proceeded to open it out, the rich creamy paper like a piece of fabric on the table. Eleanor looked at the drawing on it.

'Oh, it's Milfleet,' she exclaimed as she recognised first the tower and then the stairs to the great hall.

'It is,' he agreed, 'but not this section.' He pointed to the opposite corner. Eleanor frowned.

'No, you're right, that's different.' She was confused. 'We don't have rooms over there.'

'Not yet.' He smiled down at her, his eyes lit up with excitement. 'These are my plans to build a new wing. I had them drawn up in London and I hope to start organising the building of this latest part of our home whilst I'm here. It will make the place almost twice the size and who knows, maybe next year when the king and queen go on their summer tour, they'll visit us here.'

'Greville,' she breathed, 'that would be the most wondrous thing to ever happen to us. I wish it may be so. This new wing is huge though. It's very ambitious. Do we have funds? Can we afford it?'

'Of course we do, due to your saffron creating our new-found wealth. Which is why I've made the decision to change something else.' He pulled the rolled-up corner of the plan out flat and nodded his head towards the title, written at the bottom. For a moment, although Eleanor was looking at it, she couldn't understand but suddenly it dawned on her. Where it had originally said 'Milfleet', the title had been scored through and in elaborate penmanship, it was now inscribed 'Saffron Hall'.

'Saffron Hall?' She ran her fingers over the words. 'Are you changing the name of our home?'

'I am. We are. This is a new era for us and our family; I can feel it. And we wouldn't be able to achieve this without the spice you've grown in our fields. It's only right that we reflect the magnificence that has been brought upon us by acknowledging it. And in future, our crest will include an image of crocus flowers.' His face was split with a huge grin and his chest swelled with pride.

'Oh, thank you, Greville.' Her eyes welled up as she threw her arms around his neck, squeezing him tightly. 'This is the greatest honour you could bestow on me. I'm so pleased.'

She was as happy as he was, overseeing the planning of the new building for their home with a new name. He instructed Hugh to organise the removal of stone from the now derelict priory to be used for the new building. Eleanor wasn't happy about the use of the hallowed stone, but knew that if Greville wasn't using it, then someone else would. She tried hard to suppress her loyalty to the now departed brothers.

Every night Greville would tumble into bed beside her and they'd make love behind the drapes in the dark, afterwards lying together close in each other's arms, Eleanor demurely covered by her night rail and sticking slightly to Greville's bare, sweaty skin. Then, he would expand on all the plans he was forming to make the family as great as their neighbour, the Duke of Norfolk. How much grander Saffron Hall would be when the new work was completed, and how he was taking on a lease for a larger, smarter house in London.

He told Eleanor of the fine fabrics he was now importing in larger amounts than ever: the rich velvets that came from Venice, financed like almost everything else with the profits from the previous year's saffron.

'Are others at court jealous though?' she asked. 'Of your rise in finances and stature?' Whilst she was immensely proud of what he'd achieved because of her own contribution, she was worried he would attract the displeasure and envy of others. She knew there was always someone ready to try and pull another down so they may rise in his place. But Greville just laughed at her concerns and reassured her he was perfectly safe from anyone who may be envious of what he'd achieved.

She couldn't share his confidence though and would lie awake at night remembering the litany of names of people who'd fallen foul of the king. She was becoming scared of what she had unwittingly created. She had set her husband on the path he now trod, his elevated position at court, but equally if he fell foul of anyone, the responsibility would be hers. It was a heavy burden to bear.

314

Before long it was time for Greville to return to join the court on their progress, and Eleanor couldn't stop the tears welling up when he told her.

'I know you've enjoyed being at home,' she pointed out, her chin wobbling, 'and we love having you here. We're a proper family. Jane and Henry enjoy having you about, and Tom does I'm sure, even though he can't tell us. The whole house is happier so why don't you stay? You don't need to be at court, to be seen to be successful. Everyone knows you're rich now; surely you have nothing left to prove.' She couldn't voice her real worries, the danger of flying too close to the sun, to the king. She was too afraid to say the words.

'My dear, I will always have something to prove. To show my wealth continues to grow and that I'm popular. What I'm doing now is improving our family's standing so that Jane and Henry and God willing any more children we may have, and yes perhaps Tom as well, may marry into fine families with all the wealth and trappings they deserve. But to do that, I need to attract the right sort of friends, and contacts. I can't achieve anything stuck here in Norfolk. I must be in London where the king is. And now I hold a position at court, we're on our way to having all we desire.'

All that Greville desired was more to the point, Eleanor thought as she watched his panniers being filled ready for him to leave. Her delight at his ascendance was starting to wane. Although she, with her reckless flaunting of the law and the irresponsible concealing of the prior and Brother Rufus, could have so easily lost them everything they possessed. Including their lives. Perhaps, she reminded herself, she should be thankful they were still all together.

'Will you return to oversee the building work soon?' she

asked on their final night together as they lay side by side in bed. She hadn't yet slipped back into her shift and with the drapes slightly open and the cool draught blowing in, the full moon shone through the window and lit up the outline of her naked skin, its dips and rounded curves. Greville ran his fingertips down her thigh and over her hip to her waist, cupping her breasts with his warm hand and making her shudder with longing for him.

'I don't know. Hugh knows everything that is to be done, so you don't need to concern yourself with it. You have enough to do running the house and growing the saffron crops. Before you know it, it'll be harvest time once more.'

'We have planting before that,' she reminded him. 'We lifted the bulbs last year to split them.' She felt guilty at lying to him, but she needed an excuse for the dozen extra sacks of corms secreted in the tower room, her reward from the priory for helping the prior escape and in turn betraying her husband and his loyalty to the king, which had been moved from the barn where they'd been left. She hadn't told anyone they were there, but she'd asked Simon to plough a further two acres for the crocus stand. And, she told herself, Greville wouldn't be unhappy when the gold angels were pouring into his coffers again, once the spice had been sold.

Once he was back with the royal court, his letters continued to arrive, containing lavish tales of the progress as they slowly moved around the country. As the new building work on Saffron Hall continued, life for the rest of the family carried on much the same as ever before.

In July, Eleanor wrote to Greville.

My dear, I am so excited to tell you that I am once again with

316

child and I expect it to be born sometime in January. A new baby for a new year who will grow up to run through the rooms of our much-enlarged Saffron Hall. We are truly blessed.

She added that she hoped he may be home for Christmas and New Year, and be able to stay on to see his new child. His next letter acknowledged her news, expressing his delight, but he made no comment regarding whether this time he'd be at home for the birth. His omission spoke volumes.

Further letters told of his journey as they arrived in Pontefract and of the wondrous jousting and entertainment laid on for the king and queen. Then came one that was even more exciting, Eleanor's hand shaking as she read it.

My re-acquaintance with Francis Dereham has paid the dividends I was hoping for. He has arrived in Pontefract and been taken on as a secretary to the new Queen Catherine, with whom as you recall he had an affection when they resided under the same roof. And now due to our friendship, I have an appointment as well, assisting Dereham in his secretarial duties.

Her husband was working directly for the queen. She could hardly believe it; it was a dream come true. His letters were full of tales of Francis and himself, Queen Catherine and her ladies, and the entertaining times they were having at the great houses they visited as they made their way to York, where the king would be meeting up with King James. Eleanor couldn't imagine the exalted company Greville was now moving in.

'If Greville hadn't rekindled his friendship with Francis, this may never have happened,' she reminded Joan.

'Yes, how fortuitous that has turned out to be,' Joan replied with a pout.

Eleanor looked sideways at her friend, usually the most positive and relaxed of people. She realised that maybe Joan was becoming a little fed up of the tales of luxury that continued to be fed back through Greville's letters, compared to their humdrum lives governed as always by routine. Especially as Eleanor had confessed to her one day she'd suggested to Greville that Francis Dereham would have made a good match for Joan, but he'd disagreed.

Now Eleanor was concerned that every letter, every description of the gilded court life was a tiny stab in Joan's heart of all she'd missed out on. If Greville had agreed with Eleanor's suggestion then maybe it would have been she, Joan, following the king and queen, possibly even as one of the queen's ladies whilst her husband was the secretary. It was really no wonder that Joan was looking dissatisfied, her life drifting slowly past. All that was left to her was living as a companion, sister, and maiden aunt to Jane, Henry and the new baby, already growing visible under Eleanor's dresses. Even to Tom who continued to silently drift in and out of rooms so stealthily he was often in and gone again unnoticed.

Despite living vicariously through Greville's exciting life, nevertheless Eleanor still needed to manage the planting of her additional crocus corms. She didn't want to leave it to Simon to oversee the work, and even though her back throbbed and burned, she helped the farmworkers, pushing the bulbs into the carefully prepared ground. It took four full days until they were all planted, and after asking Joan to rub some ointment made with bay berries onto her back, Eleanor took to her bed for twenty-four hours.

When she finally emerged from her room a day later, it was to find another letter from Greville, this one sent from York where they were still waiting for King James to arrive. Apparently they had been waiting for over a week, which astonished Eleanor; who would keep the great King Henry waiting? Greville was most out of sorts at the sitting around, especially as the weather was as wet and dismal as it had been in Norfolk, and York smelled bad. No worse than London would, Eleanor thought spitefully. If he wanted fresh air he had a beautiful country estate he could return to. He also mentioned a new member of the queen's followers, a Thomas Culpeper who seemed to suddenly be in favour. Reading between the lines, Francis, and therefore Greville, appeared to have been pushed to one side by Culpeper and neither seemed very pleased with this new interloper.

As summer progressed the spindly pale green shoots of the crocus flowers emerged, shining against the hush of the muted brown earth. Finally the sun began to shine sporadically between the heavy clouds, and this was welcomed as the crops began to grow and only an occasional shower prevented everything completely drying out.

Two weeks later, Eleanor received a hastily scribbled note from Greville, saying King James had not appeared in York at all, and they were now on their return journey to London. They had moved on to Hull, but apparently the king was in the foulest of moods, and hadn't even visited the queen in recent days, so all was very subdued and quiet. He'd hoped to stop off in Norfolk on his way home but now felt it was imperative he remained with the court.

She remembered fondly the saffron harvest of previous years and had fervently wished that Greville could be excused from court to once again be at home to help, so this latest missive was a big disappointment. Last year Henry had been little more than a baby and now he was a proper little boy, talking non-stop and running everywhere and Greville was missing out on seeing him grow up. The child was immensely popular with the household, and was often found cadging sweetmeats from Cook who adored him, or running about outside with one of the farmers' boys. Nell had all but given up trying to make him behave like a gentleman's son, and she didn't hide the fact she preferred Jane with her quiet, delicate, feminine ways.

Eleanor thought it was doing Henry no harm to have the chance to run wild for a few years. Before he knew it he would be in breeches and a jerkin and sent away to school, or being brought up in a great house elsewhere. She knew Greville was hoping that with his rising fortunes and the distant family connection to his friends the Derehams, Henry may be offered a place at Framlingham, the Duke of Norfolk's grand home in Suffolk. But only time would tell. At least Tom would never be sent away. She put her hand down and sure enough touched the top of his head. He was always there, in the folds of her skirt stood at her feet, silent and waiting.

The sun brought the crocuses into flower a full week earlier than Eleanor was expecting. She had taken to walking the familiar path each morning, her shoulders slumped and her heart heavy as she remembered walking it with Greville the previous year, usually with Tom hopping silently between the footprints behind them. Even his clogs seemed as quiet as he was. And she recalled how they'd take the white manchet bread and fresh figs together with a flask of small beer and sit on the crisp dry grasses that skirted the field to break their fast. But this year she made the trip every day on her own.

The crocus stand was now huge. Indeed it was in fact two stands, as Simon had ordered the ploughing of common land beyond the meadow for planting. There was plenty of common land around the hall so she wasn't taking pasture the villagers used to graze their animals on.

She was not expecting the saffron to be ready quite so early. But, as she approached the field, shielding her eyes with her hands against the rising sun that splintered through the trees, she could see the tell-tale shivering, a sea of fluttering lilac petals, swaying and rolling in the early morning breeze, as far as the eye could see. They stretched to the horizon, dipping and bobbing. Turning on her heel she almost tripped over Tom stood behind her.

Holding his face in her hands she said, 'Time for the saffron harvest, Tom boy. We're going to be very busy, and your parents will be richer than ever.' She smiled at him and he smiled in return even though she knew he didn't understand a word that she had said. Leaving him on the path she went to find Simon to organise the workers.

The harvest was hard. Eleanor was relieved that her pregnant belly was still quite small and compact and so did not prevent her from joining in, both in the fields and in the drying room. Each day all the flowers that had opened needed to be picked during daylight hours so every available pair of hands had to be in the field, or in the hall below the tower room carefully plucking the saffron threads.

Nobody worked harder than Eleanor did, helping with both the harvesting and the de-threading of the flower heads long into the night. Finally, after the longest, most exhausting few weeks of her life, Eleanor stood in the middle of the tower room surveying the fruits of all their labours. Piled up in the room was sack upon sack of saffron cakes, the last batch still laid upon the remaining trestles, finishing drying.

A substantial amount was already stored downstairs in Eleanor's stillroom.

No surface of the house could escape the discarded petals from the flower heads which, now withered and dried, were being swept along by the ladies' skirts to all corners, despite the best efforts of a young servant girl, who'd been tasked with sweeping them up. She was thwarted in her job, however, by Jane, Tom and Henry who kept piling them up and launching themselves into the soft heap, spreading them far and wide. Eleanor couldn't help laughing, Tom clapping his hands in excitement and Nell scolding Jane for her unlady-like behaviour. Henry, however, did not receive a cross word as he gleefully scattered the petals, throwing armfuls into the air, and at anyone who got close to him.

Watching him, Eleanor wished once again Greville was at home. Not only because he'd have helped with the sheer exhaustion of organising the harvest, and the workforce, which had all fallen to her – Simon could arrange workers, but she'd agreed at the beginning that she would need to tell them when and where to harvest – but also to see the children enjoying themselves.

He would of course see the finished product, already the *Elizabeth Jane* was moored at Blakeney awaiting the sacks of spice. This year it was all bound for Calais where he could get a higher price than even the king's Clerk of the Spicery would pay. She wondered what sort of inferior saffron would be flavouring the court's dishes. As a memento of the harvest he hadn't seen, Eleanor had pressed a single crocus under the weight of several larger tomes. Once it was completely dried and flat, she transferred it to her book of hours.

If she was hoping for a visit home, or even a letter with his effusive thanks for the effort undertaken in producing such a significant crop of saffron and the riches it had produced, Eleanor was to be disappointed.

Instead, the next missive she received contained barely two lines acknowledging that his ship had arrived safely at its destination and his merchant there, along with Ralph, had sold it for a record fee. The letter mostly complained they had now returned to Windsor and the ambience was not as sunny and happy as it had been when they'd left. She was concerned at the change of circumstances, his letter so different from the ones sent during the summer.

From what she could make out, Francis was in a foul mood. He was no longer in favour with the queen, her new friend Thomas Culpeper the only person she talked about and Francis was not happy about the situation. Confused, Eleanor couldn't understand what Greville was alluding to. She read the letter out to Joan, who pursed her lips and shook her head.

'I thought Francis was the queen's secretary?' she asked. 'And Greville assists him?'

'Indeed, this is what I thought as well. I do not understand why so much of this letter is complaining about her spending time with this Thomas fellow. Why does he care so much? And he barely mentions the king. His previous letters have been all about seeing his Royal Highness, and dancing at wonderful feasts. Now, it's just about sitting in a little office scribing letters and listening to Francis moan.'

'Then why does he stay? There's the building work here to oversee, and you've just had to manage the whole of the saffron harvest on your own. You have another baby on the way. I do not understand why he's so determined to be at court if there is no more fun and jollity to be had?'

'Nor me,' Eleanor admitted, 'but he has always insisted the way to get on in life is to be noticed by the king. That way even greater riches lie, not just for us but also our children. So we must carry on here and hope he will return in time for the New Year celebrations, and the arrival of this new child.'

Eleanor didn't reply immediately to his morose letter; she was having trouble thinking of anything to say to him. If she pointed out once again that he didn't need to be seen at court all the time and perhaps now was a good time to return to his family, she'd be branded as a nagging wife, and a day-by-day account of their lives never changed so there was little to tell him about. Then a further letter arrived.

She was sitting in the office writing out the household accounts, when Hugh appeared at the door.

'A letter from London, mistress.' He stepped inside the room, bowed and handed it to her.

'Oh, thank you, Hugh.' She took it from him, her surprise evident on her face, and he raised his eyebrows in question. 'I received a letter only a couple of days hence,' she explained as she broke the seal. 'I hope Greville hasn't fallen ill. His last letter said there is sweating sickness and the court may be on the move again.' She opened the stiff paper carefully, pieces of the dried brittle wax falling to the floor as she spread the sheet out. She was aware Hugh was hovering and looking worried, so she let him wait whilst she quickly read, her heart thumping as she looked for mention of illness.

'No, he's not ill,' she reassured him, 'this is just about the king.' He nodded and gave her a perfunctory bow and left the room. Eleanor leant back in her chair. She had lied. It wasn't about the king but rather about the queen and she didn't really understand. She needed to read it more slowly, because the words weren't making sense. Instinctively she moved her hands to cover the swell of her belly in protection as a prickling of cold sweat crawled down her spine making her shudder. Suddenly she felt very afraid.

Chapter Thirty

2019

'Well that's the end of that plan.' Amber and Becky were back in the library. Amber was peering out the window at the oppressive scaffolding that still rang with the continuous hammering and thumping from above their heads.

'No it's not.' Amber's response came out sharper than she'd intended, but the more Grandad had presented reasons why she shouldn't go up the tower, the more she was desperate to do it. 'I'll just have to be more careful.'

'Seriously? You could get hurt. Or worse. This is mad, Amber. And as there isn't a key – you'll have to go up the scaffolding. How are you going to do that, without your grandfather seeing you?'

'I know it's daft, but I can't stop myself. I'm not going up the scaffolding; I'll go up the stairs. I can go at night while he's asleep. It takes a lot to wake him up.'

'I expect the tower crashing to the ground with you under it will manage to wake him though,' Becky pointed out shortly.

'I'll find a crowbar for the door.' Now she'd made a decision, Amber was in full planning mode. 'In fact we have one back at home. I'll call Jonathan and ask if I can collect it. Actually, maybe he could bring it over. We might need to use brute strength. I knew his university rowing days would come in useful one day. I'll invite him for dinner. Grandad would like to see him, then once it's all quiet we can sneak up there.'

'Do you think Jonathan will agree to your going up there, knowing it's unsafe? Because I don't.'

'I accept he may take some persuasion, but I know him. If I'm going up he won't let me go on my own in case it's dangerous.'

She was captivated that they'd suddenly realised the tower possibly held a secret the house had been holding at its heart for hundreds of years, each generation preventing the next from investigating by frightening off anyone from going up there. Maybe the forgotten family jewels would be piled up in a cupboard like Aladdin's Cave. She smiled; it was a nice thought, but unlikely. More importantly, she had the strongest feeling that some special connection to Eleanor was up there, pulling her towards it. A bond with the past and she knew she wanted, no needed, Jonathan by her side when she finally got into the tower to investigate. She put her hand against her heart. It felt like there was a butterfly in her chest, fluttering its wings in an attempt to break free.

Jonathan, surprised by her offer of dinner with the caveat that he brought his crowbar, nevertheless readily agreed. Any time he could spend with his wife, he'd grab with both hands. Unfortunately work commitments decreed he'd be

328

unable to get to the hall until the following Monday. Amber silently ground her teeth in frustration, but politely thanked him and told him truthfully she was looking forward to seeing him. Even without the anticipation of the tower investigations, she realised how much she wanted to feel his arms around her, holding her close. Her desire to hide away from the world was fading, finally being blown away by the cold winter winds.

Amber spent the next few days hard at work cataloguing Grandad's books, the evenings devoted to continuing her analysis of the book of hours, meticulously reading each page and making notes. There was another entry by Eleanor, but it was simply a recipe for some of the coloured inks she was using. Nevertheless, she translated it alongside the psalms, prayers and other entries. Amber was intrigued to see that under the recipe, Eleanor had also noted: *Tom was able to assist with this preparation using his hands and cards to talk for him. His eagerness to help is increasing his abilities far beyond what others have expected of him, I have been proved correct in my faith of him and my decision to make him a part of our family.*

She looked back through her notes to find other references to Tom. Why did others not want him as part of the family? Had they taken him in? She knew it would not have been unusual for a child or orphan to be taken on as a servant but not usually welcomed into the family unless he was a relative. It sounded as if he were disabled the way she described him, but she'd probably never know.

Finally, Monday arrived. Jonathan called to tell her he'd leave home as soon as the evening rush hour had passed, and expected to be with her around seven o'clock. For Amber, who'd been counting the hours since they'd made the arrangement, the time ticked past excruciatingly slowly. After a slow day in the library where she couldn't settle to anything, she'd gone upstairs to shower and change at five o'clock. Dinner was a simple roast and the meat had been in the oven on a low heat for most of the afternoon. Mindful of what she would be doing later, she pulled on some jeans and a jumper that would offer her some protection against any creepy-crawlies and dirt.

Grandad, who had told her twice already how much he was looking forward to what he kept referring to as the 'dinner party', frowned as she walked into the lounge.

'Not dressing up then?' he asked.

'Why would I? It's Jonathan. I haven't invited royalty.'

'It's always nice to make an effort, especially for your husband,' he reproved, and she was ashamed to notice that he had indeed put on a clean shirt and a tie. But, she reminded herself, he wasn't crawling about in dark and possibly dank places later. Goodness knew what she may encounter.

Jonathan arrived as ever, at exactly the time he said he would. If it had been anyone else, Amber would have imagined they'd sat at the end of the drive in the village until one minute to arrival time, but she'd been on enough journeys with him to know his timing was impeccable. Another of the things she loved about him.

'Hello.' Amber hugged him hard, holding him against her for several moments, breathing in his familiar musky aftershave and resting her head against the comforting warmth of his chest before reaching up and kissing him softly. She closed her eyes and wished it could go on forever. 'You're looking well.'

'You too,' he replied, 'you've filled out and you're a better colour now.' She knew from looking in the mirror every morning that the pale luminosity that had left her skin dull and opaque and the flat look in her eyes, was slowly being replaced with some of the glow and sparkle she used to have.

Amber looked behind him. 'Did you bring your tools?' Her voice was slightly accusing, worried he'd arrived empty-handed.

'Yes, yes, you sent enough texts reminding me.' Laughing at her impatience he went to the boot of his car and returned with the old canvas bag of tools she immediately recognised. Passed on to him by his mother after his father died, it seemed to contain every tool for any occasion. She was certain he'd be able to find something they could use to jemmy open the door.

'Put them back for now,' she whispered frantically, 'and whatever happens, do NOT mention to Grandad that I asked you to bring them, okay? I'll explain later.' He looked puzzled but nodded his agreement.

The dinner was a joyous occasion, and although Amber was on edge the whole time wanting to get it over with, eager to start her investigations of the tower, she couldn't deny she'd had a lovely evening. They were in high spirits, helped by the wine that flowed freely and the appetising food. There was only one uncomfortable moment when, not realising he was about to stir up a hornets' nest, Jonathan asked how the repairs to the tower were going, and Grandad explained how Amber had asked about going up there.

'He's told me not to – apparently it's some old family folklore about not setting foot in the tower,' Amber hastily told Jonathan as she passed round cups of coffee, hoping to divert the conversation. 'I still fail to see what the issue is.'

'There are things best left untouched,' Grandad reminded her sternly, getting to his feet and taking his coffee cup into the sitting room. Amber frowned.

'I don't like doing things he disapproves of,' she admitted, 'but I'm going up there. I really feel this is going to help me unravel Eleanor's message. I know she's depending on me — I have to do it.'

'Wait,' Jonathan hissed, 'is that why you were so insistent that I brought the tool bag? You're not seriously contemplating going up there? For goodness' sake, Amber, the tower is only being held up by that metal frame around the outside. It's not safe!'

'Shhhh.' She looked over at the open kitchen door. 'Don't let Grandad hear you. I have to go up there and see what's at the top. I must. For hundreds of years, my ancestors have been too frightened to go up, and I want to know why. And more importantly, Eleanor needs me to understand why. I think that's where she hid the prior and whoever was with him, and I want to see for myself. Since Kenny announced he'll have to take the tower apart, the sense of urgency I've felt from Eleanor has become more intense. And it's now or never before even more of the tower disintegrates. You don't have to come up, but I do need your assistance in getting the door open please. As you heard Grandad say, there isn't a key. But in all honesty, I would love you to be with me. Whatever was up there, or is up there now, I want to find it with you by my side.'

Jonathan pursed his lips and said nothing, but she could sense the extreme displeasure emanating from him in waves.

Eventually after watching the news, Grandad said goodnight to them both, and went to bed. Amber listened to every creak of the floor above their heads until she was content he was asleep and wouldn't be appearing behind them to ask what they were doing. They hurried through the house to the hallway at the base of the tower. Amber could feel the heavy oppressive weight of anticipation from above them, a collective holding of breath. Whatever her family had shunned for hundreds of years was now waiting for this night. She was scared, but knew she had to continue, and she was thankful that Jonathan was with her. He tried lifting the latch and giving the door a hard shake, but it didn't shift.

'It's definitely locked,' he announced.

Amber looked at him and rolled her eyes. 'Which is why I need your lock-picking expertise,' she told him, 'and if that fails, something big to wrench open the door with.'

'Well I have zero skills unpicking locks. I'm afraid I failed my burglary GCSE so crowbar it is.' He lifted the heavy object and held it out as if exhibiting an item at an auction. Amber gave him a thumbs-up before putting her fingers in her ears and wincing as the wooden door and frame began to splinter under the force of being prised open.

The ancient, fragile timber only took a couple of minutes to part company with the door as it swung out into the hallway, revealing a small space behind and a set of stone steps that disappeared around to the left, curving away into the dark. The air smelled musty and dank and Jonathan screwed up his face a little.

'It doesn't smell very pleasant,' he stated the obvious.

'You spend your life between churches and old people's homes – you should be used to it,' Amber retorted, rummaging through his tool bag looking for the torch she knew he kept there. Her hand curled around it and she pulled it out.

'Who's going first then?' she asked, raising her eyebrows and looking at him. 'Me?'

'No, definitely not you – I will.' Jonathan took it from her. 'We don't know how safe it is. You can follow. Have you got a torch of your own?' Wordlessly she pulled out her mobile phone and switched it on, before slowly beginning to climb the steep icy-cold stone steps behind him. They were damp and slimy with a thin film of lichen coating them, lit from time to time by arrow-slit windows in the external wall.

Finally they reached the top, and out of breath they held on to the rough-hewn stone and flint walls as Jonathan, who'd had the forethought to carry the crowbar with him, forced the door at the top of the stairs. With a loud crack it fell open, flooding them with fresh air from above, and they climbed the last steps into the room, a sanctuary for the family's secrets.

'Wow, it's amazing.' Amber turned in a three hundred and sixty degree circle, taking in the stone mullion window and ancient tiny leaded panes of glass, which was still in situ. The other window and a small piece of wall were missing, revealing the tranquil night yawning wide, the darkness of an eternity watching them. On the wall opposite the windows stood a blackened fireplace, a gaping hole still coated in soot, which stretched up the wall behind it, waiting for a fire to be lit. A rough wooden trestle table, feathered at the edges with splinters, stood against another wall. The floor was ankle deep in a mixture of stone dust and fragments of leaves that somehow hadn't disintegrated over the years. An occasional twig or piece of dry grass could also be seen poking out.

Amber was certain she was being watched, every atom of

air holding its breath in anticipation as if it had been waiting for her, for five hundred years.

'So what was the big secret up here?' she asked, holding her arms out. 'Why was it so imperative nobody came up, every generation resolved to scare the next and keep them away? There aren't any cupboards or alcoves to hide treasure, let alone monks. Nothing. I think I made a mistake, maybe translated the book incorrectly. There isn't anything here, apart from a thick layer of dust and ancient debris on the floor.' She slid the side of her foot into a big arc, pushing the floor covering to one side and revealing the old slabs beneath.

'Wow, these flagstones look old. Really old.' Jonathan crouched on his haunches and swept more of the floor with his hands, revealing the slabs beneath. 'They can't have seen the light of day for centuries, until that bolt of lightning and the builders getting up here.'

'No,' Amber grumbled, 'because my weird family have been determined to keep this room as some sort of shrine, or mystery.'

'Let's clear the floor,' he suggested as he began to sweep across it with his foot as Amber had done. 'If there's anything underneath all this we should be able to feel it as we clear it away. Do it slowly and methodically though, so we don't miss anything.'

Feeling disappointed and let down by the lack of any great reveal, Amber despondently joined in sweeping the floor as best she could and when the dusty leaves and hay were in a pile in the corner of the room, she removed her jumper, flicking it across the slabs to reveal them properly.

'It's a lovely room,' she said. 'Just imagine having this as a study. You'd never get any work done with views from the window like these. Look, I can just about make out the village church and the pub. I bet in daylight you can see the sea.'

'There's something wrong with the floor here,' Jonathan interrupted her as she gazed out of the window. She looked across to where he was crouched on the floor. He'd been banging his feet close together, slowly making his way cautiously across the room.

'Listen,' he said, holding his hand up as she opened her mouth to speak, but he started stamping down on various slabs. 'This one sounds different. I think maybe there's something under here. It sounds hollow as if there's a space underneath. That may explain what Eleanor wrote in her book. I know from previous reading that when Cromwell's commissioners came looking for Catholic heretics they were often hidden in spaces between walls, or under floors. A priest hole. I wonder if that's what is here. Although, if it is, I have no idea why your family have been so determined to stop anyone coming up here. We already know they got away.'

'Maybe for safety reasons?' Amber suggested. 'So no exploring child accidentally shut themselves in? Although I've always considered health and safety a twenty-first-century obsession. Is there a way we can open it?' She added, 'It might be full of Tudor gold – a pile of family treasure would be rather nice.'

Jonathan laughed. 'That would be good yes, but don't get your hopes up. Here, give me a hand. There's a small lip here under the edge but my hands are too big. It needs small slim fingers like yours.'

Amber knelt on the floor where he'd been and found the

tiny space. It wouldn't have been visible to anyone unless they knew it was there, especially with the floor covered in rushes, or a carpet.

Once she had pushed her fingers under as far as possible, she muttered, 'One, two, three,' and bracing herself as she counted, she pulled up sharply. The stone lifted slightly, and Jonathan quickly put his hands under, helping her to move it to one side.

'That wasn't as heavy as I was expecting,' Jonathan said, peering into the dark hole they had exposed. 'Blimey it really smells, doesn't it?'

He wasn't wrong. Amber had her hand over her nose and mouth, but nothing could stop the damp, stale, fetid stench that rose from the dark, turning her stomach and making her eyes water. She took a step backwards. All around her the darkness swirled and shifted, moving about, and she felt as if she was falling. The edge of a knife slicing through the air between her world and the past. Jonathan picked up his torch and Amber watched, as if he was down the wrong end of a telescope, far away. She heard his questioning voice as he peered in, but he sounded distorted and strange, muffled.

Someone else was standing there, close beside her without making contact. She didn't need to turn her head, or move a hand to feel her. She knew who it was. The smell from the hole at her feet had been displaced by the soft scent of warm hay, honey, and crushed pepper, which swirled around, enveloping her.

Jonathan swung his powerful torch beam into the space. 'It's quite deep, about five foot I would say. There's something at the bottom. I think it's a bundle of rags.'

'It's a baby.' Amber heard her voice although she hadn't realised she'd spoken. 'Not rags, a baby. It's Mary, we found her.' She felt a flood of warmth, love, and gratitude spin through her just for a moment, and Eleanor was gone. Putting her hands to her face she realised her cheeks were awash with tears.

'You can rest easy, Eleanor,' she whispered into the silence of the tower. 'I'll look after your daughter now.'

Chapter Thirty-One

2019

The hall had been swamped with police for what felt like weeks, but had actually only been a matter of days. Amber felt exhausted as she hid in her bedroom away from the noise and mayhem. She knew it was protocol that the tower was now a crime scene – even the library was out of bounds – and despite her insistence that the bones in the linen wrapping Jonathan had taken from the hole under the floor would be a five-hundred-year-old infant, they still had to be forensically examined and a full coroner's inquest instigated.

Grandad found her one evening making a cup of tea, the house strangely quiet after all the comings and goings. There had been numerous villagers who suddenly found the need to trek up the long drive with a spurious reason to visit. Thankfully a local bobby had been positioned outside the house to deter people from knocking at the door, and also to prevent the local press from calling. The national papers had lost interest when it had been confirmed this wasn't a

339

murder investigation and they were ancient bones, and the local television van had only bothered with a quick two-minute piece from the car park at the priory ruins.

'Why don't you go and stay with Jonathan for a few days?' Grandad suggested as he watched her abandon her tea to gaze absentmindedly out of the window. 'You've nearly finished archiving all my books, and you need a few days' break. Then you can come back if you like, finish off here and decide what you want to do with the rest of your life.'

Amber smiled. He made it sound so simple, and thankfully now maybe it was. Already she'd had emails from HR asking about a return date. Saffron's birthday was less than a month away.

'That's a good idea,' she told him. 'Will you be okay here though, if I went home for maybe a week?'

'Don't be daft.' Grandad waved his right hand at her. 'I've lived here all these years on my own and your stay was always going to be a temporary one. Go and spend some time with that husband of yours. Do you want to take the book of hours with you?'

'No, it can stay here. It belongs here at least until I finish reading it. Eleanor is gone now, I'm certain of it. I haven't felt her since we found Mary. I'll call Jonathan and let him know I'm coming home for a few days, if you're sure.'

'Sure I'm sure.' Grandad smiled. 'Go home to your husband.'

Within twenty-four hours it was all arranged. Amber had packed up her laptop and some clothes and was driving back to the vicarage, looking forward to being at home. Becky admitted that although she'd miss Amber, she was delighted her friend was getting away from the sadness still hanging in the air at the hall. And she was hoping that they would soon be back working together. She'd also suggested that she and Pete meet up at the pub with Amber and Jonathan in the near future, and Amber readily agreed.

Jonathan managed to move most of his work commitments so they were able to spend some time together. It was almost like a second honeymoon, each day filled with carefully planned activities and usually involving a long walk – Jonathan even suggested a dog might not be such a bad idea after years of resistance – followed by a pub dinner and far more wine than either of them were used to. Amber was happy to share their bed again and it felt natural and right that when they lay together each night they resumed the lovemaking they'd both missed.

Even going with him to visit Saffron's grave no longer consumed her with grief. She was still sad, and knew that the fast approaching anniversary of that day would be difficult, but the raw sharpness of the pain was now smoother at the edges, a dull ache that would remain with her forever, but she could accept as part of her life. Standing in the nursery and looking out over the graveyard to where her daughter lay now gave her a tiny sliver of comfort, just as it had been for Jonathan when she'd accused him of not caring. He'd just been caring in his own way; she could see that now.

The morning she was due to return to Grandad, as they sat eating a leisurely late breakfast, Amber's phone rang with a Norwich number she didn't recognise, although she instantly recognised the voice of PC Whitlock with his familiar local accent.

'Just to let you know, the coroner and the osteologist have completed their findings on the bones found. There'll be a full report at a later date but as you suspected, they came from a female baby, somewhere around seven months' gestation and about four hundred and fifty years old. We can hand the remains over to the council who'll organise a burial, or you can have them back if you'd like to sort it.'

'Yes, yes please.' Amber spoke quickly. 'We'd like them back. My husband is a vicar – he'll arrange a burial.' She pointed at the pad and pen at the end of the table and Jonathan quickly passed them to her. Scribbling the details of the mortuary where the remains were being held, she thanked the policeman before saying goodbye.

'I hope that's okay.' She pulled an apologetic face at Jonathan. 'I said we'll organise a funeral for Mary, but I want to do it, for Eleanor. It's what she asked to be done and I feel it's me she was waiting for, to unearth what she was trying to tell us. We had an affinity. Mary had been left beneath her feet, and now she deserves a proper, Christian burial. She's waited a long time for it. I wish I could inter her with Eleanor where she really belongs, but we've never found any grave or records to indicate where that is. I wonder if that's why the family were always so keen to prevent anyone going up in the tower – because they knew she was up there.'

'It's more likely that before it was used as a hole for hiding religious runaways, it was used to hide their wealth so whoever was the lord or lady didn't want any nosy servants going up, in case they found the family treasure.'

'And all these years she's been up there resting until I could find her. If I hadn't been at the hall when we had the storm that damaged the tower, who knows when the book, and her message, would have been discovered. But now I can do as she asked, all these hundreds of years ago, and make sure Mary is buried in consecrated ground.'

'I think we should do it here,' Jonathan suggested, 'bury her next to Saffron. After all Eleanor may have been an ancestor of yours.'

'Thank you, I'd really like that.' She was warmed by his thoughtfulness, another of his characteristics she'd closed her eyes to. She'd been so short-sighted. 'Do you think it will be okay?'

'You told me that neither of her parents or siblings are buried in the village. So let's have her close to us eh? Where she's got someone to look over her. Eleanor would have wanted that.' He smiled at her and raised his eyebrows, waiting for her to agree.

'You're right, of course you are. You always know the correct thing to do. I'm so thankful to have you.' She took his hands in hers. 'Let's organise it together.'

And so it was on a windswept afternoon with soft white clouds scudding across a cobalt blue sky above them that Amber, her grandfather, and Jonathan laid Mary's bones to rest beside Saffron, in the children's corner of the graveyard. The bones and her linen shroud were enclosed in a tiny white coffin. Together, Amber and Jonathan shovelled the earth back into the hole whilst Grandad walked slowly back to the vicarage. It was so small it only took them fifteen minutes to complete the job. Amber took a bunch of gypsophila and divided it, putting some on the mound of bare damp soil and some onto Saffron's grave now covered in grass.

'Once the grave has settled, we'll get a headstone, shall we?' Jonathan suggested, his hand slipping around hers, and she nodded. She waited for the tears, and then realised they weren't coming.

'And I shall plant crocus bulbs for her,' she answered.

'So what happens now? Have you given it any thought, where we go from here?' Jonathan asked, brushing the wet earth from his hands, before taking her fingertips in his and gently stroking the mud from hers.

'Yes, of course I've thought about it. About everything. It's all so different now, compared to how I felt when I went to stay with Grandad. I'm still sad, of course I am, but back then I couldn't see any future because it wouldn't have Saffron in it. All our plans were suddenly blown apart and if I didn't want to be with myself, why would you or anyone else? I hated myself.'

Jonathan took her shoulders in both of his hands and looked down into her eyes. He was frowning as he told her, 'I never thought that though. I always wanted for us to be together.'

'I know, but I had to work that out for myself. To realise that life does go on, that we have to keep breathing and have hope. And that we do have a future even though it's not the one we planned.' She paused for a moment and took a deep breath. 'Saffron will always be a part of us though.'

'Of course she will, she's our firstborn. And perhaps one day she'll have siblings and we'll tell them about their sister with the yellow-gold curls. Do you think so? Maybe?'

Amber drew in a shuddering breath before smiling softly and replying, 'Yes, yes I do, I'd like that.'

Jonathan put his arm around her shoulder and held her tight as together they walked back to the vicarage. For the first time in almost a year, there was no distance between them. Not physically, not emotionally.

Later, Amber drove Grandad home, her suitcase once again in the boot of the car. She had some important tasks she wanted to complete before she returned to work in two weeks' time. There was the archiving of his books to finish, and she needed to read to the end of Eleanor's book before she handed it over to the museum. She was certain it held one final secret – the reason why none of the family were buried nearby, and why Mary had been hidden by her mother in a hole under the floor in the tower.

Chapter Thirty-Two

1541

As Eleanor finished reading Greville's letter to Joan she looked up from the page, her face white as the blood drained from it.

'So what does it all mean?' Joan asked, her voice squeaking a little, belying the uneasiness she tried to hide.

'I'm not entirely sure,' Eleanor admitted, 'but I'm sick with worry. Everybody sounds so furtive, as if they're all hiding secrets. The queen is being kept in her rooms by her ladies, and nobody may enter. She's been visited by this . . .' she paused to look at the letter '. . . Thomas Wriothesley, and apparently he is usually sent to investigate any wrongdoings. If he turns up at your door you would be right to be scared. And the king is in a really bad mood so everyone is staying well out of his way. Greville sounds . . . I don't know, confused I think. He may act as if he is well used to the ways of court, but I suspect he isn't, really. Perhaps as the king has a reputation for being

347

hot-tempered, court often gives way to these violent and dramatic outbursts. I'm worried that Greville even sent a missive like this: suppose someone had intercepted it? The court is in turmoil and he is inadvertently inviting danger to his door and indeed to our home, if anyone caught wind of what he has sent.'

'Do you think the king has had enough of Queen Catherine already?' Joan suggested. 'Although that does seem unlikely. Remember Greville told you how besotted the king is? How young and pretty and flirtatious she is? Surely he must be hoping to beget another son with her, since it is a good few years since our sweet departed Queen Jane gave birth to Prince Edward. He's probably just ill or feeling his age, or his leg is paining him again and before you know it Greville will be writing with happier news about gay times and festivities at court,' she reassured.

Eleanor nodded, but in her heart she didn't feel as optimistic as her friend. There was something in the letter that hadn't been said, something between the lines she couldn't understand and it filled her with apprehension. More, it was what her husband hadn't told her, rather than what he had. Why was he telling her the minutiae of day-to-day happenings at court, letters Francis had been told to scribe, the comings and goings from the queen's chambers, that had nothing to do with him? An icy-cold panic was fluttering in her chest. This would have been sent over a week ago. What had happened since then?

The feeling of unease that his letter had brought refused to leave Eleanor. She couldn't shake off the unsettled thoughts taunting her, a spiteful whispering that grew and grew until in the dark of the night with just the soft calling of the owls and the turning and kicking of her baby for company, her head was spinning with fear for her husband.

She desperately wanted Greville back home with his family at Saffron Hall. It had been five months since they'd lain together, planning the extension to their home, the excitement of it being renamed Saffron Hall. And they'd created the new baby that now stirred inside her. A black shadow of guilt and doubt sat on her shoulders out of her eye line, but she knew it was there. If she hadn't been so successful in growing the saffron, Greville's finances wouldn't have increased and he wouldn't have moved into the wealthy circles that had raised his profile at court. The ones that meant their neighbour thought him worthy enough to be introduced to the queen. To be working for her. To be caught up within her circle of acquaintances and close friends.

She tried to put her worries to the back of her mind during the days that followed, instead concentrating on making the medicines and ointments she knew the household would require during the oncoming winter. With the monks no longer at the priory and their infirmary gone, the villagers would be turning to whoever they could to cure illnesses or mend their injuries, and she was now the most proficient person in the area. She'd already patched up two separate nasty gashes caused during harvesting, her poppy stalk and honey poultices preventing the wounds from becoming infected. Going out to collect the plants and flowers she required gave her the peace she needed to mull over the demons that continued to haunt her.

When Hugh came to her with another letter not ten days after the previous one, Eleanor's heart lurched and she felt a surge of acid bile rise in her throat. Her eyes caught his and he looked at her gravely.

'Do you know what's in this?' she accused, her voice sharp as she took it from him.

'No, mistress.' He shook his head vehemently. 'See, the seal is not broken. But I too have received a missive from the master, and the contents are somewhat disquieting.' He turned to go but Eleanor touched his arm, stopping him for a moment.

'Wait, please, while I find out what he says?' She also wanted to know what Hugh's letter said as well, given how worried he looked, but first she needed to read her own. Taking it to the window she cracked the seal as she ran her finger across the thick vellum, opening it. She read through it twice, her lips moving and her hands shaking so violently it made reading difficult, and eventually she looked up. Hugh had been joined by Joan and they were standing together in the doorway. He must have gone to look for her, although Eleanor hadn't noticed.

'This is even more concerning and confusing than the last letter.' Her voice came out as a croak.

'What does he say?' Joan asked. She gently moved Eleanor to a chair and pushed her down into it. Her knuckles shone white where she held fast to Eleanor's shoulders, as if she might flee at any moment.

'He says there are rumours the queen is to be taken to somewhere called Syon House. And that Francis Dereham has been accused of piracy when he was in Ireland, and taken to the Tower, for questioning.'

'Is that all he says? Will he be going with the queen? Is he still working for her if Dereham is arrested?'

Eleanor held her hand up to halt the barrage of questions.

'I don't know.' Her voice wobbled as tears clogged her throat, threatening to choke her. 'He doesn't say.' She put her hands protectively around her belly as if shielding her unborn baby from the sticky, tangible fear that hung in the air as they breathed out. 'What did your letter say, Hugh?' She looked across, willing him to give her some positive news, but the look on his face told her she wouldn't be getting any. He paused before taking a deep breath.

'Nothing more than yours, mistress.' He looked at the floor and Eleanor knew he wasn't telling her the truth. Hugh had been hostile towards her when she had first arrived in Norfolk. It had been obvious he didn't think such a young girl should be married to his master and be the mistress of the house, and back then he'd made his feelings known. Slowly though, over the intervening years, his attitude to her had mellowed, and she'd started to believe that now he held some respect for her, but this was about to be tested.

'Hugh.' Her voice was sharp and his head jolted up. 'What did it really say?'

Joan's head was twisting between the two of them unsure of what was going on, having taken Hugh's word for what he had said.

He gave Eleanor a wry smile. 'You're clever, mistress,' he admitted, with a tight smile. 'Sir Greville told me the court is in turmoil and he thinks the charges against Dereham are trumped up. That actually his arrest is something to do with the fact that the king keeps to his rooms all the time, and the queen is shrieking and wailing all day and all night. And that other man, Thomas Culpeper, is also in the Tower.'

'Could it be that Francis has caused a rift between his

Majesty and Queen Catherine?' Eleanor asked. She remembered how good-looking and debonair he had seemed on the day they visited him at Crimplesham. With his dark shining curls and deep velvet eyes, his sensual lips and sharp cheekbones, the way he'd flirted even with her, his confident self-assurance. Any young woman may have her head turned. Especially if Greville's description of the queen was true: that she had a coquettish nature, and liked to surround herself with handsome young men. That description certainly fitted Francis and they of course were old friends. More than friends, she remembered. No wonder Greville had been quick to quash any idea of her matching Francis with Joan.

'I don't know, I can't see how,' Hugh replied. 'The letter doesn't say that. He just asks that I take care of you and his family, and the house.'

'Take care of us? But why? Where's he going? Why doesn't he just leave court and come home?' Eleanor's hands twisted together.

'I think we'll just have to wait and see what news comes next,' Hugh placated them. 'There's nothing more we can do at present. Not until we know more.'

'I'm going to write to him, right now,' Eleanor decided, 'and ask him to return home. I won't refer directly to what he's told us or mention Dereham, but he needs to be back in Norfolk as soon as possible.' She told Hugh to ensure there was a boy and a horse ready to take her letter and she began to sharpen a quill. When she was on her own again, she looked at the last lines of her letter, which she hadn't read out to the others. *I think of you always, my sweet croker, with the pale blanket of lilac crocuses, which was our destiny, laid out before you*. It seemed so final, as if he was telling her something she didn't dare understand.

The next fourteen days dragged interminably. Eleanor had ordered the lifting of all of the crocus bulbs so they could be planted in fresh grounds the following year. She was relieved that Simon didn't question her decision; she had a terrible feeling in her gut and she wanted her biggest commodity to be in the hall with her, not hidden beneath the cold, hard earth outside. The winter weather was beginning to close in, sudden squalls of rain that held flecks of ice, which stung faces and caused skin to become red and chapped. Lips and fingertips began to peel and split, and Eleanor barely had time to leave the stillroom as she prepared ointments to be smeared onto sore skin. Keeping busy, however, didn't prevent her mind from wandering constantly to London and fretting continuously over where Greville was, and what was happening. Her body trembled with worry from the moment she woke up from her fitful sleep and her darkest fears edged back into her head, jostling for attention amongst the day-to-day concerns.

She had no idea whether everything had blown over and the king and queen were happy once more and making the baby everyone hoped and prayed for. Perhaps Francis and Greville were so busy with their work there was simply no time to write a letter home. She bolstered herself with these thoughts to try and find some comfort, a reassurance, but deep down she wasn't being fooled. Until word came, she couldn't relax.

When a boy eventually arrived with a letter, she was too afraid to open it. This time there was only one, nothing for

Hugh, and he stood in front of her waiting for her to read it. Breaking the seal, she opened it and read slowly.

As she read the short passage slowly her eyes grew larger until with a keening howl she dropped the letter to the floor and covered her eyes with her hands. Bending and scooping up the piece of parchment, Hugh called out for Joan who came running from the kitchen.

'What is it?' she cried. 'Is it the baby?'

'Another letter.' Hugh held it up for her to see but carried on reading what it said.

'Well, what news?' Joan crouched down beside Eleanor, clutching her cold hands in her own.

'Francis Dereham is being held in the Tower charged with treason. Of lying with the queen,' Hugh read out. Joan gasped and crossed herself and Eleanor's crying grew louder. 'Apparently they considered themselves betrothed when they lived with the Dowager Norfolk at Horsham and Lambeth, but that was before the queen was even at court. And now Dereham has been put on the rack. And that Culpeper, he's also to be executed for treason.'

'But what does this mean for Sir Greville?' Joan asked. 'He hasn't done anything wrong!'

'Indeed,' Hugh agreed grimly, 'however, merely the fact he is a friend of Dereham's and being there at court means he may be accused of helping the couple to meet and carry out any infidelity. He says he is worried for his own safety, but is not allowed to leave. He fears he may be the next to be arrested.'

'What will happen if he is?' Joan couldn't stop herself firing questions at Hugh.

'What do you think?' shouted Eleanor, tears and spittle

flying from her face. 'They'll torture him too until he admits things that never happened. He shouldn't have taken that position with the queen. If he'd just stayed as he was, none of this would be happening.' Even as she uttered the words, she knew nothing could have been done to change the course of events. From the moment she'd pushed that first crocus bulb into the dark, sticky soil, she, Eleanor, had put him on the road that led to this moment. She had sealed his fate. It had been God's will that had made the saffron grow so well, year after year. The strong and fruitful harvests, the new bulbs growing on the old ones and increasing their yield. The sacks of corms that had arrived from the priory. Every single action had steered Greville's path to where he was today. A rich and well-connected merchant and courtier whose old family friend had given him a helping hand to be working on the fringes of the queen's inner circle, and who may now possibly lead to his downfall. It was all in God's plan, but executed by herself.

'Shall I send the boy back to London with a reply, mistress?' Hugh asked, his calm voice cutting into Eleanor's tears.

'Yes, of course. I don't know what to say that I didn't say in my last letter, but it may help him to know that everything is as it should be here at home and the children are all well.' At the thought of Jane, Henry and Tom her eyes filled with tears again. Getting stiffly to her feet, she went to her desk and tried to think of a way of wording her letter without including anything that could incriminate Greville if it fell into the wrong hands. In the end she simply wrote a few lines with general household news and saying how much she missed him, especially when she was only a few months away from her confinement. She doubted her news could in any way influence anyone if they wanted to take him away for questioning, but if someone wanted to read her words the wrong way, however innocent they were, she had no doubt it would be done.

It was almost as if time stood still at the newly named Saffron Hall. No longer could Eleanor pretend everything was normal. Every time she thought she heard the pounding of horses' hooves she hurried to the window to see if it was a letter from London, but nothing came. She had no energy as she dragged her heavy body from room to room, her hands wrapped protectively around her swollen belly, or sitting close to the fire, but shivering from an icy chill deep inside her that wouldn't leave. She tried to smile and look interested when the children came to see her, but her eyes were blank and eventually Nell kept them out of sight in the nursery, carrying their food up there as well.

The exception was Tom, who'd never conformed to Nell's rules – she suspected he used his inability to hear as a reason to ignore her – and he continued to sit in silence beside Eleanor. He didn't need words to know what the salty tears that dripped off her chin and onto his soft hair meant. His small hand would steal into hers and he would sit on the floor beside her for hours like a faithful hound.

Joan, worried about Eleanor's lack of appetite when she should have been eating for two, flitted constantly between the kitchen and her companion, tempting her with hot sweet drinks made with eggs, milk and honey, and jellies. Usually Tom was the willing consumer of these offerings the moment Joan's back was turned, and Eleanor continued to grow paler, her face as wan and grey as the landscape beyond the windows.

Finally, late one afternoon on a day when the mist had

not lifted since morning, the damp clinging like ivy to the windows, the household heard the muffled thunder of horses approaching. The sound of hooves was followed almost immediately by the great gates opening, and shouting and confusion in the courtyard. The weather had cocooned them in silence all day and there had been no warning of people approaching. Eleanor sat in the great hall beside the fire and waited, her body stiff with fear, her breath stalled in her lungs whilst Hugh went outside to see what was happening. Two of the deerhounds were growling low in their throats. She desperately wanted it to be Greville returning home, but deep down she knew that it wouldn't be. These were strangers.

Sure enough, Hugh walked back in followed by two men, dressed in the gold and yellow livery of the Duke of Norfolk. Had they come from their neighbour at Framlingham Castle? The pounding of Eleanor's heart raced faster as she got to her feet, although her knees were still trembling. The men bowed and one of them stepped forward and held out a letter to her. She took it, expecting to see Greville's handwriting and seal but it was not in a hand she recognised. Opening it she began to scan the words, but she only needed to read the first two lines before the letter fell to the floor and her legs gave way as she too crumpled onto the dry rushes at her feet.

He was gone. Greville was dead.

Chapter Thirty-Three

1541

All at once there was commotion around her as Hugh shouted for assistance and the servants and Joan came running. Eleanor was helped back into her chair beside the fire, a thick knitted shawl draped around her shoulders and warm spiced wine held to her lips. Quickly Hugh retrieved the letter and read the contents, before sending the two messengers on their way. They protested that their horses needed to rest, but he wasn't listening and within minutes they'd ridden off into the murky landscape, continuing to complain about the possibility of falling into a ditch in the thick fog.

Hugh returned to where Eleanor was still sitting, trembling violently, and sent the servants away. Taking Joan to one side, he quietly read out to her what was in the letter. Eleanor fervently wished she couldn't hear what was being said, that she inhabited a silent world as Tom did. Joan's face drained as the horror of what he was relaying sank in.

'Dereham has been convicted of treason?' she asked, biting at her bottom lip. 'Are you sure?'

'He'll die a traitor's death,' Hugh confirmed, 'at Tyburn. Sir Greville was accused of treason simply for being associated with him, for being his friend. This letter says that the master died in the Tower, whilst being tortured.' His voice broke as he uttered the final words and tears spilled silently down his face. He turned away as if embarrassed at this rare show of emotion. At hearing him say it out loud Eleanor began to howl, a raw animal moan of agony as she rocked back and forth on the chair.

'No,' whispered Joan, 'it cannot be true.'

But Hugh's grim face confirmed that it was, white and drained with shock, as if cast from stone.

'There's more bad news,' he added hoarsely. 'The king's men will seize this house, and everything in it. All that belonged to Sir Greville is now owned by the crown.'

'But where will we go?' Joan was confused, unable to take in what she was being told. 'This is our home. Henry's inheritance. They can't just take it.'

'Of course they can,' Eleanor shouted, her angry voice cutting across Joan's. 'They can do what they like. They've killed my husband, an innocent man, and now they'll take everything. All that he owned. It will all be seized. He's gone and we have nothing.'

Chapter Thirty-Four

1541

The next two days passed in a stunned silence, a tangible quiet that echoed around the solid hall walls before dissipating. The work on the new wing had stopped and the lack of the stonemasons' noise, the disappearance of the constant tapping and chipping, added to the stillness. The thick cold air, the sullen winter cloud muffling the sounds of birds and animals, enclosing the hall in its silent tomb as if the world was holding its breath. Greville was dead and now life had stopped for them all.

Eleanor sat hour after hour in the great hall beside the fire, which despite the huge logs burning brightly, failed to warm her. After her initial tears she had fallen into a silent state of lethargy, rocking back and forth in her chair as she stared at the flames with her hands wrapped around her unborn child within, as if trying to gain warmth or solace from it. Hugh drifted from room to room but was unable to issue any orders. He was there physically, but emotionally he was lost. Joan took over the running of the household, finally finding her voice, although she would have traded her new-found status in a heartbeat to see Eleanor with some of the spirit she used to have. The servants tiptoed about and communicated in whispers, as shocked and stunned as their mistress. Some of the older staff could remember Greville being born and nobody wanted to believe he was never coming home.

There was no noise from the nursery, the door kept shut to prevent stray sounds seeping along the corridor. As ever though, Tom managed to slip away, and one afternoon as she awoke from a nap beside the fire, Eleanor was aware of the warm weight of his slight body against her legs where he had positioned himself at her feet. She let her hand slip off her lap until it reached his head and she stroked his hair. He turned, his big eyes dark and solemn as he searched her face, looking for the emotions he could read her by. She had no idea how someone had relayed the terrible news, but there was no doubt that he knew, the sadness reflected in his grey, pinched face.

Only her unborn child, oblivious to the sorrow it would eventually be born into, continued to be as active as ever, turning and kicking. No longer did the movements please Eleanor. She couldn't even imagine where she'd be when it came time for her confinement. She remembered Greville's pride when he'd seen Henry for the first time, but now this baby would never meet its father.

On the third day after they'd received the missive from London, Joan came to find Eleanor, sat in her usual place beside the fire like a cold stone sentinel, her arms around herself as she tried fruitlessly to get warm. Hugh had followed and stood just behind her.

'Mistress, we cannot tarry for much longer,' he said gravely. 'There's been word from London that the king's men will be leaving soon to come and confiscate the hall and estate. We need to be gone, or risk being thrown out. Or worse.'

'Then we don't have much time,' Eleanor replied blankly, shaken out of her misery by the stark facts that had been presented to her. 'I for one do not intend on being here when those crows arrive to pick over our home and our belongings.'

'Hugh and I have been discussing where we may be able to go. Would your cousin take us back at Ixworth?' Joan's hands were gripped together, continuously wringing out a cloth that wasn't there.

'What, with my husband now dead and considered a traitor? No, I suspect not. And with Greville's heir as well? Even less likely, and I'm not having him treating my children as badly as he did me.' For a moment a fleeting mental image of herself as the innocent young girl she'd been danced across her mind. How the last four years had changed her. And now, she would need every ounce of strength she ever had. All that God could grant, and complete trust in the Lutton family motto she saw every time she opened her prayer book: 'While I breathe, I hope.'

'But if not Ixworth, where else can we go? Do you think Prior Matthew would take us in?' Joan, who had always walked in Eleanor's shadow, was finally finding a voice and strength of her own.

She was thankful for it, but it wasn't right. She couldn't leave it all to Joan now at this crucial hour. She had to find some momentum from deep within her, to remind herself why Greville married her. It was because he knew she had an inner strength, and that she could fight anything thrown at her. Now, for him, she needed to show she was able to.

'Yes, that's a good idea. I'll send a letter by first light tomorrow. He and Brother Rufus are now settled at an order in France near a place called Lyons. I'll ask him to secure us some lodgings somewhere near to where he lives. If that letter can be taken immediately to King's Lynn to find the next boat that is sailing . . .' She looked across at Hugh who, if he was surprised that she was in contact with the missing fugitives from the priory, didn't show it. He gave a quick nod of acquiescence. 'Then he should get it before we arrive. We'll need to ascertain whether there's a boat that can take us, preferably from Cley but if not, Blakeney – they're quieter than Lynn so our leaving will not be as noticeable. I'm sure someone there will know of my husband and be happy to provide us with safe passage. I can pay them to take us to Calais, or Antwerp.' She took a deep breath. It was the longest speech she had made in days but she felt the stirring of fire deep in her soul and knew her true self was there within. She was still breathing and she still had hope.

'I'll send someone out to enquire first thing,' Hugh promised, 'and I'll have the carts brought around and prepared for loading.'

'Good, then we shall start tomorrow,' Eleanor said. 'Joan, please speak with Nell. She'll need to pack the children's clothes into chests. Hugh, I'd like you to explain to Simon and Cook what we are going to have to do. I don't know what will happen to the servants when we've gone.'

'I can do that, my lady.' He turned to go, then paused. 'I have no family and have always worked for Sir Greville. I grew up in this household. I would like to come with you. You cannot travel without protection.'

Eleanor looked up into his face. Always grave, always solemn, she'd disliked his singular allegiance to her husband from the moment she'd met him. And he hadn't cared if she knew of his disapproval of her. Greville had laughed at her when she'd complained of his attitude. Yet now, with her husband gone and all around her dissolving into tatters to be blown away by the wind, he had transferred his loyalty to her, Greville's widow. Suddenly, she was flooded with relief, thankful he was there.

'Thank you, Hugh.' Her eyes filled with tears as they met his. 'I am so grateful you are prepared to do that. I know Sir Greville would have been proud of how you're helping us.'

He bowed and without a further word he disappeared into the kitchen. As soon as he left, Eleanor felt the sudden burst of strength drain out of her and she slumped against the chair. How would she cope with a long journey at a time when she should be in her confinement, with young children in tow and in a country whose language was probably very different from the court French she had been taught? All whilst grieving for her husband, a man she loved so deeply? She let Joan help her to her feet and, holding her friend's hand, wordlessly walked upstairs to her bedchamber. Now she needed to fan the flames of the determination flickering inside her. She would need to draw on it to fight all that they may endure in the coming days.

Chapter Thirty-Five

1541

Awake in the early morning darkness, Eleanor lay on her back, her silent tears rolling down the sides of her face and soaking into her hair, which lay tangled on the pillow. She couldn't believe that Greville would never again run his fingers through it, or comb its long silky length while she sat in front of the fire in their room on winter evenings.

She remembered their wedding night and how he'd carefully taken all the pins out, releasing her head from its painful braids. The glorious deep red hair that matched the saffron she'd grown and that her husband had adored. The saffron that had ultimately led to her husband's downfall and death. She would never escape the blades of guilt that tortured her.

Beneath her pillow lay her book of hours where she could slide her hand under and feel its familiar shape and the indentations on the cover. She didn't need to look at it to know every inch of it. *Dum Spiro Spero*. Now, more than ever in her life, she needed to believe in her family motto and to live by it. While she kept breathing, she had to have hope.

But he wasn't coming back to share her bed again and her heart was breaking. It was so painful she thought it would burst from her. She'd grown to love Greville so fiercely and supported his ambitions, even though she'd never properly understood why he needed to be successful and well respected at court. And now where was he? She didn't even know where the bodies of traitors – and that was what he was now considered, even though he'd done nothing worse than join an old family friend in the queen's retinue – were buried. Not in consecrated ground. Would he be wandering forever in purgatory?

She needed to pray for his soul but she couldn't spend all day on her knees in the chapel when she had so much to organise. Sliding from the bed onto the floor and not noticing the icy draught that cut under the door and whistled around her bare feet, her lips silently mouthed the words from the office for the dead.

By the time it was light the fog had started to lift outside and Eleanor was wrapped in her robe with her letter to the prior written and sealed. She'd kept the information short and factual and didn't mention why she was asking him to help her. Just that she was confident he would be able to secure her and her entourage somewhere close by to live.

In the great hall, the few servants who were eating at the long table scuttled away as soon as she appeared, pushing the remainder of their meal into their mouths. Eleanor couldn't face breakfast and after taking a couple of mouthfuls of ale she walked through to her stillroom, shrouded in the semi-darkness. She lit some of the candles and looked around her. What to take and what to leave? There would be precious little space on the carts for what she wanted, so she needed to be ruthless. Only pack the items she thought she may not be able to find in France. Surely they would have similar common herbs there?

She ran her fingers lightly over her beautiful glass still, the globe-shaped flasks and beakers stood on metal frames so they could be heated from beneath to distil the medicines she made. She could remember her excitement the day she had finally collected together the component parts and could put it all up. She didn't want to leave it behind, but the glasswork had come from France originally, so it shouldn't be difficult to set up a replacement in her new home, wherever that may be. It was more important to take the medications she had already prepared and a selection of her tiny copper and lead pans.

She swiftly began to stack the items she couldn't bear to leave behind on her work table, with some jars of rare plants added. Then she collected all the saffron cakes from the pantry, and the priceless *saffron du hort* from her own shelves. She could sell them if she needed to. They were as good as money in her pocket and she'd make sure none of it was left in the house when the king's men arrived. She made a mental note to ensure she remembered the sacks of corms now neatly stacked in the tower room. Her intuition that something was amiss had been correct and she was so relieved that she had decided this year to lift them all after the harvest, and move them to a fresh ground, because otherwise they'd have been left behind under the earth. Gold for someone else.

She found Hugh and Joan talking together in the hall

and she explained to them what needed to be packed from the stillroom.

'I wondered where you were when I awoke,' Joan scolded her, 'and here you are in your robe and night rail wandering the house.'

'Not wandering, there's no time for that. We have so much to do. I couldn't lie in bed, when I needed to be getting on.'

'You need to think of the baby you're carrying, and rest.'

The truth was, Eleanor had not given much thought to the baby, who would be born on French soil and never know its father. But Joan was trying to remember the things that Eleanor simply didn't have time for. The details that were pushed to one side, her head so full of the most immediate problems.

'The cradle. We'll need to take the cradle,' she said. 'Will we have room for it, do you think? And all the baby swaddlings, and clothes?'

'I'll ask about the cradle. We may be able to find space, but we have so many belongings. No, we don't have to take it. We can make a bed for the baby in anything if we need to. I shall task Nell to pack as many of the baby items as she has room for.'

'Thank you.' Eleanor placed a hand on Joan's and squeezed it. 'I couldn't get all this organised without your help. You are truly my sister.'

'It's not really me you should be thanking.' Joan's eyes were full of tears. 'I don't think Hugh went to bed last night. He has done so much. He was just telling me that all Greville's paperwork in his office, his business dealings and anything with reference to his contacts, has been burned. Everything else in there: your inks, quills and paper, the seals, whatever else you may need is now packed in a coffer. You should get dressed now, then we can pack away the night rail you're wearing.' Joan tried to usher her upstairs, her arm around Eleanor as if to hurry her along. 'Hugh says if at all possible we must leave tonight. It's too dangerous to wait here any longer.'

'But will there be a boat ready so soon? Our letter to France is only leaving today.'

'He hasn't yet heard, although he's sent word. We can stay at an inn for a couple of days. It will still be safer than being here. But we really need to get the last pieces onto the cart.'

'Yes, of course,' Eleanor agreed as she made her way upstairs. 'Then we have a lot to do before tonight if we are to be ready to go then. And you and I need to bring the crocus corms down from the tower room. I will not leave them behind.'

'Why don't I get one of the lads to carry them down? The stairs are steep and not safe for someone in your condition.'

'No.' The reply was emphatic. 'You know why I don't want anyone up there, and that hasn't changed. I promised Greville. If anyone ever realised we hid the prior and Brother Rufus that time, they could inform the authorities before we are gone and we'll be burnt as heretics. Nobody goes up there, but you and me.'

The rest of the day was a blur of activity as beds were dismantled and loaded onto the carts with mattresses, the best tapestries, and as many chests as they could fit. Joan had appointed herself in charge and was ordering the staff about as if she were the mistress. Eleanor tied her book of hours to her pocket to ensure it was with her and not lost some-where amongst the packing, before filling Greville's wooden chest from the office with all the gold and jewellery she knew to be in the house. Unfortunately, the saffron profits had been at Cheapside, which no doubt had by now been ransacked. It was lost to them, but she had enough to start a new life, although it would not be the life she was used to. She would take her crocuses and rebuild her world again.

The poor light, dull and murky all day, faded as the afternoon wore on, although Eleanor was too busy to notice the black inky night creeping in from outside. Nor did she see the heavy, sullen clouds that had crawled over them during the day, matching the mood of the house. Hugh had told her the kitchen staff were making a feast, as much food as they could cook, both for them to eat on the journey and one last meal for all to share.

She walked into the great hall, and found everybody sat at the tables. The tenant farmers, the out-of-doors servants, the children, everyone. A huge gathering as if it was New Year. There were two chairs empty, hers, and Greville's. The sight of his empty space was almost her undoing as she held on to the edge of the table with her fingertips and felt herself start to sway. In front of her everyone stood up from their seats, their heads bowed waiting for her to say grace.

After she said it, there was a pause, before a subdued 'amen' was murmured around the table, many roughly wiping tears away with sleeves or cotton rags.

'Let us eat then,' Eleanor declared, her smile wavering as she looked around at everyone, her friends sat at the table. Her smile didn't reach the haunted look in her eyes though, as she sat down and the platters of meat were brought through from the kitchen. They were using some old wooden chargers, the pewter now packed and on the carts outside.

Jane and Henry were both fractious after an unusual day,

following none of their usual routines. Jane refused to eat and kept crying for her papa, which just made everyone around the table sob as well. Henry was too young to understand the gravity of all that was happening around him and decided to throw his food about and although both Eleanor and Nell told him off, the manic squeal of delight from Jane and smiles from Tom simply encouraged him to carry on.

Eleanor was by this point exhausted, and she snapped at Nell to take the children away. She knew she'd pay for it with the maid sulking during the journey because she'd been made to leave the dinner early, but she was too tired to care. Her belly felt heavy with an uncomfortable dragging sensation that had started a few hours earlier and she knew she had probably overdone the physical activity. But she still had one vital task to undertake.

'How long before we leave?' she asked Hugh.

'We should be gone in the next four to six hours,' he told her. 'I've had men stationed on the London Road and there is a party of the Duke of Norfolk's men heading this way. They are about half a day away but I assume they'll stop somewhere for the night. They'll be on the road again at first light though, so we need to get away as soon as possible. We'll take four of our guards. You never know what ruffians you may meet on the road. We'll need good protection.'

'Thank you, Hugh, I appreciate that. And I know Sir Greville would have been proud of all you have done.' She waited until he left the table then whispered to Joan. 'We should get the sacks from the tower.' Joan nodded, and unnoticed, the two women slipped away.

Eleanor stopped at the now empty office to collect the key to the tower. She looked around the room, desolate and barren without the chaos her husband used to leave in there. The two bare desks were side by side and she remembered how she had sat there as a new bride only four years earlier, confused and angry with everyone. And how later, she and Greville worked together, laughing and chatting occasionally or just being companionably quiet. How she'd gone from hating him, to loving him so desperately. The stiff pain wedged in her chest would never heal.

Now the room lay silent, and he was gone. She crawled under his desk to find the key to the tower, and followed Joan up the steps, each one feeling steeper than the last as she dragged her feet, her belly feeling increasingly heavy as it weighed her down.

At the top, it was freezing. Their breath formed clouds of icy condensation that clung to their faces. Even with the candles lit it was difficult to see, and with a sinking heart Eleanor spotted the occasional snowflake drift past the window. That was all they needed, but they couldn't delay their journey.

'I don't think you should be carrying the sacks.' Joan eyed them, stacked up six high all around the room. She hadn't realised how many there were. 'They're too heavy. I noticed there's ice on some of the steps as we climbed up, where the windows are.' Eleanor had indeed felt her foot slide slightly as they had walked up, but she had deliberately not mentioned it.

'We have no choice,' she told Joan abruptly, picking up the first sack. 'Everyone else will be too busy with other tasks and we have little time remaining, so let's hurry.' She slowly began to descend the stairs, leaning her shoulder against the damp external wall to guide herself down.

Eleanor was exhausted by the time they had half of the sacks in the bottom vestibule, but she knew she had to carry on. Afterwards, she was not able to remember how it happened, but as she edged down the stairs her leather slipper slid on the icy step and suddenly she was falling, still clutching the bulbs until she came to a halt at the bottom of the stairs.

Joan, who had heard the sudden shout of surprise, ran down from the tower as fast as she dared.

'Are you hurt?' She tried to help Eleanor to sit on the sacks they'd already brought down.

'I don't know. I'll be all right. I didn't fall too far; I was close to the bottom anyway. We mustn't stop though, there's no time. Go back up, I'll be right behind you.'

Joan frowned. 'Why don't we just get one of the lads to help us? They won't see anything on the floor. It's almost dark and with the remains of the old strewings scattered about . . .' But her suggestion was cut off as Eleanor gasped, her eyes wide as she looked up at Joan and held her hands up. They were wet.

'Have your waters gone?' Joan whispered, and Eleanor nodded, dumbstruck, before climbing slowly and painfully to her feet and walking back up the stairs to the tower room where she lowered herself onto the floor, her back leant against the fireplace. Her face, now only just visible in the dim candlelight was covered in a sheen of cold sweat.

'The baby's coming,' Eleanor whispered, rubbing her arms across her belly and groaning softly.

'It can't, it's too early. It can't come now, we have to leave.' Her eyes were wide with fear.

'I know. But I can feel the pains starting and I'm losing blood as well. When I fell down the stairs I must have hurt it. I've lost Greville and now I'm going to lose our baby.' Her face stilled for a moment as if made of stone, the ashen skin caught in a display of the distress that passed over it. Then she gasped as another contraction, stronger than the first, engulfed her.

'You can't stay up here,' Joan said urgently. 'You need to be in your bed.'

'What bed?' Eleanor laughed hollowly. 'My bed is on the cart. Besides, I don't think I can move now. You'll have to carry down the last few sacks. I won't leave them.'

'Yes, I can do that.' Joan was getting impatient. 'But you'll freeze up here. Let me help you back down.'

'I'm not moving,' Eleanor repeated, pausing as the pain in her stomach intensified, 'and we have no time for the midwife. Go and find some blankets quickly, and bring back faggots and wood so we can light the fire in here. We can both remember what needs to be done.'

The remainder of the sacks were quickly removed and somewhere below her, Eleanor could hear Hugh organising them being put onto a cart. Joan had returned with as many blankets and quilts as she could find that hadn't been packed into chests, but even wrapped in them, Eleanor couldn't stop shivering. She wasn't sure whether it was fear, or cold. Or both.

Her pains increased rapidly: there was none of the slow build-up as there had been in Henry's labour. This was raw and harsh, fierce pains that attacked her one after the other, washing over her until she could do nothing but give her body up to them. She no longer cared if she died, if only it would make them stop.

After just an hour she felt the hot burning, the violent tearing apart of her body that she remembered from Henry's

376

birth, and suddenly there on the straw at her feet lay a tiny baby, so small and scrawny, pale blue and covered in blood. Bending close, she could see its lungs were moving quickly, like when the dogs panted if they lay too close to the fire.

'A little girl,' Joan breathed. She took a piece of linen, an old embroidered shift that was thin and soft with age, and wrapped the tiny child before handing it to Eleanor. The baby was making no noise, opening her mouth but unable to cry.

'My daughter,' Eleanor whispered against the perfect miniature skull, still wet from where she had been inside, 'so precious, and so perfect. I shall call you Mary for our Blessed Virgin.' She continued to sit on the floor in the quiet, gently rocking the tiny baby as it breathed out for the final time and then lay still in her mother's arms. She was numb. The tears she expected frozen within her. She just wanted to lie down on the floor and never wake up.

Joan did her best to help Eleanor get cleaned up, but there was blood everywhere and she refused to let go of Mary.

'Eleanor, we have to leave very soon,' she explained gently. 'We have already delayed and we cannot wait any longer. You will have to leave Mary.'

'But she must be buried. I can't just abandon her.' Her eyes were wide, the whites showing around the iris as she gripped Joan's arm with one hand, digging her nails in hard.

'We can't bury her, don't you see? She was not baptised and it is the middle of the night. The village priest cannot be fetched now.' Joan wrapped her arms around her friend, her sister, and pulled her head onto her chest, gently stroking her hair and rocking her.

Eleanor nodded slowly. 'You're right, I know you are. But someone must help her, somehow. I'll hide her, and leave a message so she may be found and buried properly, later. I don't want the king's men finding her. I know what I must do.' She paused, then turned her head towards the corner of the room where she had hidden the prior and Brother Rufus months before. Joan followed where she was looking.

'There? Are you sure?' She was incredulous.

'Of course. I can't think of anywhere else where she won't be discovered easily. I'll write in my prayer book, and leave it in here. No heathen soldier is going to be looking through that. Then all I can do is pray that one day someone reads it and finds her and gives her the Christian burial she deserves, baptised or not.' She hesitated as if something had just occurred to her. 'Can you fetch me a piece of rosemary please, from the kitchen?'

With Joan gone, she got stiffly to her knees. Her whole body ached, but she couldn't tell between the after effects of giving birth and grief. Despair upon despair, would this nightmare never end? She heard a scuffling on the stairs, a movement that made the flames on the candles dance and sway momentarily in the draught. Had Joan decided against going to the kitchen? Please God the king's soldiers hadn't arrived already. As she looked across to the door, she saw not her friend but instead the small shadow of a creeping child that grew as he turned the final few steps and Tom slipped into the room, darting around the edge of the door and to her side.

Eleanor lifted her hand to shoo him back downstairs, then let it drop back to her side. It didn't matter if he was in the tower room, he could never tell anyone of what he may see.

Pressed against her side, Tom leant over and pulled away the bloody cloth she was still clutching to look at the baby in her arms. His worried face shrouded in shadow turned to hers, and she shook her head. Her tears dripped from her jawline and onto his head as he wrapped his thin arms around her waist and squeezed her tightly.

Shuffling on her knees over to the piece of flooring she wanted, crawling painfully and pausing to pull her skirts out from beneath her legs, she started to lift up the slab and instantly Tom jumped to his feet to help move it out of the way. Lying on her belly she leant into the hole as far she dared, but Tom put his hand on her arm to stop her and before she knew it he had slipped over the edge and was stood in the bottom of the hole, holding his arms up. He had no words, but she knew he shared her pain, she could see it in his eyes as their eyes met and she understood what he wanted her to do. She placed Mary, the tiny weightless body in his hands and watched him, barely visible in the dark as he knelt and placed her gently on the floor, soft dark movements against the black backdrop.

Putting his arms up he gripped the top edge; pulling sharply on his elbow with one hand under his armpit, she hoisted him back out. Together they silently replaced the slab and shuffled the rushes back over the top.

'Now, leave.' Eleanor held his chin, turned his face to hers and mouthed the words, but in the dim light she doubted that he'd seen. She gave him a gentle push towards the door and flapped at him with her hands, showing him that he needed to return downstairs. He turned to go but then wrapped his arms briefly around her and held her for a moment, his face buried in her skirts, still sticky with blood and with pieces of dried grass and seeds stuck to them. Then, he was gone. She knew he could never divulge what he'd just helped her do, and she was thankful for that. Just as she was grateful that he'd been there when she'd needed him most.

Staggering to the bench and trestle table beside the window, she slumped down. The quill and ink left behind from her record keeping during the saffron harvest were rough, but they were all she had. Slowly she began to write.

infans filia sub pedibus nostris requiescit . . .

When Joan returned with a small twig of rosemary, the symbol of remembrance that would have been carried if they'd been able to give Mary a fitting funeral, Eleanor placed it with the crocus flower she'd pressed for Greville, inside the front of her book and laid it on the windowsill. The tiny flower she'd saved as a symbol of their successful harvest in happier times as a gift for her husband. Now being used as a commemoration of a life that wouldn't be lived.

'We need to leave now,' Joan said. 'Are you ready to go?'

'I am. I'm sad to be leaving our home, but we will make ourselves a new one somewhere else. We don't have Greville, but we have his children, and we have the crocuses. Like us, they'll grow again. As we both did when we came here to Norfolk. One day, all will be well again. For while I breathe, I hope.' She locked the door and slipped the key to the tower in her pocket, and followed Joan outside.

Beneath them the cart creaked and began to roll slowly over the frozen earth. A fine layer of snow had already settled on the tarpaulin that covered their belongings. Turning, Eleanor kept her eyes on the dark outline of the tower, praying that it would not be her daughter's final resting place, until finally they turned the corner and it disappeared from sight.

Chapter Thirty-Six

2019

The final pages came out of the printer, and Amber added them to the folder she was holding.

'Well, that's it, Grandad. Every book in the hall is catalogued in here, and packed away in the boxes, other than the ones I've returned to the library shelves. It's up to you now if you get rid of them, but at least you know what you've got. And you'll never get lost in London, eh?' She grinned at him and he gave a wry smile. They could both remember the conversation about the road maps, but it seemed so long ago. She'd been a different person then, so fragile and remote.

'I shall spend this afternoon reading the last section of the book of hours and when I return to work, I'll hand it over to the museum. I hope Eleanor would have been happy with that.'

'And you're leaving tomorrow?'

'Yes. Most of my things are already packed. Jonathan's got

a meeting tomorrow morning, but I told him not to cancel it. I don't want a big song and dance about me moving back in; I just want to return to normal. Well, our new normal.'

Grandad smiled and patted her hand, and left her to her last few tasks.

Amber sat in the corner of the library. After all the work she'd done, it still smelled musty and old, as if dust and time had just been lurking, waiting to settle again the moment she left. The tower renovations were almost complete: within a couple of weeks the scaffolding would be down and everything would return to the state it had been before. The house, like Grandad, did not enjoy change. Carefully she turned to where she had previously read, and carried on turning the pages, looking for the entries in Eleanor's familiar hand. Somewhere she was sure would be the answer to what had happened to Eleanor and her family and Amber was desperate to find out, to get closure. The laptop, fully charged, sat ready for any transcribing required.

The first page she found had line after line of cramped writing. This wasn't a list, or a recipe, but a proper diary entry and she felt her heart beat faster and the hairs on the back of her neck stand up.

Today we visited our neighbours. I wore my lovet green wool gown with new sleeves, which Joan has been sewing for me, and I was pleased I was so well dressed as the Derehams are wealthy and well connected. Their son Francis is recently returned from Ireland. He is very handsome and I would like Greville to try and make a match for him with Joan, but he says not. Francis will soon leave for London and, he hopes, court. Greville is most keen that they meet up there, as Francis is an old childhood friend of our Queen Catherine.

Amber's eyes grew wide. The research department would be delighted at this reference to Francis Dereham, but she wanted to shout at the book, to tell Greville to steer well clear of him. She knew what was in store for the ex-lover of Queen Catherine. Her fingers were trembling now as she tried to turn the page. Pleased she was wearing her ever-present cotton gloves, she felt her hands prickle with sweat. There were precious few pages left in the book and the mention of Dereham's name now gave the volume an ominous, dark air. She was desperate to read more.

The next two pages held beautifully illuminated inscriptions of pleas to Saint Philip and Saint Francis. Amber recognised now those that were original to the book, and those that Eleanor had added, and these were definitely the latter. The following page, however, was dated 2nd September 1541 and she read on:

I have received two letters from my husband, whom I miss, but they bring me much pride as he sends news that they are now at Pontefract, and he has secured a position as a secretary alongside Francis Dereham in the queen's court. He regularly sees the king himself and I am much pleased. I hope that one day I may join him at court, but for the present I am with child and I cannot travel.

On the opposite page, it stated that the saffron harvest had begun at first light and that heavy work would be required. Underneath Eleanor had added:

Harvest is now over. We have worked for many days but all the saffron is in and I believe it will bring us great riches. There is more spice than I could have ever dreamt possible.

Amber sat staring at the page long after she had finished reading it, a sense of foreboding weighted in her chest. So much money for such innocent little flowers. Delicate lilac-coloured blooms from innocent crocuses that gave forth the sharp, acrid spice so valued the world over. It was responsible for Greville's rise in the world and ultimately, she began to fear, his downfall. She was almost too afraid to read further, but she still needed to discover why Mary had been left behind in the tower.

The next entry brought all her concerns to a head.

Today we have heard from Greville that Francis has been arrested, accused of piracy whilst he was in Ireland. Greville knows no more. He says that he cannot get close to Her Majesty to ask if it is true. Her ladies keep her away from everyone. I fear greatly that there is something he's not telling me. I have replied begging him to return to Saffron Hall so he may be here for Christmas and when the new baby comes in the New Year.

Amber couldn't stop a smile spreading across her face at the mention of Saffron Hall, her family home, seeing it written in Eleanor's hand as she turned the page, desperate to see if there were any more entries but she found only one.

He is gone. Dereham was found guilty of treason and they took my husband to the Tower and tortured him and now he is no more. His worldly belongings are now owned by the king, and even as I write his men are on the road to Norfolk.

We have to escape; we have but a day to prepare and leave. I have sent a missive to the prior asking him to find us lodgings close to him in France. I can only take Nell and Joan and the children. I will have to leave the servants behind, although Hugh, so faithful, requests that he may travel with us. Even now our belongings are being loaded onto the carts. I have already sent this year's saffron to London so that is lost, but I have my bulbs, so we may grow them again wherever we find ourselves. Where my new child will call home.

Dum Spiro Spero.

The rest of the pages were blank. The final entry had been dated 16 November 1541. She would have to double-check her history books, but she was fairly certain that November 1541 was when Catherine Howard had been accused of treason. Carefully she checked the date above the message in the front. The original entry that she had read: 17 November. Something had happened as they prepared to leave, and she must have given birth to Mary prematurely. It seemed she'd had no time to bury her, so she'd hidden the body and left those cryptic lines for someone else to discover. And it had taken nearly five hundred years for that to finally happen. It explained why neither Greville nor Eleanor and the children were buried at the church. Did she get to France? Amber may never know, but she hoped so. Or perhaps Henry Lutton returned as an adult and reclaimed his father's property, wrongly stolen from him, and as she'd hoped, maybe Amber was a direct descendant of Eleanor's. Either way, the precious book of hours had somehow been hidden away in the family home all these years, waiting for someone to find it and solve the mystery of the baby it was protecting.

Closing the book, Amber wrapped it for a final time in its tissue shroud. The frayed old linen she had found it in she was certain was from the same piece that had been wrapped around Mary's body, and was all the more precious because of it. She'd take it with the book when she left the next day. Now that Mary was gone, the house didn't need to harbour Eleanor's secret anymore.

Amber left the house the next morning, putting her bags into the boot of her car and leaving with minimal fuss. She didn't want to remember the person she'd been when she arrived, a ragged husk who'd teetered on the brink of mental anguish every day, ready to fall in. She gave Grandad a quick kiss.

'I'll be over in a week or two,' she told him. 'In the meantime go through the sheets I've left you and tick anything I can get rid of, or what you want to send to auction.'

'I will.' He nodded. She thought he may have been sad that he was going to be on his own again, but actually he appeared relieved he was able to enjoy the solitude and his routines with no one making a comment if he wanted to have a Pot Noodle or a can of tomato soup for his dinner. She'd left the fridge full of nutritional food, but she would bet money on it all ending up in the bin by the end of the week. But just as she was about to turn away he pulled her into his arms and held her there. She felt his chest move as he inhaled sharply and she heard him sniff. She must have been mistaken: Grandad wasn't the sort for tears. Or so she thought.

He bundled her quickly out of the house and shut the front door sharply. As she got in the car and switched on the ignition she saw him standing at the window, his frail, slight body ghost-like behind the glass.

She pulled out of the drive and drove slowly down the village high street and past Becky's house. In the front garden Pete was digging a flower bed and she spotted Becky pushing a wheelbarrow with Callum knelt inside clinging to the sides with his head back, laughing. She tooted her horn and the three of them waved.

The sun shone as she drove home, and she turned the radio up and sang along, feeling buoyant. She stopped briefly at the supermarket on the edge of the village, before pulling her car onto the empty drive at the rectory.

As she expected, Jonathan was not home, but the house felt warm and welcoming. She was back where she belonged, and it felt right. She nipped into the bathroom then left her bags in the bedroom to unpack later. Before she went back downstairs she stood at the door of the nursery. It was still bare and echoing, but it no longer felt as if it was accusing her. Her sadness hadn't left her and now she understood it never would, but she could live with it, accept it. Helping her remember Saffron was a positive thing; she needed to remind herself of that.

Downstairs she put the kettle on and wrote a note for Jonathan in case he arrived home. At the bottom she printed in large letters *Dum Spiro Spero* and propped up the positive pregnancy test she had just done in the bathroom – although it only confirmed what she had suspected for a few days. Sipping her cup of tea, she walked towards the graveyard to tell Saffron, and Mary, her good news.

Acknowledgements

Although writing is a mostly solitary profession, I couldn't have written this book without a whole host of wonderful people who have helped me along the way. So many in fact that I may accidentally leave people out here (and if I do I'm sorry!), but I am extremely grateful to every one of you.

Firstly, I must say thank you to my brilliant editor at Avon, Bethany Wickington, who saw the potential in *The Secrets of Saffron Hall* and gave me the chance to fulfil my dream of being a published author. She has been a source of superb advice to help bring out the best in Amber and Eleanor's story. And of course everyone else in the team at Avon, who have worked very hard on my behalf to make this book a reality.

The second person to thank is my lovely agent Ella Kahn at Diamond Kahn and Woods Literary Agency. Her support and enthusiasm has helped me as I traverse this new road, and thankfully she doesn't mind when I ask some fairly idiotic questions.

A special thanks to Dr Calum Maciver, University of

Edinburgh, for his help and expertise with the Latin passages, I am very grateful for your help.

I couldn't have got to the point of having written this book without the Romantic Novelist Association. In 2016 I was lucky enough to gain a place on their New Writers Scheme and the encouragement I have received from so many other members has been amazing. Especially those of my local Norfolk and Suffolk chapter who have been wonderfully enthusiastic and encouraging, you are all brilliant. A special shout out must go to my virtual office buddy Jenni Keer, who meets me every morning at the virtual water cooler for a gossip. She has been my number one cheerleader since I joined the RNA – I couldn't have done it without you buddy! And also the incredibly helpful Heidi-Jo Swain and Rosie Hendry, thank you so much for all your sage advice and pom pom waving.

Thanks as well to a bunch of very special friends who shall remain nameless (but you know who you are) who have helped with the more specialist paths of my research, in particular the ecclesiastical ones.

I also need to say a huge thank you to my husband Des who has been so supportive whilst I've been writing this book. Without a word of complaint he spent many, many weekends driving around Norfolk with me, visiting the ruins of monasteries and castles as the ideas for this book grew and took shape. You deserve a medal Des, and instead all you got were bowls of pottage. And last but not least, thank you to my children. Most of them have now flown the nest, but they've still received numerous updates on my writing journey – guys you have always been tirelessly enthusiastic, for which I am very grateful.